Two Ov‹

MW01095063

## Advance Praise for
### *Two Over Easy All Day Long*

Replete with entertaining small town characters, a dead body, humorous exchanges, a dog named after a popular teabag, and a dose of surprising sweetness, Shari Lane's novel tells a moving tale of transformation, mystery . . . and perhaps redemption.

> Stephanie Barbé Hammer, author of *Pretend Plumber* and *Journey to Merveilleux City* (and finalist for the Forwards INDIES Mystery Book of the Year award)

Mystery enshrouds the small town of Motte and Bailey, Oregon, when the privileged CEO of ABC Toys from New York is sentenced to community service there, after one of his toys causes the death of a young girl. Giles-turned-Tony wears an ankle monitor while dishwashing in Sunnyside Up, a diner, alongside a cast of characters who have their own penance to perform. Among the many personalities are a Vietnam vet gone AWOL, a young man who can't read, a detective investigating a drug ring, and a pregnant woman hoping to recapture her life and finish her accounting degree. Shari Lane creates characters with elegant humor, wit, and irony, revealing in surprisingly poignant scenes each character's potential for evolving beyond their frailties and past sins, through their work together and compassionate influence upon each other at Sunnyside Up.

> Kip Robinson Greenthal, author of *Shoal Water* (Pushcart Prize nominee, Landmark Prize for Fiction, Silver Medal from Nautilus Book Awards)

In *Two Over Easy All Day Long*, Shari Lane brings a small-town cast of characters to life with affection and humor. Sunnyside Up, the diner where they all work, is the kind of place you wish you could frequent, even at the risk of getting hot coffee poured on your head if owner Nancy Marone thinks you're up to no good. Don't let the whimsy fool you, though–there's deep emotion and pathos here, too. A must-read.

> Charlotte Rains Dixon, author of *The Bonne Chance Bakery* and *Emma Jean's Bad Behavior*

Good pacing, humane but honest characterizations, flashes of humor in the details–the gloved handshake, the urinal smell in the back of the bus....It starts with a child's avoidable death, and that moment is terrifying ... but Lane doesn't milk it. It happened, there is some measure of accountability, and off the story goes.

> Rachel George, *Old Books on Front Street*

Clueless corporate executive makes a big mistake, finds himself exiled to a small town with an ankle monitor and a new name. And a thankless job at a diner straight out of the 1950s, run by a team of lovably weird charcters. Shari Lane's distinctive take on a fish-out-of-water tale is delightfully quirky, engrossing, and poignant.

> Deborah Guyol, author of *Elderberry Wine Vintage 2010: Writings from the Clark College Mature Learning Program*, co-author of *Pride and Prejudice and Kitties*

# Two Over Easy
# All Day Long

## Shari Lane

*Golden Antelope Press*
715 E. McPherson
Kirksville, Missouri 63501
2024

ISBN:     978-1-952232-86-2

Library of Congress Control Number: 2024934338

Published by:
Golden Antelope Press
715 E. McPherson
Kirksville, Missouri 63501

Available at:
Golden Antelope Press
715 E. McPherson
Kirksville, Missouri, 63501
Phone: (660)349-9832; (660)-229-2997
http://www.goldenantelope.com
Email: ndelmoni@gmail.com

# Contents

# The Poppy Panda Incident

Libby Morales wasn't the first child to choke on a Poppy Panda, just the first who didn't make it.

She'd been chewing on it, absently, tasting the black velveteen ear, then the plush nose, then the smooth surface of one of the plastic eyes, exploring with her tongue all around the edge and even under the eye. A little tug with her teeth, and the eye popped off, and was pulled backward in a swift inhale of surprise, into Libby's throat, where it lodged. A perfect fit.

It took a while for anyone to notice that she'd toppled over on her side, to see the place where the panda's eye had been, to miss the rise and fall of Libby's chest. Her mother tried the Heimlich maneuver, and when that failed, she thumped on the tiny fragile space between Libby's shoulder blades, the place where her wings would be if she was a bird, or a butterfly. And then her mother shouted *You're too old to chew on your toys,* because rage was preferable, maybe, to the other emotions hammering on the doors of her mind just then.

# Chapter 1

*Giles Anthony Maurice Gibson Was Not A Bad Man.*

Giles was reasonably certain that's what his epitaph would say. The other tombstones in the quiet green cemetery had been erected to *A Loving Husband and Father; Taken From Us Too Young; Until We Meet in Heaven; My Angel On Earth.* But there would be no adoring inscription for Giles, who was unremarkable in every way, except that he had never intentionally done anything truly wicked.

It turns out that was not enough.

There were some things Giles could not remember for the life of him, such as where he put his favorite tie pin, the one from his grandfather with the tiny sapphires, but there were other things he knew he would never forget. If he closed his eyes, shut them tight against the cool blue air and the overly-brilliant sunshine and the moss-covered headstones, he could still see the worn defense table and the courtroom's dirty speckled linoleum and flickering fluorescent lights, could feel the breath of dozens of reporters washing over him like a salacious tsunami. And though it had been more than a month since the sentencing, and he was standing in a cemetery with intermittent silence as his only companion, he could summon in an instant the memory of the hearing, the low growl of Judge McCormack's voice reverberating through the incredulous halls of his mind.

The family of five-year-old Libby Morales had filed a lawsuit against ABC Toys (America's Best Company Toys, an acronym Giles admired as clever, until he saw it splashed across the news over and over and over again). Other families whose children had been harmed by the toy joined the lawsuit. When the families learned, through the course of the litigation, that the Chief Safety Engineer had recognized the problem—the eyes on Poppy Panda were a little loose, attached with too little thread to withstand sustained pressure—but assured Giles it was "an acceptable risk," when they saw in the documents that Giles had signed off on that *acceptable risk*, then the lawsuit was amended to include Giles personally.

Martin Wallanby, the company's lawyer, argued variously that: the statute of limitations had run (that is, the families had waited too long, in their grief, to sue); the plaintiffs had failed to state a claim upon which relief could be granted (because a claim of negligence requires showing a duty of care to the injured party, and since when did a toy company have a duty of care to its customers?); and finally, the president was a mere figurehead, with no meaningful involvement in the product decisions, so he could not be held personally liable for injury to the children whose families purchased his company's toys.

The judge in the civil case, a wisp of a woman with hard eyes and a hard mouth, heard the arguments in the company's defense, and said everything except what she was clearly thinking: *Bullshit.* But it didn't matter what she thought. A settlement was offered, and accepted. Sixteen million dollars. The going price for a child's life, apparently.

By the time the criminal case was on the docket, the world (or at least New York City) was aware ABC Toys had essentially escaped justice, and the jury set out to right that wrong. After the guilty verdict, Judge McCormack issued his sentence. Tall and square and shaped more like a linebacker than a magistrate, his face purple with righteous wrath, he spoke to the jury first. "For the defendant ABC Toys," he said, "nothing less will suffice than the maximum monetary fine allowed by law."

"For the defendant Giles Gibson," (a phrase Giles could never, ever unhear), the judge imposed a year of community service in Motte and Bailey, the town in Oregon where Libby had lived, and died.

It was going to be so very odd, Giles thought now, as if the idea had just occurred to him but didn't really matter. He'd spent the last ten years living in Manhattan. He grew up on Long Island (pronounced LongIsland, all one word, with a hard "g," unless you were from anywhere else), and spent his summers at Martha's Vineyard, attended Yale in spite of a mediocre intellect, and married Caroline Hathiason, whose family also spent summers at Martha's Vineyard, because his family expected him to, and because she had a charming, earthy laugh that made him feel as if he was sailing forward with purpose and meaning, instead of drifting according to the tides of others' design. His entire working life had been wrapped up in ABC Toys, his father's company, in spite of the lack of any meaningful business acumen or interest in toy-making. Or affinity for children, for that matter. He was a healthy, well-dressed man smack dab in the middle of his thirties, but no one would describe him as handsome, or give him a second glance on the street. Until the trial, most people had never heard of Giles Gibson, or had any reason to know he existed.

In other words, he'd been a nondescript man living a privileged but nondescript life right up until the Poppy Panda incident.

Life was fine.

What's wrong with fine?

"That's what I want to know," Giles said, addressing his mother's grave. "What's wrong with fine?"

Fine was better than Motte and Bailey, population just under four thousand souls (according to Wikipedia). And fine was certainly preferable to banishment to a tiny town named for a type of castle by white settlers hoping to replace indigenous nomenclature with something vaguely European-sounding and therefore sophisticated. (This information, too, was gleaned from Wikipedia. There was, it seemed, not much else to know about the place.)

"You will come down from your sheltered, comfortable life," Judge McCormack had said, "and you will live among the people you have harmed, and you will work to improve their community." He waved a thick, fearsome finger at Giles. "And you will not be living on the state's dime while you're there. We have arranged for you to work a minimum wage job, to support yourself." He took a breath, and let it out slowly, with a sound like the distant whine of a bomb being dropped. "Maybe then you will understand," he said, "how it feels to be accountable for your actions, to know that a screw-up will make you lose your job." And then the explosion: "You will go where you are nobody, nobody except the man who killed a child because your profit margin was worth more than her safety."

Though prison was never really on the table for the icon of the ABC Toys legacy, still everyone on the defense side was astounded when the sentence was read. Martin urged him to file an appeal. No higher court was going to uphold this preposterous sentence, he said, spluttering over each *s* in *preposterous*. The judge couldn't just order someone to work in the middle of fucking nowhere.

Giles waited until Martin had expended his indignation, and then he said, "It's all right. I'll go."

"But why?" Martin said, spluttering again.

"Because she's dead," Giles said. "If you appeal we'll have to start all over again with the arguments and the pictures, to remind every-one what was lost." He paused, and the word lost hung in the air with grievous onomatopoeia.

"I'll go," he told Martin, "and I'll do whatever it is they tell me to do, and then my year will be up and I can come home and it will be over."

He was flying to Oregon tomorrow. He would begin his exile in Motte and Bailey on a Sunday in the middle of June, as if he was setting off for summer camp where he would learn Personal Respon-sibility and Archery and Beginning Guitar, all in one fell swoop.

This morning, after discussing his wardrobe with his personal as-sistant, Adalbert-from-Poland (that's how he'd been introduced, as if it was a title, or a new product on the shelves, though he'd quickly been re-christened simply "Addy," because that was easier to say), Giles asked Caroline her opinion about what he should wear when working in rural Oregon. She stood at the window of their bedroom, looking out over the glory and chaos and hope and fear and faith of the streets of New York, and shrugged, sloughing off his question and the venerable old city in one small movement of her shoulders. He followed her into her closet, thinking irrationally that maybe she had changed her mind about joining him. In the warm twilight he turned to her, but she pulled away, as if she was just reaching for the pale pink cashmere sweater with the abalone buttons, or the matching shoes sitting next to the sweater.

"I'm leaving tomorrow, Mom," he said now, speaking to the mute monolith where his mother had been laid to rest, "but Caroline's not coming with me. It's eight hours of flying, with a layover in Dallas, and a long bus ride at the end." The miles of air and road stretched out before him, as if he'd already put the distance between this life and the new life he'd been ordered to lead. "Caroline is staying here," he said, in case the dead had missed it the first time.

When he'd instructed Addy to take him to the cemetery, Addy'd crooked an eyebrow and asked, "The cemetery where the little girl is buried, sir?" And Giles saw in the crook of that eyebrow the whole universe of actions he could have taken, the cornucopia of people he could have been. He could have driven off into the sunset on a motorcycle. He could have studied the Tao. He could have been the kind of man who flew to Oregon, taking his personal assistant with him, so he could visit the place where the child his negligence had killed was buried.

But he was not. He was the kind of man who instructed his personal assistant to drive him to his parents' gravesite so he could complain to his mother's ghost about the discombobulation of his tidily ordered existence and the fact that his wife refused to *stand by her man.*

And so he patted the foot of the oversized stone angel that marked the final resting place of several generations of Gibsons, and drifted out of the cemetery to the parking area where Addy waited.

Addy was scowling as Giles approached. He would soon be out of a job, Addy had told Caroline's personal assistant, and there was no point in pretending to like his boss or his work. No need to put on a happy face, he'd said. (Giles had overheard, and tried not to feel shocked.) Now that he was nearly unemployed, Addy was free to let his face fall where it would, and its natural habitat, it seemed, was a frown.

"Thanks for waiting, Addy," Giles said.

Addy looked up, *both* eyebrows bent in surprise, and the reprimand in those eyebrows was unmistakable: in the ten years Addy had been driving Giles all around the Eastern Seaboard and penning thank you notes and running errands and helping select the right clothes for each occasion, Giles had rarely said thank you.

"They're making me fly coach," he told Addy as he eased into the gleaming interior of the car and settled onto the leather seat, "and I have to live in a Sleepy Time Motel." Addy closed the door after Giles buckled his seatbelt, opened the driver's door, and slid into the driver's seat. "And I'll have to wear an ankle monitor, so I can't escape."

"I don't think," Addy said, his thick accent slightly softened as it floated back from the front of the car, "there's anywhere to escape *to.*"

Giles couldn't be sure, but he thought he heard a hint of malice in Addy's voice.

"I looked it up on the Google," Addy said. "It's a leettle place.

Miles of farms all around." And then he added, as if it was an afterthought: "Sir."

"I hope they don't have bedbugs at the Sleepy Time Motel," Giles said. "I've heard bedbugs are a problem in American motels lately."

Somehow, in the panoply of Things to Feel Sad About, the potential for bedbugs was the final insult, and Giles wondered for the umpteenth time why he couldn't have simply paid the fine and called it good. It wasn't as if he'd deliberately ignored a clear and present danger (was that what you called it when the danger involved a teddy bear?), or put those damnable things on the shelves himself.

His resolve to accept his sentence and avoid further unpleasantness wavered. Again.

But it was too late for second thoughts. He was flying out tomorrow, laying over in Dallas, and he was flying alone.

"I hope they don't have bedbugs," he said again.

"Yes sir," Addy said, and then he started the car and drove Giles home, one last time.

# A 62.5 Degree Egg

There is a special kind of hell that is flying coach on a commercial aircraft.

Giles feels as though his senses are under assault: the stale smell of other people's breath, the irritable sounds of a restless child a few rows back, the painful angle of his legs crammed against the seat in front of him, the plastic taste of the food, as if the utensils and the food are made of the same substance.

What he wouldn't give for a 62.5 degree egg, the creamy concoction available only to those who have the special equipment to cook an egg, delicately, until it reaches precisely 62.5 degrees Celsius.

Often served over lobster, with tarragon sauce.

For hours he flies above the clouds, watching the world slip away beneath him, until he lands in a place called Portland, Oregon, and tries to take comfort in the fact that it shares its name with Portland, Maine. It's not so foreign, he tells himself.

And then there is the Greyhound bus from Portland to Pendleton, where the odor of urinal cakes is almost but not quite powerful enough to overcome the rank sweat of the large, apparently overheated man sitting across the aisle from Giles.

Giles watches the ridiculously green and brown scenery sliding by the windows, missing its beauty and seeing only its not-homeness. He thinks of the morning, so long ago, twelve hours or maybe twelve millennia, remembers grumbling to Caroline *It can't be morning yet I swear I just closed my eyes*, and Caroline looking at him in the dim dawn with her attractive hazel eyes that see through and in and past him, saying *You're going to be okay, Giles.*

He clings to the memory, though it hurts, because it hurts less than being here, on his way to Motte and Bailey. He squeezes his

8

eyes against the present tense, and replays in his mind the words *I'd be more okay if you came with me,* replays her answer, that pierces him like a long thin needle jabbed somewhere sensitive and vulnerable and unexpected: "I can't," she says. "I'm having my hair done today."

And he thinks, snatching at a wisp of hope, perhaps it's just easier to say *I'm having my hair done* than *Goodbye, I can't face what you've done and what you have to do now.*

At the bus station in Pendleton, he fills his mind with the remembered sight and smell and feel of Caroline's hair sliding through his hands, concentrates on the memory so as to leave no room for considering the fact that a man from the sheriff's office is affixing an ankle monitor to his bony ankle. The man is a caricature of a rural sheriff, overweight and gruff, using words like *ain't* and *bullcrap,* and Giles is jolted out of his determination to focus on Caroline by the strangeness of the speech. The man tells him the monitor will be activated remotely, once he has checked into his motel in Motte and Bailey, and he will be notified later in the week what his community service assignment is. Then Giles gets into the backseat of an unmarked police car and they drive to a town that looks to be a few hundred yards from end to end, and he is deposited at the front desk of the Sleepy Time Motel with his two rolling suitcases, like a foster child who was rejected for adoption because he was too fractious or recalcitrant or obtuse.

Or because his company's toy killed a child.

And then the man from the sheriff's office drives away.

The woman behind the desk checks him in, and Giles learns he will be living in Room 202 for the next year, and all he can think is: Two hundred and two bottles of beer on the wall, two hundred and two bottles of beer, you take one down and pass it around, two hundred and one bottles of beer on the wall.

It's too clunky to sing that way, and he wishes, momentarily, that he'd been assigned to room ninety-nine. That's the song, isn't it? *Ninety-Nine Bottles of Beer on the Wall.*

What use is beer on a wall? he thinks.

And then: I hope I'm allowed to have beer during my exile.

Or scotch.

Thirty-year old single malt Macallan scotch.

# Chapter 2

"I can't do it," she said, smacking her gum at him, chewing apparently a substitute for the words she couldn't or wouldn't say. "I can't call you Giles."

"Mr. Gibson, then?" he suggested hopefully.

More gum-smacking. "Not hardly. What's your middle name?"

"I have two middle names," he said. "Anthony and Maurice."

"Tony it is," she said. "You sure as hell ain't no *Tuesdays with Morrie*, so we're going with the Anthony one, only shorter, so it sounds more, I don't know, normal."

Nancy Marone was the owner of Sunnyside Up, a true diner (though she optimistically referred to it as a café). Nancy told Giles she knew he was in Motte and Bailey as a punishment for some crime, though she did not know the nature of his misdeeds. "I know you're in trouble, *big time*," she said, "and I don't need to know no more."

According to Nancy, nobody else in town was aware a criminal had been foisted upon them for reparations and, possibly, rehabilitation. The details were certainly not common knowledge, in spite of the presence of the media throughout the trial. It was New York media, after all, and everyone knows you can't trust *that*. The judge had announced the community service portion of the sentence *in camera*, "To protect the privacy of the family, and the community," he'd said, "not *your* privacy, Mr. Gibson."

Libby's parents had moved away, Giles was told, fleeing the memories. There would be no one waiting for him at the town's entrance to tar and feather him, literally or figuratively, and he was grateful for that small mercy.

Judge McCormack's clerk had called all the restaurants in and around town (there were six, including a McDonald's and a coffee truck) to find out who was hiring. Nobody was, it turned out, but the clerk talked Nancy into taking Giles on by explaining that the court would deduct and pay over to Sunnyside Up all of Giles's wages out of the fines collected by the court.

"Which was a relief, let me tell you," Nancy told Giles. "It's not like I have two nickels to rub together around here."

Also according to Nancy, the judge's clerk had indicated the matter was confidential, and inquired whether that would be an issue.

"I told her I can keep my mouth shut," Nancy said.

Standing in front of the cash register, Nancy looked at Giles as if he was a side of beef and she wasn't sure there was going to be enough of him to go around. "Too bad about your name," she said. "But I'm in the same boat. My middle name is Tauitau. I'm named after a Cayuse Indian chief. The Cayuse lived around here a long time ago. Some of 'em still do. My mom says we have some Cayuse in us, and she wanted to honor that, you know? 'Giles Anthony Maurice Gibson' is kind of a mouthful compared to Tauitau. But still, I bet they made fun of you when you were a kid, yeah?" She paused, apparently waiting for confirmation that Giles had been mercilessly bullied (perhaps by the other children the nanny brought over to play with him?). When he neither confirmed nor denied the facts as they had been presented to him, she pointed to a table.

"I don't suppose you know anything about waiting tables, or cooking?" she asked, and there really was a question mark at the end of the sentence, as if she thought there might be more than one possible answer.

"No," Giles said sadly, feeling truly apologetic and inadequate. Why hadn't anyone ever taught him to cook?

"Well, Tony, it's never too late to learn," she said.

She gestured around herself, as if taking in the sweep of a vast establishment. "Sunnyside Up's open Tuesday through Sunday, breakfast and lunch only," she said. "That means you have to be here early but you're generally done by two o'clock, three o'clock at the outside. After that, maybe you have your community service, I don't really know anything about that part, or if not, then you can do whatever you want." She looked at him expectantly, and he wondered what *whatever you want* could include, here in this tiny town.

"Follow me and I'll show you around the place," she said, when he failed to say hooray or something similarly appreciative of having his afternoons off. She pointed to the kitchen, and as he headed in that direction she patted him on the behind. Giles was too surprised to say a word. Then he thought: Oh, was that sexual harassment? He felt like Lucy in *A Charlie Brown Christmas*, like maybe he should be shouting *Help I've been smacked by a Nancy, get hot water, get some iodine!*

He wasn't sure which was more disturbing, being patted on the behind, or being renamed without his consent. He was going to be hard-pressed to remember to answer to Tony.

It was eight in the morning on the one day the café was closed (Monday), and Giles-*cum*-Tony suddenly realized he hadn't eaten anything substantive in over twenty-four hours, other than the lukewarm plastic tray of what was allegedly chicken cacciatore, served by a flight attendant with thick burgundy-colored lipstick. Maybe Nancy would teach him how to make an omelet, he thought.

No such luck.

As she showed him the workspace, Nancy made it clear he was going to start—and likely finish—as a dishwasher. The dishwashing station was a good fifteen feet long, with three deep stainless steel sinks and a monster of a machine for glasses and cups and plates and flatware. There was soap in giant tubs, for the dishwasher, and a walk-in pantry about the size of his closet at home. The shelves were lined with clean dishes and biscuit mix and Lowry's Seasoned Salt and beef broth and tabasco sauce and cans of Crisco. The combination made for a slightly sweet and strangely comforting odor.

Nancy talked and trying-to-remember-to-be-Tony listened, but mostly he looked. He noticed the gray scratches on the dull white plates, and the glasses cloudy with age. He looked at Nancy, and saw a woman who was short and just this side of plump, with dark hair obviously dyed to hide the creeping gray, a generous bosom, and small, capable hands. She had a bit of a frog-bottom, he noticed, derriere slightly flattened and splayed like a frog in the middle of leaping from one lily pad to the next, one safe space to another, which was surprising since she had a modest amount of padding elsewhere on her body. The overall effect was pleasant. No one would call her beautiful, sophisticated, or distinguished, but she made him *feel* what Caroline had said yesterday morning: he was going to be okay.

"Tony," she said. "That judge's girl didn't tell me what all happened, but she told me enough. She said you're the president of a company and you let your folks get away with something they shouldn't of. I don't know whether you're really a bad man or you just didn't know what was going on. Now I think about it, you *should've* known what was going on. I run this place, and I know enough to only hire somebody who can cook the eggs just right, and I know which of my servers can make Jems and Crackers leave a tip, though they're about as penny-pinching as it gets. I've never really been out of Motte and Bailey, except for a couple of volleyball tournaments and a 4-H show, and I went to Mexico a few times on vacation, but I was drunk the whole time and don't really remember it, so that don't count. But I read lots of books, and I watch movies, and I know you're from New York City," she said it like the old television advertisement for salsa, "and I'm telling you, if you haven't already figured it out, you're not in Kansas any more. Meaning you're not in the big city. We don't pass the buck here. Well, the mayor does, probably, but most of us poor piss-ants in town know what the rest of the poor piss-ants are up to, and the man what used to be sheriff eats breakfast here just about every day, so when he's trying to hide something I know that, too."

Giles hoped she wasn't expecting a response, because he hadn't followed anything after *as penny-pinching as it gets.*

"Just make sure the dishes are clean before you put them back on the shelf and keep up with the dirties so we can serve people. Wipe down the tables and fill the salt and pepper shakers and make sure there's enough sugar and Sweet 'N Low. I was going to say something about keeping your nose clean but I guess I don't really care what you do with your nose when you're not at Sunnyside Up."

"Thank you," Giles said. It seemed the safest thing to say.

"And Toni-o," Nancy added. "Don't ever let me smack you on the backside again. That was a test, and you failed."

"Okay," he said, even more uncertain.

"I don't smack you, and you don't smack me, and we'll all get along just fine."

The thought of all that smacking made him feel dizzy, or maybe that was just hunger, so he thanked her again, and wandered back to his room at the motel.

# Chapter 3

Sleepy Time Motels are the same everywhere. That's their charm, if you like consistency and predictability. Giles would have said he liked consistency and predictability—he had two twelve-ounce low fat lattes every morning before heading to the office, for instance—but he found nothing reassuring about the dull blue carpet and the gray walls.

He caught himself counting the orange squares on the slippery polyester bedspread.

More than once.

He called home, using the bedside phone in his motel room, but no one answered. No cell phone, no laptop, no internet access, Judge McCormack had said. Cruel and unusual punishment, Martin had said when relaying that part of the sentence to Giles, and then he'd laughed, and brushed a couple of croissant crumbs from his lap.

Giles tried to turn on the television, but discovered it was not functioning. Do I have the right to tell them to fix the TV, he wondered, or is that part of my punishment?

Sleepy Time Motels don't have an attached restaurant and room service, or at least this Sleepy Time Motel didn't, so he wandered back out as soon as he'd checked with the front desk, to see if there were any messages for him. Perhaps the message light on his room phone wasn't working? But no, there were no messages.

Two blocks away, further down the town's main street, he found Tio Mio's Mexican Restaurant Lunch and Dinner Served Every Day. Giles had been to Spain (which, like Nancy's trips to Mexico, didn't count), and he'd seen Taco Bell ads, and of course when he was at Yale there was a hole-in-the-wall Mexican restaurant outside campus, as there is outside nearly every American campus, but he'd never eaten

14

at Taco Bell or the hole-in-the-wall restaurant outside campus. He had never learned Spanish (and therefore didn't realize "Tio Mio" was not, in fact, proper Spanish for anything). The end result of all that inexperience and ignorance was that after he was seated he had no idea what to order.

A rotund waiter emerged from the kitchen, puffing slightly, rivulets of sweat wending their way down his broad face, and Tony wondered what a waiter does in the kitchen that makes him out of breath. Lift weights? Slaughter the animals? He'd never been even a little curious about what goes on behind the scenes in a restaurant, or in his own kitchen for that matter.

Probably he'd find out, working at Sunnyside Up, he thought.

He asked the waiter what he recommended, and shortly after that a large platter swimming with melted cheese and red sauce arrived. There was some kind of shredded meat hiding under the cheese and sauce, and the waiter brought a cold beer, and warm salty tortilla chips.

It was, Giles decided, the most delicious food he had ever eaten in his entire life.

After he had eaten and paid for his meal and left what he hoped was a generous tip for the world's best Mexican food, and worried, briefly, whether whatever he made at Sunnyside Up was going to be enough to allow him to eat at Tio Mio's every day, he wandered aimlessly until he came to a Safeway. He went inside and picked up a newspaper, *The Umatilla News*. He asked the checkout person whether they carried *The New York Times*, but she shook her head. "We can order it for you, if you want," she offered. Suddenly, Giles was afraid. Wouldn't they know it was him, the child-killer, the toy-maker-monster, if he ordered a New York newspaper? He told her that was fine, he was just curious. He left *The Umatilla News* on the counter and went back to get a paperback (unsatisfactory, but at least it was on *The New York Times* bestseller list), and a box of chocolate covered raisins (he was the only person in the wide wide world who liked chocolate covered raisins, according to his father).

"You know those are made by Chase Chocolates," the checkout person said. She had freckles and strawberry-blonde hair and a pug nose, like a caricature of a little girl who'd grown up but never stopped living in the body of a chubby toddler. Her nametag said *Hi I'm Leesa.*

"They are?" Giles said.

"Yep," Leesa said. "I never eat anything made by Chase. They sell formula to moms in poor countries and the babies die because they're not getting breastfed."

Perfect, Giles thought. Even the candy I like is evil. He grabbed a generic chocolate bar instead.

"Child slave labor," the clerk said. "In Africa."

Giles had never been a conspiracy theorist, but he was beginning to feel just a wee bit paranoid. He gave up on the candy and bought the newspaper and the book, and went back to his room in the motel, plodding through the shimmering heat. It was mid-June, and although he knew it made no sense, Giles suddenly missed the oppressive humidity of home. He missed the terrible smell of the city in the summer—an odor like no other, as if the foundation of the island was slowly and not-so-subtly rotting away. He missed the sounds, the horns blaring, dogs barking, people yelling, babies crying, vendors shouting, brakes squealing, never-sleeping sounds.

Most of all he missed being known. "What can I get you, sir?" "Dinner will be served at seven, Mr. Gibson." "Have you seen the latest numbers, Boss?" "Pass the sugar, sweetheart." Being known here in the middle of the middle of nowhere would be disastrous. But that didn't make it any easier to be unknown.

\* \* \*

"I saw you at Safeway yesterday."

Giles felt as if he'd been caught in a crime. Again.

It was the same strawberry-blonde with the pug nose and the freckles who had warned him about the hidden injustice in his candy bars, only now she was standing in the diner wearing a Sunnyside Up apron.

"This is Tony," Nancy said to her. "He's going to wash dishes."

"Got tired of dishwater hands, Nance?" the young woman said. Turning to Giles, she said, "I'm Leesa. That's L-E-E-S-A."

"Hello L-E-E-S-A," he said, thinking furiously *I'mTonyI'mTony-I'mTonyI'mTony*.

"I work part time at Safeway, and here part time. And I babysit." She looked him over, appearing to be assessing him. He hoped his wardrobe choices (or rather, the wardrobe choices Addy had

suggested)—khakis, a light blue polo shirt, and Sperry top-siders—
were nondescript enough to avoid uncomfortable questions. "I have
to pay the rent, you know," she added. Tony nodded, as if he did
know.

"I'm sorry I gave you a hard time about your candy yesterday,"
Leesa said. "I just think, well, geez, I mean Jesus Christ, this town is
so *narrow-minded* and *stifling.* I have to bring a little worldly wisdom
around here."

He nodded again, unsure what the proper protocol would be for
this conversation, unsure what she wanted him to say or be or do.

"Did you ever find a New York newspaper?" she said.

Nancy rescued him from the question by steering him back into
the kitchen, which was now a scene of chaos unlike any he'd ever
experienced.

A tall, grizzled man was standing in front of one of the wide stainless steel counters, peeling onions and feeding them into a food pro-
cessor. A giant bowl with an equally giant whisk held eggs ready for
scrambling, a pool of golden eyeballs floating in egg-white goo. Broken shells were scattered like bones around the bowl, most of them
oozing and dripping onto the counter. A dozen half-empty ketchup
bottles stood open, and a large container of ketchup was upended
into a funnel perched in the mouth of one of the smaller bottles, both
precariously balanced against the wall. Another enormous bowl held
the beginnings of biscuits, judging by the box of Mom's Best Biscuit
Mix standing beside the bowl, and the carcasses of what must have
been fifty oranges were piled next to a massive juicer.

"I heard," the man grunted, before Nancy could introduce them.
"You're Tony, you're going to wash dishes. I'm Walt, and I don't like
chitchat."

Walt's long white hair was standing up in every direction, and
his long yellow-white beard was bound into a sort of ponytail with
kitchen twine. Walt had mean eyes, Giles decided. Walt was wearing
ragged fatigues, and ancient army boots with the sole visibly coming
apart from the shoe on the right foot.

"Hairnet," Nancy said, staring into those mean eyes with the authority only the boss can wield, with a look that said I know you're
a cranky old fart and you hate rules, and I know you cook like nobody's business, but I'll fire your ass if you don't do what I say. "And
gloves."

Walt dropped his gaze and put on a hairnet. And food service gloves.

Nancy spoke loudly, so Leesa could hear her from the kitchen. "First aid and CPR training Friday, after we've cleaned up from lunch. That means you, too, Tony," she said.

That means me, too, Tony, he thought.

And just like that, he was Tony. For the rest of the day, he only had to remind himself again once. When he called Caroline that night, it would be *Hi honey, it's Tony.* Giles was gone and there was only Tony.

It was a relief, really. Tony hadn't destroyed his career, Tony hadn't accidentally killed anyone, Tony didn't have to worry about anything except washing dishes and filling salt and pepper shakers and—apparently—taking a refresher course in first aid and CPR.

"Redemption at Sunnyside Up," he said, and then he realized he'd said it aloud. Nancy looked at him as if he was insane, and maybe contagious. Walt stopped beating the eggs, set the whisk down (on the counter, unfortunately), delicately, as if it was made of fine china, and slowly came around the counter toward Tony. Tony flinched, deeply afraid Walt was going to punch him.

Walt extended his hand, encased in a clear plastic food-service glove. "Welcome, brother," he said.

\* \* \*

The first wave of people came into the diner, mostly old white men, Tony noticed, stoop-shouldered, wearing long shorts with wrinkled pale knees poking out, some of them wearing black socks and white bargain-store tennis shoes with their shorts. At first, Tony glanced up every time the door chime announced a new arrival, but soon, prodded by gentle and not-so-gentle reminders from Nancy, he was too busy to look.

Tony was responsible for filling the water glasses on the front end of every meal, filling and refilling coffee cups as needed, and clearing the table and wiping it down after guests left. When instructed, he set out fresh napkins, silverware, cups and glasses, and checked the levels of essentials like sugar and salt. And, of course, he washed dishes.

He couldn't help but compare the cheap paper napkins and dull stainless steel flatware to the linens and gleaming silverware he and

Caroline were accustomed to at home, and once he caught himself scrubbing a knife obsessively, trying to make it shine. But the frenetic pace and the monotony (strange how the two can co-exist, he thought) drove philosophical musings out of his mind.

"Gloves," he said, once again not realizing he had spoken aloud. The scalding water and harsh detergent were taking a toll on his smooth pink hands—the hands of a wealthy corporate executive who'd never had to wash a dish in his life.

"Under the sink," Walt grunted.

"I've always wondered why we're called white," Tony said, rummaging in the cupboard under the sink. "I'm more of a speckled peach color, normally, and now I'd say my hands are an angry red."

"Nancy says Table Two needs water," Walt said.

Apparently their brief kinship was over.

"You're new," said the old man at Table Two, inclining his head graciously as a king might acknowledge a young squire. A sparse ring of hair circled his head like a furry gray halo, and watery blue eyes smiled kindly through thick glasses.

"I'm—Tony," he said.

"Welcome, Tony. I'm Roj. That's short for Roger, in case you're wondering. Roger Lanyard. I just live down the road. Nancy can tell you, Sunnyside Up's my favorite place for lunch."

"And breakfast," Nancy said, giving him a strange, twisted smile.

"And breakfast," Roj agreed, patting her arm conspiratorially as she passed.

Tony wasn't sure, but he thought he saw Nancy flinch.

"I was the sheriff around here for years," Roj said, and it was clear he expected some sign of deference from Tony.

"Interesting," Tony said cautiously, unsure if that was sufficient.

"Table Four needs coffee," Walt shouted from the kitchen, and Tony was sure he wasn't just imagining it: there was definitely hostility in the shout, aimed not at him, necessarily, but in the general direction of Roj.

"Well, nice to meet you," he said to Roj.

\* \* \*

In his first-ever shift as a dishwasher and busboy at a diner, *Tony* spilled coffee on a patron (he apologized profusely, and the old man said it was all right, not to worry about it), nicked his thumb on a knife (Leesa showed him the first aid kit and told him to write it down on the Incident Log, in case it got infected and fell off and he was permanently disfigured and disabled and had to file a workers' compensation claim), knocked over a bucket of dirty dishes waiting to be stacked in the dishwasher (breaking four plates and two glasses), and stepped on Nancy's foot three times.

As he walked back to the motel that afternoon, he realized he had inadvertently managed to annoy or genuinely piss off almost everyone in the diner, all in one day. He wasn't used to being disliked, and it hurt, though he reminded himself these were not "his" people, he was only here for a year, and it was okay if nobody liked him, he'd soon be home to Caroline and Addy and all the others who were nice to him.

Except Caroline didn't answer the phone when he called that night, and he remembered belatedly that Addy had taken another job in anticipation of his employer being gone for a year.

The television was working now. Tony-who-used-to-be-Giles wasn't sure how it got fixed, but assumed it was some sort of electronic miracle. He slipped under the bedcover and watched a little of *The Colbert Show*, a dose of semi-erudite patter to counteract the hours spent side by side with the uncommunicative Walt. He decided to ask Caroline if she would order him some of that special salve from the Vermont Country Store for his hands, the kind with Bay Rum in it. And that made him think of rum, and he wondered where he could find a liquor store, and wondered again whether there was something in the judgment about not buying liquor. And whether he'd be able to afford it, once the meager amount of cash in his wallet was spent.

He probably should have read the court's order more closely.

On the show, a female guest talked about the disconnect between the wealthy few and the *hoi polloi,* and then he remembered that he was Giles Gibson, exiled from the life of "the wealthy few" because his carelessness had killed a child, and he felt simultaneously suffocated by guilt and bereft of all that was familiar, lying under an ugly polyester bedcover watching a television that was bolted to the wall so he wouldn't be tempted to steal it, and he wept.

# Chapter 4

He was twenty-three the first time it happened. Addy's predecessor had driven him to Saint Laurie, one of the finest tailors in New York City. Even for the wealthy there is no parking between Fifth and Broadway, and there wasn't time to make an appointment for a home fitting, so the pre-Addy-personal-assistant had dropped him off in front of the store. As he crossed the sidewalk to the door of Saint Laurie, he saw an old man sitting against the wall of an adjacent building. He had a filthy gray cap on the ground, to collect the coins and occasional dollar bill people would toss at him, and he was singing *Bridge Over Troubled Water* in a quavering, raspy voice. "I will ease your mind," he sang, and then he faltered, and sagged, and fell over onto one ear, as if he had just decided to take a nap.

A woman who was pushing a toddler in a stroller stopped, and crouched in front of the old man, and shook his arm. A young man in a turquoise velour jogging suit stopped his mincing "power walk" and leaned over the woman.

"Does anyone know CPR?" the young man shouted, as the woman fumbled in her purse for a cell phone.

Giles knew CPR. His father thought it imperative that everyone in the family, and all the household staff, learn basic first aid and CPR, because they traveled abroad, and you never know what kind of medical care you can get in some of those places, his father said. (Giles sometimes wondered if his knowledge of CPR would have saved his father, had he been there when the heart attack occurred, but he was away, skiing in the Swiss Alps or watching a crew race on the banks of the Housatonic River—he could no longer remember where he'd been at the time—and so he was left an orphan at the ripe old age of nineteen, slated to graduate in the ordinary course and take the reins of company leadership from Jack, his father's right hand-man who acted as a sort of regent until Giles graduated from college. So much for Knowledge Equals Power.)

Now, standing in front of Saint Laurie, Giles started toward the small group of people surrounding the no-longer-singing man. He went over the CPR steps in his head: check for breathing, check for pulse. . . . And then he stopped. The man was clearly homeless, and hadn't had a shower in quite some time. What if the singer had some sort of disease? Was there a medical condition that made you want to sing Simon and Garfunkel tunes on a sidewalk in Manhattan? What if it was contagious? He didn't even really like Simon and Garfunkel. Surely someone had called 911 by now. Perhaps the man was dead already. What would be the point of administering CPR to a dead man?

And so he turned away, and went into Saint Laurie, hanging his head because even at twenty-three he knew a little about cowardice, and apathy, and the inertia of being the kind of man who gets his suits from Saint Laurie.

*       *       *

Just before the CPR and First Aid refresher course on Friday, Nancy gave them all a stern lecture about paying attention, as if she'd assembled a group of middle school students who were more likely to make wisecracks and do rude things to the first aid mannequins than learn how to save someone's life. "And the no-cell phones rule applies in CPR class, too," she said.

"What?" Giles said.

Nancy grabbed Giles's elbow and physically dragged him out the door and pointed to a sign in the window that he'd somehow failed to notice: *No Cell Phones Try Talking To Each Other.*

He nodded, feeling pleased rather than otherwise. The judge's prohibition on cell phones and other devices would sting ever so slightly less if he wasn't the only one unable to lose himself in a screen.

"Of course, if someone's actually dying," Nancy added, as Giles followed her back inside, "you can use your phone to call 911."

During the class, Giles was surprised to find he was enjoying himself: One-two-three-four *breathe.* One-two-three-four *breathe.*

"Bravo, Tony, you're a natural," the instructor said.

As he lay in bed each day after that, before getting up to face the day, he said it to himself like a mantra, like a prayer. One-two-three-four *breathe.*

It was different from the way he'd been taught all those years ago, at his father's instruction, and a few days later Giles overheard Walt explaining to Leesa that the old fart who'd led the refresher course had it totally, completely wrong, but Giles decided he didn't care, he was sticking with the magic mantra and hoping he'd never actually have to use it. (Thirty-five years of avoiding saving someone's life seemed like a pretty good track record, and he hoped that trend would continue.)

On the evenings when Caroline didn't answer the phone, he'd say it to the bedside lamp, resting his elbows on his knees and closing his eyes to shut out the sight of the cheap white lampshade, thinking ferociously of how Caroline's body felt next to his, remembering the sound of her gentle snoring, remembering how she liked her tea with a little cream, because that's how her mother, imported from London like a fine antique or a purebred dog, took her tea.

One-two-three-four *breathe.*

\* \* \*

"This is Nareen," Nancy said.

It had been a week since the CPR refresher course, nearly two weeks into a one year sentence, and already Tony was ready to be done with new introductions. Every day was filled with new faces and names, and he was haunted by the fear that he wouldn't remember one of the names. Not remembering when you're the president of a company is a gaffe you can overcome with charming self-deprecation, but he wasn't sure how well charming self-deprecation would go over from the busboy slash dishwasher at Sunnyside Up.

Nareen was Black, and so far Tony had met or seen only various shades of white in Motte and Bailey. Meeting Nareen made Tony think again of home, where the word "rainbow" was entirely insufficient to describe the glorious panoply of humanity in New York City: the hues of skin and eyes and hair, maxi skirts with Jesus-sandals and navy blue suits with narrow leather shoes, same-gender lovers and opposite gender and both gender, short and tall and average, downy-smooth skin smelling faintly of baby powder and leathery hides so

deeply wrinkled it looked like the fissures formed during a few millennia by streams flowing over insensate rock.

Except it turned out Nareen was from Portland, Oregon, and it just
doesn't get more unexotic than that, Tony was pretty sure. Although
Motte and Bailey might have even Portland beat.

Nareen was also, at first glance, unhappy, which made Tony more
than a little nervous. He was used to being around people who were,
or at least pretended to be, happy.

After Nancy had done a little training, she turned Nareen over
to Leesa to finish showing her the ropes, before the first customers
arrived.

"So, what's Portland like?" Leesa said to Nareen, when there was
a brief respite from customers.

Listening in on the conversation as he checked the salt and pepper shakers and the napkin dispensers, Tony was surprised to hear a
sharp, whittled sound in Leesa's voice, the small-town easy-going lilt
disappearing from her voice as if she was *trying* to sound edgy.

"Look," Nareen said, "just to get it over with, I'll tell you the deal
and then I'd appreciate if you wouldn't ask any more questions, just
leave me alone and let me do my thing." She took a breath, and Tony
and Walt stopped what they were doing and listened without looking
at her.

"I'm pregnant," she said, "And no, I don't have a husband."

Tony wouldn't have been surprised if she'd said something about
fish and bicycles, her voice and her eyes daring anyone to tell her she
needed a man.

"I'm a junior at PSU," she continued, clutching one hand in the
other as if holding on for dear life, "and I got pregnant, and my
boyfriend wanted to get married and my mom wanted me to have
an abortion and my grandfather told me he'd give me money to buy
a car if I'd dump my boyfriend and quit school and come work for
him, and I took his money and I got on a bus to Spokane where my
cousin lives. I just needed to be someplace . . . not home. Someplace
I could hear myself think, so I could figure this out. The bus broke
down outside Pendleton, so they took us in taxis to the bus station. I
texted my cousin to see if she could come get me but she told me her
car is in the shop and anyway she decided she doesn't have room for
me in her apartment. Smiley emoji times five gets you out of being
a good cousin, I guess. Nancy found me at the bus station and said

she could use some help here a few days a week and she has an extra room above her garage where I can live, so here I am."

She crossed her arms against her chest, a corporeal barrier to her heart. "I don't know how long I'll be staying," she said. "My due date's December 11." And then, before anyone could say or do anything with all that information, she added, "If I decide to have it."

The silence in the restaurant was palpable, an absence of clanking silverware and frying things and bustling.

"One-two-three-four *breathe*," Tony murmured.

"What?" Nareen said.

Before he could answer, and apologize, and think of something more appropriate to say, Leesa said with the tiniest of swaggers, "So sorry you're stuck in this backwater town, man," and she stressed the word *man*. "That's just the *shits*, y'know?"

Tony almost laughed, but he caught himself in time and turned it into a cough. Even as an out-of-touch rich guy in his thirties he knew the signs of a girl-crush. Leesa was in love, if not with the real Nareen, at least with the image of urban Black woman her mind had conjured.

"Knock it off, Leesa," Nancy said. "Next you'll be telling her your favorite rap star."

To save Leesa from further ingratiating self-abasement, Tony said, "Have you picked out a name for the baby? If you decide to have it, I mean?"

"No," Nareen said, and for just a minute she looked less like she would take a piece out of anyone who asked her a question.

"'Ophelia' is pretty," Walt said, coming out of the kitchen with a half a tomato in his hand, bleeding juice between his fingers onto the floor.

"Ophelia went mad and drowned herself," Tony pointed out.

"Well look who's a literary genius," Walt sneered.

"I'm moving to Portland," Leesa said, still talking a little too loudly.

"You are?" Tony said.

"Some day," Leesa said. "You don't think I'd stay here in Motte-*fucking*- Bailey for the rest of my *fucking* life, do you?"

It was a little like a slap, or maybe more like a near-miss kick to the groin, watching the freckles dance across Leesa's nose as she dropped the f-bomb. Tony started to say something, but a customer came in and they all went back to their respective restaurant roles and left Nareen to be confused in peace.

As he wiped down tables and washed dishes, trying to minimize the number of damaged and broken pieces, he mused on the apparent dichotomy that was Nareen. She had started out telling them all to back off, then unburdened herself in a torrent of words. Perplexing.

And here was another puzzle: just before Tony left for the afternoon, Walt said, quietly, as if he was speaking only to himself, "I wonder what Nancy was doing at the bus station?"

*  *  *

"Listen up Tony, and you too, Nareen," Nancy said the next day, as they were getting ready to open. It was Sunday, their busiest day, which meant everyone who was on the schedule had to arrive extra early and stay later than usual. Nevertheless, Nancy had ruthlessly ordered them to come in even earlier, so she could share with the two newbies the mysteries of Diner-Speak.

"I should have trained you on how we talk, Toni-o," she said. "On your first day, I mean. But since Nareen is here, there's no time like where we're at now."

Tony started to correct her, to tell her the saying is *There's no time like the present*, but he wasn't sure that was true: the past was pretty nice; the present was just barely tolerable, most days.

"You have to get the lingo right if you're going to work here," Nancy said. "If I tell you to *check the sand* it means check that every table has enough sugar."

"Okay," Tony said.

"And it could be the fake pink packets or the real stuff, so check them both."

"Okay," Tony said again.

"If I tell you to *check the twins* it means check the salt and pepper." She pointed, in case being a criminal meant he was unfamiliar with salt and pepper shakers.

"And we've got special names for the food," she continued. "*Eve with a lid on it* is a piece of apple pie with ice cream."

At the rate things were going, Tony didn't think he'd ever be in a position to take food orders at the diner, and if someone ordered pie he'd likely just take the pie out of the pie case and serve it up

himself. But he liked the sound of the phrase, so he squirreled it
away for future use. Maybe he could surprise Caroline someday in a
restaurant. "I'll have an Eve with a Lid On It," he'd say to the waiter,
and Caroline would look at him quizzically, but he wouldn't explain,
he'd just smile at her beneficently.

"*Heart attack on a rack* is biscuits and gravy. It don't matter how
many times they say you should eat less fat and less red meat, people
always love biscuits and gravy."

Nareen nodded as if this was serious business. Tony looked at her
looking at Nancy, and decided he should be *serious*, as well.

"*Paint it red* means with ketchup. So, of course, you know what
*Paint it yellow* means."

Tony thought briefly, wildly, about a piece of performance art he'd
seen last year, where a middle-aged woman stood naked on a stage lit
only with ultraviolet light while young men in white glow-in-the-dark
leotards splashed yellow glow-in-the-dark paint on her body.

"Mustard," he said, going with the safer option.

"*Give it shoes* is a takeout order. We don't do those, so just tell
'em no, if they ask. *Indiana Jones* is a customer who comes in just
before closing. *Chud* is a bunch of doofuses who come in and order
only coffee, and then they sit on their brains forever, yakking."

Tony thought of all the times he'd sat on his brains, yakking, and
felt a keening ache for a life where that was still an option. He
glanced at Nareen, wondering if she was thinking something similar, she whose life was about to change, perhaps, in ways far more
drastic than a one-year exile, whose days of lingering over coffee in
a restaurant would likely come to a screeching halt in a few months,
after the baby was born.

If she decided to have it.

"And eggs," Nancy finished. "Eggs are what we do, so pay attention. *Wreck 'em* means scrambled. *Sunnyside up*—that's where
the restaurant got its name—means fried eggs that don't get flipped.
*Drown 'em* means boiled. *Chicks on a raft* means eggs on toast."

"That seems kind of sexist," Tony objected, looking sideways at
Leesa, hoping for a nod of approval that, whatever other flaws he
might be hiding, sexism was not one of them.

"Not if you like boobs and eggs and boats," Nancy said. "But you
can call it eggs on toast if you want."

"*Why bother?* is decaf coffee with non-fat milk," Walt shouted from the kitchen, punctuating his sentence with the clang of a frying pan as he slammed it onto the counter. "For obvious reasons." More clattering. "Unless you're a philistine," he added.

Tony was surprised to hear a reference to philistines from the short-order cook who had apparently—judging from his fatigues and army boots—served in some military capacity prior to becoming a short-order cook in a small-town diner. True to his initial introduction ("I'm Walt, and I don't like chitchat"), Walt spoke rarely. But so far, every time he'd opened his mouth, he'd said something unexpected.

"And don't forget *over easy*," Leesa said. "Eggs over easy are flipped and just cooked gently."

Tenderly, Tony thought. I'd like my eggs cooked tenderly, compassionately, benignly. Solicitous of the fragile yolks.

"Oh, and when you want everything all together on the plate, you ask for it *all day long*," Nancy said.

"Yeah," Nareen said softly. "Like I want everyone to just back off and leave me alone *all day long*."

"My kind of girl," Walt said, grinning through the order window.

A smile on Walt was alarming, Tony thought. Not just because it was rare and unexpected. There was something maniacal in his eyes and in the curve of his mouth, mostly hidden by yellowed mustache and beard, and the hint of crazy just expanded when he smiled.

Roj was the first customer, clanging the entry bell almost as soon as the linguistics lesson was over. He surveyed the restaurant briefly, as if choosing one course of action among many, before sitting down at the same booth and ordering the same thing he'd ordered the previous day. And every other day he'd come in, since Tony started his sentence.

Nancy smiled at Roj, and Tony once again thought he saw a little steel in that smile, and wondered.

Nareen took his order. Roj gave her the same gracious nod he'd given Tony, and then, resting his gnarled hand on her smooth forearm, he asked her where she was from.

"Why do you want to know?" Nareen asked.

Tony expected Roj to look flustered, and he expected Nancy, who was watching from behind the counter, to reprimand Nareen, but Roj just chuckled and Nancy pursed her lips and closed her eyes as if she was praying.

* * *

Caroline answered her phone that evening.

Tony had arrived in mid-June, and it was now nearly the end of June; in the intervening two weeks there'd been one, and only one, conjugal telephone conversation. Nothing at all the first week, and Tony thought and then closed his mind to the thought that this was Caroline's way of leaving him, as if she could simply slide out of his life by refusing to answer the phone. And he wondered if she was busy, maybe even out with someone else. Since arriving and being tagged with a monitor like a wild animal under observation, he'd called her every single evening, and every single evening—except one—the call had gone to voicemail. The sound of the voicemail message and his wonderings pinging endlessly in his brain generated physical pain, so he'd stopped thinking and turned his attention to the television or a book or sleep.

But tonight he didn't have to find a substitute for Caroline's voice.

"So they're calling you Tony?" she said, even though this was a topic they'd covered in the earlier conversation. Obviously, she was just filling air time.

"Yes," he said, feeling the strain of trying to act like everything was fine from thousands of miles away.

"Well, I suppose it's nice to be incognito," she said. "We can pretend you're a spy, undercover for some kind of corporate espionage gig."

"Bond, James Bond," he said, and he giggled, feeling insuppress-ibly happy that she'd said *we* can pretend, the two of them together, pretending.

Caroline had a Bridge date tomorrow night, she said, and a board meeting the next day, and she was scheduling interviews for a new personal assistant. It turned out Addy and Caroline's girl Martha had been having an affair, and when Addy left Martha did too, so now Caroline had to find a new one.

"The flat seems very empty without you or Addy or Martha," she said.

It burst his happiness-bubble a little to know they were all of a kind, personal assistants and husband, but he refused to dwell on it.

"We hired a new girl at the restaurant," he said. "She's young and pregnant and single. As far as I can tell, Nancy finds stray people and takes them under her wing like some people adopt stray dogs or cats."

"So does that make you a lost puppy or a lost kitten?" Caroline wanted to know.

Tony liked being a spy better than a lost pet, so he switched topics. "How's Jack doing?"

"He seems to be enjoying his role as usurper of the crown," Caroline said. Jack Tollefson had been a sort of regent over Giles and, by proxy, ABC Toys, after Giles's father passed away. But then Giles graduated, MBA in hand, and Jack was re-relegated to second-in-command. Tony had never really trusted Jack, and he trusted him even less now.

"I assume he's doing a marvelous job," Caroline said, and she sounded bored. "I don't really keep tabs on the company, you know. But he's always wanted to run the show, and now he's getting his chance."

Once again, Tony felt desperate to get back, to be Giles again, to make sure Jack didn't take over and fulfill his role too well or too thoroughly. Which was odd, because even as "Giles Gibson, President," he'd never really cared that much. Work was a place you went and signed papers and made phone calls and attended meetings so you could go home and eat dinner and make love to your wife at the end of the day.

"Well, he doesn't have what it takes to run the show," Tony said flatly. "So he'd better not get too comfortable."

Caroline didn't answer, and Tony couldn't tell if that was because she didn't expect him to come back and take up his place in the company again, or if she simply didn't care who was running the company. Instead, she asked how his community service was going. More pain, because she clearly didn't remember what he'd told her in the previous phone call, that no one had reached out to give him an assignment, and he didn't know whom to ask, so he'd just let it go. Sleeping dogs and all that, he'd said in the call last week.

"Still no word," he said. "Anyway, you remember I told you about the other young woman at the restaurant, Leesa? She told me she's twenty-three, but she acts younger. Maybe that's what growing up in a small town does to a person." Once again, Caroline had no comment, and he kept talking, filling the silence, hoping to hit upon the words that would elicit some response. Any response. "So Leesa, has a crush on Nareen. A crush as in she idolizes her, I mean. Leesa follows Nareen around trying to sound tough. It's ridiculous, but I think she's trying to sound *Black*. Which is funny, because out here in Oregon—it's pronounced *Or*-eh-gun, apparently we've been saying it wrong—everyone talks like everyone else, as far as I can tell. No Boston or New Jersey or Texas accents. Just a flat kind of affect. And Nareen's not even a little tough, she's smart and just trying to figure out what she wants, but she's stressed and that makes her a little . . . gruff, I guess, and I think all Leesa sees is someone from a big city who is going to college and who has, I don't know, *choices*. Everything Leesa doesn't have, maybe." He realized he was babbling, trying to keep Caroline from signing off, and he resisted the urge to tell her she should come out to *Or*-eh-gun to visit him.

He knew he and his room at the Sleepy Time Motel had nothing to offer.

They talked a little more, a very little, but there was a buzzing or a roaring sound in his ears and in his heart, the droning sound despair makes just before it overwhelms hope and optimism and everything good, so he said he'd better go, though where or for what purpose he couldn't have articulated, and he forced himself to sound cheerful as he signed off with his best imitation of light-hearted: "Love you."

After the call, he went back to the Mexican restaurant for dinner, over to Safeway for some fair-trade non-baby-killing chocolate-covered raisins, and home again to watch *The Colbert Show*.

And that's when he realized: he liked Nancy and Nareen (but not necessarily Walt), he liked watching TV with chocolate-covered fruit, and he was looking forward to finding an opportunity to ask Nancy what she'd been doing at the bus station.

Not for the long term, of course, but for now, two weeks into his one year sentence, he thought maybe it wouldn't be so bad. Maybe he could survive his sentence, and return to his real life as though it had all been nothing but a surreal and only mildly unpleasant dream.

# A Bad Egg

Tony paces the halls as if he's sleepwalking.

It's Monday, a little over a week since Nareen landed in their midst. The diner is closed, and he has nowhere to go, nowhere to be. No one to be.

He could go to Tio Mio's for dinner but he knows it will be crowded, people yelling Hey did you catch the game and No the boss made me work late and children asking for a Shirley Temple or a Roy Rogers and a wizened *abuelita* (that's what the mother calls her) patting little knees and admonishing No more growing up, si? Being alone in all that togetherness is almost unbearable.

Staying in rather than going out for dinner means he is free, free to watch the minutes tick slowly by or walk the dingy, drab halls of the Sleepy Time Motel. He chooses the latter.

He measures his steps by the diamond-cluster pattern in the carpet, one stride for every three clusters of peach-colored diamonds on a faded blue background. He believes VP Jack Tollefson would refer to this—this carpet, this pacing of the hallways, this life—as a clusterfuck.

He's a caged animal, a lost Boy Scout, a *Stranger in a Strange Land.*

It's not as if he's never seen dreary carpets or drab halls. Every business has them, and ABC Toys is no exception. As company president, it was incumbent upon Giles to see and be seen, periodically, and so every few months he would leave his gleaming office with its perfectly maintained antique desk and beautifully framed art, and allow himself to be transported to one of the warehouses via Rolls or Mercedes or private jet, and then he would shake hands with the foremen (and forewomen, Caroline's voice in his head reminds him) and inspect the assembly lines and breathe the air permeated with cotton batting and crayon wax and tempera paint. The brightly colored toys could never quite dispel the gloom that shrouded the factory, the Barbie's Dream Homes and Matchbox Lamborghinis and lime green Playdoh no match for the cement floors and the pall cast by ugly fluorescent lighting.

The visits were temporary, over in a few days, at most. At the end of the visit, he would be transported via Rolls or Mercedes or private jet back to his gleaming office and then later back to his spacious and well-appointed flat.

But now, now he is relegated to these unsavory conditions *all the time.*

He meets no one else in his perambulations. To all appearances, the motel is empty. Apparently, bumfuck Oregon is not a hot destination. At least not on a Monday, not at the end of June, when the air is aiming in the direction of the hundred-plus temperatures that will soon suffocate the valley.

He tries to access his inner company president. Time for action. Stop pacing, get out of this hall, out of his head. He takes the world's slowest elevator down to the first floor, smiles at the woman behind the front desk in what he hopes is an ingratiating way (he can't be sure of the effect—when people are paid to like your smiles you don't worry about such things, you just know they'll smile back). She is middle-aged, wearing a faded button-up shirt with a Peter Pan collar, which looks the tiniest bit absurd sitting under her round, tired face. Her name tag says *Hi I'm Irene.* She is staring at a cell phone on the counter in front of her, motionless except for the rhythmic swiping and typing on the screen of her phone.

"Hello Irene," Tony says. "Is there a restaurant in the motel?" As though she might have been hiding a secret entrance under her feet for the last fifteen days. As if there might be a hidden passageway through the door marked Clean Linens. Irene looks vaguely like Nancy in a way he can't quite pin down, and he remembers Nancy mentioning her Cayuse heritage. Maybe this woman is Cayuse, as well.

The woman looks up from the cell phone, likely noticing his existence for the first time, shakes her head in response to his question, points to a vending machine near the motel entrance, and goes back to staring at the tiny screen in her hand. For reasons he can't explain at the time, and regrets ever afterward, he puts in a twenty dollar bill

and chooses an egg salad sandwich, a candy bar, and bottle of something that purports to be orange juice, with Sunny-something-or-other
in the name, evoking images of palm trees and Florida beaches and
happy families romping under blue skies (without the alligators, poi-
sonous snakes, or sharks), but which turns out to contain mostly high
fructose corn syrup and artificial "sunny" orange food coloring.

Next to the vending machine is a framed informational poster
about the local confederated Tribes, including the Cayuse. Tony un-
wraps the candy bar and reads the poster. After all, he's got nothing
better to do.

He reads about the missionary family that brought measles and
grief with their bibles, and thinks to himself that there seems to be
no end to the mischief wealthy white people can do to brown people,
and he thinks of Libby, and wishes, momentarily, that he was other
than white, or other than wealthy, or both. As if that would bring
Libby back. As if he would never have signed off on the Poppy Panda
if he'd been anyone other than wealthy, white Giles Gibson.

He reads about the famous chief whose name Nancy shares,
Tauitau. There is a photo of the chief, sitting in a chair surrounded
by the accoutrements of his tribe and his culture. His face is settled
into a "Really?" look. He seems to be asking the photographer if this
is all the photographer sees, beads and feathers and a wide-brimmed
hat, a caricature of the settlers' idea of *Indian*.

He eats his sandwich next, washing it down with juice that tastes
nothing like a Florida orange, and reads of Tauitau's bold statesman-
ship, and the ferocity of Five Crows, another Cayuse chief. He smiles,
thinking he can see a little of that ferocity in Nancy, the way she
intimidates the oh-so-intimidating Walt and freezes out Roj, about
whom there is some suggestion of unsavoriness, though Tony's been
unable to identify the source.

And then he returns to his room, and is ill, sickened by vending
machine food just as the Native Americans were sickened by the settlers' unfamiliar diseases, though he knows somewhere in the back
of his mind that the comparison isn't apt, isn't fair, isn't reasonable.
In that same corner of his brain that can still articulate thoughts he
thinks maybe this is retribution, the land that watched mutely as the
white people abused the native inhabitants belatedly exacting a small
revenge from one white man. *You're being ridiculous*, he whispers to
his brain, and then he throws up, and sleeps, and wakes up feverish

and delusional, and throws up again, and again, and again. He sleeps through his scheduled shift the next day, and thinks he's seeing visions when the front desk woman leads Nancy into his room to check on him. "Egg salad," he croaks. "Vending machine."

Nancy says, "Ah, that explains it. You'll be okay soon."

Or maybe, "Ah, that drains it. You'll die soon."

He can't be sure.

Three more days he sleeps, and vomits, and sleeps again. He sleeps right through Thursday, the Fourth of July. He thinks he hears a parade, and fireworks, but knows he must be dreaming. This town is deserted. There are no children to wave tiny plastic flags, no Elks Lodge members to ride in be-flowered convertibles, no baton-twirling pre-teens or women wearing jodhpurs and riding horses with their tails braided (the horses', not the women's). Certainly there are no marching bands playing trombones and drums slightly off key and off beat.

He's in bumfuck Oregon, after all.

And he's alone.

# Chapter 5

"There's a body in the dumpster."

Walt leaned through the order window to speak to Nancy, who was standing on the other side. His body and his voice said casual, noncommittal, as if it was something he'd had to speak of a thousand times before, and Tony, lifting his hands out of the dishwater, wondered briefly (before moving on to more relevant queries) what Walt's history was, whether the ragged fatigues Walt wore every day were simply a fashion choice or really did signify time in the military, and if that was why he could speak of dead bodies in the same tone one might use to describe the weather, or comment on a new and unflattering haircut.

"What the hell are you talking about?" Nancy said.

"There's a body in the dumpster," Walt repeated, his voice low but somehow still carrying over the clatter of restaurant noises.

Nancy left the order window and came around the corner and through the swinging door like a mini-mack truck at full speed.

Nareen, who was on her way out of the kitchen after her break, stopped moving to avoid a collision with Nancy, doing a fair imitation of a comedy director's instruction: *Nareen stops in her tracks.* Unfortunately she stopped and Nancy kept going, and of course they crashed into each other—or rather, Nancy crashed into Nareen, and Nareen dropped the cup she was carrying, absentmindedly, out of the kitchen.

At the sound of the shattering cup Leesa abandoned the coffee set-up she was working on and rushed in to see if Nareen was okay.

"Walt said something about a body in the dumpster," Nareen said, pushing Leesa away.

"What?" Leesa said, and it sounded like a cross between a shriek and a squeak.

"Who is it?" Nancy said, visibly shaken.

"Is it a man or a woman?" Tony said, genuinely curious. And then he realized how removed he must be from the experience of tragedy, that his first thought was not sorrow for the life lost but idle curiosity about the gender of the deceased.

It was a thinner, weaker Tony who had finally managed to drag himself back to the diner on Friday. Shortly before opening, he joined the other staff scheduled for that day (Walt, Nareen, and Leesa) to receive the weekly paycheck. "Uh, Tony?" Nancy said. "You don't have no sick leave. You know that, right?" When he looked at the check, he realized what that meant. His entire paycheck wouldn't be enough to cover his room, even at the Sleepy Time Motel's economy rates. "Can I eat here next week?" he asked, too tired even to feel humiliated. Nancy rolled her eyes and said of course.

Other than the meager paycheck, Walt's announcement about finding a body in the dumpster was the most interesting thing that had happened to Tony since he'd stopped throwing up.

"Come again?" Nareen said to Walt.

Walt looked at Nareen's worried eyes and took a step back, and then "Oh my God," he said. "This isn't Perry Mason, people. I found a dead cat."

The others were furious. Leesa said it wasn't good for the baby to scare Nareen like that (Nareen looked concerned but not frightened), and Nancy told him he'd better go back to shutting up (Walt agreed), and Tony felt disappointed that there was no mystery to solve.

"I'm going home sick," Leesa announced a few minutes later. "I keep thinking about dead bodies and it's making me want to puke." She held up her phone and Nancy gave her a warning look, but Leesa said, "Oh keep your shirt on. I just used it to call Scooter and he said he'd fill in for me."

Tony dropped the glass he was about to put in the dishwasher. Number eleven on the broken dishes tab. "Who is Scooter?" he said. He'd known a couple of Scooters in his life, but they were all really Morton Alexander Scotts or William James Alden the Thirds. He didn't think there were many William James Alden the Thirds here in Motte and Bailey, but perhaps he was wrong about that.

Leesa didn't answer, but very shortly Scooter showed up to take over. It was after the breakfast crowd and before the lunch crowd, so the café was somewhat quiet and Tony had a moment to take stock of his newest acquaintance. He looked to be in the twenty-fivish range, about the same as Leesa, though there was something in his eyes that said he didn't suffer from the same perpetual childhood. He was sandy-haired with pale skin and violet-colored eyes, wearing the kind of dull tan pants that Catholic school students wear, a little too tight around his skinny waist, and a little too short, with a faded green polo shirt, the shade of green a pale kid with pale sandy hair should never wear. The overall effect was of a man afraid to grow up, shrinking into his childhood clothes as if he could thereby avoid adulthood altogether. He stood in front of Tony during introductions, rubbing his hands along the sides of his legs as if his palms were perennially sweaty (which they were, as Tony discovered when Scooter shook his hand), and then scurried away quickly.

Tony pulled Nancy aside and said cautiously, "Is he the last one?"

"The last one what?" Nancy said.

"The last person who works at the restaurant," Tony said. "The last one I haven't met before today. I'm worried I'm going to have a hard time remembering everybody's names, if there are any more."

"What, a big fat cat company president like you?" Nancy said, incredulous. "I would've thought you'd be good at schmoozing and pinching babies' cheeks and remembering everybody's name. And their wife's name, too, if you needed to."

"Who's a big fat company president?" Leesa said, coming up behind them as she was getting ready to leave.

Nancy did a semi-visible hand-over-the-mouth-oops move and then she said, "Tony here wants to be a CEO or a company president some day, so I told him he'd better get used to remembering new people's names."

"Huh," Leesa said. "From nobody to company president." She moved in closer, eyeing him shrewdly. "Nancy told us not to ask you any questions about where you're from and stuff," she whispered. "She said you were running away from something and we shouldn't ask. But if you ever want to tell me, Mr. I'm-going-to-be-a-big-shot-someday, I'm all ears."

And then she left, presumably to go home and puke.

"Guess you'd better come up with a story," Nancy said. "Leesa'll never give up until you tell her something. First it'll be subtle hints, then she'll act like she's trying to be nice, give you a chance to get it off your chest, as if she was doing *you* a favor by listening. Then she'll make it sound like you're a big blue meanie, keeping it from her, like she's got some constitutional *right* to know your secrets." She picked up a dishrag, clean but stained, and a bottle of bleach water for disinfecting the tables. "And yes, Scooter is the last person who works here that you haven't met yet," she said, finally getting back to Tony's question. "He's been in Ohio visiting his grandma these last few weeks. He works here some days, and he works part-time at the gas station."

"Oh," Tony said. That seemed to be his go-to response these days, which was disquieting.

"Anyway," Nancy continued, "I'm sorry about Leesa and her being so nosy and all." She moved to the counter to clean up the coffee grounds Scooter had spilled almost immediately upon starting to work. "I really tried to get everyone to just back off, but Leesa's insatiable."

"She's got nothing better to do with her time," Walt said, looking up from where he was separating English muffin halves. "She's a smart cookie, and she's just withering away here. You're about the closest thing she's seen to excitement in a long, long time—or you were, until Nareen showed up."

Tony wondered whether Scooter's presence would change things. Until Nareen came along, there seemed to be exactly enough people to do the work: Nancy and Leesa waited tables, Walt cooked, and he (Tony) did all the rest, except for early morning setup and afternoon clean up, which he shared with Nancy and Walt. After Nareen arrived, Leesa and Nancy and Nareen waited tables, which meant Leesa was no longer on the schedule every day, and also meant Nancy did more sitting around supervising. He was reasonably certain Nancy would give the employees as many hours as she could, because she knew they were all counting on the money, which begged the question: how could Nancy afford to have three wait staff in a restaurant that was only open for breakfast and lunch, Tuesday through Sunday, with seating for forty-two people at full capacity (four booths, five tables, and six barstools at the counter)?

Later, after the lunch rush was over and Scooter had taken his ineffective self home and Nareen had taken her slightly more effective self back to the apartment above Nancy's garage, Walt reappeared and said quietly, "Nance, I need to tell you something."

Tony hadn't been included in the invitation, but something in the quiet demeanor of the ragged aging hulk suggested this was a serious conversation. Tony felt rather than thought that he'd like to be there to protect Nancy, which was a surprising way to feel, but he didn't question it, just walked behind her into the kitchen, trying without success to look as though he was not following her, only had an errand in the kitchen that just happened to coincide with Walt calling for a private conference.

"It wasn't a cat," Walt said, without further preamble.

"Holy shit," Nancy said. "Sorry, Tony."

How did I become a person around whom others apologize for swearing? Tony wondered. "It's okay," he said graciously, realizing belatedly that accepting the apology reinforced the idea that it needed to be made.

"You've left a body rotting in the dumpster all day?" Nancy said.

"I really didn't think Nareen needed that in her life," Walt said. "Or Leesa. I was trying to say it quietly, so only you would hear, but she did hear, and then she freaked. So I made up the cat story to throw her off. I think I know who it is, but I don't know what to do about it."

"Show me," Nancy said.

"C'mon Tony," Walt said. "You're here, you might as well come with us."

Tony had never smelled a dead body. Even pets had been quickly removed after expiring, officious house staff working quickly to sanitize death for him. The smell from the metal container that had been sitting in a hundred degree heat for the better part of a day was overpowering: decomposing eggshells and pancake remnants and orange peels and bacon bits and dried ketchup and over and under and through it all the odor of death and decay that so quickly, eagerly takes over our bodies as soon as it can get its foul fingers into them.

Nancy held her breath and peered into the dumpster.

"It's Sam, isn't it?" she said. There were tears trickling from the corners of her eyes, and Tony wasn't sure if she was crying because of the smell or because it was someone she knew.

Walt nodded, and closed the dumpster with a clang that sounded like a bell tolling.

"Who is Sam?" Tony asked.

"Roj's bastard kid," Walt said. "One of them, anyway. I've lost track, but I think he's up to, like, ten, maybe fifteen kids? Twenty? Who knows. Sam's stupid. Correction: Sam *was* stupid. I don't just mean he wasn't smart. I mean his mom didn't know she was pregnant, and she drank, and Sam had fetal alcohol syndrome. He never really had a chance to be anything but stupid and a loser. Nobody loved him, nobody wanted him. His mom OD'd on booze and other stuff by the time he was seven, and his relatives took him in but one by one they gave up. Now he has no one except his dad, who mostly just pretends Sam doesn't exist." He looked down, and shuffled a ragged-booted foot back and forth as if contemplating planting the boot in Roj's backside, and then he added, "Roj takes a kind of perverse pride in his bastards, but Sam was a blot on his record, I think."

It was the most words Tony had heard Walt use at one time, and he wanted to thank him for the explanation, but he couldn't think of a single thing to say that might convey his gratitude and keep the flow of information coming.

"Oh," he said.

Again with the *oh*.

"Roj did it," Nancy speculated darkly.

"He doesn't have enough balls to kill someone," Walt said. "Not with his own hands, I mean. And he's not strong enough to lift a body and put it in the dumpster."

"So why are we just standing here?" Tony asked. "Shouldn't we call the police?"

"We don't really have police around here," Nancy said. "I mean, we have a part-time officer who comes over from Pendleton a few days a week, mostly to give safety talks at the elementary school and take reports on stolen bicycles and vandalized cars. For real law enforcement we have to rely on the county sheriff's office. Roj used to be the sheriff, and he knows everybody there."

"He *owns* everybody there," Walt said. "Look, Tony, I just said I don't think Roj actually killed Sam, but I wouldn't put it past him to have hired someone to do it, and no matter what he'd have a finger in investigating it. My bet is if he was behind it he'd cover it up, or maybe even frame someone for it, if he thought he might get something useful out of being able to hold murder charges over someone's head."

Tony thought of the genial face and monk-like head. How could someone who looked so much like Friar Tuck be evil?

"Couldn't it have just . . . happened? Why do you think he was murdered?" Tony said.

"Well, he didn't put himself in the dumpster, for one thing," Walt said. "But even without that, I don't *think* someone killed him, I *know*." After that, there was no question. Nancy and Tony accepted the verdict as if it was the result of long deliberations by a full twelve-person jury.

"But we can't just leave the body here," Tony said.

"No, we can't," Walt agreed.

There was a long silence, while they stood in the impossible heat trying to not breathe the impossible smell wafting from under the closed dumpster lid.

"Tonight," Walt said finally. "Four o'clock, so we'll have time to get back and get to work. Which means I'm really talking about tomorrow, I guess. Anyway, four o'clock. Meet me here. We'll put his body in the back of my truck. If anyone sees the truck parked in the alley they'll just think I'm here for prep work. We'll take Sam out to the woods and bury him. It's really the only decent thing we can do."

Tony absorbed the idea slowly. He wanted to protest, but he kept getting hung up on the word "decent." It was a strange and new feeling, wanting to be the kind of person who did the decent thing—even if it involved burying someone nobody loved in the woods at four in the morning.

"Oh, but my ankle monitor won't let me go more than five miles from town," he said, and then he swore, softly, apologetically, genteelly. He hadn't meant to let Walt know he had an ankle monitor.

"Forget it," Walt said, as if Tony's ankle monitor and criminal past and genteel cursing were of no interest to him. "We'll find a place within five miles."

"I won't be part of this," Nancy said quietly.

"I don't expect you to," Walt said. "But some day you might feel differently. Some day you might want to take a stand."

Tony had no idea what Walt was talking about, but there was a miasma of fear and sadness and even guilt that haloed Nancy like the after-effects of a day off gained by falsely claiming you needed to care for your ailing grandmother, or the remorse that comes from a less-than-little-white-lie, so he didn't ask.

* * *

He wanted to tell Caroline about his secret plan to do *The Decent Thing*. Or Addy. Or even the ever-untrustworthy Jack, who might right this minute be taking over ABC Toys, making Tony—making *Giles*—superfluous. But he couldn't tell anyone, least of all Caroline, who refused to come to the trial or the sentencing hearing, and refused to come to Motte and Bailey with him, because, she said, she didn't want to get mixed up in any "unpleasantness." It was the first time he'd knowingly withheld information from his wife in over a decade of marriage.

When they spoke that night, he told her about how Walt had said there was a dead body in the dumpster and everyone got upset but then Walt said it was only a dead cat. Caroline listened politely and told him she had won a couple of hands at Bridge, and then asked him unexpectedly out of the blue, joyously, marvelously, if he missed her.

"Yep," he said, and then they signed off for the night.

Gotta go bury a body in the woods, he thought.

* * *

It was almost cool enough to be pleasant in Motte and Bailey in the wee hours before dawn. Walt was waiting behind the restaurant, leaning against a massive 1976 Ford F-150. The truck was painted in shades of tan and brown, although most of the paint had long since ceded to rust. "I usually just drive my hog," he said, jerking his head toward the truck, "but this is what we need right now."

"You ride a *pig*?" Tony said.

Walt grunted, and it might have been a laugh or it might have been a sound of irritation. "Where are you from, 'Tony'?" he said.

The removal of a dead body from a dumpster full of rotting food does not bear describing. Walt managed it with minimal help from Tony, for which Tony was enormously grateful. Then Walt placed the thing that used to be Sam gently on a tarp in the back of his truck, wrapping one side across Sam's face and tucking it under the other side of Sam's body, so it wouldn't be immediately obvious that there was a dead man in the back of his truck, if they passed anyone on the road on their way out of town.

Tony was surprised by how strong the old man was, and simultaneously ashamed at his own squeamishness. He was beginning to realize how extraordinarily incompetent he was at just about everything, everything that mattered, anyway.

Tony climbed into the cab of the truck, looked around in vain for seat belts, and finally tucked his feet gamely under the seat, figuring if worse came to worst he'd grab hold with his toes.

"Five miles," he reminded Walt.

"Got it," Walt said.

If Tony was hoping for a repeat of the almost-garrulous Walt of the afternoon, he was disappointed. Walt said not a word as they drove through town, turned onto first one and then another country lane, and then onto a barely graveled track that dove into a sparsely wooded area, where a half-moon lay indolent fingers of light, making suggestions of silhouettes rather than actually illuminating anything.

Walt pulled off the track and parked in front of a clump of saplings and blackberry vines and hemlock bushes.

"Wait here," he told Tony.

Tony tucked his feet further under the seat, as if by sitting primly he could turn the event into something clean and tidy, something *Leave It To Beaver*-ish or at least *The Wonder Years*-ish. The floor of the truck was littered with papers, and his Sperry Topsiders slid noisily across the floor every time he moved his feet. Tony pushed the papers to one side of the floor, but they floated gently back to the center again, unwilling, apparently, to occupy any space other than the one they had occupied before Tony intruded.

Then, and only then, did his brain kick in. He was a convicted criminal, being monitored by the sheriff's department—a nest of vipers, according to Walt and Nancy—so-called law enforcers who may or may not have murdered someone, a someone that he and Walt were now going to bury in the woods in the middle of the night. Surely that was illegal, even without the element of possible involvement by a corrupt sheriff's department. What, oh what, was he thinking?

After a few minutes, Walt came back, and motioned for Tony to join him. Reluctantly, Tony got out of the truck, and stepped gingerly through the dry grass behind Walt, until they came to a place behind the bushes. Walt handed a shovel to Tony, and grunted in the direction of a clear-ish patch of land under a wizened clump of bushes.

Tony attacked the ground with good intentions but little gusto, and very soon Walt grabbed the shovel from Tony's hands.

"You're a complete girl, you know that?" he said roughly. "I'm staring down seventy, and I can dig faster than you. Hell, my three-year-old niece could dig faster than you."

"I didn't know you had a three-year-old niece," Tony said.

"I don't," Walt said, "as far as I know. But if I did, she'd be better than you."

At long last the job was done. The pit was dug, the tarp-wrapped body was further entombed in several old blankets (to minimize the chance that the coyotes would smell it and dig it up, according to Walt), the earth was tamped down over the soil, and dead leaves and other natural detritus were scattered over the top of the grave.

"Let's go," Walt said.

"Shouldn't we say something?" Tony objected.

"Grace," Walt said.

Only it wasn't a joke, like a kid at a table smirking and wanting to say "Grace" and get on with the meatloaf or the roast turkey sitting succulently in front of him; it was a powerful, deep growl of a prayer, a one-word summons to provide postmortem what Sam had so desperately lacked during life.

Walt dropped Tony off behind Sunnyside Up. "I'm going to rinse out the truck bed and change," he said. "*You* should go home and shower. You stink to high heaven."

As Tony was getting out of the truck, one of the papers from the floor stuck to his shoe and fluttered to the ground. He picked it up, intending to hand it to Walt, but Walt reached across the seat and pulled the door shut and drove away. It was too dark to see what kind of paper it was, so Tony folded it and stuffed it into the front pocket of his jeans.

Only then did he realize he was alone in the dark in the alley where a young man had been killed and stuffed into a dumpster.

# Chapter 6

Giles had never in his life washed his own clothes (or anyone else's clothes, for that matter), but Tony was going to have to learn.

Before he left New York, he instructed Addy to prepare his wardrobe. As always, Addy complied, purchasing ten pairs of Levis, ten pairs of Dockers khaki pants, a pair of Sperry Topsiders, a pair of Adidas, and a one-month supply of underwear, socks, and tee shirts.

It had now been one month.

In addition to having used all his underwear, the clothes Tony had been wearing during the early morning activities had absorbed a stench so deep that he was assaulted by the smell when he walked into his room after his shift at the diner, as if the whole room was on its way to becoming a morgue, or a city dump, or some combination thereof.

He was so tired, so tired from his grave-digging and his dishwashing, and he wanted nothing more than to collapse on his miserable bed until the next day's shift. Or maybe until his year-long sentence was up. But he had not forgotten that the last time he gave in to despair he ate food from the vending machine and was ill for days. He knew he had to find a way to become someone he'd never been, a person who stayed awake and took care of things that needed taking care of.

The knowing was so much easier than the doing.

He carefully checked the pockets of his dirty clothes before packing them into one of his suitcases. He found the piece of paper from Walt's truck, the one that stuck to his shoe. It was still folded neatly in half and in half again, and he set it on his nightstand with a mental note to return it to Walt. Then he trudged to Safeway to pick up whatever supplies he might need, wheeling the suitcase full of dirty clothes behind him, realizing only after walking through the doors that he could have and should have left the suitcase in his room while he went to the store. Once inside the store, it took him nearly twenty minutes to consider his options: with or without fragrance, all natural, biodegradable, compostable, liquid, powdered, unholy mixture of every toxic chemical known to man.

Then he trudged back to the motel (for the first time truly appreciating the meaning of the word "trudge"), still dragging his suitcase behind him and also carrying a grocery bag with laundry detergent, liquid fabric softener, stain remover, and dryer sheets. He asked Irene (aka The Surly Woman Behind the Front Desk—did she ever leave the Sleepy Time Motel or was she somehow permanently affixed to her chair?) where he could go to get his clothes washed. She looked at him with distaste. "You mean a laundromat?"

When he found the laundromat, he discovered you have to have quarters, and the machine to convert bills to quarters only took ones and fives. Flipping open his wallet, he found a single twenty-dollar bill, the very last of the cash he had brought with him. From here on out, he would survive—or not—on his wages from Sunnyside Up.

Still tired, so tired, he ventured back out into the onerous afternoon heat, back to Safeway (once again pulling his suitcase behind him and now also carrying the bag of laundry supplies), exchanged the twenty for three fives and five ones, returned to the Laundromat, got a mountain of quarters from the change machine, read the instructions on the back of the bottle of laundry detergent, compared those instructions to the poster on the wall, decided it probably made no difference, and washed everything in hot water.

He picked up a weary-looking paperback someone had abandoned on one of the hard plastic chairs, and tried to concentrate on the words, to resist the soporific sound of washing machines and dryers. A young mother came in carrying an enormous canvas bag of laundry (Tony was grateful he at least had a suitcase on wheels), followed by a small boy whose preferred form of entertainment, it turned out, was running his tiny toy car over the legs of others waiting for their laundry and chortling gleefully when his mother scolded him. Tony could feel his eyes closing, in spite of the book and the chortling child, and sleep won the battle at some point, until Tony was jolted awake by the sound of the book falling off his lap and hitting the floor.

Finally the washing machines holding Tony's clothes signaled that they were done, and he glanced at the young mother who was ferrying some of her laundry to one of the dryers even though she had come in after he did. He wondered if there was some secret to making the washing machines go faster, some arcane esoteric knowledge of which he, the president of ABC Toys, was ignorant. He reached into a machine and with one hand grabbed a bundle of his wet clothes and with the other opened the door of the nearest dryer. As he tossed the bundle in he noticed: his tee shirts and underwear were not *exactly* tie-dye, but close enough that a nearsighted hippie might think he had tried.

* * *

"Nice tie-dye," Nancy said the next day. "Did you do that on purpose?"

Nothing had been said between the three of them about the body, or the burial, but Tony was used to being around people who didn't talk about problems, just pretended they didn't exist. It was the Gibson family way. That's how it came to pass that his closest confidant was his mother's grave. He was mildly surprised to discover it was also the way things worked in a small-town diner, though in this case it might be simply the fact that yesterday (the Decent Thing day, in Tony's mind) was Saturday, and today was Sunday, the busiest day at the diner, with little time and space for secret confabulations. Whatever the reason, he was grateful to be talking about his clothes rather than the dead body of an unwanted son.

"It was an accident," Tony said. "I guess I did my laundry wrong."

Leesa and Nareen looked at him quizzically, and Leesa started to ask him something (probably how could a man make it to somewhere between thirty and forty and not know how to wash his own clothes?), but Nancy interrupted.

"Nareen," she said, "you don't have to go if you don't want to, but I signed you up for those whaddyacallem' classes—birth-thingy, erm, prenatal, that's it—over at the community college." She handed Nareen a glossy pamphlet with a photo of a fat baby on the front: *Blue Mountain Community College, serving Morrow, Umatilla, Union, Wallowa, Grant, and Baker Counties.*

"They got a new class that starts every month," she said. "There's one starting tonight, but you can start another time if you want. Or you don't have to go, if you don't want to. Like I said."

*Nervous* was not a frequent visitor to Nancy's face, in Tony's brief experience, but it was definitely hanging about now.

Nareen took the pamphlet, and Tony expected her to say something sarcastic about not needing a stupid class, or maybe to remind them, again, that she hadn't decided whether to continue with the pregnancy, but all she said was, "Thanks."

"I'll go with you," Leesa said, and they could all hear how desperately hard she was trying to sound casual, not like she was begging to be allowed to go.

Walt, Nancy, and Tony held their collective breaths.

"Okay," Nareen said.

And then the Sunday breakfast rush hit, and everyone dove into action.

Crackers and Jems were the first to arrive, two more old white men who came every Wednesday and Saturday, sat in the same booth every time (á la Roj), and ordered fried eggs and hashbrowns and link sausages. When Tony first met them, Nancy told him Crackers's real name was unknown to anyone except his own mother. May she rest in peace, Nancy said. Maybe a few other people, she added, like the clerk at the county recorder's office, and the doctor who delivered him. Probably his kindergarten teacher. But not me, she said. When Tony asked where the name Crackers came from, she said even that was boring, since everyone knew it was just because, for a few months when he was about two years old, he refused to eat anything but soda crackers.

Jems was short for Jeremiah, Nancy'd told him.

They were the most nondescript people Tony had ever met, sitting quietly and unobtrusively in "their" booth and mopping up fried egg goo with their buttered white toast, but he treasured the fact that he knew their order and their schedule, knew their place in the warp and weave of the fabric of Sunnyside Up.

Except that today was Sunday.

And today, for some reason, they were talkative, and vociferous.

"We just got back into town," Crackers said loudly, when Tony set their water glasses on the table.

"Whoo boy, it was a long trip," Jems said, just as loudly.

"Where did you go?" Tony said, wondering what two people who could easily be mistaken for furniture or lawn ornaments did for excitement.

"Well, you know, sometimes one just has to get away," Crackers said.

And Jems said, "Can't stay 'round here all the live long day, you know. Just hafta get out somehows."

Tony had noticed before that Crackers spoke precisely and carefully, sounding more like an English teacher than a farmer in rural Oregon. He always wore a short-sleeved button-down shirt, usually pale blue or ivory or peach colored, sometimes with a bolo, and shorts that looked as though they had been carefully pressed before wearing. His friend Jems, on the other hand, sounded and looked like a cowboy just in from the range.

Nareen rescued Tony from the conversation by taking their order.

"How's the baby treating you?" Crackers asked Nareen.

"I think I felt it move," she said shyly.

"Got a name picked out yet?" Jems asked.

"Ophelia, maybe," Nareen said, looking down at her fingers, the pen, her order pad. "If I decide to have it," she added.

If either of the men was shocked, they hid it well. "Ah," Crackers said. "'Farewell, Ophelia, and remember well what I have said to you. 'Tis in my memory lock'd, and you yourself shall keep—"

"Fried eggs, hashbrowns, and link sausages," Jems interrupted, and when Nareen looked at him, he grinned.

She grinned back.

Tony took his break at eleven o'clock, and asked Walt, as humbly as he could, for an omelet.

"What kind of omelet?" Walt said, and Tony knew it was a loaded question.

"Whatever kind you feel like making," he said, thinking what a strange sensation it was for the heir of the ABC Toys legacy to be afraid of offending a short-tempered short order cook.

Walt made a concoction of gruyere cheese and caramelized shallots that was, quite simply, stupendous. Tony said as much, but Walt turned on him with such a fierce look that Tony flinched, and subsided.

"Only use free range eggs," Walt said a little later, as if the conversation hadn't lapsed. "I grow the shallots myself, in my back yard."

"You grow shallots in your back yard?" Tony said, truly amazed by the multi-faceted Walt.

"Got nearly an acre behind the house, and Taylor, the landlord, let's me do whatever I want with it. Don't tell Nancy, though. The feds don't like me bringing in home-grown food to a restaurant. They'd rather have stuff grown in Florida with a heavy coating of pesticides, picked before it's ripe and blasted with radiation to finish the job, then shipped across the country in a truck that gets about three miles to the gallon."

Tony thought a man who drove an ancient Ford pickup probably shouldn't cast stones about gas mileage, but wisely kept those thoughts to himself.

"So I just bring 'em in on the sly. Onions and shallots and potatoes and lettuce."

Later, Tony caught himself humming the theme to Green Acres, picturing Walt in overalls.

And tattered army boots.

With his long white hair in a braid down his back.

Just before leaving at the end of her shift, Leesa pulled out her phone, surreptitiously, and took a picture of Tony in his almost-tie-dye shirt. "In case I need to bribe you with something," she said, chortling.

Scooter came in to work the lunch rush, and Tony tried to engage him in conversation, but Scooter scrunched his shoulders and gave only monosyllabic answers, seemingly terrified by the attention, so Tony gave up.

And then Roj came in. It was the wrong time (nearly noon), and he sat in the wrong booth ("his" booth was taken), and there was something wrong with his smile.

When Nareen asked him what he'd like he said, "I want to talk to Nancy."

Tony did his best imitation of a person who wasn't listening, which wouldn't have fooled anyone who was paying attention, but fortunately neither Roj nor Nancy was looking at him. He heard Roj say tersely, "Sam's missing. Have you seen him?"

Nancy didn't miss a beat. "Nope, but it seems to me he often disappears for a while," she said. "He's in with a bad crowd, you know?"

"I know," Roj said, and for a moment he looked sincerely troubled. "Maybe I should get involved."

"Little late for that," Nancy said.

"Why do you say that?" Roj said sharply.

"He's thirty-two," Nancy said.

Was thirty-two, Tony thought.

Roj grunted, looking less kindly and monk-like than Tony had yet seen him. "Well, ask around, will you? I'm worried."

"I don't believe for a minute that man is really worried," Nancy said later, after Roj had gone.

"He seemed worried," Tony offered, tentatively.

"I'll give you this," Walt said. "Roj ain't never been no kind of actor. And yes, I'm aware that's a triple negative," he sneered, turning on Tony as if Tony had lectured him. "Roj deserves a triple negative. If I could have worked in a fourth, I'd have done it."

"That's true," Nancy said, ignoring the comments about grammar. "Roj has an evil laugh, when he knows he's got someone over a barrel. And he likes to toot his own horn, so to speak. He'll tell the world when he sticks it to someone."

"But maybe murder's different," Tony said.

Walt and Nancy looked at him. "No," they said, almost simultaneously.

"Word is, Roj is no stranger to murder," Walt said. "Not with his own hands, like I said before. But ordering someone else to do it, not a problem for him."

Tony didn't ask, didn't want to know. He wanted to go back to not talking about it, to pretending there was nothing wrong. He turned to the sink, and gave his full attention to the massive pan soaking in greasy gray water, hoping the conversation was at an end.

Nareen came through the swinging doors and said quickly, as if getting the words out would end any indecision, that she was going to go to the prenatal classes. She looked ever so slightly defiant. Nancy said, "Great!" and Walt nodded with a grimace that might have been intended as a smile, and went back to cooking, and the rest of the day slogged along like any other day, until it ended, as days always do.

Leesa showed up shortly after the Open sign was turned off, even though the prenatal class didn't start for another hour or so. Her hair was pulled into two tight pigtails, and she was wearing cutoff shorts and a low-cut tee shirt with hearts and daisies on the front. She sat on one of the barstools and heckled Scooter about a spot on the counter he'd missed, and couldn't he take down the coffee service without spilling it all over the place? Tony looked at Scooter, expecting him to be annoyed, but he was grinning good-naturedly, and even at one point did a mock bow and said, "Yes, your highness, right away." It was a side of Scooter he hadn't seen before, hadn't even known was possible.

At the appointed time, Leesa and Nareen left together, Leesa visibly fawning and Nareen visibly exasperated by the fawning. They promised to give a full report on Tuesday (since the next day was Monday, and the diner was closed).

After everyone was gone except Tony, Walt, and Nancy, Tony mopped the floor, expecting and also dreading that someone would say something about Sam, or about Roj, but Walt and Nancy seemed lost in their own thoughts. Nancy's eyes were uncharacteristically vacant as she pulled the cash out of the till and counted it and pushed the buttons on what she had referred to as the goddamnedest fanciest POS machine she'd ever seen, could probably say her prayers for her and cook her dinner, if she just knew how to program it. Walt pulled out a CD player bathed in dust and unidentifiable schmutz, and played a ZZ Top album while banging about in the kitchen, presumably cleaning or doing prep work, or both. Tony stifled the urge to say something to Walt about being too old fashioned for Spotify or one of the other music streaming services, guessing that would only earn him one of Walt's terrifying glares.

*Jesus just left Chicago, and he's bound for New Orleans.*

Why New Orleans? Tony wondered. Why not New York? Or Motte and Bailey? He smiled at the thought of a robed and sandaled savior walking the quiet streets of town.

"Crackers and Jems were certainly talkative today," he said finally, in the silence between songs. "They kept going on about how they'd been out of town."

"What did you say?" Walt said, switching off the CD player and coming out of the kitchen.

Tony repeated himself, and Walt waved at Nancy to stop what she was doing and come over to where they were standing.

"Have you ever known those two to go anywhere further than Walla Walla?" Walt said to Nancy, squinting ominously.

"Walla-who?" Tony said, genuinely taken aback.

"Don't start," Nancy said.

"You sure have some odd names in Oregon," Tony said.

"Walla Walla's in Washington," Walt said. "Washington state, not

D.C., and it's just over the border, about twenty miles away. And anyway, New York's got its share of weird names."

Tony started to protest, but then he remembered Cheektowaga and Poughkeepsie and Schaghticoke. (Caroline always said when she saw "Schaghticoke" it made her think some tycoon from the soda behemoth was doing the naughty with a pretty young thing from Los Angeles. "And Lord only knows what people must think of when they see 'Coxsackie,'" she'd say after that.) And then he wondered: how did Walt, who gave every indication of being a small-town man from Motte and Bailey or its immediate environs, know the names of tiny towns in upstate New York?

"Now that you mention it," Nancy said, taking up the thread of Walt's question, "I've never known them to go anywhere at all. Sometimes they go over to the river, or down to the reservoir outside Pendleton, but Crackers is scared of drowning, so they don't do that real often." She paused, rubbing the end of her nose thoughtfully, and when she was done there was big gray smudge, and Tony had an almost irresistible urge to take a napkin and wipe it off for her. "And when they do go anywhere," she said, "they always tell us before they go, and tell us all about it when they come back."

"But not this time," Walt said.

"Those two are good and scared of Roj," Nancy said to Tony. "Roj has always used it against 'em, knew he could make 'em do just about anything and they wouldn't fight back."

Tony saw an unspoken agreement pass from Nancy to Walt and back again: later, they'd interrogate Crackers and Jems, ask them where they went, see if they knew anything about Sam's death. "Why wait?" he said, and then realized the point of a secret unspoken agreement between friends is that no one gives voice to it. "I mean, why can't we go visit them today?"

Nancy shook her head, and there was a finality to the gesture, a warning to leave it alone.

"I'm not doing anything after work," Tony said, ignoring the warning.

"Stop digging," Walt said shortly.

Tony recognized the reference to the old adage *When you find yourself at the bottom of a hole stop digging,* and then he thought with some resentment that it was the second time in as many days that Walt had told him to *stop digging.*

* * *

Another unbearable Monday. Tony tried on daytime television, as if it was an outfit from Walmart that might look okay if you squinted but, much like wearing khakis and doing his own laundry, was ultimately a poor fit. He used the microwave in his room to warm the food Nancy'd sent home with him yesterday, read, napped, paced the halls, tried (unsuccessfully) to engage Irene-the-front-desk-woman in conversation, tried to call home to talk to Caroline (also unsuccessfully), and then spent a fair amount of time feeling sorry for himself.

Until he reminded himself it could be worse; he could be a dead man nobody loved, buried in a shallow unmarked grave under a drought-stunted shrub less than five miles outside of town.

* * *

Leesa and Nareen arrived at work the next day at the same time but in two very different frames of mind.

"We went to that class on Sunday," Leesa said, checking the ketchup and mustard levels as she talked, "and they showed videos of the miracle of birth." She set the bottles on each table, the clank of glass against Formica emphasizing her words. "Man, those women *screamed*. It was like that scene from *Alien*. Made me decide right there and then there's no fucking way I'm ever having a baby. The camera got right up in there, in between their legs, and there was blood and guts and stuff you just never want to see."

"But then you have a beautiful baby," Nancy said, giving Leesa the oh-my-God-stop-talking look.

"It would have to be some baby to make it worth all that," Leesa said, shaking her head.

Walt didn't rely on subtleties. "Shut it, Leesa," he said.

Nareen muttered something about morning sickness and *not too late to change my mind* and rushed out of the room.

Only then did Leesa seem to realize what she'd done. "I'm sorry," she said, looking stricken.

"It's okay," Tony said, thinking he knew something about hurting people without meaning to, and how that can prey on your mind afterward, when it's too late to do anything to fix the hurt you've caused.

Roj came in at his regular time, and sat in his regular booth.

"Found Sam yet?" Nancy asked pointedly.

Roj just grunted, his characteristic smug look uncharacteristically missing.

Nareen recovered enough to take care of customers. Leesa apologized profusely, but as far as Tony could tell, she was not forgiven.

"I don't really need the two of them here at the same time," he overheard Nancy tell Walt, "now that I've got Tony here to bus tables. I'll just alternate their schedules for a while until Leesa grows a brain."

And when will that be? Tony wondered.

Have I grown a brain yet? he thought.

Does it hurt?

* * *

That night, he saw the piece of paper he had inadvertently stolen from Walt's truck sitting on the cramped desk in the corner of his motel room. He didn't *mean* to snoop, he told himself, as he started to unfold the paper. And then: I'm the president of a thriving company, I don't need to explain anything to a short-order cook. He heard himself practicing how he could apologize and say the paper had fallen open when he picked it up. And then he realized with a clenching pain that started somewhere in his gut and spread upward to his chest and downward to his buttocks and his legs that this was how he ended up here, in bumfuck Oregon, by ignoring the voice in his head that said *don't.*

So he didn't.

The next day, he handed the piece of paper to Walt. "The other night, when I got out of your truck, this got stuck to my shoe," he said.

When your face is grizzled and pock-marked and lined with years of anger and grief, it isn't really possible to look ashen, but Walt's face did a passable imitation of blanching.

"Did you look at it?" he said grimly, in the same tone of voice a man might say *Will it be hanging or the firing squad?*

"No," Tony said, meeting Walt's eyes.

Walt shoved the paper into one of the pockets of his ancient fatigues, and turned back to the onions he was chopping. After that, the only sounds from Walt for at least an hour were the rhythmic whack of the knife against the cutting board and the angry whir of the blender and the whining scrape of metal whisk against metal bowl.

# Chapter 7

And then there was the day a stranger came to town.

Tony was affronted. It was the last Friday in July, and he had been in Motte and Bailey for almost seven weeks (but who's counting?), long enough to be yesterday's news even in this place where "news" consisted mostly of who had accidentally ignited a house fire with weekend grilling, who was in jail for driving under the influence (again), and whose kid was on the honor roll this month. Nareen was a freak (not Nareen personally, just the fact of her existence here, a young person who had come *from* the big city *to* this town in the middle of nowhere, rather than the other way around). Everything else was regular and predictable, and Tony had just about figured it all out. He knew all the employees at Sunnyside Up, of course, and he knew the regular customers: Roj; Crackers and Jems; the handful of people who actually seemed to have a job, who came in right when the restaurant opened to grab a cinnamon roll or a doughnut and a cup of coffee before heading to work; the young families who allowed themselves the luxury of breakfast out before church on Sundays, who squabbled in whispers over the prices, saying, "You and your brothers can share—you don't need a whole stack of pancakes to yourself." He knew Nancy's mother, who sometimes forgot to change out of her dirty pink slippers before popping into the restaurant for a cup of coffee (when she wasn't traveling the backroads in their fifth-wheeler or snow-birding it in Florida), and Nancy's sister, who said almost every time she came in that she was going to get the hell out of Dodge one of these days, and make something of herself. Less than two months into his sentence, working six days a week from open to close, Tony knew them all, knew their schedules and what they'd order and even where they'd sit when they came in, and he liked things to stay the same once he'd achieved that state. Actually, he'd been in the habit of *insisting* that everything stay the same, comfortable in the knowledge that change could only happen on his say-so.

So he was offended when a shifty-eyed Mexican in slightly worn, too-big dress slacks and a dingy white button-down shirt showed up at the restaurant, sat in Roj's booth, and asked if anyone knew where he could rent a room for a few weeks.

Nancy had supplied the "shifty-eyed" and the "Mexican" when describing the newcomer to her sister. The two of them were sitting at the counter after the restaurant had closed for the day, Nancy supervising the end-of-day clean-up and her sister flinging gossip with the casual aplomb Walt used on breakfast potatoes. "Not that his race has anything to do with it," Nancy added loudly, speaking in the direction of Tony, as if he by virtue of being foreign to Motte and Bailey were more likely than anyone else to be offended by racism.

"I believe 'Mexican' refers to country of origin, not race," Tony offered helpfully.

"Well, we got plenty of Mexicans around here, and they haven't ever been any trouble," Nancy said, still speaking loudly.

"That's right," her sister said. "We wouldn't be able to run the farms without 'em. And that family what owns the restaurant in town, they seem real nice."

"But this one, he's new, and he won't say what his business is," Nancy said.

Apparently, Tony thought, you're supposed to announce your intentions at Sunnyside Up when you first come to town. The poor schmuck had just arrived and already he'd broken the rules all unknowing.

Notwithstanding his sympathy, Tony had to agree: the newcomer was shifty-eyed.

For one thing, he seemed to be asking a lot of questions. After his initial appearance he started showing up every day, shortly after the diner opened, wearing some variation of the same dreary outfit, and he'd ask whoever was serving him, or sometimes the occupants of the booth or table nearest to where he was sitting: Do the local schools have a War-on-Drugs program? What's the graduation rate from the high school? From Blue Mountain Community College?

About a week after his arrival he directed a question at Nancy that made Walt and Tony stop what they were doing and exchange glances while trying to look as if they were not exchanging glances: Has anyone gone missing recently?

"If they had we'd call the county sheriff," Nancy said.

"Or," Nareen interjected, fixing them all with her fiercest stare, "people could just leave other people alone." She handed a menu to a man who had just come in, whose paunch was so sizeable he had some difficulty squeezing into the booth, and then she turned again to Nancy and the shifty-eyed newcomer. "If a grown woman wants to disappear for a while," she added, "she has the right to do just that, without having some baggy-pants P.I. sniffing around after her like she's a criminal."

It had not occurred to Tony (or to Walt or Nancy, for that matter) that the newcomer could be after Nareen rather than Sam. When the questions started, Tony assumed he was a journalist, or an undercover cop. He also assumed, based on what Walt had told him about Sam's life and his death, that drugs were involved in the investigation, more particularly the purchase and sale of drugs, not just personal use, which was why it made sense to him that there would be media or law enforcement involved.

"My pants are baggy because I recently lost weight," the shifty-eyed man said, sounding smug. "And why do you think anyone would care where you are?" He waved at Nareen dismissively.

"I'd care, if I'd lost her," Nancy said angrily.

"We all would," Tony said, finding a vehement loyalty springing up from some unexpected place in his heart.

"So you *are* a baggy-pants P.I.?" Scooter said, surprising them all.

"I'm just passing through," the man said, sounding sullen.

"Then why are you asking so many questions?" Nancy said.

"I just like to get to know a place when I'm passing through," he said.

"Bullshit," Walt said from the kitchen, startling everyone in the restaurant, including the few customers who had been eavesdropping on the conversation.

"Watch your mouth," Nancy said. "There's customers here."

"Poppycock, then," Walt said, poking his head through the pass-through window. "At least you could tell the truth if you want us to believe you. Nobody just wanders into Motte and Bailey and stays for a whole week, and nobody who's just passing through asks all kinds of questions about drugs and missing persons."

"He's got a point," Tony said. "Who are you, and why are you here?"

"I'm nobody," the stranger insisted. "Why don't you people just leave me alone?"

Tony had never been a very effective company president, but he knew how to take control of a meeting, at least. "I think we got off on the wrong foot," he said, wiping his hands on his apron and taking a seat across from the man. "I'm Tony. Welcome to Motte and Bailey."

"Luis Delgado," the stranger said.

They shook hands, both eyeing each other with distrust but both obviously familiar with the social protocols for pretending they trusted each other.

Another surprise in this surprising day: Scooter sat down next to Tony, across from Luis. He said nothing in the interchange that followed, just glared at Luis and visibly tried to look menacing.

"Where are you from, Tony?" Luis said, sipping his coffee and grimacing at the taste. (Nancy only believed in one kind of coffee: airplane-fuel strength, and that was especially true of the decaf coffee Luis had ordered. She seemed to feel you had to do *something* to make up for the lack of caffeine).

"Wisconsin, originally," Tony said, lying with a facility he didn't know he had—never having had to lie before, he had supposed it would be difficult. "My family moved to New York City when I was a kid. My parents passed away when I was in college, and after my inheritance was used up, I came out here. I used to have an aunt in Seattle, and I was on a road trip to visit her but only got as far as Motte and Bailey before the money ran out and my aunt stopped returning my calls." He figured that was enough misleading information to keep Luis from finding out his real identity. He knew he sounded like an East Coast person educated at Yale or someplace similar, so any tale of being a local would never fly, but a once-rich-now-down-on-his-luck story was more plausible, or at least he hoped it was.

"Your turn," he said with practiced civility.

"My turn?" Luis said.

"Where are you from, and where are you 'passing through' to?"

"Ohio," Luis said. "By way of Portland. I don't know what comes after Motte and Bailey. I just go where they send me." He pulled out a badge and flashed it at Tony and Scooter, too briefly for any of them to see the jurisdiction or even whether it was a fake badge from a party store. "PDX Detective Delgado," he said. "And your cook's right, I'm not just passing through."

"What are you investigating?" Tony said, still keeping his voice pleasant.

"I'm not at liberty to say," Luis said.

Scooter listened, his eyes wide and his nostrils flaring.

Walt came all the way out of the kitchen, and extended his hand with a look that was anything but welcoming. "Walt Whitman," he said. "Don't ask about the name." And in case the subtext was unclear, he said, "We don't take to strangers here."

Luis stood and took the proffered hand and shook it, and for a moment it looked as if the two men were engaged in a game of chicken, neither willing to release the other's hand first.

"Were you in the service?" Luis said, eyeing the ragged fatigues and decrepit army boots.

"I was," Walt said.

"Which branch? Where did you serve?"

"I'm not at liberty to say," Walt said, dropping Luis's hand.

Damn! Tony thought. For a split second, he had hoped he might finally learn something about Walt.

"Order up," Nancy interjected, looking pointedly at Walt. "Shit on a shingle."

"'Shit on a shingle'?" Tony repeated, bewildered. He was reasonably certain that had not been one of the terms in the Sunnyside Up lingo training.

"Creamed beef on toast," Nancy translated. "Scooter, Mr. Delgado here hasn't ordered his food yet, and I'm pretty sure he didn't come in to enjoy your company. Table four needs coffee, Tony."

They dispersed reluctantly, but all that day Tony felt as if invisible lines connected him to Nancy, Walt, Scooter, and Nareen. They watched each other and Luis, knowing that the slightest tug on those invisible lines would bring the others to the center, no longer one person facing the unknown but a body with multiple fronts.

"We're staying late to clean the ovens and replace the broken trim on the counter," Nancy said that afternoon, "and then we're all going out for a drink."

Tony nodded, not sure if there was a hidden message.

"We're going to Joe's," Nancy said. "It's less than five miles away, so you won't have any problem going there because of your, ah, you know . . . ."

There *was* a hidden message—he was being invited out for a drink after work, with his co-workers and his boss. Tony wanted so badly to hug Nancy he actually leaned in, but thought better of it.

"Okay!" he said instead, bouncing up onto the balls of his feet with happiness. "All righty then!"

"You're weird," Nancy said.

Weird Tony, that's me! Tony thought.

* * *

Joe's Bar & Grill was dark, and quiet. Not the place to be in Motte and Bailey, even on a Saturday night, apparently, or maybe five o'clock was just too early for the regulars. Although smoking in restaurants and bars had been illegal for quite a while in Oregon, the upholstered booths and dingy carpets exhaled decades of old smoke. A pool table with worn felt stood empty in the back of the bar, forlorn and unloved like an old dog in an abandoned junk yard. Tony peered into the gloomy corners, curious. He'd had cocktails with important work-related contacts at glittering venues in Manhattan, but he was unfamiliar with the practice of gathering *en masse* with a motley assortment of one's peers at a dive bar.

They sat in a row at the bar, and Tony imagined how the montage would look captured in a glossy magazine photo: at one end, Nancy, probably a full two feet shorter than Walt (the tallest person in the group), her hair shot with gray, her bottom spilling ever-so-slightly over the edges of the barstool, a worn pale blue sweatshirt with faded lettering hiked up on her comfortably– but not overly–wide back, something in the posture clearly suggesting the others in the line answered to her; then Tony, his ever-present khakis wrinkled and stained from the day's work, the cut of his hair still reminiscent of a man who has his own personal barber, but overly long and shaggy now that he's been without a haircut for two months; then Nareen, young, attractive, fashionably-dressed—if the photographer stood behind them, he'd miss the intelligence in her eyes, and the bemused look that said how-the-hell-did-I-end-up-here-with-these-people?; then Walt, hunched over the bar like a cantankerous Father Time, leaning ever so slightly toward Nareen, as if by his mere presence he could protect her. And what would the caption read?

*ABC Corp President Checks Out Oregon Market By Having a Drink With Prospective Customers?* More likely: *Crew of Local Café Enjoys a Beer at Joe's.*

Tony had a beer, and then another, something with the word Rogue in it (libertarian beer —who knew?), an unfamiliar brew but enjoyable. Nareen had a Shirley Temple. She was just going to order a club soda but Nancy insisted on ordering something more festive for her, something that at least looked like a cocktail. Walt remained taciturn through two whiskey and sodas, with Nancy as the foil chattering on about nothing in particular, even though she joined Nareen in the Non-Alcoholics club. "Drank too much as a young woman so now I just stick to diet Coke," she said.

Leesa joined them after Tony's third beer, filling the last seat at the end of the bar, and Nareen looked away, clearly still annoyed, or terrified, or perhaps both.

"Who're you texting with?" Nancy said to Nareen, eyeing with distaste the thumbs flying over the screen.

"My mom," Nareen said, without looking up.

Tony was surprised to find Nareen was in contact with her mother, but then again, it wasn't as if Nareen had been sent away. Unlike Tony, Nareen had chosen to leave home for a while, to "hear herself think."

Had it worked? he thought.

After a couple of hours, when some of them were pleasantly buzzed and others (*i.e.* Leesa, who had been drinking steadily since she arrived) were smashed, Nancy said to Walt, as if they had just been discussing it, as if she wasn't responding nearly a month later to Walt's half-overheard mutterings, "In answer to your question, Mr. Nosy, I was at the bus station to pick up my daughter."

"Your daughter?" Tony said.

"Her name's Gertrude," Nancy said. "I know, it's a funny kind of name, but it was my best friend's name growing up and I knew if I ever got the chance I'd name my daughter Gertrude, so when the time came, I did. I think my friend said her parents named her after Gertrude Stein or something. I looked up Gertrude Stein but now I can't remember why she was important."

Tony made a mental note to request a book about Gertrude Stein at the local library, and bring it to Nancy. She should know something, he thought, about the woman who was responsible for the name of her best friend and, by extension, her daughter.

"Gerty's in town?" Leesa said.

"No," Nancy said shortly. "She left again on the next bus when she heard Roj hadn't moved away like he threatened to do."

"Roj is Gerty's dad," Leesa explained.

Tony felt in danger of falling off his bar stool, like a cartoon character demonstrating the vaudeville interpretation of *astonished*. Solid, stable, down-to-earth Nancy, and sleazy, disingenuous, possibly-murderous Roj? He wondered briefly whether there was anyone in town Roj *hadn't* bedded or fathered. He thought of Sam, the body disintegrating more slowly than the memory of him, and he thought of Walt's comment that Roj took a perverse pride in his bastard children, except for Sam.

"So you raised your daughter alone?" Nareen said, and Tony knew the others wondered, as he did, how Nancy would finesse her answer to avoid causing further anxiety for Nareen while also steering clear of false assurances.

"Yes," Nancy said shortly.

"But don' worry," Leesa interjected. "It'll be easier for you." She leaned over Walt and tried to pat Nareen's leg, missing by a few inches. "Big city like Portland. No racism. Y'know. People 'spect single moms. And, y'know, black moms."

There was a heartbeat of silence in which to wonder which part of Leesa's pronouncement was most outrageous and most ignorant, and whether Nareen would respond.

"'No racism'?" Nareen said, and it was as if she was just too tired to be angry. "What planet are you living on, Leesa?" She looked as if she was going to say more, but instead took a long pull at her ridiculous pink drink and then slid off the barstool and went to the restroom.

A little later, when the others were occupied with their conversations, and the noise in the bar (which had become more crowded as the night wore on) enveloped them in privacy almost as effectively as walls, Nancy leaned over and said, "You handled that guy Luis pretty well, Tony. That's the first time I've seen you act like a big shot company president."

Tony grimaced because he wasn't sure if it was a good thing to act like a big shot company president, but the warmth in Nancy's eyes seemed to speak of appreciation, not criticism.

"We woulda never got the truth out of him otherwise," she said.

"We still don't know what he suspects or who he's after," Tony pointed out.

"I'd bet my bottom dollar we'll find out soon," Nancy said.

And then, though he knew he had no right to ask, no right to know, he said, "How old is your daughter?"

"Thirty-four," Nancy said.

Nancy had mentioned once that she was forty-nine, and she was going to do something big to celebrate the big five-oh when it came around in February. Roj looked like he was in his seventies.

Maybe it wasn't as bad as killing a little girl with a stuffed panda, but it was bad, nonetheless.

They stayed and talked and drank for several hours. Tony was reluctant to leave, not wanting to go back to his empty motel room, knowing it was too late to call Caroline, with the time difference, but eventually he said his goodbyes and headed out. As he was crossing the gravel parking lot, he heard the door swing shut. It was Leesa, and she yelled for him to wait up.

He waited, and she caught up, and leaned drunkenly against his arm. They stood at the edge of the tiny parking lot, the dust kicked up by their footsteps swirling and sparkling in the dim blue light of the streetlamp, and then without warning Leesa pulled Tony close and whispered, "I saw your ankle-thing. When you were sitting at the bar, and I was coming back from the ladies' room. Your pants-leg hiked up, and I saw it. You must be a criminal. That is so sexy."

And then she kissed him, until he pulled away. "You're not driving are you, Leesa?" he said gently.

"Nope," she said, and she giggled. "I walked. Will you take me home with you?"

"I'm married," he said, thinking how easy it would be to kiss this girl with her freckled nose and her utter naivete about the world and her ludicrous attempts to sound tough and urbane.

But he didn't want to kiss Leesa. He wanted to kiss Caroline and sleep in their eight-hundred-thread-count organic cotton and satin-blend sheets imported from Italy that had been ironed by Addy or whoever Addy's replacement was, and he wanted to get up in the morning and order people about from his many-windowed office at ABC Toys HQ. He wanted to be Giles, not Tony, not the clumsy busboy who worked at a diner in Motte and Bailey, who knew that a kindly-looking monk-like old man had apparently taken advantage of every underage girl in town and then left her to fend for herself and her illegitimate child. He wanted to be someone who didn't know where one of those illegitimate children lay decomposing, after it had been tossed into a dumpster.

"Come on, L-E-E-S-A," he said. "I'll walk you home."

"It's not really L-E-E-S-A," Leesa said. "I jus' tell everyone that. 'L-I-S-A' is so fucking boring."

"I'll bet your mother didn't think so," Tony said.

They walked the few blocks to Leesa's apartment. Or rather, Tony walked, trying gamely to steer Leesa along a reasonably straight path. Leesa wobbled and weaved and laughed over nothing at all, and once she said, "I think I just peed my pants."

Leesa lived in the Garden Glade Apartments, a bunker of a building obviously constructed in the sixties, with a couple dozen units and a sign that said *Vacan y I quire Withi* propped against the corner, faintly lit from above by an anemic flickering spotlight that couldn't seem to decide whether it wanted to be on or not. The sign was flanked by two dusty flower beds housing bedraggled marigolds and black-eyed susans and stunted dahlias, stoop-shouldered and gasping for water.

Tony helped Leesa navigate the lock, propelled her gently inward, and flicked the switch in the entry. The apartment was dilapidated but tidy: clean dishes in the rack by the sink; brown braided rug in front of a plaid sofa in the living room; a couple of thriving spider plants by the window. A plaque over the kitchen counter said *Don't Bother Me I'm Busy Living Happily Ever After.* Tony guided Leesa to the sofa, where she sat with a slightly pained sigh.

"See you tomorrow, Leesa," he said.

"No you won'," she said, and she giggled, as if it was funny, not seeing him. "Not working a' Sunnyside Up tomorrow." She cocked her head and looked up at him with one eye closed. "Do you think I'm cute?" she said.

"Yes," Tony said.

"Nareen's cuter. Do you think she thinks I'm cute?"

Before Tony could answer, Leesa said, "I'm not a lesbo, you know."

"It would be okay if you were," Tony said mildly.

"I know, I know. It's just that sometimes I don't know what . . ." the thought trailed away into the night, and Tony thought: yes, sometimes I don't know what, either.

He engaged the doorknob lock and shut the door behind him, and suddenly there was Luis again.

"Ubiquitous," Tony said, frowning at the shifty-eyed countenance he was sure was squinting at him in the dark.

"No idea what that means," Luis said. "And I don't really care. What I'd like to know, Tony, is why you're wearing a dog-collar around your ankle."

# Chapter 8

"You're not here to investigate me," Tony said, and it wasn't intended to be a these-aren't-the-droids-you're-looking-for kind of statement, only the truth. The proceedings against his company were a matter of public record, and local law enforcement was aware of his real identity. He was only a mystery to the residents of Motte and Bailey. Giles Anthony Maurice Gibson, *aka* Tony, was not, or shouldn't have been, a proper subject for police investigation. He'd already been tried and found wanting, as the old lady says in the modern version of the movie *The Ladykillers*. Or was that a G.K. Chesterton quote?

Lost in his thoughts, he almost missed the detective's retort.

"Don't tell me my job," Luis said.

Tony sighed, deeply, trying but failing to exhale the fog of alcohol and sadness from his veins. "Let's go to my hotel room," he said.

"Okay," Luis said. "But I'm armed."

"Fine," Tony said, because that seemed the appropriate response, "but I'm not."

In his room in the motel, Tony sat on the bed, his head spinning from the oddly-named beer and the lack of dinner.

Luis sat in the armchair upholstered with oversized red poppies. The springs squeaked as he shifted around to try to get comfortable (or perhaps trying look more intimidating—the chair was lower than the bed, leaving Tony in the physically superior position).

"Where are you *really* from?" Luis said.

Tony lifted his leg and showed his skinny ankle with the clunky device. "I have an ankle monitor, so you should be able to figure out my history without questioning me," he said. Luis's gloomy face, the red poppies on the chair, the cheap polyester bed covering . .

. with every passing minute this encounter felt more surreal. He wrestled with the sensation, and attempted to channel his company president persona. "I'm being monitored at all times," he said, by way of additional explanation. "So it's extremely unlikely I'm involved in whatever you're looking into."

Luis squinted at him, and his expression said *Why won't you answer my question?*

But that wasn't the question Tony wanted to answer, and that's the thing about power and privilege: you get to decide what the question is.

"Look," he said. "Part of my sentence included the extremely unusual requirement—unheard of, probably—that I live here, in Motte and Bailey, perform community service, and work at Sunnyside Up to pay for my living expenses. My whereabouts are monitored to ensure I don't leave town." He spoke carefully, fighting against the sensation that this was all a dream, a nightmare. He was pretty sure if he didn't guard his speech the next thing out of his mouth would be *Beware the Jabberwock, my son! The jaws that bite, the claws that catch! Beware the Jubjub bird, and shun The frumious Bandersnatch!*

"The Bander-who now?" Luis said, more than mere puzzlement in his eyes, and Tony realized then that he hadn't been careful, hadn't guarded his words, he'd quoted nonsense and now Luis thought he was crazy as well as guilty of some crime or crimes unknown.

So much for the position of power and privilege.

"I'll look up your history," Luis said. "But what about that community service? I've been here for over a week and I haven't seen you picking up litter on the highway or planting flowers in the town square. What's the deal there?"

Tony had honestly forgotten about the community service (again) until the shifty-eyed man sitting across from him raised the issue. No one had ever reached out to give him an assignment, and as he'd told Caroline when she asked, he was determined to let sleeping dogs lie. Maybe someone somewhere had decided working in a diner was enough of a punishment.

He could only hope.

He stroked his chin as an excuse to cover his mouth, to prevent more beautiful nothings from escaping. He crossed one foot over the other, obscuring the ankle monitor, and then, to distract the detective's gaze from his ankle, he said, "You know, I arrived less than two months ago, and I know very little about the town or anything going on around here. I do hear things, working at the diner. All of us do. I could probably be useful to you, if I was so inclined, and if you told me what you're looking for. Otherwise, I'm a dead end."

Luis seemed to digest the information, looking for a reason to argue. Tony waited a small eternity, and finally Luis shrugged, seeming to accept Tony's statement.

"I can't tell you what I'm looking for," he said. "That's confidential information." He stared pointedly at the ankle monitor and added, "Even if I could tell you, I probably wouldn't. I don't trust you. Call it intuition. It's not just that you're a convicted criminal, you just seem . . . weak."

" 'Weak'?" Tony said. He was almost but not quite too tired to be offended. Was the downward spiral of his life ever going to end? A year ago he was having poached eggs on toast in a gleaming dining room in his Manhattan flat, thinking about a round of golf at the Inwood and enjoying the sight of his lovely wife across the table from him. Now he was sitting on a lumpy bed in a musty hotel room being called "weak" by a tattered detective.

"It's time for you to leave," he said.

"Mind if I ask to see your driver's license?" Luis said, getting up slowly.

"Yes, I do mind," Tony answered. "I've done nothing to give you reasonable suspicion that I'm currently engaged in illegal conduct. I'm tired and hungry and a little unpleasantly buzzed, and I'd like to be alone in my misery."

Mustering his last ounce of mental clarity, he steered Luis toward the door, and watched him exit. He closed the door behind Luis and locked it, and rested his forehead briefly against the cold metal plate running along the edge of the door. He could hear the detective's shuffling footsteps as they came to the end of the hall, and the ding as the elevator announced it had reached the second floor, and the whoosh of the doors as they slid open, and then closed again. Prying himself away from the door, he collapsed on the bed without flossing or brushing his teeth, or washing his face, or changing into his silk pajama pants, and slept the sleep of the damned.

\* \* \*

"We need to talk," Tony told Nancy and Walt the next day, rubbing the stubble on his chin irritably (they all looked a little worse for the wear, quite frankly). "Luis followed me home last night."

Walt looked murderous, and Nancy looked alarmed.

"If you can stand to be here on your day off," Nancy said, "We could meet here on Monday, when the restaurant is closed."

Mondays had been a special kind of torture for Tony. Time with nothing to do and no one to talk to, time to realize how unnecessary he was to the wheeling and turning of the universe. His only plan for tomorrow had been to check out the library for that book on Gertrude Stein.

"Sure," he said, as if it made no difference to him either way.

"I was going to do some canning tomorrow," Walt growled, and Tony couldn't stop himself from staring. "Early tomatoes are about ready," Walt said. "But I can come in first thing."

"'First thing' for Walt is about eleven," Nancy told Tony.

"On my day off it is," Walt said.

A few minutes later, just before opening, Nareen came in. She said nothing but "Morning," to the others, and spoke in quiet mono-syllables to the first round of customers. "I need a break," she told Tony. "My feet are swelling up."

"That's not good," Nancy snapped at Nareen, as if she was angry, as if Nareen had been unforgivably negligent in allowing her feet to swell. "You shouldn't have swelling feet at—what are you now, about four months . . . no, wait, like five months?" Nareen nodded. "Let's get you to the doc next week."

Nareen looked like someone trying not to look worried, and, turning back to Tony, asked if he would take care of the family at Table Four.

Tony smiled, all wistful thoughts of his past swept away by the joy of being asked to play hero in Nareen's hour of need, and being entrusted with the critical function of waiting tables. Quickly, he tried to go over the list of phrases in his head, and then he panicked: *heart attack on a rack* was the only one he could remember (other than *sunnyside up*, of course). What if someone wanted something other than biscuits and gravy or gently fried eggs?

The three boys at Table Four wanted the Short Stack with Bacon, mom visibly wanted pancakes but ordered the Yogurt Cup instead, and dad ordered the Farmer's Omelet and Home Fries. Easy enough, Tony thought. He refilled the adults' coffee, wiped the table when

Kid Number One spilled his juice, and remembered to bring the hot sauce dad said he liked to put on everything ("Keeps the wife and kids from eating off my plate," he said).

And that was the way the day went, with mostly happy customers, nothing other than small disasters, no Roj, no Luis, a break for lunch with the best French Dip sandwich in the universe ("I put a little fresh thyme and a splash of balsamic in the *au jus*," Walt said), clean up and refill and restock, then out the door and down the hot, dusty street to his motel. He planned to call Caroline, read a little, maybe catch a nap, then head back out for dinner. A day he could almost bring himself to call *pleasant*.

And then without warning a thought descended, a palpable, oppressive presence like the heat: the pleasure of waiting tables and helping Nareen, the smell of sizzling bacon, the sight of kids blowing bubbles in their chocolate milk—it was all a false peace, a comfortable routine that masked the rot underneath. Nothing could make up for the fact that there was a body buried just outside of town and a shabby detective sniffing around and a murderer in their midst.

* * *

"Do we know what he's investigating, yet?" Nancy said without preamble.

They were gathered around a table in the far corner of the restaurant, mostly hidden from the view of anyone walking by, so it wouldn't be obvious from the street that they were inside the closed restaurant. ("Some fool'll be bound to bang on the door thinking if we're inside we might as well open up and serve them," Nancy observed, "If they can see us in here, I mean.")

Walt had made sour cream coffee cake for their meeting, with raspberries and hazelnuts worked into the crumble-top. The cake part melted in your mouth, but when Tony said how unutterably wonderful it was, Walt pursed his lips.

"No," Tony said, in response to Nancy's question. "He asked me about my ankle monitor, and I told him I'm not the guy he's looking for."

"What, like Obi-Wan Kenobi?" Nancy said, smiling.

"If he backed off, then you're right, it's not you." Walt said. "He didn't seem interested in Nareen, so it's gotta be whatever Sam was mixed up in. Probably drugs, maybe worse."

"'Worse' like what?" Tony asked.

"Quiet little town like this can hide a lot of dirty little secrets," Walt said. "Human trafficking, child porn, mafia stuff."

Tony thought of his own dirty little secret and grimaced. He caught Nancy's eye and knew she knew what he was thinking.

"He's a police detective, not a private P.I., so it'd have to be something that affects a lot of people." Walt continued. "Probably just garden variety drugs," he said. "Miles to go before I sleep and no one watching the henhouse but the fox...."

Tony resisted the urge to point out that Walt was mixing not only metaphors but also literary allusions.

"That's probably the real reason Roj was so concerned about Sam's disappearance," Nancy said with a flash of insight. "I don't think for a minute he gives a damn about his son, but if Sam is—or was—a tool in one of his schemes, and he goes missing, there goes Roj's retirement plan."

"What kind of drugs?" Tony asked.

"It's easy enough to grow weed out here without going through all the rigamarole of getting licensed," Walt said. "But you could also live off the grid and make a whole lot of meth, and no one would ever know."

Tony felt instantly out of his depth. Even though he had lived for most of his adult life in the heart of the city Henry James called "appalling, fantastically charmless and elaborately dire," he'd been mostly protected by the bubble of wealth. Making meth was not in the wheelhouse of a toy company executive who grew up in Oyster Bay Cove on Long Island.

"I still think we need to talk to Crackers and Jems," he said, thinking out loud and forgetting for the moment Walt's admonition to stay away from that subject. "I mean, they're obviously hiding something."

Nancy sighed, and rubbed her temples. "Crackers and Jems are 'partners,'" she said. "Everybody knows it but nobody says it. If we start asking questions they'll squeal like stuck pigs and claim we're harassing them because they're gay."

Tony thought that was the most surprising thing he'd learned about this surprising backwater town so far—that a gay couple should decide to stay in what had to be an overtly homophobic community, and that the likely-overtly-homophobic community mostly refrained from persecuting them.

"Which would be stupid," Nancy continued, "because the secret's been out ever since Crackers chose Malibu Barbie over a Fisher Price dump truck when he was three, at the Community Center Christmas celebration." She ran her fingers through her hair, with disastrous results, and then somewhat self-consciously tried to smooth it over. "I remember how he stroked the doll's hair and said *Pretty* over and over," she said, her face holding that inward-looking stare you get when you're playing the reel of old movies in your head.

"And nobody's ever bothered either of them about it," Walt said. "Motte and Bailey folks are every kind of small-town and small-minded, but we protect our own."

*We protect our own.* What a strange thought. As a member of the Long Island Gibsons, Giles had carried a bubble of protection as a birthright. Now he was outside the bubble, looking with unexpected longing into a circle of wackos and weirdos who would, just like the illustrious Gibsons, protect those who by fortune or fate were inside the circle when it was drawn.

"What if I just asked them? Casually? You know, 'I'm new around here, looking for somewhere to go, somewhere to get out of town for a while.' They mentioned last week they'd gone out of town, I could just be . . . following up."

Walt scowled, and looked as if he was planning once again to reject the suggestion out of hand, then he nodded. "Might as well try," he said.

"But we still need to figure out what to do about Luis," Nancy said.

Tony looked at the remainder of the coffee cake, wondering whether it was socially acceptable to ask for another piece, and then decided this was a moment for executive action by Giles, not tentative cake-lust by Tony. He reached across Walt and scooped himself another generous helping.

"They sure didn't teach you any manners in New York City," Nancy said, raising an eyebrow. "You could have just asked me to pass you the plate."

"Good god, you're from New York City?" Walt said. "No wonder." He left that thought unfinished.

Ignoring the jibe, Tony said, "If we think Luis is here about drugs, and about Sam and Roj and whoever else is mixed up in it, then we're more or less on the same side as Luis, aren't we? So why not work with the detective rather than around him?"

It didn't occur to Tony until later that the three of them had shifted, without realizing it, from hoping the news of Sam's death would never surface, to investigating the situation themselves, and now to "working with" a detective who might or might not be investigating Sam's death.

The prospect of collaborating with the mealy-mouthed shabby detective was unsavory to Tony, and it was obvious from their expressions that Nancy and Walt felt the same, but after a highly-charged second or two Walt said reluctantly, "I guess that makes sense. If we work with him we can control what he finds out, to some extent, and make sure he focuses on criminal activity instead of poking around in everyone's dirty laundry."

"Exactly," Tony said.

"What did you do in the Big Apple anyway?" Walt said unexpectedly.

"Company president," Tony said without blinking an eye or pondering Walt's sudden change from taciturn to curious.

Walt whistled. "Never would have guessed. Not in a million years."

"What did you do in the army?" Tony said.

"Went AWOL," Walt said.

* * *

That night Caroline called Tony—for the first time since he'd moved to Motte and Bailey. And another first: he wasn't sure what to say to her, even felt a little impatient that she was taking up precious time when he could be strategizing for the next day. He told her about the coffee cake, but she'd never been as passionate about good food as he. Food could transport him. The savory and sweet smells that assailed him when walking into Tulsi, the Indian restaurant in uptown with curtained tables and high-backed chairs of exotic dark wood, where he sometimes dined with Caroline or a business partner, those odors made him understand the word "swoon" on a visceral level. And the opposite was true, too; a disappointing meal ruined Tony's mood for a long time. But if somebody served Caroline something she didn't like, she just didn't eat it.

They talked for a little while about the unyielding heat in Motte and Bailey, an oppressive force by mid-afternoon, like walking into an oven, and about how much Tony missed the cool breezes that curled off the bay over his childhood home.

"I miss you," Caroline said, and Tony suddenly found it hard to breathe.

"Do you remember a few years ago at that horrendous Thanksgiving at your Aunt Zelda's?" she said. "How we pretended you had to go check your email but we hid in the billiards room closet and made love?"

Tony did remember, the warm tan smell of cards and poker chips and wooden backgammon boards and ivory chess pieces, and the muffled sounds Caroline made and the sweetness of release when it came, all too quickly. It's like waiting for cookies to bake, Caroline once said; there is crazy anticipation while the heavenly smell floats through the kitchen, and then almost without any intervening time there is the sudden realization that you've eaten the last warm cookie, and there are no more. The pleasure is always over too soon.

They shared a few more do-you-remembers, and Tony felt the strands of that life pulling him back, and he couldn't tell if the web that bound him to Nancy and Walt and Nareen and Leesa and Scooter was expanding to incorporate his old world or stretching to the breaking point as he vacillated between the old and the new.

* * *

The next day, Luis came in and sat in the booth behind Roj's booth, and within a few minutes Roj came in and took up his usual post.

Good, Tony thought. I'll tackle Luis, and Roj'll overhear. Maybe I can put the fear of God in him. He watched the two men for an opening, and noticed that for the first time Roj seemed to have dressed for the sake of being inconspicuous. Normally he wore a short-sleeved shirt in bright plaid or Hawaiian-style flowers, and jeans or slacks that announced long before he opened his mouth to speak: Don't mind me, I'm just a retired county sheriff who goes to church, a pillar in the community who loves to play with his grandkids. Today he was wearing a tan shirt and faded jeans, as if he could fade into the woodwork by dint of wearing unremarkable clothing.

It was now or never, Tony decided. "So Luis," he said, sliding into the booth across from the detective.

"So Tony," Luis said. "If that is your real name."

"It is," Tony said, thinking having *Antonio* for a middle name made that close enough to the truth. "I'd like to get you off my back, so I've decided to help you."

"Yes?" Luis said, looking guarded.

"You might want to start by speaking with the man sitting in the booth behind me—his name is Roger Lanyard. Roj for short. You might want to ask him about his offspring. He's apparently got more children than you can shake a stick at. A true Casanova, I've heard, and he never hangs around afterward to raise his bastards (and I use that term in the formal sense). It's my understanding that if there's ever anything shady going on, Roj has his fingers in it. He's the former head of the Sheriff's Department, but don't let that fool you. According to the locals, that never got in the way of doing anything that might profit him. He's been asking about one of his sons who has apparently gone missing. This particular son had a well-known history of addiction and drug abuse."

Luis absorbed this information slowly. "Why are you telling me this?

"I want you to leave me alone," Tony said, flattening his palms on the scratched table between them.

"I can't promise to do that," Luis said. "You're already involved because you know what you just told me. On top of that, you're a convict."

Tony stiffened. He'd rarely thought of himself as a convict. Just a man caught in the crosshairs of corporate problems. He felt nailed to the floor by the word, as if he was no longer Giles, average golfer, company president, husband to the lovely and charming Caroline, scion of the Long Island Gibsons. He wasn't even Tony, bumbling and largely inept server in a tiny town in the middle of the middle of nowhere. Just a convict.

"Whatever you think you need to do," he said, sliding out of the booth and standing up. "I just thought you'd appreciate the information."

As he walked away from the table Tony glanced at Roj. He'd heard. There was rage haloing the round face, and a thin veneer of to-hell-with-you, and something else: pain?

Nancy had been listening as best she could through the bustle and clank of restaurant sounds, and Tony could see that she must have reported what she'd heard to Walt, who had stopped making even a pretense of paying attention to his cooking and was now swearing eloquently over burnt eggs. Tony bussed a table, brought the dishes back to the kitchen, and was greeted with a furtive thumbs up by Nancy and a nod of approval by Walt (an admirable feat, accomplished without even a moment's hiatus in the profanity streaming from his lips).

Luis didn't take action immediately. He continued to sip his decaf coffee long after it was stone cold, watched the passers-by out the window, read the local paper. At one point he took his phone out of his pocket and started to look at it, but Nancy bustled over and rapped irritably on the table. "Sorry," Luis said. "I keep forgetting you don't allow cell phones in here." And then he said, "As long as you're here, I'd like to order a couple of pieces of toast. Dry, please."

"What the hell?" Walt muttered.

"That's the cleanest expletive I've heard from you yet," Tony said, grinning.

"Every day he orders the same thing: decaf coffee and dry toast. Dry toast is pointless," Walt said. "Might as well order a cardboard box to eat. And what is he playing at? Roj isn't going to stay here all morning just to give him an opening."

And yet as the morning wore on it seemed that was exactly what Roj intended to do. He ordered his usual, barely opening his mouth to form the words. He ate slowly, deliberately, and then allowed his coffee cup to be filled over and over. He got up, and the Sunnyside Up crew tensed, thinking he was leaving and Luis was going to miss his chance, but it was only to visit the Men's room. The breakfast rush cleared out, and then at long long last Luis stood up and moved to Roj's table.

"I'm Luis," he said without preamble. "I imagine you overheard my conversation with Tony. He was obviously talking loudly, hoping you'd hear. I apologize for intruding on your time—" (now it was Tony's turn to mutter what-the-hell? Luis hadn't apologized for intruding on *his* time) "—but I do need to follow up on every lead."

Roj waved at the seat across from him. "I don't know why I'm a 'lead' just because some second-chance jailbird tells you I've got kids out of wedlock," he said, "but as a former law enforcement officer I understand you've got your duty."

Ah, Tony thought. That was it. Luis and Roj belonged to the Club, and he, the Convict, did not.

"Is it true a son of yours has gone missing?" Luis said.

"Well now, it's hard to say," Roj said, and the veneer of cooperation was sickening. "My son Sam has had quite a few run-ins with the law. I tried to help as best I could," (playing the part of the grieving *paterfamilias*, Tony thought), "but there's only so much a father can do. After a while, I kind of gave up." He shook his head sorrowfully, a sad little smile playing about the corners of his eyes. "But I do try to check in from time to time, and I haven't been able to reach him lately. I have to confess it's got me worried."

Walt had to physically restrain Nancy from charging out onto the floor and calling Roj's elaborate bluff.

Luis nodded. "I can understand that. Is it true he, ah, suffered from addiction?"

Tony knew that hesitation; that was the "ah" of someone who didn't believe one "suffered from" addiction, someone who thought anyone with enough backbone and integrity would never *allow* himself to become addicted, but who understood that "suffer from" was the socially-acceptable terminology.

"It's true," Roj said. "Funny how that happens."

"Depends on your definition of 'funny,'" Nancy whispered furiously to Tony.

"Preachers' kids go to sinning, doctors' kids smoke cigarettes, and sheriffs' kids do drugs. Why do you suppose that is?"

Even Luis looked a little bored with the act. "Don't know," he said shortly. "Have you taken any steps to locate your son?"

"Just asked my boys over at the Department to keep an eye out," Roj said.

"Do you have any reason to believe your son was involved in selling or manufacturing, as well as using?" Luis asked.

"It's possible," Roj answered. "But I'd have no way of knowing."

Nancy broke free of Walt's grip and descended on the two men like a flat-bottomed middle-aged avenging angel. "You sure as shit would know!" she shouted. "You'd know because there's never been a single joint or ounce of smack in this town that hasn't greased your palm along the way!"

Roj looked up, and smiled gently, as if bestowing absolution on the local lunatic.

"Nancy is the mother of our daughter, Gertie. Gertie is a good girl, unlike Sam, but Nancy's never quite forgiven me. Y'see, Luis, I asked Nancy to marry me, and she turned me down. Then times got hard, and she begged me to ask her again, but I'd moved on by then. Met and married my beautiful Josie, and started a family with her. Josie passed away a few years ago, and I think Nancy's been hoping I'd reconsider ever since. You shouldn't mind what Nancy says. It's just her broken heart talking."

It was Nancy's—and Roj's—misfortune that she had been holding a nearly-full pot of coffee when she paused to listen to the conversation. That pot was now upended on Roj's shining, mostly-bald head. It was hot enough to sting but, sadly, not hot enough to scald, and when it was empty Nancy lifted the pot with the obvious intent of bringing the whole thing down on Roj, until Tony intervened.

Luis arrested Nancy on the spot, and they all waited until the sheriff arrived to take her to jail.

Leesa showed up just as Nancy was being ushered into the patrol car.

"Tell Nareen I won't be home tonight," Nancy told her, grimly, just before she took her seat in the back of the car.

In a rare display of circumspection, Leesa asked no questions until after the patrol car was gone.

"Why didn't you stop her?" she demanded of Tony.

"I tried," he said, feeling helpless.

"Walt could have stopped her," she said.

Tony sighed, wondering why this freckle-faced woman-child in this nowhere town had the power to make him feel such strong emotions (incompetent being the feeling of the moment).

"Where *is* Walt?" she said.

And that's when he noticed that Walt had disappeared. He could not imagine Walt abandoning his friends, and assumed there must be a rational explanation, but the fact remained that he was nowhere to be found, and the lunch crowd was beginning to trickle in.

"Do you know how to cook?" Leesa said.

"No. Do you?"

"I eat Kraft macaroni and cheese and Top Ramen," she said shortly. "I know it's not good for me," she added, as if Tony had given her a disapproving look (he had not). "But we're all going to die sooner or later, and what have I got to live so long for?"

Tony circumnavigated the area around the restaurant, including the alley behind the building. When he found neither Walt nor his motorcycle, he went back inside and announced that unfortunately Sunnyside Up would be closed for the day, as their cook was unavailable.

There was grumbling and sighing. A few who had come in right after Nancy'd been driven away, who hadn't yet heard the gossip from others in the diner, assumed Walt must be sick. "Tell the old bastard to get well soon so he can get back to making my lunch," one old-timer said gruffly. And then the customers trooped out and Tony flipped the Open sign to Closed.

"You kind of looked like you knew what you were doing there, Tony," Leesa said. "You kind of took charge. I like that."

Turning away from the signs of eminent mooning he said, "I wonder where Walt went?" And then he remembered: Walt had defected from the army. Though he didn't seem to be concerned about Roj, or even Luis, he probably didn't want to risk any encounters with unknown local law enforcement. Questions might be asked and the federal government might be alerted and what some might consider a long overdue prison sentence might be imposed.

And then we'd both be convicts together, Tony thought, but the thought did not make him smile.

# Chapter 9

The nearest jail was Pendleton, a little less than thirty miles from Motte and Bailey. Because of his ankle monitor, Tony couldn't join the rest of the crew when, an hour or so later, they descended on the diner with an almost-fully formed plan to visit Nancy in jail.

They went together: Leesa, Nareen, and Scooter. Walt was still MIA (an acronym that seemed grotesquely apt when it surfaced in Tony's mind). When Leesa asked if he was coming, Tony shook his head, and said he'd hold down the fort until they returned. Another military phrase. What're you going to do? War is everywhere, he thought. Or maybe the saying is *war is hell*. He couldn't remember.

Leesa seemed to guess his reluctance to join them had something to do with his ankle monitor, and she whispered discreetly, "Walt might know how to rig that thing so you could get away."

"I can't take the risk," Tony said sadly. "You go and give my love to Nancy, and when you come back I want to hear what happened." She nodded, absently, but he held her eyes. "Every detail," he said.

He was glad concern for Nancy and the need to get moving prevented Leesa from asking more about the whys and wherefores of his ankle monitor, as she so visibly wanted to do.

He watched as they crammed into Scooter's ancient Toyota Corolla. You wouldn't think "crammed" was the way of it for three people in a four-door sedan, but the back seat and floor on the passenger side were taken up with wood scraps that Scooter intended to use, he explained, for some as-yet-undetermined project. There were so many, piled higgledy-piggeldy in a dangerously tottering heap, that the passenger seat had to be positioned all the way forward, leaving little room for an actual passenger of any reasonable size and shape. Tony gave Nareen a hand folding her awkwardly swollen body into the abnormally small space in the front seat, but by the time he had come around to the other side Leesa was already buckling herself into the back, next to the heap of wood. She smiled at him mistily, obviously pleased at the thought that he had intended to help her into her seat.

"Aren't you worried the pile of wood scraps is going to fall on you?" he said, eyeing the heap nervously.

"Nah, I can handle it," Leesa said.

And then he went back into the empty diner and waited, first perusing last week's *Umatilla News*, then heading to the dusty, deserted Sundries store for a used paperback, then back to the diner to make a cup of bitter coffee (Nancy'd never shown him how) and a microwaved Butterhorn topped with a scoop of melting margarine, then finishing the last of the dishes from the customers who'd been served before Nancy's arrest, and finally going back to the booth to stare at the words in the paperback though his brain registered nothing, absolutely nothing.

After an hour or so, Walt showed up again, stomping into the kitchen through the back door as if nothing had happened. He nodded at Tony and went to work in the kitchen, presumably doing prep work for the next day, humming a Grateful Dead tune. (Tony only knew that's what it was because Walt said gruffly, "Hope you don't mind listening to the Dead," and when Tony looked at him quizzically, Walt sighed, and explained, "The Grateful Dead.") It was a tune called Friend of the Devil, Walt said. Tony wondered if Walt was the friend of the devil in this situation, or maybe Walt considered Tony Satan's compatriot. It was always hard to tell, with Walt.

In between pretending to read and listening to Walt humming tunelessly, Tony thought about what it would feel like to live in fear of being caught. Walt had said nothing more about being AWOL, and Tony was too young to have worried about war or being drafted. But, he thought, whatever Walt had done, it must have been years ago. Decades ago. Surely the army wouldn't still be after him now?

Though personal devices had been banned by the judge, no one had said anything about staying away from others' computers. On his next Monday off, he could go to the library and do a little research, he decided.

Except that the idea of presenting information to Walt was more than a little daunting, and he rolled his shoulders, sloughing off any intimation of responsibility for his fellow man.

Finally, the rest of the crew returned, and assembled in Sunnyside Up to give their report to Tony and Walt.

Highway 11 is pretty much the only road that runs between Motte and Bailey and Pendleton, Leesa explained, for Tony's benefit. She'd started to tell him about the jail, but he interrupted and asked about their route. He wanted to picture the journey, since he couldn't go and see it for himself, and he reminded her of her promise to share every detail.

"There's nothing much to see," she said dismissively, "unless you count dusty farms." She rubbed her nose thoughtfully. "Well, there is Athena. Got a few hundred people, maybe, people who didn't know any better or didn't have a choice. But that's about it. Pendleton feels like a goddamned bustling metropolis after Athena."

"It's called a 'micropolitan' area," Walt said, laconically.

"Yeah, because that sounds so much better than No-the-hell-where land," Leesa said.

"Hey, did you notice they're having their Doggy Dip Daze again?" Scooter interjected. "That's where they fill the pool with water but no chlorine, so people can bring their dogs to swim," he explained to Tony. "I was thinking of bringing Missy."

"Missy is Scooter's dog," Leesa said, in case that was not obvious. "She's sweet but dumb as a bag of hammers."

"I always wondered how a town that's even smaller than Motte and Bailey took on the name of a Greek goddess," Walt mused. "There's a couple of old buildings and a Scottish festival with bag-pipes and guys wearing skirts, but nothing that might make you think of Greece. No ocean or vineyards or ruined temples, anyway."

Tony wondered briefly if Walt had ever been to Greece, thinking Walt was a man with many hidden facets, so it wouldn't necessarily surprise him to learn Walt had been a world traveler before hiding out in Motte and Bailey.

"I suppose that's no odder than naming a patch of desert in the wild wild west after a kind of medieval castle, though," Walt added.

"You forgot to say there's a dirt bike factory in Athena," Leesa said.

"Is that where you got your hog?" Scooter asked.

Walt gave him a withering glance. "My Harley is not a dirt bike."

Scooter reddened and Leesa saw his face and changed the subject. "Who d'you think came up with the saying 'dumb as a bag of hammers?'" she said. "Hammers don't even have brains. Why would a bag of hammers be dumber than one hammer?"

"Oh my god," Nareen said. "Trying to get information from you all could drive a person insane. I'm sorry, Tony."

Tony had actually been enjoying the meandering conversation. "That's okay," he said, in case she was advocating for him.

"Nancy was still pretty mad when they finally let us in to see her," Nareen said, taking up the thread of the story. "Apparently she gave the poor young deputy an earful from the back of the patrol car. All the way to Pendleton." She grinned.

"She's got a mouth like a sailor," Leesa said, as if that would come as a surprise to anyone. "Do they call a woman sailor anything different than a man sailor?"

"I don't think so," Tony said.

"Luis was in the cell with her, trying to get some information," Scooter said.

"It was sort of like watching a young veterinarian try to trim the nails of a pissed-off cat," Nareen said. "Without a sedative."

"Did he find out if it was true? Did Roj really ask her to marry him?" Tony asked.

"Yes, it's true," Walt said. "But it was less like asking and more like suggesting he'd make her life a living hell if she didn't marry him."

"And he wasn't desperately in love with her or anything romantic like that," Leesa said. "He was running for county sheriff again, and us little people were on to him, so even with whatever he always did to rig the elections he needed something to boost his credibility with anyone who didn't know the real Roger, something nice and stable like a wife. A wife who ran the local diner that makes everybody happy."

"She turned him down," Walt said. "Pretty much spit on him and his offers and his threats."

"He won the election anyway," Scooter said.

"She calmed down when she saw us," Leesa said, returning to the story.

"A little," Nareen added.

"She wanted to know why we didn't bring her any goddamn food," Scooter said, wincing as he repeated the expletive.

"Are they going to let her go?" Tony asked.

"Only if she can make bail," Leesa said. "They've got her on disturbing the peace and assaulting a former officer of the law."

"The coffee was still hot," Nareen added, by way of explanation.

"But in the jail cell she went down the list of all the lowdown rotten things Roj has done over the years—at least the things she knows about—and I think Luis believed her when she said she couldn't really have done anything else, under the circumstances."

Luis went up a notch in Tony's opinion. "How much is bail?" he asked.

"Fifty thousand buckaroonies," Leesa said.

"What the hell?" Walt said. "Do they think she's a flight risk or something? She's got nowhere to go, and it's not like she can skip town and leave the restaurant. It's how she pays the bills."

"My guess is Roj got to 'em and said to set the bail high," Leesa said, and Scooter nodded in agreement.

"Even Luis seemed surprised when he heard the amount," Nareen said. "He asked the deputy why they were setting it so high."

Another notch. Maybe two.

"What did the deputy say?" Tony asked.

"He just shrugged."

"She doesn't have that kind of money," Walt said sourly. "And neither do we. So we're just going to have to keep the restaurant going until she gets out. *Capiche*?"

It should have sounded silly, a mafia-style warning issuing from the grizzled long-haired short-order cook about the dire consequences for anyone who didn't do his part to keep the dilapidated diner running, but Tony admired the implied we're-in-this-together attitude, and he nodded. "Got it," he said.

"Do you think Luis will lay off whatever he's investigating now?" he asked.

"No," Nareen said. "Unfortunately. Before we left the jail, he pulled me aside and told me he wants to meet with all of us later this week. Maybe Thursday or Friday, he said."

There was a collective groaning and rolling of eyes, but they had, it seemed, no choice in the matter.

"Why you?" Tony said. "Why did Luis pick on you to demand a meeting?"

Nareen shook her head. "I don't know. Maybe because Leesa and Scooter are obviously such babes in the woods."

"You sound almost maternal," Tony teased, gently.

"God help me I do," she grinned, and it was the first time Tony had ever seen a wholehearted smile on Nareen, untainted for just that millisecond by fear and uncertainty about the future.

\* \* \*

The five of them willingly dove into action the next day, doling out shifts and parsing out tasks to make sure Sunnyside Up kept rolling.

"You're the prettiest, so you should be the main server," Leesa said to Nareen.

Tony looked at Nareen, realizing he hadn't noticed how or whether she was "the prettiest." She had high cheekbones and fathomless dark eyes and a full mouth that looked as though it might prefer to laugh rather than always pressing its lips together in anger or worry or exasperation. Tony wondered whether she had been angry before the unexpected pregnancy interrupted her life, or whether this was a relatively new state for her. The first time Nancy brought her to the diner, her hair fell in short semi-ringlets around her face. Since then, it was either wild and free or pulled back severely and tamped down with some kind of oil or gel, reflecting, perhaps, that its wearer had decided *I like it like that, boogaloo baby, I like it like that.* She had a slender, bird-like frame (except around the middle where the baby was making a whole new body shape), and her small ears and nose and chin seemed to fit her head in precisely the right proportions. Tony searched himself, a little anxiously, for signs of desire before recognizing what he was feeling was protectiveness. And sadness. Nareen couldn't stay here forever, he understood now as if for the first time, and though he, too was a temporary denizen of Motte and Bailey the thought made him wistful. She was smart, ambitious, and she had a family who loved her and missed her; she had a life outside this town, and one day she would go back to that life.

Would he? It was an odd question. Images and impressions crowded into his brain, new pressing in on old, as if it was a wrestling match: the smell of Sam's body, putrid and forlorn; the scent of coffee made from freshly-ground beans, served in a delicate cup that had been in the Gibson family for five generations; the almost imperceptible earthiness of Nancy's voice, a huskiness threaded through each word that softened even the sharpest rebuke; the gentle rustle of Caroline's fingers turning the pages of *The New York Times*; the shocking clatter as he dropped and broke yet another plate when trying to transfer it into Sunnyside Up's industrial dishwasher; "Would you care for crème brûlée with your coffee, sir?"; "Stop digging." Images of *now* and *before* competed in his brain. Would he go home today, if he could? Shouldn't the answer be obvious?

And then he thought: Would Caroline welcome him back to the world of poached eggs on an antique tray that had once belonged to Napoleon, after this tiny town had regurgitated him?

"Snap out of it," Walt said roughly, so Tony snapped, and they got to work.

They had a larger-than-usual crowd, since the news of Nancy's arrest had spread. There was a lot of jovial banter among the patrons, with many I-wish-I'd-been-there-to-see-Roj-get-what's-coming-to-hims.

Roj did not make an appearance.

Crackers and Jems arrived at their appointed time, and sat in their appointed booth. Tony jumped in before Leesa or Nareen could do anything.

"Coffee?" he said.

"You're not going to dump it on our heads, are you?" Crackers said, grinning.

"I wasn't planning on it," Tony said, "but 'the day ain't over yet.'"

Both men laughed loudly. "That's from the movie *City Slickers*," Jems said, looking as if he was seeing Tony for the first time. "I never would have pegged you for a *City Slickers* fan, Tony."

"I'm just full of surprises," he said. "And speaking of surprises, I'm going stir crazy around here. I really am a city slicker, and I need to get away. You said you went on a trip last week. Where'd you go?" And then, so they wouldn't think he was prying, he added, "Just looking for suggestions. It seems to me you just hit more farmland whichever way you drive around here."

Jems nodded. "You got that right. We just went to Port—"

Crackers cut him off. "We really can't help you," he said. "I'm sorry, Tony."

Jems looked abashed. "Yeah, we don't go nowhere interesting," he said, mispronouncing and over-enunciating each syllable: *in-ner-es-ing*.

"Ah," Tony said. So they *were* hiding something. He felt almost triumphant, and then immediately realized that he'd learned nothing of any value to the investigation.

"No go," he said shortly to Walt, when he was back in the kitchen. "They wouldn't tell me. Jems started to say something about where they went—Port-something, I think, I assume he must have been about to say *Portland*—but Crackers practically shouted Jems down to keep him from telling me where they went."

"Might be suspicious," Walt said, turning over a half dozen fried eggs with astounding tenderness. "Or could be they just went to Portland for some supplies for the farm. Or maybe they just got tired of buying their clothes at Rancho's. That's a place that has a selection of spurs next to the cowboy boots, you know. Biggest advertising push is they have Levi's *and* Wranglers *and* Carhartt. Or they just went away for a romantic weekend and didn't want anyone to know."

Tony's lips involuntarily curled. At an especially deep glowering from Walt, he said, "Well. You know." He threw up his hands. "I mean. They must be in their *seventies*."

"You'll be in your seventies some day," Walt said, grinding a generous portion of pink Himalayan salt over the hash browns, then adding an apparently-carefully calculated sprinkle of cayenne and sage. "When you get there, you'll be grateful for a little intimacy, I assure you."

Tony was chastened. Walt was right, of course, but then he thought, that's the prerogative of the young, to think pleasure is their provenance and the old have no claim to it. Thirty-five wasn't the same as eighteen or twenty, but if he was reading their ages correctly it was younger than Crackers and Jems and even Walt by about half.

"Well anyway," he said, "I didn't get any information."

"Didn't think you would," Walt said.

Tony bit back an angry retort; he wanted some of those hash browns when it was time for his break, and it seemed prudent to refrain from challenging Walt. At least until after he'd eaten.

"Well, I tried," he said.

\* \* \*

Two days later, Luis dropped Nancy off in front of the restaurant. Everyone stopped and went to the front door to stare in amazement.

"How did you get out?" Leesa asked.

"Got a hearing in a few weeks," Nancy answered. "Halloween, actually. Isn't that, whatchacallit, ironical? The devil puts me in jail and I'm going to court on Halloween."

"Yeah, but how did you get out?" Leesa persisted.

"Did someone convince the judge to waive bail?" Nareen asked.

"Uh huh," Nancy said. "They told the judge I wasn't no flight risk."

"Don't you trust it," Walt said harshly. "It was Roj, I'd bet dollars to doughnuts. He's going to use it to try to blackmail you, Nancy."

"Keep your britches on, Walt. I know who sprung me. It was that shifty-eyed Mex—" She caught herself, and *abashed* was written all over her face. "It was that detective what started it all. Luis."

"Really?" Scooter said, voicing everyone's surprise.

"Yup," Nancy said. "I'm out on my own whaddyacallit. Recognition. Reconnection. Whatever." Then she clapped her rough hands together with a sound like an old dog's bark. "Enough of that," she said. "Let's get to work.

"And thank you," she said, looking around at their expectant faces, "for all you did. Seeing you at the jail was just the cat's meow, made me know I was missed; and keeping things going here while I was gone was a real nice thing. I don't know what I'd a' done without you." She looked dangerously close to tears so Walt said loudly, "Tony kept the books while you were out so all the numbers should be good but I'd check him. He could have made a mistake."

Tony wisely refrained from protesting. He understood Walt was just trying to distract Nancy, and anyway, his math skills never had been all that great. Really, Walt was right; he could have made a mistake.

After the lunch rush he followed Nancy into the pantry.

"I tried to post your bail," he said. "But I was reminded that I have no access to my money until I've served my sentence."

The conversation with Caroline had been physically painful, and humiliating. She was far too genteel to simply refuse, but the message was unmistakable. For as long as he was *Tony*, working off a manslaughter conviction, she was not going to make any effort to keep him connected to the privileges *Giles* enjoyed. She certainly wasn't going to arrange bail for some strange woman in a tiny town in the middle of nowhere, Oregon. "I don't want any entanglements of gratitude," she'd said.

Tony was shaken out of the remembering when Nancy pulled him close for a ferocious hug, and tried to plant a kiss on his cheek. He moved his head in surprise, so it landed on the side of his nose.

"Thank you, Tony," she said.

"What for?" he said. "I couldn't get bail."

"For trying," Nancy said.

Tony smiled. "I wish it had worked. That's really the best thing about having money. You can help people when they need it."

"Huh," Nancy said. "I would have thought the best thing about having money is you can have a fancy car. See, me? I've always wanted a tricked-up Chevy truck in cherry red with shiny chrome wheels. If I ever win the lottery that's what I'm gonna get."

\* \* \*

The meeting with Luis was put off until the following Monday so the whole crew could meet, off duty, in the diner, without the risk of eavesdropping customers.

Tony couldn't decide if Monday came too soon or was too long in coming. After a lifetime of simply letting life come at him, he felt a sudden desire to be a man of action, and he wanted to know what Luis was going to say and whether the conversation was going to lead to something definitive.

On Monday morning, he forced himself to walk slowly as he made his way down main street from his motel to the diner. He knew he was unprecedentedly early and no one would be there to let him in. He took in his surroundings as if for the first time: dusty, cracked asphalt with faded paint dividing the road and demarking the parking spots. An empty movie theater with signs in the window that said *Opening again soon,* but the signs were faded and the window was so thickly coated with dust that Tony wondered whether "soon" was defined in terms of eras (Mesozoic, anyone?), or whether the sign was the embalmed remains of a plan that never materialized. The drug store advertising Get Your Little Blue Pills Here And Jump Start Your Love Life. His favorite Mexican restaurant Tio Mio's—still his preferred dinner spot, which was unfortunately beginning to show in his mid-section—closed for now, but proudly announcing Open For Dinner Seven Days A Week. A veterinarian's office, a law office (who knew? Tony hadn't noticed it before), and a store called Trish's

Place that appeared to sell a combination of homemade candy, used Tupperware, antiques, and party supplies.

Further down the road, Tony could see the glowing golden sign of the only fast-food place in town (technically on the *outskirts* of town). In a place as flat as Motte and Bailey, pretty much everything was visible from the center of the town, and even a slight breeze carried every scent straight through from one end to the other. Tony could smell frying grease and the unique, addictive, but slightly off smell of the restaurant's fried breakfast sandwich. (Eating fast food had been one of many *firsts* for Tony. He had enjoyed it enough that it had become his Monday morning go-to place, until Leesa caught wind of it and heckled him with stories of abused workers and chemical pesticides and tortured farm animals, after which he continued to eat there on Mondays with guilt as an added condiment, like a dollop of ketchup left out in the sun.)

There was a little bit of garbage in the gutter, but not as much as he would have expected. The overall impression was not so much of refuse (the detritus of a populous too busy to pick up after itself) as abandonment. There was nobody around to toss garbage into the street.

Tony felt restless and distressed by the forlorn town. It was a relief, when he reached the diner, to stand outside Sunnyside Up, looking in. Even without people, the drab linoleum, aluminum-bordered counters, and round red bar stools spoke of busyness and purpose. The line of coffee makers hanging about like union workers before the whistle blows, and the napkin dispensers tidily filled and standing at attention on each table, they made it clear: here was a place where people gathered, where *bustling* happened.

While he stood staring through the window, his forehead pressed against the cool glass, he became aware of sounds behind and around him. Cars. A voice here, another down the street. The jingle of keys in a storefront door. Maybe, after all, the town wasn't abandoned. Maybe it was just New York hubris (and ignorance) to expect a small town to show signs of life at the crack of dawn.

He didn't know what to expect from the meeting. Of the Sunnyside Up crew, only he, Nancy and Walt knew the answer to the question *Where is Roj's missing son, Sam?* Leesa, Scooter, and Nareen were presumably clueless about that and every other aspect of whatever Luis was investigating. Did Luis suspect Nancy knew more than she'd let on? Or Walt? What did Luis hope to gain from the conversation?

Tony had been pacing and musing for nearly an hour when Nancy finally arrived and let him into the diner.

"I walked," she said, though he hadn't asked. "Got to do something to keep up my girlish figure." And then she laughed, that warm, husky sound Tony sometimes caught himself trying to elicit, though he didn't have a comedic bone in his body.

The others trickled in and took their places in and around one of the booths. Scooter practically pushed Walt aside and plunked himself down next to Leesa, which must have taken inordinate courage, Tony thought. Nareen pulled up a chair and sat at the end of the booth, facing the others. Luis sat down last, looking as if he wished he'd thought to take a chair, but finally slid into the booth next to Walt, blinking nervously. Tony stood to one side.

"Thanks for meeting with me," Luis said, when they were all gathered.

There was something different about him, Tony thought. He seemed to be addressing them as members of his team instead of suspects in a police line-up.

Walt remained visibly unconvinced. Apparently, getting Nancy's bail waived was not enough, in Walt's mind, to make up for the fact that Nancy wouldn't have needed bail waived if the shifty-eyed newcomer hadn't inserted himself in everyone else's business. Tony understood. The last time they'd seen Luis, he'd been unctuously buddying-up to Roj, and then arresting Nancy for doing what any reasonably sane person would have done under the circumstances.

Tony assumed neither Walt nor anyone else at the table was familiar with the art of engendering cooperation from opposing parties for the sake of achieving a common purpose, and so he stepped into the leadership role. "You're welcome," he said, in response to the *Thanks for meeting with me* opening salvo.

"It looks like it's to my benefit to trust you," Luis said, and they all flinched, the nascent confidence dying before it could take root. "As unlikely as it sounds, we've traced a pretty significant drug ring to Motte and Bailey."

Walt grunted an I-knew-it.

"The road from Los Angeles to this godforsaken town is littered with dead bodies," Luis continued. "I still don't know why the road ends here, but I assume there's someone—

"Roj," Nancy interrupted.

"I know that's who you think it is," Luis said quietly. "But I can't arrest someone just because he's an asshole."

Nancy smiled grimly.

"What about statutory rape?" Tony said, thinking of Nancy and all the other underage women Roj had apparently impregnated.

"Unless it's happened within the last ten years, I can't do anything about that now," Luis said. "And you should know if the girls were sixteen or seventeen, that's a hard case for the prosecutor to win. Juries seem to assume it was consensual, even if the young woman testifies that it wasn't. Apologies to present company," he nodded toward Nareen.

Nareen exploded out of her chair. "Why the hell would you say that?" she shouted, her voice echoing off the walls of the empty diner, a tinny chorus of outrage. "I wasn't underage when I got pregnant, and it most certainly was consensual. I was in a long-term relationship with a really good guy, a guy who probably would have agreed to get married if I wanted to. But I didn't want to. I wanted to finish college and work as a CPA and buy a nice house in one of those neighborhoods where the houses are older than I am and everyone has a lawn that stays green all summer because they water it practically every day, and I wanted to get a couple of dogs and a cat and only then was I going to even *consider* having kids. You can bet your tired old detective ass no one has *ever* touched me unless I wanted them to."

She looked so fierce they did not doubt her for a second, did not doubt there would be serious consequences for anyone who dared to disrespect the almost visible boundary around Nareen's body, a line like the silhouette around a body at a crime scene, only this line was drawn by and ferociously defended by the living presence vibrating and twanging and bouncing within.

"Sorry," Luis said, sounding more exasperated than apologetic.

Nareen looked at him and grabbed her belly and opened her mouth, most assuredly to hurl more invective but instead she said, "Ow."

"Ow?" Nancy said.

"I think I need to go to the hospital," Nareen said.

* * *

Everyone could do the math; five months' pregnant was way too soon to be having pain, so Nareen was right, the hospital was clearly the next move.

"The closest hospital we got is in Walla Walla," Leesa said, for the benefit of the people in the diner who didn't know (Tony and Luis and Nareen). "That's like, twenty miles away. In Washington."

Luis offered to drive, but Nareen shook her head, violently, vehemently, so Nancy ran home to get her car. While they waited, Scooter (whose car had refused to start after returning from visiting Nancy in jail) rubbed Nareen's shoulders and breathed slowly and loudly, telling Nareen to breathe with him, *hoo hoo hee hee,* and Tony was irrationally proud of the timid pink and speckled little man for knowing just what to do.

Nancy and Nareen sat in front, and Scooter, Walt, and Leesa sat in back. Tony closed the door once everyone was buckled in, noticing the scratched and dented brown paint and the crack in the lower corner of the windshield. When Scooter asked if he'd be following with Luis, Tony decided it no longer mattered who knew he was a convict and who didn't, and he explained to the assembled occupants of the car that he couldn't leave town because he was wearing an ankle monitor. Every ounce of him, every atom, longed to join them, to be part of the pack closing in protectively around its (potentially) wounded member. But it didn't matter what his every atom wanted, and that hurt more than anything.

No one said *That's okay* or *Thanks for letting us know* or even *Don't worry about it.* But then, it wasn't okay, and he was worried about it.

Nancy rolled her window down and encouraged the others to do the same. "The goddamn air conditioning's broken again," she said, while Leesa sang *On the road again,* warbling nervously and off-key, and neither Nancy's words nor Leesa's singing completely drowned out Nareen's anxious *hoo hoo hee hee.*

As they drove away, Tony fixed in his mind the image of the determination stamped on Nancy's face, a statement that no harm would come to the woman sitting beside her if it was in her power to prevent it. He remembered a line from that Christmas movie Caroline loved: "Dear father in heaven, I'm not a praying man, but if you're up there and you can hear me." He'd always thought it was odd, that there was an end to it after "me." That was the prayer: If you're up there and you can hear me. There was more, after a pause, but that was separate. First and foremost, please be in heaven looking down on us, and please be listening. Please don't let there be only and forever a vast insensate cosmos glittering coldly and unfeelingly over my puny existence.

"Back to you and me," Luis said, when the car was no longer visible.

"You're annoying, you know that?" Tony said.

The windows of his eyes drew closed, and Luis sighed. "I know," he said.

# Chapter 10

"We might as well keep talking," Tony said, still staring at the spot on the flat horizon where the car used to be. "What were you hoping we could do to assist in your investigation?"

"Several things," Luis said. He pulled out a small notebook, spiral-bound at the top, and an equally small, eraserless pencil.

Tony could imagine, if he tried, that police department PIs didn't make a lot of money, but he didn't think they'd be reduced to swiping tiny pencils from golf courses or church pews. "What's with the miniature writing utensils?" he said. "Why don't you take notes on your phone like everyone else?"

"I like to write by hand," Luis said, sounding peevish.

"As Leesa would say, 'Whatevs.'"

"You don't look like the kind of man who says 'Whatevs,'" Luis said.

"What kind of man do I look like?" Tony challenged.

Luis looked at him slowly, appraising him inch by inch from the feet up. "The kind of man who went to Harvard, lives in a penthouse apartment in Manhattan, and had to ask his butler what the little people are wearing these days so he could pretend to fit in."

"I don't have a butler," Tony said, matching Luis's peevishness. "And it was Yale. Weren't you going to tell me what you wanted us to do?"

"Yes," Luis said. As he spoke he made a notation with his diminutive pencil in his diminutive notebook. "Number one: those two old guys. Crackers and Jems. They keep going out of town. I need to know where they go. You know, the first time I heard someone use those nicknames, I thought it was Crank and Jeez." He waited, but

Tony didn't laugh. "They've gone out of town both of the last two times a shipment was noted," he said.

"'Noted'?" Tony asked. "Don't you intercept the shipments?"

"If we did, the shipments would stop. We have to figure out the source first, or we just end up shifting the problem to someone else."

"Ah," Tony said, feeling once again out of his depth in spite of or maybe because of his education at Yale and his flat in Manhattan. After a few seconds of silence, broken only by the sound of a car passing, he said, "This will sound odd, since I'm the one who offered the Sunnyside Up crew as partners (for lack of a better word) in your investigation. But aren't you worried that, by telling me Crackers and Jems are suspects, we'll turn around and, I don't know, tip them off?"

"Yes," Luis said. "And no. I don't trust any of you, but I've also been working on this case long enough that I'm reasonably certain none of the Sunnyside Up crew is involved in running drugs."

I guess that's something, Tony thought. "So you're going to, what, tail them? Follow Crackers and Jems everywhere and see what they're up to?"

"It's not that simple," Luis said. Another car went by, raising a tiny tornado of dust around the two men. "In a town this small there's no friggin' way to be inconspicuous. It's pretty obvious that you're following someone if your car and theirs are the only ones on the road for a hundred miles."

"I don't know that we would have better luck," Tony said. "But I'll tell the rest of the group and we'll see what we can do." And then he added, "They're gay, by the way."

Luis pursed his lips. "Now it's my turn to ask. Why are you telling me that?"

"Because what you might think of as surreptitious and therefore suspicious behavior could be simply an attempt to protect their privacy in a small, extremely conservative town."

"Good thinking," Luis acknowledged.

"What's number two on your list?" Tony said.

"Figure out who saw Roger's son Sam last, and where."

"Saw him alive, you mean?" Tony said.

"Who says he's dead?" Luis said sharply.

Tony immediately realized his blunder, but years of presiding over executive meetings stood him in good stead. "I assumed," he said. "It sounds like he's a ne'er-do-well, and it sounds like he's been missing for a while."

Luis's eyes narrowed. He looked inclined to pursue the issue, so Tony said quickly, "Number three?"

"Find out what Nareen is doing here," Luis said.

Tony had never been a violent man—there had never been a need, for a man to whom everything was handed, for whom every need was met almost before it had been expressed. But as he thought of Nareen under surveillance, followed and interrogated by the likes of this mealy-mouthed detective, all the oddly protective emotions he'd begun to feel for her, for Nancy and Scooter and Leesa and even Walt percolated to the surface, and he found his fists clenched and the muscles in his arm primed to reach back, back, back into a life he'd never had and a man he'd never been, all the way from New York to Oregon, gathering force over the miles in between, and it took every ounce of strength to stop this other man's fist and this other man's arm from punching Luis squarely between the eyes.

Luis stepped back, sensing the barely-suppressed rage.

Tony unclenched his fist, and dropped his arm back to his side. "You'd just throw me in jail," he said. "You're not worth it."

"I thought you just said none of us are suspects. So why on earth is Nareen on your list?" Tony said finally.

"She's not necessarily a suspect," Luis answered slowly, carefully, "but she is certainly out of place here in Motte and Bailey—"

"—and she's Black," Tony said.

"In case you hadn't noticed, I'm Latino," Luis said. "I'm no stranger to prejudice. Why do you think I became a detective?" He looked down, and kicked a piece of loose asphalt. "I got tired of being pulled over for 'driving while Mexican,'" he said, when it was clear Tony wasn't going to speculate. "Nareen is not a 'person of interest' because of the color of her skin," he continued. "But she is new here, and she's young, urban, and educated. You have to admit this is a strange place for her to land."

"This seems to be the end of the line for a lot of unexpected people," Tony pointed out.

"Like you," Luis said.

"Like me," Tony agreed. "But I can tell you Nareen's story. She's from Portland (Oregon, not Maine), and she was a junior in college when she got pregnant. Everyone was pulling her in different directions, telling her abortion, adoption, get married, quit school, don't quit school. The term was over, I guess, she was free for the summer, so she hopped a bus to Spokane to visit a cousin, just to give herself a little space to think her own thoughts, is how she put it, only the bus broke down outside this godforsaken hole (her words again, not mine). She called her cousin, who made it clear she wouldn't be welcome, leaving Nareen stranded and abandoned at the bus station, which is where she met Nancy."

He folded his arms, considering the most judicious and efficacious way to make Luis see. "Nancy takes in stray people like some old ladies take in stray cats," he explained. "And I very much doubt that Nareen will be here for much longer," he said. "She has a life to go back to, she's just here while she figures out what that life looks like now." He paused again, trying to gauge the effect of his explanation. "So that's her story," he said.

"So *she* says," Luis said.

"Good god man, have you looked at her?" Tony expostulated. "She's twenty-one and pregnant. What exactly do you suspect her of doing or being other than twenty-one and pregnant?"

"Stranger things have happened," Luis said.

Tony started to say something snide, but Luis wasn't done.

"And then there's Walt," he said. "There's no such person as Walt Whitman living and working in Motte and Bailey, not in any official record." He jerked his head at the diner's entrance. "Sunnyside Up's crew may not be running drugs, but you're all damn suspicious, as far as I can tell, the whole friggin' lot of you."

"Do me a favor," Tony said. "Just say fucking and get it over with. We're all fucked, and it doesn't improve the situation to claim we're 'frigged' or 'frigging,' whatever that might mean. Have the courage of your convictions, please, and swear like a real man."

\* \* \*

"It turns out bail was waived," Tony told Caroline when they talked later that evening.

"That's good, I suppose," Caroline said. Tony could have done without the *I suppose*. "I just don't understand why you wanted to post bail. What do you care about this Nancy woman?"

Was she jealous? Tony wondered. "I was trying . . . I don't know. It would have been an act of charity," he said, because he knew Caroline understood philanthropy. "And selfishness. Without Nancy I have no job. I don't want my sentence extended when there's no work to do because my boss is in jail."

The words "sentence" and "jail" hung between them like rotting fruit hangs from a branch; you walk around the swollen and blackened orbs, afraid to brush against them lest you accidentally release the sickly smell, and there's nothing else for it but to tread carefully, until they fall of their own accord and finish decomposing.

"Nareen went to the hospital today," he told Caroline, to break the uncomfortable silence. "She had contractions but she's only about five months along, so she shouldn't be having contractions. I haven't heard yet whether they're going to let her come home."

"She's beautiful," he blurted, trying to capitalize on what he hoped was jealousy.

"She's a beautiful, penniless, pregnant, college drop-out," Caroline said.

"Yes," Tony said, deflated.

"Jack is making some organizational changes to ABC Toys," Caroline said, and Tony was instantly gripped with elation (she's trying to make me jealous, too) and fury (how dare Jack make changes without my approval).

"He can do whatever he wants while I'm gone but there will be hell to pay when I get back if he's screwed something up," he said evenly. "What changes is he making?"

"I haven't paid too much attention," she said. "I don't know why, but he's invited me to the Board meetings. I had nothing better to do, so I went to the last one. I think he was talking about separating the company into divisions. You know, infants, preschool, dolls, blocks—something along those lines. He seemed to think it would be more efficient."

*More efficient.* Jack was more everything, Tony thought. More handsome, with his cleft chin and his patrician nose and his piercing gray eyes, all framed by his perfectly cut black hair ever so slightly lighter at the sideburns, suggesting gravity and dignity rather than senility. More decisive, as if he rather than Tony had been born into a decision-making role. Taller and more broad-shouldered and more effortlessly flirtatious.

Giles had never liked Jack, when you get right down to it.

And just like that, he was Giles again, and not the wealthy business tycoon who was interviewed by *Time* magazine but the wealthy business tycoon who had been banished to Motte and Bailey in disgrace.

"I hadn't realized we were lacking in efficiency."

"I suppose every company can be more efficient," Caroline said.

"Different isn't necessarily better," he said.

"If you say so," Caroline said. She spoke languidly, and the tone evoked images of Caroline in her lavender nightgown, the one with the lace hugging the plunging neckline, where a small movement to one side seemed like an invitation to see and touch and kiss the breasts just barely hidden from view. He pictured her lounging on their bed, the comforter ever so slightly rumpled under her bottom, the pillows pre-fluffed behind the graceful arch of the small of her back.

And then she spoke, and the image exploded, leaving only a residue of longing. "Well," she said, "I guess I should sign off for the night. Let me know how the pregnant college drop-out is doing,"

"I will," he said.

* * *

"Just a little false labor brought on by stress," Nareen told anyone who asked, repeating it word for word like a mantra. That's what the doctor at the emergency room had said. And he said Nareen could keep going as she had, no need to change anything, maybe just try a little harder to avoid stressful situations. "Nothing upsetting, irksome, annoying, aggravating," he said. "Oh, Jesus, Dan, give it a rest," the nurse said, at which the doctor held up his phone so Nareen could see the *Thesaurus.com* entry on his screen, and then Nareen smiled, which was likely the intended result, so it was all good, she said.

It had been a little over a week since the emergency that wasn't, as Walt called it. When Sunday rolled around again, Nareen and Leesa attended the prenatal class together, as usual. With the diner closed on Monday, Leesa'd had to wait until Tuesday to give an update on the latest class, and now she was giving the others a blow-by-blow account.

*Sans* terrifying gore, this time.

"Scooter, come here for a minute." Leesa spoke as One Who Must Be Obeyed.

Meekly, Scooter dropped what he had been doing (literally—he dropped the packet of napkins he'd been using to refill the dispensers), and hurried to Leesa's side.

"You never learned to crawl, did you?" she said.

"What?"

"Your mom told me something, ages ago, back when my cousin Lucy's baby was just scooting along and then suddenly, bam! he learns to walk, with no crawling in between. Your mom said that's why your nickname is Scooter, because you went right from scooting to walking."

Scooter turned brilliantly red. "Yeah," he said. "That's what everyone said. Kind of an army crawl thing is what I did."

"Well, we learned in class on Sunday that when a baby doesn't learn to crawl it makes it hard for the kid to learn to read. There's some connection, some brain-thing."

"Neurological," Nareen supplied the word. She was not on the schedule for today, but she'd announced that she had nowhere else to be and she was bored out of her mind, and Tony immediately thought of Caroline, who went to business meetings because she was bored.

"That's it," Leesa said. "Neurological. Anyway, did you have a hard time learning to read?"

The shade of Scooter's cheeks deepened impossibly, until his face was an uncomfortable magenta.

"Why are you talking about me?" he muttered, barely moving his lips.

"Just trying to make sure Nareen's kid doesn't have the same problem," Leesa said, apparently oblivious to Scooter's discomfort. "They showed us how you can teach your baby to crawl, if he's not getting it on his own."

"It's a she," Nareen said. "The baby's a girl. They did an ultrasound when I went to the hospital and they told me it's a girl."

"Hey that's great!" Walt shouted from the kitchen.

The entire crew turned and stared at Walt.

Nancy said what they were all thinking: "Don't think I've ever heard you say the word 'great' about anything."

"What would you call it?" he snarled.

"Great," she snarled right back. "I've just never seen you . . ."

" . . . express enthusiasm," Tony finished for her.

"Then you've never seen me harvesting shallots," Walt said.

They tried not to, really they did, but in the end they couldn't help themselves: they laughed. A little snicker at first, then a couple of guffaws, Walt glaring at them and then giving in to the moment and smiling at his own expense, and then they were leaning against the leatherette booths and the Formica counter and the faux-wood tables and each other, laughing as if they had to get it all out at once because they were afraid they'd never laugh again.

Later, Scooter approached Tony, and it wasn't clear whether his face had not yet recovered from its earlier blush or had recovered and then started all over again.

"Tony, can I talk to you, kind of, you know, privately?"

"Of course," Tony said. He wiped the dirty suds from his hands on the torn and graying rag hanging from his apron ties. (When he started the job, he had observed how men were supposed to wear an apron—at least men working in a diner in Motte and Bailey—with the ties wound all the way around the waist and back again so there was a handy line in front to hang things from.) Wiping dirty suds on a dirty rag had become second nature faster than he ever would have thought possible. A little over two months was all it took to get used to constant ubiquitous grime, it seemed.

They moved into the pantry for a little privacy. This, too, had become second nature, this retiring to the pantry for a private conversation. Tony allowed himself to revel in the smells while Scooter worked up the courage to tell him whatever it was he wanted to say, breathing in the baking mix and powdered milk and Crisco, the dim smells mixing with the dim light from the single bulb hanging on a dangerously ancient wire from the ceiling. On that very first day the odors had seemed strangely comforting, for a man who had never been exposed to such odors. Now, they smelled like home.

"Y'see," Scooter said, running his fingers through his short sandy blonde hair, "I mean, it's just that . . . ."

"You're in love with Leesa," Tony prompted him.

"What?" Scooter said.

Tony had never seen anyone look more like a frightened rabbit than Scooter did just then. "You're in love with Leesa," he said again.

"I—that's not what I wanted to tell you." Scooter shook his head, but it was more that his head wobbled on his neck rather than a decisive rejection of Tony's statement. He wiped his perennially sweaty hands on the sides of his too-small pants, and then on the front of his plaid short-sleeved shirt with the frayed collar, and finally on the apron with the Sunnyside Up logo on the pocket. He shuffled his right foot forward and backward, the rubber squeaking a little against the cement floor.

Tony waited.

"She changed her name," Scooter said. "She told me she changed it because she didn't want to be ordinary, like some boring old Lisa from some boring little town in boring old Oregon." Clearly, he was quoting.

"I know," Tony said.

"What I wanted to tell you," Scooter started again, and he took a deep breath. "What I wanted to tell you is I can't read."

"What on earth?" Tony said. He could not recall ever in his life having been so surprised, so completely taken aback.

"How—how did you make it through school?"

Scooter shrugged, apparently frustrated with Tony's response. "I faked it until I couldn't any more, and then I dropped out."

"How do you take orders?" Tony said.

"Well, I've always kinda memorized a few words whenever I need to, and I memorized the stuff on the menu. I watch people's eyes and see what they're looking at when they read something," he explained. "It helps that Nancy uses her finger when she's reading. She points to the stuff as she says it. I practiced writing the words at home after I figured out what went with what." He shook his head, as if to deny whatever it was Tony was thinking.

"The menu's been the same the whole time the restaurant has been open," he added. "And I know the prices," he said. "I mean, I can read numbers. That's why I can make change and work at the gas station. I even did okay in math, except I had to have someone else read me the word problems. Leesa sometimes did that, when we were in grade school. But words," he said, and he left it hanging there, as if his feelings on the subject were self-evident.

"Words?" Tony prompted.

"Well, they just look like bird tracks on the paper," Scooter said.

"I think that is the saddest thing I've heard in a long time," Tony said.

"Why?" Scooter said.

"Because you can't lose yourself in a good novel, or read a newspaper with your morning coffee." He raised his eyebrows suggestively.

"Or write a love poem to Leesa."

"I don't want to write a love poem to Leesa," Scooter said stiffly. "I just wanted to tell you because I was hoping you'd get her off my back about this crawling thing. It's stupid anyway. Why would crawling have anything to do with reading?" He waved his hand, making it clear he wasn't interested in an explanation. "It doesn't matter, I just want you to help me make sure Leesa doesn't know. I don't want her to find out I can't read."

"You can't read?" Leesa had come into the pantry behind them. Her voice was shrill, and accusatory. Scooter pressed his lips together, visibly steeling himself against crying.

"What the mother-fucking-hell is wrong with you, Scooter?" She had moved from shrill to all-out shouting. "I'm your friend. You didn't think to tell me?"

And here was another surprise. Tony could see Scooter had been prepared for humiliation, abuse, and insults, but not this.

"I could have helped. I tutored that snot-nosed Harker kid next door. I taught him pretty much everything he knows. I could have taught you how to read. But noooo, you have to make it a big god-damned secret."

"Leave him alone," Walt said, peering around the corner.

"What the hell is going on?" Nancy said, crowding into the already crowded pantry.

"Nothing," Tony said firmly. "Nothing is going on. Leesa, go back to work."

He moved around Scooter and pushed Leesa, none too gently, out of the pantry. "We'll talk about it later."

Nancy looked at him questioningly, but he shook his head. Walt went back to juicing oranges, and Scooter was left alone in the poorly-lit richly-aromaed room.

And then, as if they hadn't had their fill of unpleasant surprises, there was one more waiting in the wings, as if the author of this drama or this slapstick comedy that made up their lives just couldn't resist a plot twist: Roj walked in, took a seat at his booth, and said to no one in particular, "I'll have the usual."

As if nothing had happened.

Walt had to physically restrain Nancy. "Control yourself, woman," he said grimly, standing behind her with his arms locked across her chest while she struggled and made kicking motions with her feet, as if she could land a well-placed foot from where she stood in the kitchen. He spoke low and stern, with his mouth right next to her ear. "You don't want to end up in jail again."

"I can't stand to see him acting all innocent like he didn't do anything," she said loudly, ignoring Walt's efforts to keep the argument quiet.

"I get that," Walt said. "But you can't go bashing him in the head with a coffee pot again." He tightened his hold across Nancy's collarbone. "Or kicking him in the *cojones*," he added.

"Let me go!" Nancy said, still struggling and showing every indication that bashing Roj in the head or kicking him in the *cojones*—or possibly both—was exactly what she intended to do.

"I'm not letting go until you promise to behave yourself."

"I'll behave! I'll behave!"

He released her, but stood tensed and ready to spring into action if she made a break for it.

"Sheesh. It's no wonder you don't have a girlfriend," Nancy said sulkily. "Manhandling people like that. And that damn beard of yours is scratchy."

"I don't have a girlfriend because I'm old and ugly and taciturn and I live in the middle of nowhere," Walt said.

"I don't think you're ugly," Nareen said. She had popped into the kitchen when Roj showed up, to make sure Nancy didn't go ballistic.

"Then you're a fool, and a blind fool too," Walt snarled.

Nareen was no shrinking violet. "I think you're a romantic at heart," she said, and she sidled up to him, managing to look somewhat sultry and flirtatious in spite of the fact that she was over five months pregnant and wearing baggy old sweatpants that had likely belonged to Nancy at some point.

"I am not!" Walt said.

"You are taciturn, I'll give you that," Tony said.

The dark storm of Walt's eyes flashed (apparently it was fine for Walt to practice a little self-deprecation but it was *not* okay for Tony to pile on), and Tony flinched for the second time in their short affiliation.

Leesa joined them in the kitchen and wanted to know what was up and had they noticed that that fucker Roj had come in and ordered the same fucking thing he always did, as if nothing had happened.

"I wish you wouldn't swear," Tony said suddenly. "Or at least I wish you'd use a milder word." (The irony and the hypocrisy and the sexism didn't hit him until later—hadn't he just told Luis to swear like a man?)

"Why? Because a prissy fucking Manhattanite can't handle the fucking word *fuck*?" Walt sneered.

Suddenly Nancy was in charge again.

"Walt, I hired you to cook. So cook Roj his fu—, uh, cook him his breakfast. Leesa, go ask Scooter to serve Roj."

"Scooter left," Leesa said, looking down at the scuffed toes of her high-tops.

Nancy sighed. "Then you take his table," she said, turning to Tony.

"I'm on it," Tony said, glad of a chance to put some physical distance between himself and Walt, whose eyes were still shooting thunderbolts in his direction.

Tony refilled Roj's coffee cup without a word, and served his breakfast in silence, when it was ready. Taciturn is the word of the day, he thought. As he turned away, after refilling Roj's water glass, Roj put a hand on his arm. "Wait," he said.

"Why should I?" Tony said.

"I'm many things," Roj said, "but I'm not an idiot. I know I'm not welcome here. I came because I need help. I really do think something must have happened to Sam."

"Nice try," Tony said. He looked at Roj, the bald head with its fringe of gray hair, the grizzled and patchy stubble on his chin and cheeks, the ruddy complexion of a man who had been overly fond of beer and stronger stuff than beer for an overly-long time, and that's when he noticed with distaste that there were tears in the old man's eyes.

"Sam was the only boy," Roj said. "Out of all them, fourteen kids—that I know of—all the rest were girls. I wanted him to be something, something more than he was. Nancy won't tell you, but I tried to come around once in a while, play with him, take him to a ball game. I might have even married his mom, but she was a drug addict." Tony rolled his eyes. "Even before I met her," Roj added, seeming to guess Tony's thoughts. "Anyway, he was kind of screwed before he ever had a chance. But I've always hoped he'd find a way to straighten up and fly right."

"Funny," Tony said. "I heard you used him to run drugs."

"You heard wrong," Roj said.

"Well," Tony said, relenting a little, if only to keep the conversation going, "when was the last time you saw him?"

"A couple of months ago. End of June, maybe? The sheriff's department sponsored an upgrade to the soccer field, and I was there to cut the ribbon. Sam was there too. He liked to play soccer, when he was younger. Even got kind of good at it, but he dropped it just like he dropped everything, including school. Funny thing is, he looked good. Clean, sober. Happy even. I asked him if he wanted to go have a beer or something—"

"—that seems like a bad idea for an addict who appears to have sobered up," Tony interrupted coldly.

"Yeah, you're probably right," Roj said. "Anyway, he turned me down. Then about a month ago, must'a been about the middle of July? A little earlier? I went to his house to ask him if he wanted to come to a Timbers game with me. They're the pro soccer team in Portland," he explained. "Anyway, I went to his mother's old house. I bought it when she was pregnant with Sam. I own most of the real estate around here," he added.

"I'll bet," Tony said. "And I'll bet you charged her a bundle to live in some run-down shack."

"I don't charge *Sam* anything," Roj said stiffly. "Anyway, he wasn't there, which isn't anything new. But there was garbage and dirty dishes everywhere. Sam's never been no kind of housekeeper, but he would at least know to throw away the wrappers from the fast food joint."

Tony leaned on the table, making himself a physical presence in Roj's personal space. "You're going to have to get your information somewhere else," he said, keeping his voice light and pleasant but making no attempt to hide his meaning. "You need to stay out of Sunnyside Up, and leave Nancy alone."

Roj nodded, apparently respecting the message, albeit begrudgingly.

"However, I'm sure the detective would be happy to hear from you," Tony said.

Roj shook his head. "He don't know nothing that could help me."

"Well, maybe *you* know something that could help *him*," Tony said.

Roj shook his head again. "I was telling the truth to that shifty-eyed Mexican," he said.

Tony was surprised to hear Roj speak of Luis in the same terms as the others, and he felt a momentary empathy with the detective: it hurt afresh every time he remembered that his entire character, body and soul, had been reduced to *convict*; he could only imagine what Luis must feel like knowing he was nothing more than a *shifty-eyed Mexican*.

"When I told him I asked my boys down at the department to keep an eye out," Roj continued, "I was speaking true. But nobody's seen him."

Damn, Tony thought. He was no expert at reading people, but it appeared Roj really was ignorant about Sam. Which meant they were back to square one in figuring out what had happened and who was responsible, and getting rid of their . . . shifty-eyed Mexican.

# Hard Scrambled

From end to end, Motte and Bailey is less than half a mile long. That means Tony can walk the length of Main Street, when Monday comes around again, without setting off any alarms from his ankle monitor. He pictures a broad-waisted sheriff in a brown uniform watching a little red blip on a screen somewhere, a blinking light that represents Tony, tracking the blip as it moves from the Sleepy Time Motel to Sunnyside Up to Tio Mio's and then back to the Sleepy Time Motel. Occasionally to the laundromat, the grocery store, the library.

And once, a short distance out of town in the middle of the night to bury a dead body.

He imagines the sheriff wondering when the hell Tony is going to do anything interesting, anything other than taking up space and wasting everyone else's time. Tony resolves, again, to check into the community service part of his sentence, and just as quickly changes his mind. Again.

If the police and the courts and the whole universe of people who are supposed to be tracking his progress don't care what he's doing, whether he's fulfilling his community service requirement, why should he?

He catches himself counting his footsteps, and then losing count. He reaches the edge of town and stands directly in front of the sign hailing visitors: *Thank you for coming to Motte and Bailey!* Beyond the sign, Main Street becomes Highway 11 once again, stretching on before him, straight and sure, like the life Tony had before he was Tony, a clearly-marked path forward, without deviation.

Is that how it was for Sam, before death intervened—a clear path, a known future? Not necessarily a bright future, but at least a host

111

of tomorrows unfurling before him. Or was it always a "long and winding road," with hidden menace around every bend?

He leans against the cheery sign and looks into the distance. Through the shimmering haze (the result of high desert sun and the dust generated by miles of crops and livestock), he can see the Blue Mountains, craggy snow-capped peak after peak. It is breathtakingly beautiful and simultaneously sere and bleak to a man whose horizons normally include forests of skyscrapers and fields of taxis and herds of humans.

Somewhere in his consciousness he knows he should enjoy the lovely scenery, find pleasure in the moment, and count his blessings that he is not a forgotten drug addict moldering in a dusty grave. But he is not up to the task. The mountains glower at him disapprovingly, and he turns away. If even the very stones of the earth find him deficient, what hope is there for him?

Then again, perhaps they are just mounds of stone, and he is imagining that they care whether one mewling man learns to appreciate his brief moment under the sun.

# Chapter 11

It's funny how life just keeps going.

Here he was, an exile from his elegant, easy life in New York, stuck in the middle of a police investigation—an investigation that, although Luis didn't know it yet, was likely to expand to include the murder of the bastard son of the former sheriff. He vacillated between worrying about what fresh hell his conviction might visit upon him, what information Luis might unearth, and whether his wife was going to leave him and run off with his second-in-command, who was at this very moment trying to usurp his position at ABC Toys. But every day he got up, and every day (except Monday) he came to the diner. He filled the napkin dispensers, and prepped the coffee, and checked the salt and the pepper and the sugar and the fake sugar. He wiped tables with a rag that looked as though its sole purpose was to smear bacteria on every available surface. He washed dishes, and tried to stay out of Walt's way, and kept an eye on Nareen to make sure she wasn't having contractions again, and looked for opportunities to point out to Leesa what a good guy Scooter was. When his circumstances threatened to overwhelm him, he slipped into the pantry and stood for a moment, inhaling the silence and the friendly odors. Once, he realized he was making a mental inventory, noting it looked like they were getting low on lard and ketchup.

Day after day, life went on, and day after day, nothing changed at Sunnyside Up. Nareen continued to be pregnant (though she chipped away at those nine months and got a little closer to giving birth, of course). Walt stayed curmudgeonly. Nancy continued to be furious at Roj for everything that had ever gone wrong in her life. Luis continued to hang around but seemed no closer to solving the mystery he had come here to solve.

A couple of weeks after the blessed moment (Nancy's words) when Tony had ordered Roj to stay away from the diner, the crew decided to go on a picnic—or rather, Leesa decided they should go on a picnic, and her powers of persuasion were formidable, so they went.

The Motte and Bailey lagoon was four miles outside of town, which meant Tony could go, as long as he didn't decide to take a long hike in the other direction, away from town. It was Monday, so the diner was closed, and both Leesa and Scooter weren't scheduled at their other jobs until the evening. Walt said he'd make fried chicken, and Tony felt his saliva glands quicken at the words, a proverbial Pavlovian response, except that he doubted Pavlov had ever fed his dogs anything as good as Walt's cooking.

September had arrived, but summer hadn't noticed. The weather was a tease in the morning: a hint of freshness and sweetness, like the breath of a child who has been chewing bubblemint gum and demands *Smell this don't I smell good?*, her small face screwed up with the agony of hoping you'll say *Yes, sweetheart, you smell delicious.* But it was all a lie. By the time five people and one dog (Scooter's) had squeezed into Nancy's car, driven to the reservoir, parked, and unpacked themselves and the picnic accouterments, the air was gleefully hot and oppressive.

Walt arrived on his motorcycle while they were unpacking the car, with a roar of wickedly gleaming metal.

"God, I hate being pregnant when it's hot," Nareen said, easing herself into a sitting position on the blanket.

"Hey, wanna hear a good pregnancy joke?" Leesa said.

"Sure," Nareen said. "I could use a laugh. But just know that if the joke sucks I may have to hit you."

Leesa looked uncertain, but took that as sufficient encouragement to proceed. "Okay, here goes. What is the most common pregnancy craving?" she said.

"Pickles and ice cream?" Scooter said.

"Don't be stupid," Walt said. "It's a joke, not a serious question."

"I never craved any of those things," Nancy said. "I craved steak, and chalk."

"There's a name for that," Nareen said. "I forget what it is, but it means you're lacking some important nutrient, if you crave chalk."

"Did you eat any chalk, Nancy?" Scooter wanted to know.

"Nah. I knew it was just some crazy pregnancy shit."

"Don't you want to hear the punch line?" Leesa said.

"I do," Tony said. "What *is* the most common pregnancy craving?"

"For men to be the ones who get pregnant," Leesa said, chortling at herself before she even got the words out.

"Okay, you get a pass this time," Nareen said. "It wasn't exactly funny, but at least it wasn't about being fat."

"Oh, that reminds me of another one!" Leesa said. "Why do women always smile when they see another woman who's pregnant?"

Nobody said, "Why?" so Leesa answered herself, "Because she's fatter than they are—ow!"

"I warned you," Nareen said serenely. "Now I've got one for you: What does a pregnant woman say after she apologizes for her random emotional outbursts?"

No one tried to guess the punch line this time.

"Up yours and I hate you!"

Walt laughed. "You're my kind of woman, Nareen."

Tony watched the interchange, content for the moment to be here in this place with these people. The tyrant sun made diamonds on the water. The golden fields around the reservoir gave the impression of plenty, and the lone oak tree under which they had parked themselves waved gently overhead like an attentive servant fanning a family of royalty. Behind it all, the Blue Mountains made a graceful and glorious backdrop, not judgmental now, just a thing of beauty.

Scooter's dog, Missy, entertained them all with her antics. Missy was some combination of border collie and a half-dozen other breeds; she had the attractive black and white fur and half-flap ears typical of border collies, but her legs were longer than they should be and her rump was speckled, and her body was overly-barrel-shaped (though that might have been the result of Scooter's propensity for sharing Cheetos and Big Macs with her). The moment they arrived, she dashed to the shore with all the intensity of a wolf after a caribou, hurled herself into the reservoir, raced back with just as much fervor, shedding sheets of water as she came, and then shook violently as soon as she was near the blanket again. Everyone protested but no one really minded. They hadn't unpacked the food yet, and the cool water felt good (though the odor of wet dog was somewhat less refreshing).

After a while, when everyone had taken the first of what would likely be many dips into the water, they ate lunch.

"Thyme, paprika, garlic, onion powder, cayenne, and a bit of corn-meal," Walt said, in response to Tony's reverent question about the chicken. "Then I fry it in peanut oil."

Flaky biscuits, ice cold raspberry lemonade, and chocolate chip cookies completed what was surely one of the best meals Tony could remember eating. The chocolate chips had slightly melted in the sun, and the cookies were still soft, having been baked just that morning.

"Okay Scooter," Leesa said when she had picked the last crumb from her plate, "I read that it's never too late to learn to crawl, and it'll help you learn to read. So, come on, time to practice."

Four voices yelled at Leesa with some variation of *Leave him alone!* but Leesa was adamant. To everyone's surprise, Scooter said he'd give it a try. He got on all fours, and commenced to crawling toward the lagoon, while Missy circled anxiously, licked his ear and his elbow, and generally made a nuisance of herself. Having crawled to the wa-ter's edge and back, expostulating when his palm or his knee grazed a rock or (once) a star thistle, he collapsed on the blanket.

"Okay, now I'm ready for my reward," he said.

"Your reward?" Leesa said.

"What, aren't you going to feed me peeled grapes or something? Fan me with palm fronds?"

Leesa smiled. "I don't even know how to peel a grape, and there sure as hell aren't any palm trees around here. Would you go for another glass of lemonade?"

"I guess so," Scooter said.

"So Nareen, what're you going to do after the baby is born?" Leesa said.

A slow-simmering panic competed with annoyance in Nareen's eyes. She smoothed the flowered cotton tent of her maternity dress (a gift from Nancy, the fabric declaring simultaneously *Made in China* and *Nancy loves me*), and picked at the detritus that always gathers on a blanket on the ground.

"Just keep going, I guess," she said after a minute.

The collective breath-holding ended, but Leesa pressed on. "But, I mean, are you going to stay here and keep working at Sunnyside Up and raise your baby in Motte-fuck—" she glanced at Tony, "I mean, in Motte and Bailey?"

Panic won out. Nareen held herself rigidly, visibly willing herself not to cry, but a rogue tear escaped and slipped down her cheek.

"Did I ever tell you yahoos how I came to be in this flea-bitten godforsaken backwater town?" Walt interjected.

"You've never told us anything," Nancy said. "In all the years you've worked for me, you haven't said boo about yourself."

Tony remembered his first meeting with Walt: "I'm Walt and I don't like chitchat."

"Well, I'm going to tell you now, so listen up, because I'm not likely to repeat myself."

Tony rearranged his bottom so the tree root wasn't quite as improperly located. Scooter and Leesa leaned in closer, and Tony noticed with satisfaction that in the process Leesa's right leg rested against Scooter's left leg, and she didn't move it away, at least not immediately.

Walt hesitated, as if wondering whether, having broken his troth with Taciturnity, he could continue, even for Nareen's sake. He tugged at the ragged blue do-rag tied around his head that had been knocked askew when he took off his motorcycle helmet. He stroked his yellow-gray beard, and then his hand dropped to the ground, unable to find anything else to occupy itself.

"I'm from upstate New York," he said after a moment. Tony's heart did a jumping jack, to hear his home state mentioned here in the furthest reaches of the West. "Small town boy from the beginning. You might not think it to look at me, but I did well in school. I wanted to be a teacher. An English professor, actually."

"Nope, I just can't picture it," Nancy said. Walt looked sheepish, and then resentful.

Tony glared at her. "For heaven's sake, don't interrupt, or he might never finish the story," he said. Secretly, he agreed with Nancy; a beatnik nihilistic philosopher, maybe, but Walt seemed almost genetically precluded from presiding over a classroom with even a modicum of patience and compassion.

Walt continued. "My family wasn't poor, exactly. My parents ran the local lumber and hardware store. But they weren't rich, and sending me to college wasn't in the cards. So I figured I'd enlist and get college paid for.

"Even though I'm a pacifist." He gave a twisted little grin.

Scooter whistled, then clapped a hand over his mouth and looked guiltily at Tony.

"I got all the way through my sophomore year," Walt continued, "but then the Army decided I was needed in the field. That was 1970. They sent me to Vietnam." His eyes turned hard. "I'm not talking about that. You can go see all the movies if you want to know what it was like. I'm no Forrest Gump, I can tell you that. I'm no good at taking orders. And there have been a few people I would have liked to hurt, in my life, but just randomly killing people? So they don't randomly kill you? Because our governments told us to?"

He sat for a moment lost in the bubble of his memories, a younger man in an old man's body, regret clothing him like a second skin.

"After I'd been in for a couple of years, I got word that my parents had died in a car crash. They sent me home on bereavement leave, because my brother Dave was still a minor and I had to arrange for a guardian for him."

"How old were you then?" Nareen asked.

"Twenty-two."

Tony thought about that, tried to imagine a twenty-two year old man, cocky and brash and ignorant and foolish, suddenly taking on the role of parent for an adolescent boy, a person probably only slightly more cocky and brash and ignorant and foolish. He had never been entrusted with so much responsibility, not once in over ten years of running a multi-national company. Never even had to take care of a pet. Sitting on a patch of dust and prickly dead grass, a tree root working its way into the crack of his behind, he realized uncontrovertibly that if he had been that young man, put to that test, he would have failed.

"I got everything arranged. Dave went to stay with some friends from school. I signed all the papers and got the bank account all set up to support him. Got him a lifetime supply of condoms and told him not to screw up his life or anybody else's, if he could help it. And then I got in my mom's car—it was a pink Peugeot, not the one they crashed in but the car my Gran gave her when my folks got married—and I started to drive back to the airport, but when I saw it up ahead, that ugly gray clump of buildings that looks more like an elephant graveyard than anything an architect designed (I'm talking about the Albany International Airport), I just kept going. I didn't really plan it, I just kept driving." He breathed in and out through his nose, long and slow, his nostrils flaring with the effort of taking in and releasing oxygen. "The stupid thing is, that was the summer of '72."

The others looked at him blankly.

"They started pulling troops in March of '73. I could have waited and maybe never had to hide, could have finished college, could have been an English professor all these years."

"Or you could have waited and been killed before the order to withdraw came in," Nancy said.

"That was the last time I saw my brother," he said. "I sold the car, changed my name, let my hair and my beard grow out, hitchhiked across the country, stopped for a few months here, a year or two there, taking odd jobs in places that didn't ask for paperwork and didn't mind paying me under the table. Finally landed in bumfuck Oregon. I've been basically hiding out here ever since. I keep waiting for the military police to show up and haul me away. So far, I've been lucky."

He was silent again, and they thought he was done, that he'd used up all his words saying more at one time than any of them had ever heard him speak. Scooter opened his mouth to ask a question, but Walt had one more thing to say. "I never went back," he said.

He got up and walked to where his motorcycle was waiting, got on, started the engine with an angry roar, and drove away.

"Whew," Leesa said. "I wonder where *that* came from!"

"That came from him trying to stop you from harassing Nareen," Scooter said quietly.

"I wasn't—" Leesa started to say, and then she shrugged, scrunching up her face in that adorable, irritating way she had. "I'm sorry," she said to Nareen.

"You say that a lot," Nareen said. "Maybe you should think before you open your mouth, and then you wouldn't have to say you're sorry so often."

"She only asked because she cares," Scooter said, instantly changing sides.

"Whatever," Nareen said.

"How did Walt end up at the café?" Tony asked Nancy.

Nancy ran her fingers through her short gray curls as if searching for the facts, as if bits of history had leached out of her brain and migrated to the ends of her hair.

"It was over twenty years ago. God, now I think of it it's probably been twenty-five years. It's hard to remember when it seems like he's always been here." She smiled ruefully, that smile that says *How did I get here?* and *Where did the time go?*

"I had pretty much inherited the restaurant from my folks," she continued. "I liked doing it and I'd been helping out since I was a little bitty thing, and they were tired of it and just wanted to go on long golfing vacations in Florida and play with their grandbaby when they were home, so it made sense."

Tony tried to picture Nancy as a little girl, darting around a bustling café, and then as a teenager, "slinging hash" with a baby on her hip, but the images he conjured were somewhat disturbing: short and pigtailed but with the same face lined with the cares of a business-owner and the same slightly dumpy physique, and the potty-mouth Nancy had acquired working around people like Walt. He shut down the image quickly.

"We had a few short order cooks over the years," Nancy continued, "but one after another they found something better to do. So I put up another sign and posted something in the *Valley Herald*. And right away here comes Walt, looking like something out of a movie. Long hair tied back in a ponytail, long beard, mean eyes, dirty old fatigues, and scuffed up army boots." Her audience nodded, listening as if with one set of ears.

"I remember it was one of those deathly hot days when you wonder why you stay in this part of the world. The radio said we'd set some kind of record. And in walks this grungy guy wearing an army jacket that looks like it was too tore up to be a rag in somebody's rag bag."

"Why do you think he still wears army stuff when he's AWOL?" Scooter said.

"Because he's a strange old cuss with a twisted old brain," Nancy speculated. "Who knows? Anyway, I ask him why do you want the job? And he says he's been working as a ranch hand at Bob Skedgmore's place, and he says he's getting too old for that kind of work. He mostly never talks about his past, but I did find out later that he'd just bummed around the country taking odd jobs, like he said just now. Farms and ranches and whatnot, like a goddamned teenager, even though he musta been in his forties when I met him. So I ask him why I should hire him when he's got no experience cooking for a restaurant. He says watch me. And he cooks up a storm, right there in the kitchen, and it's the best damn food that kitchen'd ever seen."

Once again her listeners nodded in unison. That much they could believe, having been the beneficiaries of the best damn food the kitchen'd ever seen.

"He said he taught himself, watching the cooking shows on TV," she added. "I hired him on the spot. He had one requirement, and that was that I pay him in cash. Kind of a pain in the ass, really. All the rest of you get a check or an auto-deposit into your account, on payday. Like normal people. But I have to go to the bank and get money out before I can pay that old geezer." She gave a hoarse, low chuckle. "I knew it wasn't right when he asked, but I was desperate. My sister—she does the bookkeeping and the taxes for Sunnyside Up—she asked me, Walt's first year, why payroll was lower than before. I told her not to worry about it, wink wink hah hah, and she didn't like it but she didn't ask me about it again." Nancy stopped, and rubbed her eyes, like a child waking up from its nap, befuddled. "Anyway, I can't think Walt's missed more than a handful of days since then, and when he does, I just fill in for him. Six days a week, six in the morning to closing time at two, plus however long it takes to clean and prep for the next day. And he's off when the rest'rant is closed, of course, Mondays and Christmases and Thanksgivings and Easters. But that's about it."

"Huh," Leesa said. "I can't believe I've known him all this time and never knew his story."

"I guess that's the way he wanted it," Nancy said.

Nareen shook her head. "Good thing you've never asked me to look at your books, Nancy," she said. "I don't have my degree yet, but it's pretty obvious you'd be in a world of trouble if you ever got caught."

"Yeah, well, that's the nice thing about living in bumfuck Oregon," Nancy said. "Nobody really cares what happens here."

"It seems weird," Scooter said, and then stopped.

"A lot of things are weird," Nancy agreed. "You thinking about one thing in particular?"

"Well, yeah," Scooter said. "It seems weird that Walt's still worried about being caught. Do you really think the army would send someone all the way out here to lock him up? After all these years?"

The same thoughts had occurred to Tony, but now, though he'd never made good on his internal promise to research the issue at the library, somewhere in the recesses of his mind he recalled seeing an article or a headline or a chapter in a history book about a renewed push, in the nineties, to catch deserters and draft dodgers. He started to share what he remembered, but Nareen spoke first.

"I don't think the feds ever give up on you, if you've screwed them over somehow," she said. "But I'd guess it's more likely he'd get in trouble for not paying taxes. And you, too, Nancy. I know you said nobody cares about what you do in Motte and Bailey. But, uh, I wouldn't be too sure."

Nancy paled.

"You wouldn't ever turn us in, right?" Leesa said.

"Maybe you," Nareen said, smiling sweetly. "But not Nancy. Not Walt."

In what Tony now recognized as a classic Leesa-move, Leesa stuck out her tongue at Nareen.

A tiny breeze whiffled the surface of the water, danced among the dandelions and high desert grasses, and tickled the hair on Tony's legs. In spite of the somber conversation, everything felt just about perfect.

"What about you, Tony?" Leesa said. "Everybody else has come clean. I want to know what's up with the ankle monitor thingy. What's your story?"

* * *

Tony described the picnic to Caroline that night, leaving out the part about Walt going AWOL. Not that Caroline would care, or would ever try to use that information against Walt, but it just felt like a holy secret, a sacred trust.

Though Caroline would think that was ridiculous, he decided, as he tried to describe the motley crew and the meal they had shared.

"It sounds lovely," she said, and her words were infused with wistfulness.

Real live tears of gladness jumped into his eyes and one even escaped and spilled down his cheek and ran into his ear (he was lying on the bed while they talked).

"It was nice," he said. "Right up until Leesa demanded to know my story."

"What did you tell her?" Caroline asked.

"I stammered and stuttered like a high school kid trying to convince the homecoming queen to go on a date," he said.

Caroline laughed. "You've never had to convince anyone of anything," she said. "And I'm sure you had a date without even trying."

"A lot you know," he said, switching from crying to laughing, and the ease of it was a beautiful thing. "Junior year I asked Maryanne Stinson, the prettiest girl in my class, if she'd go with me, and she turned me down cold. Afterward I went in the bathroom and threw up. My senior year I just didn't ask anyone, so I wouldn't have to hear anyone say 'No' again."

"And then you met me, and you didn't even have to ask," Caroline said.

"Well, you were so comfortable to talk to," Tony agreed. "And then there's the fact that you started kissing me the first time we were alone together."

"And wasn't I a good kisser?" she said, and he could hear the wicked grin in her voice.

The weight of that memory was a physical force, sweet and painful and revised as all good memories are to erase the harder bits of reality and tinge the scene with lilac-scented, rose-colored mist. Her lips had been so soft, so soft, and her thick shining honey-colored hair had fallen forward and caressed his surprised cheeks. They had been studying together, facing each other with very little space between them, and he had dared to fantasize, with her delicate knees almost touching his, about putting his hand on her thigh—he figured he could make it look casual, reaching across her for a handful of the salted nuts she had set out for a study snack—when she interrupted his daydream by kissing him.

"You are an excellent kisser," he said, "and I miss your kisses terribly."

An angry pounding on the door interrupted the conversation.

"Hang on," he said, deeply annoyed that their intimate shared remembering had been cut short.

He went to the door and opened it, but there was no one there. The ping of the elevator indicated someone must have been holding the elevator for whoever knocked, to ensure a quick retreat. Tony looked down and saw a four-by-six postcard on the floor, tied with string to a newish-looking brick. On the postcard there was a message, formed from letters cut from a magazine. The letters read:

**BACK OFF OR ELSE**

"This is ridiculous," he said, returning to the phone.

"What is?" Caroline said.

"I've just received a bad-Hollywood-movie-style ransom note."

"What?" she said.

"It's not really a ransom note," he hastened to explain. "Just a note tied to a brick. It says, 'Back off or else.'"

"Back off of what?" she asked, sounding mystified.

"The only thing I'm involved in," he said. "This whatever-it-is that detective, Luis, is investigating." He still had not shared with Caroline his middle-of-the-night burial, or the fact that he'd had a very public conversation with Luis, suggesting the investigation should focus on Roj. And he hadn't told her about warning Roj to stay away from the diner. As he catalogued the things he hadn't told Caroline, he was appalled, and he started to apologize, but Caroline cut him off.

"Then do it," Caroline said. "Back off. I can't take any more of your . . . issues, Giles."

The pleading in her voice sounded like love and concern, in spite of the word "issues," and that satisfied a deep, deep longing in him. But he resisted. "I can't," he said, and then he paused. "Strike that. Reverse it," he said, calling on a line from *Willy Wonka and the Chocolate Factory*. He knew Caroline had loved the movie as a child, and he hoped she might smile instead of following her worry down its winding path. "Make that I won't. I won't stand aside and let things fall wherever they may, like I've always done. I won't."

The silence that followed was so long and so hollow, Tony had time to count the squares on his bedspread, and notice that the threads were coming loose on the sixth square from the edge.

"I don't know if I can take another legal battle," Caroline said at last, her voice sounding small and tinny and distant, as if she was talking through an antique phone in an old black-and-white movie.

And there it was. No articulated challenge or ultimatum, no one saying *You must choose*, but it was clear a choice must be made, even so.

* * *

After the breakfast rush the next day, Tony was washing dishes and thinking about the call with Caroline and the threatening note, trying to decide whether or not to share the incident with the others, when Scooter came into the kitchen for something. Walt grabbed

Scooter's elbow and steered him into the pantry. Tony stopped washing dishes so he could hear.

"Listen, Scooter," Walt said roughly. (Did he know any other way to speak besides roughly? Tony wondered). "I can teach you how to read, if you want."

"Oh no," Scooter stammered. "I'd be too scared."

Of trying and failing, or of having Walt as a teacher? Tony thought.

"What's there to be scared of?" Walt growled.

"Y-you!" Scooter said.

"Oh for crying out loud," Walt said, and then he stopped. "Okay, what if I promised to be nice?"

Scooter appeared to be considering whether Walt was capable of fulfilling this promise, but after a few long seconds he agreed, and Tony heard them set it up for every afternoon after the restaurant closed except Saturdays and Sundays. (Scooter had an early shift at the gas station on Saturday and Sunday mornings, and he said having to face Walt afterward would be too much, and Walt said fine, Sunday afternoons were for napping anyway).

The idea that Scooter was finally going to learn to read, that he would have access to the world of *New York Times* editorials, and comics and sports in the *Valley Herald*, and cheesy spy novels, and complicated instructions on the swingset for the children Scooter would someday have made Tony so happy he started to whistle the theme from *Reading Rainbow*, which was the only appropriate tune he could think of.

"Cork it," Walt said, emerging from the pantry with a nervous-looking Scooter in tow.

# Chapter 12

"Another Monday, another secret meeting," Nancy said with an exaggerated sigh.

For two whole blessed weeks, as the long hot days of summer finally ceded to the shorter and ever so slightly less hot days of fall, Tony had continued vacillating about whether to share the threatening note with the others. Day after day, he stepped on and off the trains of thought. As time passed, and nothing else happened, he told himself the whole note-on-a-brick-thing was an anomaly, and convinced himself he should just ignore it. But then he thought—and it was a new thought, fresh like the hint of a new season in the air: he'd be upset if he found out one of the others had received a threatening note, and didn't tell him about it, didn't let him carry his share of their burden.

Finally, he'd decided to bite the (figurative) bullet. "Can we meet here tomorrow?" he asked the others. "Without Luis?"

Nancy sighed. "I was hoping to take Nareen off to the big city for some maternity clothes. And by big city I mean Spokane."

Walt made a snorting sound.

"I have something to tell you," Tony said, and he hoped he didn't sound like a pre-teen pretending to be Double-O-Seven.

"Good, fine, whatever," Nancy said. "At least we won't have to look at that annoying man's face."

"Which annoying man would that be?" Walt asked.

"Luis!" Nancy said. "Well, when you get right down to it, it's all of 'em. The whole damn lot of you. Men!" she said.

After they'd convened this particular Monday meeting, and Tony had given a quick rundown of the event, the others looked at him in shock. Shock immediately gave way to outrage in Leesa, predictably, and she told Tony he should file a police report.

"What good would that do?" Walt said.

"I don't know," she said. "Maybe they could dust the brick for fingerprints, or trace the letters to some magazine only one person in town gets."

"Hold your horses there, Miss Marple," Walt said.

"Miss Who?" she said.

"The Agatha Christie detective," Nareen supplied, shifting a little so that her ample belly aimed away from the table and out of the booth.

"Oh," Leesa said, obviously not wanting to ask any more questions lest she further reveal her ignorance.

"I appreciate the thought," Tony said, "but I agree with Walt that it wouldn't do any good. It sounds like you all already suspect local law enforcement of being in cahoots with Roj."

" 'Cahoots'?" Nancy said. "What kind of word is that, Tony?" She waved her hand at him, to stop him from explaining. "I know what it means," she said. "It just sounds weird coming from you."

Tony didn't know how to respond. If he spoke like his Manhattan self, he was accused of being snooty, a man who *sounded* like he went to Yale and had a personal assistant named Addy; when he tried to do otherwise, he was "weird." Maybe silence was golden after all.

"Why don't we tell Luis?" Scooter suggested. "He's supposed to be investigating, so why don't we give him the information and let him investigate?"

"Hey, that's a good idea!" Leesa said, ignoring the groan from Nancy and poking Scooter in the ribs, which of course caused him to turn pink.

As if he'd been hanging around hoping to be invited in, Luis appeared on the sidewalk outside the diner. Tony retrieved him from the merciless mid-morning heat, and brought him inside.

Luis surveyed the group briefly before finding a chair and sliding it over to the booth where they were gathered. They in turn studied him. Short and slender, wearing what they all assumed was standard-issue undercover clothing, he gave the impression of someone who took his job seriously, but who lacked either the financial wherewithal or the fashion sense to look as neat and professional as he'd like. Every hair was in place, but he was perspiring, and his somewhat oversized slacks were wrinkled, and his long-sleeved button-front shirt was slightly yellowed and frayed at the collar.

"This was left outside my door," Tony said, showing Luis the note but omitting any mention of when it had appeared. "It was tied to a brick." He looked at Luis, trying to gauge the reaction, but Luis, presumably practiced in the art of getting a story by waiting, said nothing.

"There must have been at least two people involved," Tony said, "because the elevator dinged as soon as I opened the door."

"So?" Luis said.

Tony swallowed a grimace of irritation. "So, one person must have been holding the elevator open while someone else knocked, left the brick with the note, and then ran back down the hall. Otherwise the person who left the note would have had to push the button and wait until the elevator came to my floor."

"Yeah," Leesa said. "Some detective you are. You can't even detect that!"

Luis rubbed his fingertips thoughtfully across his upper lip, ignoring Leesa's insult. "Why would someone target you?" he said to Tony.

"Why not?" Tony said.

"Well, you claim you're not the person I'm looking for, and you claim you're not involved in the situation I'm investigating. And yet here's someone—two someones, according to your theory—who think you're so involved they see you as a threat. Why do you suppose that is? If you're an innocent bystander, as you say?"

Tony felt a little twittering of panic in his belly, worrying that Luis was about to disclose Tony's true identity right here in the diner, to all the people Tony most wanted to hide it from. Before he could think of an answer, Walt stepped in.

"Well, let's think about this," Walt said. "Tony's new, that's one strike against him right there." He held up a gnarled forefinger, with bitten-down nails and enlarged knuckles. "We may be a town full of jerks, screw-ups, and ne'er-do-wells, but we all know each other's faults. A detective shows up and starts asking questions, people around here don't think *Who committed a crime?*, they think *Who told?* They'd look at Tony here and see a big, ugly rat."

Tony tried to feel grateful that Walt was defending him, but failed, for the most part; being called a big ugly rat can make it difficult to feel gratitude.

"Then there's the fact that he works here, where Roj eats breakfast almost every day," Walt continued, holding up a second finger. "You already know everyone at this table suspects Roj of being at the center of any drug trade, and we're not alone. The rest of the town would agree if there's any funny business Roj is in on it. They wouldn't have bothered reporting anything about Roj, because they all know there's no point. But Tony, the new guy, he might have said something."

Luis nodded, apparently following his reasoning so far.

Walt was practically garrulous, and Tony wondered how much more the normally taciturn man was going to say.

"So if Roj *is* involved," Walt said, "Roj and his partners would figure maybe Tony found out something and squealed like a stuck pig."

This was getting ridiculous. Now he was a pig?

"I guess it all comes down to this: *you* were so sure Tony was involved with one thing or the other, you followed him home one night. Don't you think there are other people out there at least as smart as you?"

Luis glowered at Walt, whether because Walt was lecturing him or because of the aspersions to his intelligence, it was hard to tell. Maybe both. "Moving on," he said. "I still think there's more to your story than I've uncovered in my investigation, and more than you let on, *Tony*."

"There's more to all our stories," Nancy said quietly.

"What are you going to do about the threatening message?" Scooter said, bringing them back to the discussion at hand.

Luis pursed his lips, thinking. "I could call my department and get authorization to set up a stakeout outside the motel. The problem is this frigging town is so small everyone will know exactly what is going on if a strange car shows up and starts hanging around outside the Sleepy Time Motel."

"Wait, you live in the Sleepy Time Motel?" Leesa said.

"Like Nancy said," Tony answered, "everybody has a story." He tried to keep his voice gentle without leaving an opening for further questioning, but it turned out to be unnecessary. Leesa had already moved on from that topic.

"Why not do a stakeout inside the motel?" she said.

"We can help," Scooter offered.

"You're not properly trained," Luis objected. "It's not like in the movies, you know."

"Then train us," Scooter said.

"Headquarters'll never allow it," Luis said, still looking skeptical.

"They don't need to know," Scooter said. "You'll be doing the official watching, and we'll just be hanging out in the general vicinity when you're at the diner or interrogating someone or . . . something."

Although obviously not pleased with the plan, Luis finally agreed to educate the entire group on the finer points of lawful spying, on the condition that the minute anything happened they would call him, he would call his colleagues at the sheriff's department, and official monitoring would be set up. They moved on to logistics, and it was decided Luis would rent a room down the hall from Tony's room, and then Leesa, Scooter, and Walt would take turns sitting in the room, listening for anything suspicious. If they heard anything, they'd look through the peephole in the door to see what it was, and would immediately—"and I do mean immediately," Luis said, in case the words *the minute anything happened* hadn't sunk in—notify Luis.

Nancy didn't offer and wasn't asked to offer her services, and Nareen was exempted by mutual consent. "I'm not really into your spy games anyway," she said. "And I don't care that much."

A dark flower of hurt blossomed inside Tony, but he said nothing. Why should Nareen care about him?

There was a brief interlude of joking (*What do we do if there are no rooms free—Motte and Bailey's such a tourist destination, the motel's bound to be full up*; and *Better not let Nancy and Walt take a watch together, or we'll end up with The Love Boat old people style,*" which earned Leesa a vigorous punch on the shoulder from Nancy and a wry eyebrow-raise from Walt). And then Leesa asked the Big Question: "What do we do if we see something suspicious, like someone going into Tony's room?"

"You call me," Luis said, showing remarkable patience, as if he hadn't just explained that.

"Or, if you're me," Walt said, "you follow the bastard."

"You don't have a gun," Luis pointed out.

"How do you know?" Walt said.

Luis squinted at him, but seemed to decide not to pursue it.

Tony wondered briefly how Scooter would balance his shifts at the gas station and Sunnyside Up, learning to read, and spying. As if reading his thoughts, Scooter said, "I got nothing to do in my spare time, so it's all good."

It took less than a week for Luis to get authorization from head-quarters to rent a room—the others were pretty sure he'd said nothing to his department about enlisting their help with the actual stakeout—and by the last day of September the room down the hall from Tony's was rented under an assumed name. Luis wouldn't say what name he'd chosen, though the others teased him mercilessly with guesses, asking, "Would you like some more coffee, Myrtle May?" and "How's that toast, Fred Flinstone?" Tony quickly got into the habit of knocking smartly on the door of room 205, waiting for one of the Sunnyside Up employees to poke his or her head out, chatting for a minute or two, and then heading off to work. When he came home at the end of his workday, it was the same routine in reverse.

By the end of the first week of the stakeout, no one suspicious had appeared, no new bricks or other threatening messages had showed up, and the members of the stakeout team were complaining of boredom.

They talked about it at work, but no one seemed to have any idea what the next step might be if the perpetrators (Leesa used the word proudly and as often as possible) never returned.

One Wednesday, after a week and a half of what Leesa called *a whole lot of nothing,* the same young family that Tony had gleefully served when Nareen's feet were swollen returned to the restaurant. The three dark-haired hopeful-eyed boys squeezed into the booth across from their parents, and every few minutes there was a small eruption of poking-hitting-crying-jabbing-yelling-spilling, followed by hissed instructions to *knockitofforwe'releavingrightthisminute.* This time, Nareen didn't ask Tony to take over for her, so he didn't get to serve them, but he filled their water glasses and the parents' coffee cups repeatedly, and swooped in to clean up every spill, feeling very proprietary. Each time, the mom or the dad murmured *thank you,* looking embarrassed.

"That's odd," Nancy said thoughtfully.

"What is?" Tony said, wondering why the parents seemed so much more chagrined over their boys' behavior than last time, even though it was not appreciably worse.

"The Maxes usually only come in on Saturdays or Sundays. Tom

is the manager of the Automotive Department at Walmart, and he
works weekdays. Sandy doesn't ever try to handle all three of her
monsters alone, leastaways not in a sit-down restaurant."

Tony hadn't realized Sunnyside Up was *a sit-down restaurant*, and
wasn't entirely sure what that meant. Were there restaurants where
one walked while eating, perambulating the premises? Or lay upon
couches like toga-ed Romans, eating brined olives?

The next time Tony was needed, he said familiarly, "Hello Tom,
Hello Sandy." Before he could say anything about what nice boys
they were or make some other inane comment that would establish
that he, Tony, liked this family very, very much, Tom grabbed his
wrist. "Don't," he said.

"I don't mind," Tony said. "It's my job."

"N-no," Tom said. "I mean, don't . . . don't s-stick your nose in.
Don't get involved."

Sandy looked down at her yogurt, staring intently into the creamy
pink depths as if looking for the answers to life's little mysteries at
the bottom of the bowl. Or maybe just a place to hide.

Tony was flabbergasted.

"I'm flabbergasted," he told Walt a few minutes later.

"You aren't," Walt said.

"I'm not what?" Tony said.

"You're not flabbergasted. Unless you're a dinosaur or a dragon
in a Disney flick, you're just surprised."

"I don't see what that has to do with anything," Tony said petu-
lantly. "That nice-looking young father of three just threatened me.
Why do you care what I call it?"

"Because it's annoying," Walt said. "Take the time to pick the
right word, or else keep your trap shut."

Tony turned on Walt. "You find everything I do annoying, Walt.
I'm stuck in this town, in this diner, just like you. And just like you,
if I stray too far from Motte and Bailey, I'll be thrown in jail. Or I'll
have to pay a few million dollars more. It's not clear to me which, but
either way, I'm here for eight more months, so either help me figure
out who wants to get rid of me, or leave me alone."

"I get it," Walt said, unexpectedly backing down. "But I just can't
stand it when people are stupid about their words."

Tony was tempted to pull out a "Whatevs," Leesa-style. But he
needed Walt on his side, Walt who didn't dig like a girl, Walt who

could make a prayer of one word, Walt who worked miracles with eggs and cheese. And Walt, who had wanted to be an English teacher. "I'll try to be more careful, literarily speaking," he said, though he still sounded sulky even to himself.

"Appreciate it," Walt said. "Nancy," he yelled from the doorway to the pantry (where they'd been having their palaver, of course), "come here for a minute."

Nancy came, and Tony told her what had happened.

"You're shitting me," she said. "You couldn't find anyone in this town less likely to be involved in dirty work than Tom and Sandy. They're a little rough around the edges, but I would never have figured them for criminals."

"Or thugs," Walt agreed, nodding.

"He stuttered when he talked," Tony pointed out. "Maybe he's not used to being a thug."

Nareen joined them on a pretense of needing something from the pantry. "People aren't always what they seem," she said.

"Should we tell Luis?" Nancy said.

"Not yet," said Walt. "I'd bet my last pair of underwear they're on the bottom of the totem pole in whatever we're dealing with."

"Who'd want your last pair of underwear?" Nancy said.

Walt rolled his eyes and pressed his lips together, looking more like an eccentric queen than a grouchy old cuss. "Luis'd just arrest them and then we'd never find out who put them up to it."

Nareen backed out of the pantry (there was really no other way out, in her condition), and went back to serving, but Tony noted with satisfaction that when she removed the plates she "accidentally" dumped the last smear of eggs and cheese and hot sauce on Tom's lap, and "accidentally" bashed his groin with the plate as she clumsily tried to wipe the mess off his legs. "My bad," she murmured, barely apologetic.

She *did* care!

The Max family left, and the restaurant slowly emptied out as the morning rush ended. Finally, Nancy turned the Open sign to Closed, and the five of them (Nancy and Walt, Nareen and Scooter, and Tony) began working their way through the closing checklist.

Suddenly, Leesa burst through the door, yelling, gesticulating furiously, and crying. Leesa wasn't on the schedule for today, and in any event the diner was now closed. No one had any idea where she had

come from or why she was there. She just appeared, a strawberry-
blonde avenging Fury.

"Murderer!" she yelled, looking at Tony.

"I know what you did!" she sobbed, tears streaming over her
round, freckled cheeks. "I heard. They told me. Libby's aunt and
uncle saw you, when you were working, and they knew they'd seen
your face somewhere, and then they remembered, and they checked
in the old newspapers they kept from when it happened, and they told
me. You killed that sweet baby girl, you and your toys, that stupid
stuffed bear, and then you came here to—to what? See if you could
find some more kids to kill? What the hell is wrong with you, you
mother-fucking child-killing bastard!"

* * *

"Leesa found out about me," Tony told Caroline that night, and
he was amazed to hear the words come out of him quiet and calm
when it felt like a shriek, a howl, the anguish after the *echthroi* have
split time and space. He didn't tell her what happened next, how his
body froze, cell by cell, until he could speak no words, and make no
sounds, only look at Leesa with *I'm sorry* weeping from his eyes.

"Martin told me he thinks he can get a reduction in your sentence,
Giles," she said, as if she hadn't heard, as if it was of no consequence.
"Then you could come home."

"They all looked at me like I'd sprouted a second head," he said,
needing her to stay with him as he recounted the story. "And Nancy
sent me home." As if this place where he slept and spoke to his wife
on the phone was *home.*

"It doesn't matter," Caroline said patiently. "If you come back to
New York, it doesn't matter what someone in Motte and Bailey thinks
of you."

And Tony didn't know how to answer her, how to explain that
somehow, it did.

* * *

He wasn't sure if he was expected at work the next day, or even
allowed at work, but since he'd heard nothing to the contrary, he decided to go in, thinking or hoping maybe his white-man-with-money

skin had protected him one more time. As he walked the dim, stale-cigarette-infused hallway, with its gray walls and its stained orange-and-blue-triangled carpet, the door to Room 205 opened, and Scooter poked his head out.

"Can we talk?" he said.

Tony nodded, and followed Scooter into the room that was in every way identical to the room he had just left, except that this room had two beds and only one window, and the dim air felt like an off-kilter haiku written by a fifth-grade student: I sit here and wait, but no one appears to me, and the air is sad.

They each sat on one of the beds, facing each other.

"Why did you come here?" Scooter said.

"I had no choice," Tony said simply.

"What do you mean?" Scooter was angry, but Tony could see that he was also hurt, whether on his own behalf or Leesa's or the little girl's family or all of the above; it was hard to tell.

There was a moment, a single instant in time, where he could have refused to answer. He, Giles Anthony Maurice Gibson, owed this shy sandy-haired boy nothing. He could have said, "I'm not at liberty to say," mimicking Walt. He could have sneered, "Mind your own beeswax," as Leesa was so fond of saying. Or he could have told Scooter a sanitized version of the story, minimizing his role in the situation, making it sound like he'd been unfairly prosecuted for someone else's crime.

But here was Scooter, who had freely volunteered his time to help protect Tony, who had shown up for dreadfully dull stakeout duty even now, when he knew Tony was a murderer. Scooter could have written Tony off, but he didn't, and he deserved an answer, even if it meant Tony risked severing the nascent thread of friendship between them.

Tony counted to four, and exhaled.

One two three four *breathe*.

"The judge found that my company, ABC Toys, had been criminally negligent in manufacturing these teddy bears we made," he said. He saw the glazed look in Scooter's eyes that says *I have no idea what you're saying*. "It's a crime," he explained, "to be careless with the things a company makes, if someone gets hurt because of the carelessness."

Scooter nodded.

"We called them Poppy Pandas," Tony said. As if that was relevant. "The judge said the little girl—Libby—that her death was foreseeable. That we should have known it could happen. But the thing is, he told me—the Vice President of Product Safety—he told me the eyes on the bear were a little loose, but he said it was an acceptable risk."

He paused, looking at Scooter, to see if there was an impending exodus.

"Anyway, there was a lawsuit, and that ended up in a settlement. Sixteen million dollars. It's likely most of that went to the lawyers for Libby's family, and the lawyers for the other families who joined the lawsuit. I don't know how much the families actually got. There was also a criminal trial, where the judge fined us the maximum."

He stopped again, gathering his courage for the final blow. "The judge also sentenced me to perform community service in Motte and Bailey for one year," he said. He blew the words out, bullets spraying indiscriminately, to do their damage. "And he said I had to earn my keep at a minimum wage job, so I would know what it felt like to be the kind of person who was the victim of other people's decisions. 'You will go where you are nobody,' the judge said."

"Is that what we are?" Scooter asked. " 'Nobody'?"

"I don't think that's what he meant," Tony said. "He meant I would understand what it felt like to have no power, like you and Leesa and Nancy and Walt, no ability to escape the consequences of your actions by just waving money at the problem."

"I still haven't learned to read," Scooter said.

"That was kind of a non sequitur," Tony said testily. In the absence of complete rejection, he had fostered a faint hope that Scooter would grant him absolution.

"A what now?" Scooter said.

"A non sequitur is—what does that have to do with me being sentenced to community service in Motte and Bailey?"

"Everything!" Scooter said. "You—you're talking about not having power. I've been running away from learning to read so I wouldn't have to figure out what to do with my life. I can't go to college or move away or even ask Leesa to be my girlfriend because I can't read. Yeah, I'm, like, powerless. And there's Walt. Ever since the picnic we all know he's running away from the Army. Powerless, that's practically his middle name."

"Except over eggs. He's got a lot of power over eggs," Tony said.

Less than half a smile graced Scooter's face.

"Do you know why Nancy won't leave Sunnyside Up?" Scooter said.

Tony shrugged.

"Well, Leesa told me she thinks Nancy feels guilty for being a bad girl and getting pregnant when she was fifteen, even though that's on Roj, not her, I mean, that's Roj's . . . sin. Leesa thinks maybe Nancy doesn't believe she deserves anything better than running the diner. That's, that's powerless."

Tony wasn't sure where Scooter's words were leading, and he started to ask, but Scooter wasn't done.

"And Nareen, I mean, she's running away from her boyfriend and her parents and her grandparents so she can be confused by herself without them telling her what to do." Scooter stood up and started to pace, and with each argument he walked faster and talked more loudly, until he was nearly yelling. "We're all running away from our problems," he said. "You've got no . . . you're not the only one who feels like he's got no power. Just because you're rich, it doesn't make you special. And just because we're poor, it doesn't mean we have no power. There's nothing about being poor that makes it so I can't wake up one day and say, 'enough.' Learn to read, go back to school. You know, change."

Tony thought, wildly, briefly, of engaging Scooter in a discussion of systemic inequality and the philosophical ins and outs of wealth redistribution, but he didn't want to talk about economic and political theories. "Do you think Leesa will ever forgive me?" he said.

"I don't know," Scooter said. "She used to babysit Libby. We all, pretty much everyone in town, came to the funeral. It was horrible."

Does it need to be said that a funeral for a five-year-old girl is horrible? Tony wished he could have been spared that last sentence. "It's not like I choked her with my own hands," he said stiffly. "I had a responsibility to make safe toys, I understand that, but I didn't fly here from New York to murder a little girl."

"She was so pretty," Scooter said. He sat in silence for a while, perusing his inner photo album. Tony remembered the image the prosecutor had shared with the jury, the image burned on the backs of his eyelids, the dark-haired, honey-skinned, twinkle-eyed, elfin face that Tony could never, ever forget.

"I'll talk to Leesa," Scooter said finally. "I don't know if it will do any good, but I'll talk to her." And then he said, "It was you that sprung Nancy from jail, wasn't it?"

"I wish," Tony said, as fervently as if he had a magic lamp to wish upon. "But I tried. And I think I've just about convinced my lawyer to hire someone to represent Nancy at her hearing on Halloween. He understands if Nancy goes to jail I'm out of a job, and that interferes with me completing my sentence."

Scooter shook his head. "And we wouldn't want to mess up your life, would we?" Sarcasm didn't sit well on his open, kindly face.

"No, that's not what I meant. I meant that's what I had to say to get him to hire someone to help Nancy. And I wanted to help." He looked down at his hands, no longer pale and smooth, the nails no longer showing any signs of his last manicure several months ago. "I wanted to help Nancy. Because she's my friend."

He'd longed to share his machinations on Nancy's behalf with Scooter and the others, but he couldn't without giving away his identity. He'd told himself that was for the best, dimly recalling the apostolic exhortation: Let your giving be in secret. (His had never been a church-going family, but he'd taken Comparative Religions in college, and he understood that most of the major faiths frowned, doctrinally-speaking, on making a big show of charity.) But now he thought: nuts to that. He'd just lost the faith of Leesa with a double "e," whose opinion mattered, for reasons he could scarcely articulate, and if he had to break some commandments to get it back, well, that's what he'd do. He'd convince Martin to help, and then he'd throw a parade and carry a sign proclaiming his good works on Nancy's behalf, and maybe that would rub the corners off Leesa's rage.

"I don't think you're a bad person," Scooter said gently. It was oh so odd to hear him take a paternal tone, to try to be reassuring, but Tony felt comforted, nonetheless. Scooter would make a good mate for Leesa, he thought, if only she would give him a chance.

Even though he was already quite late, after his tête-à-tête with Scooter, Tony walked slowly, slowly down the street, delaying the moment of discovery: Would Leesa be there? Would she talk to him?

And: Would Nancy fire him? She had a restaurant to run, after all. It couldn't be good for business to have him there, the man who was responsible for the death of one of the town's children. Nancy had agreed to take him on incognito, but she might have changed her mind, now that his cover was blown. Leesa would spread the word throughout Motte and Bailey and beyond, of that he was almost certain. What would that do to the reputation of Sunnyside Up? Perhaps he'd have to start over at McDonald's or Shari's in Pendleton. Or a restaurant in Athena (No-the-hell-where-land, as Leesa called it).

But there's only so long dawdling can delay a journey of three and a half blocks, and all his questions were answered in relatively short order. Leesa wasn't not-talking to him; as soon as she saw him the tears and the yelling began again, a river of hurt and betrayal originating somewhere around her toes and traveling upward through her veins, defying gravity, gathering strength, becoming a tsunami, and Tony was caught in the force of it, circling helplessly. Nancy grabbed his arm and propelled him into the kitchen.

"Go home," she said fiercely. "Leesa will get over it, and then you can come back to work."

"Home?" Tony said, this time thinking of satin sheets and Manhattan.

"Back to the motel," Nancy said, and left him standing there.

Tony moved to go out the back door. Walt was sitting at the small table near the door, where staff ate their meals. His long gray hair was pulled loosely into a braid, but more hair had escaped the braid than had been captured in it, and most of that was standing on end or sticking out at odd angles from his head. He looked like a dangerous escapee from a mental institution, Tony thought, though he was careful not to say it aloud—both because it wasn't politically correct and because of Walt's propensity for being terrifying.

"Wait," Walt said. He pulled a piece of paper from his pocket, a piece of yellow, lined paper folded and refolded and slightly grimy around the edges, and scribbled something on it. "Here," he said, waving it at Tony. "My cell number. Call me and I'll let you know when it's safe to come back."

Tony thanked Walt, and pushed the note into the pocket of his no-longer-pristine Dockers, and then he left, with no clear idea of where he should go, or what he might find when he got there.

# A Curate's Egg

Out the back door, past the dumpster that had housed Sam's body, and down the street again. More dawdling, more pondering. He takes a few random turns, wandering streets he's never explored before. Mostly they lead to dilapidated houses staring forlornly from their window-eyes.

An inhabited house is a testament to hope. The house announces to all who pass: I am lived in, life happens here. Fat tender toddler feet will dance on my lawn, there will be lovemaking in my bedrooms, perhaps even in the kitchen; Aunt Cecelia will drink too much beer and pontificate on politics and pass out in my pantry, Marco will wrestle with adolescence on my balcony and lose the battle, parents will hang their heads in despair at the impossibility of parenting, and grandparents will sit on my porch and smile in sympathy and a little vindictive pleasure that it is no longer their burden to carry, this impossibility, they can merely watch and meddle and criticize and then go home to their own house where whining and urinating on the floor are the provenance of the senile overweight dogs, and dinner can be a bowl of mint chocolate chip ice cream if you damn well feel like it.

When no one inhabits the house, it is bereft, but still there is hope. A fresh coat of paint and a liberal application of fescue-blend grass seed is all that is needed, the house believes.

Tony passes the houses, pushing aside their silent hopes and griefs. He comes upon a massive building he hasn't seen before, a community center that was built through the generosity of John and Martha Lanyard, according to the bronze plaque on the grass. A memory stirs in his mind: *Welcome, Tony. I'm Roj. That's short for Roger, in case you're wondering. Roger Lanyard.* Presumably John and Martha are related to Roj. It seems there is no escape from the toxic influences of that man.

It is a Thursday in the middle of October. All the children who might otherwise be cavorting or lurking or whatever else a child does in a community center are presumably in school. The huge building is mostly silent. Like everywhere else in this town, the community center feels abandoned, a place for people where people aren't. He remembers reading on Wikipedia that there are fewer than four thousand people in Motte and Bailey, but most of them seem to be missing in action at any given time. In one of the vacant shops he passes every morning on his way to work, there is a newspaper article taped to a dusty window, proudly proclaiming a Revitalization Plan. He thinks back to the Latin classes obligatory in an East Coast private college preparatory high school. "Vita" means "life." Revitalization: the act of breathing life again into something dead. Can a town be revitalized if the people refuse to show up for the effort?

He walks on, shoving his hands into his pockets for lack of anything else to do with them, but that turns out to be a mistake. Someone rams into him with such force it feels like he's a building on the other side of a wrecking ball, and he crashes to the ground, face first, unable to extricate his hands from his pockets in time to break his fall. Then there is the sensation of a hard, sharp knee in his back, between his shoulder blades, and a rough hand smelling faintly of something vaguely familiar—lavender, of all things! —and an angry voice saying, "We told you to back off. Why are you still sniffing around? Why are you even still here?"

His ears are ringing from the impact, he can't see his attacker out of the one eye not pressed against the pavement, and the stinging on his cheek is quite painful. He has no immediate capacity for struggling, and all he can think to say is, "I can't leave."

It is unclear whether the someone pinning him to the ground understood his words, but the voice growls something that sounds like "Mind your own business" (or maybe it's "Mime is my business"?). Tony feels his head being lifted by the hair (maybe finally time to find a barber in town?), and then a cloth bag of some kind is slipped over his head, and secured by a string or twine or rope around his neck. The whatever-it-is is tied uncomfortably tight, but not so tight that he will be unable to breathe, and Tony is irrationally grateful, as if the person has given him a lovely gift. The pressure on his back is lifted, and there is a grunting sound of someone standing up with difficulty, and finally the sound of someone walking rapidly away.

Tony frees his hands from his pockets, rolls over, and sits up, and then with no little difficulty he manages to untie the knot in what turns out to be ordinary kitchen twine holding the cloth bag over his head. In the time it takes to free himself, he feels as if he is suffocating.

But he is not, and once the bag is off he sits and breathes, in and out, again and again and again. He'd prefer not to open his eyes, but he can feel that his face is bleeding in earnest, so he pulls off his polo shirt and mops at the side of his head, still sitting on the sidewalk, trying to decide what to do. No one has come out of the sad and hopeful houses across the street; no one has come out of the abnormally quiet community center. Looking around at the empty street, rubbing feebly at the gushing wound that, by the feel of it, covers a good portion of his right cheek and forehead, he comes to a decision: he was foolish to get involved. Caroline was right. He should just keep his head down and finish his sentence and go home, home where people know him and nobody smashes him to the ground and ties a bag over his head with lavender-smelling hands.

Right now, he needs someone to pick him up and take him to get medical care. Then he remembers he has Walt's phone number, and he fishes the paper, now even more disreputable-looking, from his back pocket.

As he unfolds the paper, he notices writing on the back. The hand-writing is meticulous, the careful cursive of the older generation, be-fore children learned to "write" using a keyboard.

> *The drooping lilac dreams of me*
> *Rosy rising in my consciousness*
> *Green respiration*
> *Birthing microscopic suns.*

For a second that stretches almost to eternity before boomerang-ing back again, Tony cannot comprehend what he is seeing. Perhaps Walt has copied a poem from a—what? From a literary magazine? Logic intervenes, and he understands that he's reading a poem Walt wrote.

"You sneaky bastard," he says aloud, and then he adds, almost but not quite grinning in spite of his pain, "I'm flabbergasted."

# Chapter 13

"That's what you were trying to hide from me, that day when you wanted to know if I'd read the papers I found in your truck," Tony said.

Walt glared at him. "You've just been attacked by the Lavender Bandit and all you want to talk about is poetry?"

Tony had limped into the community center, located the office, and convinced the young woman behind the desk that, though he was still bleeding, he was not mortally wounded, he just needed to use the phone. He called the number scrawled on the back of the crumpled paper, and Nancy answered, creating even more havoc in Tony's addled brain (though she answered, "Grumpy old cuss's phone, Nancy speaking"). She told Tony she'd send Walt to pick him up, and he heard her assure Walt she could fill in, he wasn't the only one who could cook around here, and then he heard Walt mutter something about food poisoning and not to forget to put a pinch of cayenne in the hash browns.

Walt met Tony in front of the community center, loaded him unceremoniously into the ancient pickup truck, and brought him to a surprisingly attractive little cottage. The house was sided in blue-gray shingles with white trim, the paint well-maintained, and the tiny porch swept clean. A few high desert shrubs flourished in the yard, bordered by a white picket fence. Behind the house, visible because it was wider by a considerable margin than the house itself, was what looked to be a truly massive garden, with pumpkins trailing here and there and empty corn stalks and even, if Tony was not mistaken, broccoli and kale.

It was not at all what Tony would have expected.

Walt helped Tony into the house, practically shoved him onto a

143

dilapidated couch that might once have been plaid, handed him a wad of toilet paper and a bottle of hydrogen peroxide fetched from somewhere in the bowels of the cottage, and asked him what happened. Tony squirted hydrogen peroxide onto the toilet paper and mopped at his face as he shared the basic outlines of his miserable morning (wandering the town, finding the community center, being thrown to the ground and threatened, and of course having a bag tied onto his head by an older man smelling of lavender).

"But enough about me," he said, still gamely dabbing at his wounds. "Now that I know you're a poet, I'm curious. What's your real name?"

"I'm not going to tell you that," Walt said. "I adopted Walt Whitman a long time ago. As far as you're concerned, that is my real name. Can we get back to what happened this morning before I'm tempted to bloody the other side of your damn face?"

"I'm no literary expert, and I'm not really a fan of poetry," Tony said, "but I think you're very good."

Walt made a sound that managed to combine impatience and irritation. "I'm guessing from Leesa's tirade that the company you used to be president of makes toys," he said.

Tony nodded, and with difficulty refrained from correcting the "used to be."

"So you'll understand if I don't get up and dance a jig because you think I'm good. That's like me saying I've never played with a toy in my life but I think your toys are awesome."

"I guess I see your point," Tony said.

"And you're gonna see it right on your pretty little rich boy's nose if you ever breathe a word of this to anyone else in town," Walt said.

"I think Nancy'd be keen to know her chef is a man of the arts," Tony needled.

"Shut. Up." Walt said, and each word was indeed a sentence with a period at the end, an order that needed no embellishing with frivolous adjectives or wayward adverbs.

Tony decided it would be wise to comply.

"You're sure it was lavender?" Walt said, after Tony had relayed all the additional details he could remember.

"Yes," Tony said. "Why do you ask?" It occurred to him that lavender and lemon verbena and other essential oils were the ingredients of the privileged life. He doubted Leesa had lavender-infused hair treatments, and he couldn't imagine Scooter seeking out an aftershave with a hint of sandalwood or evening primrose.

"Crackers and Jems have some land they farm," Walt said, "and lavender is one of the main crops. Smells like baby puke, in my opinion, but I guess Portlanders and Seattleites will pay big bucks for a bunch of the stuff."

"Huh," Tony said, trying and failing to picture the two bland, oh-so-generic, and going-on-geriatric men engaged in criminal assault. "If it was one of them, that would explain why my attacker seemed to have some difficulty getting up, and why it sounded like he walked away rather than running."

"How do you know it was a man?" Walt said.

"It was a man's voice, and his hands were large and rough."

"I think it's time to pay them a visit," Walt said, stroking his long beard thoughtfully.

"You do you what you want," Tony said, recalling his recent decision to avoid entanglements in others' problems. "I'm out."

Walt rounded on him. "You don't get to be 'out.' It's your fault you're here, and being here means you're involved. You work at Sunnyside Up, a man shows up dead and a detective starts nosing around and someone throws a bag over your head; you're already in up to your eyeballs, and you don't get to just wash your hands of it like some goddamned Pontius Pilate."

He stood up and paced the floor, shaking his head. "Why *are* you here, anyway?" he said. "It seems like a hell of a choice, under the circumstances."

Tony sighed. It would have been nice to explain it just once, to everyone he knew in town, and be done with it. But nice was not an option, not when you were the president of a company that had carelessly made toys that murdered little girls, and you had been sentenced to live and work in a diner in bumfuck Oregon.

He looked around at the small house, trying to come up with the most economical version of the story. While the outside of the little house was tidy, the inside reflected the persona of its curmudgeonly inhabitant, who gave the finger to social protocols such as housecleaning. Clothes were draped or dropped wherever Walt had happened to be when he took them off, and the sink was piled with dirty dishes. An ancient television squatted against the wall in the tiny living room. Louvered doors hung ajar, revealing a laundry room *cum* closet, the washer and dryer streaked with rust and caked with dust.

"I'm president of a toy company," he said, glad at least to use the present tense. "One of my company's toys killed a little girl. Killed Libby. The judge ordered me to do community service here, and ordered me to pay for my living expenses by working at Sunnyside Up. Nobody here has ever talked to me about community service, so I don't know what that was supposed to be. I'm here for a year—I can't leave until the end of May, next year.

"And I'm married," he added. "And I miss my wife.

"A lot.

"And my face hurts.

"And I'm really, really sorry about Libby. If I could take it back I would. I've wished a thousand times that I could find a genie in a bottle and undo the whole damn thing."

Walt got up without a word, went into the single bedroom, and came out with bottle of pills. "Percocet makes the world go round," he said, and he tossed the bottle to Tony.

* * *

Unlike Walt's house (which didn't match the man at all, at least from the outside), the home of Crackers and Jems was exactly what Tony would have pictured for two gay men living in farm country. A white sign with cursive lettering reading "Violet Vale" announced the farm. A long gravel drive, bordered on either side by a split rail fence, wound through apple and cherry orchards, ending in front of a periwinkle ranch-style house. Behind the house, as far as the eye could see, there were fields of lavender in every stage of growth and harvesting. The odor, sliding in through the open windows of the truck like an oil slick laminating the beach after a spill, was overpowering. Tony was momentarily disoriented, remembering the lavender-smelling hands and the string around his neck. He told himself, sternly, that he was not allowed to have PTSD or anything like it. He was a Gibson, and Gibsons did not suffer from mental illness, not unless there was an expensive and highly confidential sanitarium to which they could gracefully exit for a period of time, not to exceed three months.

Walt parked the truck, and he and Tony approached the yard, which was encircled by sturdy metal fence panels. "Goat fencing,"

Walt said, as if Tony had asked, "to keep the dogs in." The aforementioned dogs made an immediate appearance, and began vocalizing their pleasure—or displeasure, in some cases—in baritone and soprano voices. It was hard to tell in the flashing of color and sound, but Tony thought he counted seven dogs. Maybe eight.

"Oh now hush my darlings," Crackers said, appearing at the door and making kissing sounds to the hairy hoard. His words, and his kissing sounds, had no effect.

Crackers wended his way through the throng toward the gate, still calling on them to behave themselves, and even stopping to scold an enormous wolfhound, "Is that any way for a lady to act? Where are your manners, my dear?" The wolfhound looked apologetic but continued to bark.

"To what do we owe the pleasure?" Crackers said to Walt and Tony, stepping over an ancient dachshund whose long graying hair swept the ground, and who appeared to be both deaf and blind (as it was barking wheezily in entirely the wrong direction). And then, catching sight of Tony's mangled face, "Oh my good and gracious me," he said. "What happened to you?"

In a perfect imitation of every gravelly-voiced movie detective Walt answered, "We were hoping you could tell us."

Crackers opened the gate and swept his arm around in a gesture of invitation, gently moving several dogs aside with his foot as they tried to sneak through the opening. He slammed the gate shut with surprising force, as soon as Walt and Tony were inside the yard.

"This is Marigold," Crackers said, pointing to the wolfhound. "Please sit down, missy." Marigold sat and showed her enormous yellow teeth. "Don't mind her, she's smiling," Crackers assured them.

"And this is Butch," he said, bending over to pat the dachshund on the rump.

A gleaming black Labrador who leaned against Tony's leg, pinning him against the gate, was introduced as Callooh. She looked up at him with immediate and profound adoration. "Callooh Callay, you see?" Crackers said. Perhaps it was the Percocet, but Tony did not see, so Walt clarified: "Come to my arms, my beamish boy! O frabjous day! Callooh! Callay!"

Claude (the hero of the Broadway musical *Hair*, Crackers explained), a vaguely-terrier-looking animal, continued to bark ceaselessly, stopping only when he stumbled over a dilapidated squirrel-shaped dog toy, apparently bound by dog-code to attempt to tear it to shreds before resuming his barking.

Freya, a Great Pyrenees who was probably at some stage in her life a gorgeous dog but whose fur was so matted and filthy she looked like a refugee from a war-torn country, gave a final desultory bark in their direction and then curled up again in a dusty depression in the corner of the yard, her nose touching her tail so that her body formed a perfect, grimy circle. Crackers apologized for her lack of social graces. "Freya is the Norse goddess of sexual freedom and fertility," he said, as if that explained everything.

"You have so many dogs," Tony said, because he couldn't think of anything else to say.

"We need them to guard the farm," Crackers said, sounding defensive.

They made it past the gauntlet of dogs and into the house, only to discover one more canine.

"Lipton," Crackers said, "like Lipton tea." He pointed to a German Shepherd resting in a basket by a bay window in an immaculate living room. Sunlight bathed her dark fur like alpenglow on a mountain. She thumped her tail lightly at the mention of her name.

"Lipton is recovering from surgery on her leg—torn ligament," Crackers said. "And speaking of tea, can I get you boys something to drink?"

"We didn't come here to drink tea," Walt said, and simultaneously,

"Coffee would be nice," Tony said.

Crackers smiled, a worried sort of smile, and shuffled in what Tony assumed was the direction of the kitchen. "I'll just be a minute," floated back toward them. "Make yourself at home."

Tony sat down cautiously, and was immediately approached by Lipton.

"I'm a little afraid of dogs," he confessed.

"Get over it," Walt said. Even so, he tried to coax Lipton away from Tony, patting the side of the chair in which he was sitting, by way of invitation.

But Lipton would not be coaxed. Ever so gently, she rested her head on Tony's knee. Her intelligent eyes regarded him patiently, one demonstrative ear tipped forward, tail down but wagging mildly, reassuringly. Tentatively, oh so tentatively, Tony patted her head.

"Starbucks," Crackers said, reappearing with a tray of mugs.

Tony looked around, expecting to see another dog.

"No, I mean the coffee is Starbucks beans," Crackers said, guessing at Tony's mistake and grinning. "We ground the beans this morning and this is from a fresh pot."

Tony preferred a precise amount of organic half-and-half and Damara sugar in his coffee, but none was offered, so he endeavored to drink it black.

"Now then, I don't know why you'd come here after wrestling with the asphalt or trying to give yourself a sandpaper facial," Crackers said, pointing at Tony's face, "or why you'd be asking me questions, so let's start at the beginning. What happened?"

If Walt had a plan, he had not shared it with Tony, so Tony decided honesty really was the best policy, when sitting in a periwinkle house being affectionately accosted by a German Shepard named Lipton.

"I was attacked by a man who smelled like lavender," he said.

"What the hell?" Jems said, appearing in the hall through which they had recently entered. "Who done it?" For some reason, it didn't sound like irony, like he was saying whodunit?

The difference between the two men was far more striking, here in their home, than Tony had noticed in the diner. Crackers was wearing a pressed short-sleeved shirt in an attractive shade of sage green, and slacks, and he looked perfectly at ease carrying the tray with the coffee carafe and mugs. Jems was wearing dirty jeans and scuffed cowboy boots. Crackers was pale and slightly pudgy; Jems was lean and weathered. Was it that opposites attract, Tony wondered, or simply that here in this tiny rural town the soul-mate options for a gay man were extremely limited, and it felt better to have someone than no one? Strangely enough, that was the basis for many couplings in the rarefied world of wealthy Long Island families, as well; when the pool of available mates was small, you often settled rather than accepting solitude.

"Who done it?" Jems said again, when no one answered.

Walt sighed heavily, loudly, an exhalation full of irritation. "We don't know, but you're the only people in Motte and Bailey who raise lavender."

"Do we look like thugs to you?" Crackers said.

"Of course not," Walt growled (did he have any other way of speaking? Tony wondered). "That doesn't mean you're not."

"We been here all day," Jems said.

"As Jems said," Crackers nodded. "And why on earth would we want to rough up Mr. New York here?"

"We heard you was from New York," Jems added.

"And we've seen the ankle bracelet you wear," Crackers said. "You must be in trouble with the law, which means you probably had all sorts of unsavory characters after you long before you came to our little town."

"It wasn't that kind of crime," Tony said stiffly.

"It wasn't what kind of crime?" Crackers said.

"The kind that makes unsavory people want to chase after you."

"Who've you got working on the farm?" Walt cut in.

Crackers raised his eyebrows and then immediately looked down and started picking dog hair off his pant leg.

"This time of year we got about a dozen, mostly Mexicans what don't speak English," Jems answered.

"The person who attacked me spoke English, and he didn't have an accent," Tony said. "He put a bag over my head and tied a string around my neck." He tried not to cry, and succeeded.

"Does Tom Max ever do any work for you two?" Walt said.

"Tom? What could he possibly have to do with a brutal attack?" Crackers said.

Tony appreciated the "*brutal.*"

"He also told Tony to back off."

"My, but you are making friends, aren't you?" Crackers said.

"He comes of a Saturday now and again, to work on the farm to make extra cash to feed them boys," Jems said. "They eat like horses, he says."

"Was he here last weekend?" Walt pressed.

"Don't remember," Jems said. "Mighta been."

"What are you hiding?" Crackers said to Tony.

"What are *you* hiding?" Walt retorted.

"Oh get off it," Crackers said. "You know all our secrets." He looked meaningfully at Jems, still standing uncertainly in the doorway.

"We got illegals here," Jems said, as if to assert that was the only secret to which Crackers could possibly be alluding.

"You and everyone else who owns a farm," Walt said. "Is that all?"

Lipton noticed that Tony had stopped patting her head. She shoved her cold wet nose under his hand, and chuffed quietly.

"That's all," Crackers said firmly. "But Tom was here last weekend. God help us if he's mixed up in something dangerous. The whole world must be going to hell in a handbasket if that's true."

"The whole world's been there and back again many times, as far as I can tell," Walt said. "We're so far down that road we don't even notice how hot it is, or how crowded it is in the basket."

"Wait a minute," Tony said, fighting against the pale pink Percocet fog in his brain. "Today is Thursday. If Tom was here over the weekend, his hands wouldn't still smell like lavender on Thursday, would they?"

"Of course they wouldn't," Crackers said. "More likely they'd smell like automotive grease from his job at Wal-Mart. So you're barking up the wrong tree with him." He looked satisfied. "I just knew he couldn't be involved," he said.

Lipton placed one giant paw on Tony's leg, and to his surprise it was not an unpleasant sensation. He looked into her beautiful eyes, and thought perhaps Walt was right; perhaps it was time to get over his fear of dogs. He patted her again on the crown of her head, just between her ears, and she swished her tail across the floor exactly twice.

While they were all mulling over where to go from the not-Tom conclusion, a wizened, brown-skinned man shuffled in, smelling of something vaguely familiar that was definitely not lavender. He looked around the room, taking in Jems leaning against the doorjamb, Crackers and Walt seated on the mauve floral sofa, and Tony in the recliner.

"*Joder!*" he said, when he saw Tony and Walt. He looked over his shoulder as if he thought if he didn't make eye contact Walt and Tony might think the profanity was aimed at someone else, someone lurking in the hall behind him. And then, "Uh, *Jefe*," he said, still looking over his shoulder. "*Jefe*, you come quick."

"Juan," Crackers said pleasantly, firmly, "what can I do for you?"

"Come with me," Juan insisted. "I show you."

Tony looked at Juan with undisguised affection. "Well hello little man," he said. "You must be one of those illegals Jems mentioned."

Crackers and Jems flayed Tony with a glare, but he was oblivious, having suddenly become aware what a delightful word illegal was. So he said it again: illegal illegal illegal. "Don't worry," he said to Juan. "Your secret's safe safe safe with me."

"Looks like the meds have kicked in," Walt said.

"Gentlemen, it appears I am needed elsewhere," Crackers said, taking Tony's coffee cup from him with what seemed to Tony like unnecessary force. "I'll walk you to the gate so the dogs don't slobber you to death." As if his words were marionette strings Walt and Tony followed him, though Walt grumbled about being brushed off for some goddamned lavender crisis.

Juan was partially blocking the hall, shaking his head. As they squeezed past, the familiar scent-that-wasn't-lavender once again assailed Tony's nose.

"Pot!" Tony burbled happily. "I smell marijuana."

"All right, keep moving," Walt said quietly, trying to steer him toward the door, but Tony turned and grabbed Juan's hand and began shaking it happily. "I had pot once. Funny smell, isn't it, Juan? I'm so sorry I never learned Spanish, by the way. Did I already say that?" He giggled.

"'You know all our secrets'?" Walt said to Crackers, who was holding the door and staring at them with a smile fixed on his face as if by Super Glue.

"Well, well," Crackers said. "I don't know what you're talking about."

They made their way through the happy canine crowd, and after the gate clanged behind them, Walt leaned over and said something to Crackers that Tony didn't quite catch.

Back in the truck, Tony waved happily at the dogs, and at Crackers and Jems and Juan, standing in the doorway. And then he turned to Walt, who was audibly coaxing the truck to start. "What did you say to Crackers?" he asked (or at least, that's what he thought he asked. It was hard to be sure with all that cotton candy floating through his ears).

"I told him I couldn't believe all this time I've been getting my weed from someone in Jacksonville," Walt said.

# Chapter 14

Tony fell asleep in the truck on the way back to Walt's place, and slept through the rest of the day and into the night.

He dreamt that Walt had tenderly carried his limp body into the house, laid him down on the greasy couch, and tucked him in, murmuring, "You've had a rough day."

He woke up in the pre-dawn darkness to find himself still in Walt's truck, a screaming charley horse in his left calf competing with a screaming headache that seemed to emanate from the center of his brain cavity and radiate outward. And someone seemed to be repeatedly stabbing a white-hot knitting needle into his right eye socket and scraping tuberculin-infested claws across his right cheek.

"Morning sunshine," Walt grunted, when Tony stumbled through the door. "You've got yourself a shiner, I see."

Walt was sitting at a small, deeply scratched kitchen table, the kind with drop-down sides that is only about two feet square without its pop-up extensions. He was wearing a torn and stained pair of sweatpants that might once have been navy blue, and an equally torn and stained tie-dye tee shirt that said *Everybody's Dancin' in a Ring Around the Sun*. In front of him, on the table, was a pad of yellow lined paper, an assortment of pens, and an enormous cup, liberally chipped, half full of coffee. There was only one chair at the table.

"Coffee maker's on the counter," Walt said. "Grinder's there too. Coffee beans are in a bag somewhere. You'll have to wash a cup."

Tony felt weak, and angry, and desperate for coffee. Shame at his behavior the night before was also banging at the edges of his consciousness, but that was mostly drowned out by the other emotions. He squeezed past Walt's bulk, and tried to clear a space on the counter. The coffee maker was tucked behind several bowls crusted with food, four open spice jars, an enormous canning pot, and a strange tool, rubberized on one end, that looked like a minimalist sculpture of a wide-mouthed bass. He found the coffee beans, figured out how to work the grinder, rinsed the coffee pot and started another round, washed a mug, and slammed around in the cupboards and refrigerator until he located a bowl of sugar and a nearly-empty container of organic half-and-half. While he waited for the coffee to brew, he glared at the broad back and gray braid partially obscuring the words on the tee shirt: *Grateful Dead 1988.* Walt ignored him through the whole ordeal, staring intently at the pad of paper in front of him, occasionally writing a word, sometimes two words. Tony tried to read the words as he moved, cup in hand, toward the couch (the only other place to sit), but Walt covered the paper with his hands.

Tony sat and sipped his coffee, holding the cup reverently. The steam swirled around his face bringing visions or perhaps just hallucinations. The web and weave of his life, every humiliating mistake and soaring triumph, every nuanced assumption and infant hope and cradled dream seemed to converge on this moment, and it felt as though he held in his hands all that he would ever need. He wished Walt would look at him, would see the epiphany in his eyes. He felt as if he was vibrating visibly.

"I guess now we know what Crackers and Jems were hiding," he said.

"I guess we do," Walt said, without looking up.

"Why don't they just get a license? Isn't it legal to grow in Oregon?"

"I don't know why," Walt said. "Maybe it's too much trouble."

"I feel different," Tony said finally.

"It's the Percocet," Walt said.

"It's more than that," Tony insisted.

"Go back to the motel," Walt said. "I'm trying to write."

"Aren't you supposed to be at work by now?" Tony said.

"Nancy said to stay home until you woke up, make sure you hadn't died in your sleep." He didn't sound as though he had been very worried.

"What if the cuts on my face get infected?" Tony said, knowing it sounded like whining.

Walt sighed, dropped his arm heavily on the tiny table, and said, "Then go to the health clinic. It's at the other end of town."

"Why are you writing on paper?" Tony said, looking for a way to hurt Walt. "They make these things called computers."

"Don't have one, don't need one," Walt said, refusing to take the bait.

\* \* \*

Tony made his way back to the motel through the cool morning air, trying to nurse along the sense of epiphany but feeling it fade, swallowed by a rising tide of resentment at the unfairness of it all. He thought of calling Caroline, in the hope of some spousely comfort, but immediately remembered that she had thrown down the gauntlet: stay out of the town's secrets, appeal the judgment, and behave like Giles Gibson.

Or lose her.

Drinking coffee in a filthy cottage while an AWOL poet scratched away on a pad of paper was fine—What's wrong with fine? he had asked his mother's grave on that oh-so-long-ago morning, before he'd been exiled—but maybe, after all, it was not enough. He wanted Caroline, too. He wanted Nancy and Nareen and Leesa and Scooter, and if at all possible, he wanted his flat in Manhattan and Addy handing him freshly-pressed slacks and meetings with the venerable board of directors comprised of rich white men waiting for him to decide whether this year's push would be movie-themed Legos or clown dolls with the faces of famous actors and presidential candidates, and someone bringing him a double latte and telling him Sign here, Mr. Gibson.

Golf, though, he could give up. And cocktail parties. And steel cut oatmeal—he'd take one of Walt's omelets over steel cut oats any day.

He shuffled along the sidewalk, lost in his musings about what he'd keep and let go, if he were once again master of his own fate, but gradually the outside world crept in.

People. There were people around him. Cars driving down the street. A woman with impossibly curly hair unlocking the door to a salon. A grizzled lumberjack of a man coming out of the post office, a man for whom someone should have invented the verb *to hulk*. A man with a long narrow face like an iguana talking on a cell phone outside an attractive yellow Victorian house with a sign that said Vic Abrams Attorney at Law. Tony wondered whether the iguana-man was Vic, or one of Vic's clients, or opposing counsel, or just someone talking on the phone outside a law office who bore an unfortunate resemblance to a lizard.

Somehow, he had rarely noticed that the town was populated by people, people doing the things that people do.

Tony wished he had somewhere to go, somewhere he was needed. If not the boardroom of ABC Toys at least the kitchen at Sunnyside Up. If I can't have my old life I'd at least rather be washing dishes at the café, he thought. As long as I could wear rubber gloves to protect my hands.

Luis was sitting on the bench in front of the motel when he arrived.

"What the hell happened to you?" he said conversationally.

"I was attacked," Tony said.

Luis raised his eyebrows. "Let's take a walk," he said.

"I don't want to," Tony said, reinforcing the impression of a sullen toddler who very much needs a nap.

"Yes you do," Luis said. "There are two men waiting for you in your room, and I don't think they're part of the Motte and Bailey Welcome Wagon."

Now Tony felt like weeping. There didn't seem to be any part of his body that wasn't in pain, and he was so tired he felt like his feet and hands were filled with lead pellets and the earth was a magnet, drawing him down; give in, lie down, sleep, the concrete beneath him whispered.

"Okay, but I think I need to go to the health clinic. Do you know where it is?" he said.

"Sure," Luis said. "Follow me."

They walked the remaining few blocks together in silence, until they came to a surprisingly small sign announcing MB Urgent Care and Health Clinic, Emergency Entrance In Back.

The clinic was housed in a squat bunker of a building. "It looks like it doubles as a bomb shelter in case the Russians ever decide to attack the strategically critical town of Motte and Bailey," Luis said.

"That's Motte-Fucking-Bailey to you," Tony said.

Luis raised an eyebrow. Again. "Feeling a little out of sorts?" he said.

"I am," Tony said, suddenly deciding to act his age. "I apologize."

They entered through the doors in the back. Inside, scuffed gray floors and scuffed gray windowless walls lent a Kafka-esque air, but the old women at the reception desk were friendly and spoke in hushed, cheerful voices, and the triage nurse, whose name tag said simply "Steve," clucked in sympathy when he looked at Tony's mangled face.

Tony and Luis settled into two of the lime green plastic chairs to wait. A large plaque near the reception area pronounced it Lanyard Waiting Room, and in smaller letters, "Thank you for the generous donation to our clinic." Tony wondered who was being quoted, and where the money had gone. Surely they hadn't used the "generous donation" to purchase the gray linoleum squares on the floor and the lime green chairs, he thought.

And then he wondered: how many good deeds does one have to perform to make up for past evil? How many donations cancel out fathering an unwanted child with an unwilling underage girl?

And how many dishes would he have to wash to erase the stain of a little girl's death from his hands?

"Do you want to tell me about it?"

Tony was startled, thinking Luis had read his mind and was offering to assist with his moral calculus. When he realized Luis was referring to the attack, he was tempted to refuse. He didn't want to think of Luis as an ally, didn't want to confide in Luis or share information that might ultimately put Tony on the outside of the Sunnyside Up crew. In the end, he decided to treat the question the same way he addressed questions from a middle-manager at ABC Toys: the manager asks questions, the company president gives answers, but only on a need-to-know basis. Coolly, wrapping power around himself as easily as Superman dons his flying suit (but without the necessity of the now-extinct telephone booth), he described the attack, and told Luis that the person who attacked him seemed to be an older man who smelled of lavender.

"But it wasn't Crackers or Jems," he said.

"I'd already checked them out," Luis said. "Even before you got yourself mugged."

"Got *myself* . . .?" Any other words Tony might have said flew away on the wind of his anger.

"Their given names are Matthew Watterston and Jeremiah Neehi,"

Luis said, ignoring Tony's sputtering half-articulations. Smugness sat on Luis's face like a cat on a sunny window seat, as if it belonged there. As if Luis and only Luis could have ascertained that information, through his superior intellect, or sleuthing skills. "We know they operate a substantial lavender farm. I don't know why you're so sure it wasn't either of them."

"Walt saw them at the café at the same time I was being attacked," he lied wildly. "And before you go there, I don't think it was one of the farm hands, either. The man who attacked me spoke English. No accent. If I'm not mistaken, the majority of the farm workers in Oregon are immigrants, so I imagine I'd have been able to tell if it was one of their guys." And then he tried to regain the upper hand he'd had so fleetingly. "Tell me about the men who broke into my room," he said.

"I didn't get a good look," Luis said. "I'd just come to check in with Scooter. I was standing in the hall, and Scooter was standing in the doorway, telling me it had been quiet and he was going out of his mind with boredom, when we heard the elevator ping. I slipped inside the room and closed the door, and looked through the peephole. Two large men came down the hall, and one was packing."

"You mean he had a gun?" Tony asked, feeling like he'd fallen into a movie. "How can you tell?"

"He wasn't hiding it," Luis said. "It was holstered at the small of his back, and he wasn't wearing a jacket or sweater or anything. Oregon's an Open Carry state," he said, and then, seeing Tony's confusion, he explained, "where you can carry a gun openly anywhere except around a school."

A nurse in a bright yellow sweater with bright yellow hair and bright red lipstick burst through the swinging door next to the reception area and called, "Mr. Jacobson? You can come on back, now."

A young man, limping and wheezing, followed Ms. Yellow-Sweater back through the swinging doors.

"I could only see the face of the man closest to the peephole," Luis said. "He was a great big bull of a man. And not Ferdinand the bull who just likes to sit quietly and smell the flowers."

"Could you identify him if you saw him again?" Tony asked.

Luis scowled. "Thinking of taking up PI work once your sentence is over?"

"Maybe," Tony said. "But here's the however-many-dollar-question:

why the hell were you waiting around outside the hotel when I got there? Why didn't you arrest the thugs?"

"'Thugs'?" Luis said, rolling his eyes. "You really are something, Tony. The strategic decision was made to wait and see what they did in your room, then arrest them when they came out. The sheriff's people are still there, though I, of course, am here babysitting you while you get your face cleaned up."

The nurse came out again. "Martha Spigello?" she said. An elderly woman struggled to her feet, leaning heavily on her walker. Her flowered dress and pale pink cardigan seemed to be as much a part of her body as the wrinkled knees, the knee-high compression stockings, and the beige old-woman shoes. After she had steadied herself, she looked back at the seat and saw her handbag, a black patent-leather purse with a faux-gold snap. Slowly, slowly, slowly she turned and reached for it.

"Here you go," Luis said, handing the bag to her. He seemed to have moved to her side as if beamed there by an invisible Scotty or disapparated from a wizard's wand: one second he was sitting next to Tony, the next he was handing the bag to old Mrs. Spigello.

"That was decent of you," Tony said as Luis returned, wishing he'd thought of it first. They both looked back toward the chair the old woman had just vacated and saw, in the next chair over, a girl of maybe thirteen or fourteen, with lank dark hair and skin the color of amber syrup. She was wearing a sequined, low-cut dress that would not have looked out of place in a cocktail lounge, and she was barefoot, and she was crying. Her legs were impossibly scratched, and her left arm was bent in a place where no arm should bend. Tony wondered how it was that they had not noticed her until now.

Once again, Luis was here one second, there the next. "What's your name?" Luis said softly, so softly Tony could scarcely hear the words as he made his way over to where the girl—and now Luis—was sitting. She shook her head. "*Cómo te llamas, mi hija?*" Luis tried. She shook her head again, and pointed at her mangled arm, and whimpered.

"I don't think she speaks English or Spanish," Luis said to Tony, still speaking softly. "As you noted, there are a lot of immigrants in this area. Farm country." He looked at the girl, and patted the uninjured arm, then turned again to Tony. "I'm guessing maybe she's from one of the indigenous populations in Mexico or Central America.

I doubt the clinic will have a translator who can help her."

"But she needs to be seen right away," Tony said, his mind refusing to grasp the concept that a child this badly injured was waiting while the Mr. Jacobsons and Mrs. Spigellos were called back for treatment. He looked again at the girl. Tears made lines down her face, weeping rivers from her eyes to her chin.

Luis patted the girl's hand and started to get up, but Tony stopped him. "I'll handle this," he said. "You stay with her."

He approached the desk and explained the situation to the receptionists. "She'll just have to wait her turn," they said, after peering around Tony at the girl. Tony looked at Steve, the triage nurse who had been so sympathetic toward Tony and who was watching the scene unfold from his "privacy" triage cubicle, but Steve just shrugged and went back to the crossword puzzle he had been doing.

"Her turn is now," Tony said pleasantly, forcefully. "I'll pay for her care, if she doesn't have insurance." One of the receptionists opened her mouth to object, but Tony cut her off, adding, "And I'd like to go in with her."

"Are you her legal guardian, young man?" the other receptionist asked.

"Right now it looks like I'm the only kind of guardian she has," he said.

It took a few more minutes of genteel bullying, with Tony pointing out that health care providers are required by law to have interpreters available (he had read it in the *New York Times* in that long ago time and faraway place that was his life in Manhattan), and hinting that if they did not have an interpreter someone would need to report that fact to the relevant authorities, and Steve insisting they had call-in interpreters but they didn't even know what language the girl spoke, and Tony saying that's because you haven't lifted a finger to find out, but eventually Tony and the girl were led back through the swinging door.

The girl sat on the patient bed, still crying but holding her mouth clamped shut, and Tony stood nearby, wishing he knew something more useful than corporate intimidation. A doctor came in, soft eyes replacing the look of frazzled impatience when he saw the girl.

"I'm Dr. Mishigawa," he told the girl, but she didn't look up, just rocked slightly back and forth, a prisoner to pain and fear. At Dr. Mishigawa's instruction, Tony held one small trembling hand

and looked into the small terrified face and made what he hoped were soothing sounds while a sedative was administered.

After a brief evaluation, Dr. Mishigawa sent the girl away in a wheelchair, for x-rays. "I can tell you just from my preliminary examination," he said to Tony, "we'll probably have to operate before we can put it in a cast." He paused, visibly sizing Tony up. "I understand you didn't bring her here, and you're not her parent or legal guardian," he said. "Thank you for advocating for her."

"My…" Tony hesitated. How should he refer to Luis? *The annoying saggy-pantsed detective* didn't seem quite the thing. "My friend," he said at last, "who is here with me, he thinks maybe she's from one of the Indigenous populations. Mexico or somewhere else in Central America. She doesn't seem to understand English or Spanish."

"We do sometimes get immigrants from those populations," Dr. Mishigawa said, and then he said, "You understand that I'm going to have to report this."

"What, to the immigration authorities?" Tony said, incredulous. "You want to deport her?"

"No," Dr. Mishigawa said shortly. "I have to report the injury as potential abuse. It is possible to break an arm that badly without violence, but not likely. When you add the fact that she appears malnourished, and there's no adult here with her…" he trailed off. "And then there's the dress."

Tony didn't want to think about the dress. Some parents dress their children in bizarre adult fashion. Some teenagers dress inappropriately just to drive their parents crazy. The children in some poor families have to wear whatever fits out of the ridiculous hodgepodge in the donation bin. Some people just like sparkly things. Couldn't any of those explanations be the truth?

"Do whatever you have to do to protect her. I can pay for anything she needs," he said, hoping it was true, hoping Caroline would simply agree when he told her about the arm, and the tears. "I'm staying at the Sleepy Time Motel, Room 202."

The good doctor eyed Tony with obvious skepticism. Tony could picture the situation from the doctor's perspective: the man claiming to be able to pay was wearing two-day-old clothes that had been thrown against the sidewalk, slobbered on by Lipton the German Shepherd, and crammed against the door of Walt's ancient and none-too-sanitary truck, his face was stubbled and scratched, his one good eye was bloodshot from the Percocet and the other eye was swollen and bruised. And he had just admitted he lived in the Sleepy Time Motel.

"I've had a rough couple of days," Tony said, "but trust me, I'm good for it."

"I wasn't worried about that," Dr. Mishigawa said. "With or without payment, I'd make sure she's cared for. I'm just trying to figure you out. You don't look like the run-of-the-mill Motte and Bailey resident. You act like someone who is used to being obeyed, and I'm picturing a McMansion somewhere. You're filthy, injured"—he gestured at Tony's face—"and staying at a cheap motel."

"It's a long story," Tony said.

"Well, I don't need to hear it, but you will need to tell our triage nurse anything you know about the girl."

"Your triage nurse didn't give a damn about the girl," Tony said. "And your receptionists were no better. They all clucked over me like mother hens, but a girl who is brown-skinned and doesn't speak English was left sitting there to rot, and would still be sitting there if Luis and I hadn't gotten involved."

Dr. Mishigawa nodded. Clearly, this was not news to him. "I'll make sure that's dealt with," he said. "Now then, I assume you checked in for your own injuries, so as long as you're already back here I won't make you return to the waiting room. I'll take a look now, but if an emergency comes in you may have to wait."

"That's fine," Tony said. The aches and pains that had faded in the presence of white-hot self-righteous rage returned, growling with resentment at his momentary neglect. He climbed gingerly onto the examination table, and allowed himself to be gently prodded.

"Well," the doctor said, "we'll get you cleaned up and slather you with ointment. And I think at least one of those scratches could use a couple of stitches. Any chance you'd like to tell me how this happened?"

"I was attacked from behind," Tony said. "I had my hands in my pockets and couldn't get them out in time to cushion the fall, so my face got intimately acquainted with the pavement."

"Have you reported the attack to the police?"

"My friend Luis is a detective," Tony said evasively.

The doctor sighed, and shook his head. "We'll have a PA in here in a few minutes to take care of you," he said, and he left the room.

Seconds later, Luis poked his head in. "What the hell are you doing?" he said, and then, before Tony could come up with a suitably aggrieved reply, "We've got a problem," he said. He motioned to Tony to follow him down the hall. The swinging door separating the treatment areas from the waiting room had a window in the top half. Luis mimed looking carefully through the window, and Tony peered over the ledge. Every spy thriller and detective show he'd ever watched had included a scene where someone was looking through a window without being seen, and Tony had often wondered how that was supposed to work. In a normal, not-Picasso-esque person, the eyes are about a quarter of the way down the face, so by default the top quarter of one's head must be visible over the edge of a window in order to look through. He did his best to cock his head sideways so that one eye had a view of the waiting room with a minimum of forehead showing.

A massive man was standing in the middle of the waiting room, looking as if he wasn't quite sure how he got there or what he should do now.

"That's one of the guys who broke into your room earlier," Luis whispered. "I have no idea how he slipped past the sheriff's men outside the motel, or how he knew to look for you here."

Tony took in the unnaturally large and muscular torso, the disproportionately small legs and feet, the square head framed by shaggy black hair, and the mean little eyes.

"*Toro, Toro*," he whispered.

# Chapter 15

"We went out the back door after Luis made sure the coast was clear," Tony told Caroline.

It was untenable to continue keeping secrets from his wife, he'd decided. He had been mugged, his room had been broken into, and he was being stalked by two men who would be, presumably, unintimidated by Tony's best boardroom tactics. If there was a chance he was going to be sent home in a body bag, Caroline deserved to know why. He told her everything—finding Sam's body, helping Walt bury Sam, trying to help Nancy and Walt keep that information from Luis while ostensibly helping Luis with his investigation, the attack outside the community center, the emergency room visit.

"Luis called for backup, but the man gave them the slip again," he said, when the whole story was out. "There are police watching the motel now, but they're Roj's men, so I'm not sure how comforting that is."

"Who is 'Roj' again?" Caroline asked, sounding flat and cold and more distant than two thousand seven hundred and ten miles away. (He had looked it up before he left Manhattan).

"Former sheriff, not a nice guy," he said. He ran his fingers through his hair, as if a smooth coiffure could tame the rough contours of everything he had been and done and seen up to this moment in his life.

"And one other thing, while I have you on the phone." He recognized that he was speaking to Caroline as if she was his business associate, or possibly even his executive assistant. If she was going to hang up on him, he needed to make sure he had taken care of logistics first. "We'll be getting a hospital bill. Please make sure it is paid." He paused, waiting for her to speak her whys and wherefores, but

164

she said nothing. "There was a girl in the emergency room," he said. "Her arm was broken. She didn't speak English. The doctor believes she may have been abused."

He couldn't bring himself to say the words *sex trafficking* aloud. His mind flitted briefly on the thought: maybe we make our own reality by the words we choose, and the words we omit; maybe if he refused to name it he could bar its entry.

"There was no adult with her," he continued. "So I made sure she got treatment, and I told the hospital I'd pay for the services."

Empty, having disgorged everything, he waited, the chasm between them expanding like the universe, stars edging back from the black hole, nothingness crowding out the constellations.

"When you called, I was sitting here looking at wedding photos," Caroline said, speaking into the void. "Do you remember the cake?"

Fists curled as if in self-defense, feet braced against the floor, Tony had been prepared for accusations and anger. Now, exculpatory arguments and rationalizations free-floated, with nowhere to land.

Of course he remembered the cake.

The union of two prominent Long Island families was an elaborate affair, with gaudy pomp and circumstance. Mauve tulle, tuxedos with matching mauve ties and cummerbunds, a dress with puffed sleeves that could best be described as ludicrous. Only Princess Diana would understand the humiliation those photos engendered, and she was dead.

And then there was the cake. Thousands of dollars were invested in a multi-tiered white and silver-baubled creation, ordered by Caroline's mother. ("Couldn't we just have a quiet wedding in the park?" Caroline had asked. "With pie? I like pie so much better than cake." Caroline's mother had smiled, and patted Caroline's knee, and said apologetically, "You were born into the wrong family for a quiet wedding in the park, my dear.") But when they cut into the cake, they realized there had been some mistake; the gilded frosting hid a red velvet cake. The cut cake stared at the gathered crowd like a gash, an open wound. The pieces as they were distributed on elegant bone china by liveried waiters looked like chunks of flesh still partly encased in ivory skin. He'd glanced at his new bride, to see if she was as mortified as he, to see if she knew the proper response when discovering that one's wedding cake looks like a post-mortem accident. And found she was laughing. Doubled over, holding her sides, tears just beginning to leak from her beautifully-mascara'd eyes, her beautiful tiara askew on her beautiful honey-colored hair, laughing so hard it was obvious she could scarcely breathe. And that's when he knew he had chosen (or been chosen by) the right helpmeet.

"I remember," he said. "I remember the cake."

"I don't want to lose you," Caroline said. "I'm afraid for you."

"I'm afraid for me too," he said, knowing it was not the kind of thing a husband should say to his wife who is two thousand seven hundred and ten miles away.

After the call, in pain, unwashed, and uncertain, Tony stripped off his filthy clothes, and discovered he still had Walt's bottle of Percocet in his pocket. It felt like a miracle. He took one and then showered while it took hold, trying without success to wash his hair without letting the water touch his battered face.

And then he slept like the dead.

He woke up, went to the bathroom, drank a half dozen glasses of water, took another Percocet, and fell back into bed. If he dreamt, he did not remember his dreams. If he felt fear, or anxiety, or self-loathing, he did not remember. He slept, and slept, and slept.

Two days later, Nancy called him, waking him to the realization that he was hungrier than he could ever remember being, and nauseous. "Report to work on Tuesday at eleven o'clock," she told him. Tony tried to work out what day it was, and landed on Sunday. "Scooter'll take the breakfast rush, and you can do lunch," she said. "Then we'll get you back on the regular schedule." She paused, and Tony pictured her face screwed up in thought. "And for god's sake do something about your face," she added. "Walt says you're a mess."

She had sent Leesa on vacation for a couple of weeks, she told him. Tony wasn't sure an employer could do that, but then Nancy didn't seem to be up on or concerned about the dos and don'ts of employment law. "I sent her away because she kept crying and giving the customers hell if they asked for anything. I didn't want her getting snot in the food. Having you bleed all over would be even worse, so make yourself pretty before you get here."

"Yes ma'am," Tony said, heart-glad to hear her ordering him about, to know that soon he would be allowed to wash dishes and fill salt- and pepper-shakers and wipe tables with a less-than-sanitary rag.

He waved at the officer sitting on guard in a car in front of the mo-

tel, walked to Tio Mio's and ate not one but two plates of beautiful
Mexican food swimming in red sauce and melted cheese, waved again
at the officer on his way back, and barely made it into his room before
throwing up most of what he had eaten. Back outside in the glim-
mering cool of a fall night, down to the corner store for soda crackers
and ginger ale, noticing with childlike glee the inflatable spider and
the glow-in-the-dark skeleton inside the doorway, harbingers of Halloween, and back to the room with its faint odor of stale carpet and
not-so-faint odor of sheets soaked in man-in-an-opioid-sleep-sweat.
Except when he walked in, the latter odor was gone and his bed had
been made. He was momentarily stumped; someone from the motel
had clearly come in and changed his sheets, replaced the towels in
the bathroom, and tidied the room. Had someone been changing his
sheets the whole time he'd been in Motte and Bailey, and he'd never
noticed?

And then he realized that of course someone had been changing
the sheets. And someone had been vacuuming the carpet, and scrubbing the shower, the sink, the counter. Even the toilet. He had been
laboring under the misapprehension that he was cleanliness personi-
fied, that he never left hair in the shower drain, that his feces never
stuck to the inside of the toilet bowl.

In the few months since he'd arrived he'd grown just enough integrity to be ashamed.

* * *

On Tuesday morning, as if it was his first day at a brand new job,
Tony headed to work a few hours early. His regular shift started at
six in the morning, before the little town was awake, and ended mid-
afternoon, so his morning "commute" normally took place when most
people were still inside their homes, and when he walked back to the
motel at the end of his shift the town's residents were at work or at
school or (during the summer) hiding inside from the heat. Since
he had been ordered to start with the lunch shift today, his decision
to leave early put him on the streets at the same time as everyone
else, and he marveled at the busyness around him. Once again, he
wondered at his previous assumption that the town was empty, abandoned, and dead. After waving at the officer who was trying to guard
him, he sat on a bench near the diner, taking in the mothers dropping
their children off at the elementary school, the pregnant woman with

purple hair pacing up and down the block as if she could convince the baby by jiggling that it was time to be born, the man carrying an enormous gray cat with Yoda eyes.

"Looking at me, you are," the cat said with a sneer, curled malevolently in its owner's arms.

Perhaps there was still a smidge of Percocet in Tony's veins.

He shuddered. His brief foray into communing with animals—the tentative pat on Lipton's head while interrogating Crackers and Jems—had not altered his basic sense that animals were foreign, and unpredictable. And possibly sinister.

He swiveled on the bench so he could see further down the road. He knew from his past perambulations that there was a Dutch Brothers on the edge of town, but no Starbucks. He'd heard that Walla Walla had three Starbucks, but though Walla Walla was about a half an hour away, just over the state border, it might as well have been another country. Motte and Baileyites did not go to Walla Walla unless absolutely necessary, Tony had been informed sternly.

He stood up, noticing that some of the peeling paint on the bench had left flakes of faded orange on his khakis. He patted his backside, assuming there were more paint flakes there, and thought wistfully how nice it would be to have someone to ask *Do I have paint flakes on my butt?*

He gave up town-watching and went inside the diner to wait. Nareen nodded at him, carrying her stomach before her as a butler carries a tea tray set with delicate cups, cradled carefully but expertly. Nodding was better than snarling or yelling at him. Scooter also gave him a pale semi-smile before turning to one of the customers sitting at the counter. Luis was in "his" booth, with his decaf coffee and dry toast. Crackers and Jems were at a table near the back. "Your face is looking a little better, my friend," Crackers called out, giving a half-regal wave.

And that, it seemed, was that.

"As far as I can tell, by some miracle no one in town heard about the commotion," Nancy told him quietly, after he'd made his way into the kitchen. "My guess is you got lucky, since the restaurant was closed when Leesa went all full metal jacket on you, and then maybe she decided she didn't want to share the information with anyone."

Shortly after Scooter left, as Tony was still tying the strings of his apron around his waist, Roj came in.

"I can't believe he's here," Tony said to Nancy. It was aggravating that Roj felt he could ignore Tony's instruction to stay away. *Giles* was used to obsequious compliance; Tony got no such respect. Just one more sign of his descent into insignificance, a descent that never seemed to hit rock bottom.

"Figures," Nancy sniffed angrily. "Nothing gets through that thick skin." She glared at the back of Roj's head, and Tony half expected to see a mark on the bald spot, imprinted by Nancy's eyes. The sign of the devil, perhaps, or a scarlet A for Asshole.

Nareen left Roj to cool his heels for a good long time before moving to his table to take his order. "The usual?" she said, speaking coldly (which was no small feat, since a pregnant woman sounds warm and nurturing almost by default). She stared pointedly somewhere northwest of Roj's shoulder.

And then startled when Roj said, "What's 'the usual'?"

Nareen's head jerked back, a visible *Oh shit* and *What the hell?* The man sitting in Roj's booth wasn't Roj. He had slightly more hair, and had made a faint-hearted attempt at a comb-over with a few straggling strands. He was a little thinner (but not by much), and he was wearing a Hawaiian shirt with palm trees in faded colors that looked as though they might once have been bright oranges and greens and yellows.

"You're not Roj," Nareen said.

"I'm not," the man said. "I'm his cousin, Joey, from Spokane." He held out his hand, and it was a sign of how nonplussed she was that Nareen took it, and didn't pull away even when he held it too tightly and for too long.

"I can't believe I didn't realize it was Joey," Nancy said quietly to Tony, and then she said, loudly enough that the whole restaurant heard it, even over the hum of conversation and the clatter of cooking, "We got ourselves an Okie from Spokie."

A look of annoyance crossed Joey's face, but he smoothed it over quickly. "Roj figured he might not be welcome here for a while," he said. "But Sam's still missing, and he thought if anyone found out anything, you'd hear it first at Sunnyside Up." Nancy looked smug at that, and Tony had to wonder how small a life must be if your richest source of pride was that gossip came first to your diner. "He asked me to park myself here for a bit," Joey continued, "and said to let him know if anybody got a lead on Sam."

The entire restaurant had grown quiet to catch the conversation, and Nancy's "Huh" could be heard clearly.

Luis stood up, ungainly and awkward with anger. "*I'm* the detective here," he said to the back of Joey's head.

Joey turned and gave Luis a signature Roj smile: benign, patronizing, a dash of disarming charm like a coat of lacquer to bind the whole mess together. "Hello detective," he said. "What have you discovered so far?"

Obviously reluctant to give Joey the satisfaction of a "nothing," Luis shook his head and sat down again.

Loath though he was to champion the weaselly detective, Tony felt obliged to step in. He joined Nareen beside Joey's booth. "Why don't we leave law enforcement to the authorized law enforcement folks?" he said. "I don't believe an unofficial investigation is useful, especially not from the cousin of the person who, in the opinion of many, is the prime suspect in anything that goes awry around here."

"I'm just here to have breakfast," Joey said, looking up at Tony with hooded eyes, and then he returned his attention to Nareen. "Honey," he said, "I'll just have the usual. Whatever's good enough for Roj is good enough for me."

"Call me honey again and you'll get pig shit on rye," Nareen said.

The current of fear that had arced through the restaurant as the conversation escalated turned to laughter.

Joey smiled, but there was nothing of happiness or humor in his smile.

Rather than going behind the counter and talking to Walt through the order window, Nareen walked through the swinging door into the kitchen. Tony followed, hovering protectively, so closely that he came through in the same swing of the door.

"Tony," she said, turning and speaking quietly.

Walt, sensing something important, came out of the walk-in refrigerator with a carton of eggs tenderly cradled in each arm, leaving the door open behind him so that the light spilled around him like a halo around an unwilling, disheveled angel.

"Smell my hand," Nareen said.

Tony took her hand and lifted it to his nose and sniffed deeply.

"Lavender," he said.

* * *

"I can't arrest a man for smelling like lavender," Luis said, after Tony had engaged in a series of exaggerated winks and gestures designed to surreptitiously suggest Luis should meet him behind the restaurant.

"There seem to be a whole lot of reasons you *can't* arrest someone," Tony said.

"What?" Luis said.

"Well, you've done a hell of a job not-arresting the hulking maniac who broke into my room and then followed us to the clinic . . . . And you told us you can't arrest Roj for being an asshole . . . . And you told us it wouldn't do any good to arrest him for having his way with underage girls."

Luis winced. "How is Nareen feeling?" he said.

"I wish you wouldn't do that," Tony said.

"Do what?" Luis said.

"Show little particles of humanity. It really gets in the way of hating you."

Luis leaned against the concrete wall of the diner, crossed his arms, uncrossed them, waved a hand in front of his face to dispel the fetid waves emanating from the dumpster behind him, re-crossed his arms again, and finally closed his eyes, as if the day was too bright and the smell too strong, an assault that could only be endured indirectly through one's pores and one's eyelids. "I'm not going to apologize for trying to be a decent person," he said.

"She's doing fine," Tony said. "The baby's healthy. She's going to have a girl."

Luis kicked at a piece of broken concrete with his toe, making a mark on the scuffed black orthopedic shoes he often wore. Tony looked at the shoes, wondering briefly what was wrong with Luis's feet that necessitated the shoes.

The sun sparkled on tiny bits of broken glass around the base of the dumpster, and a puff of wind caught a patch of dandelions that had forced their way through a crack in the concrete, making their brilliant yellow heads dance gaily. Somehow, they had missed the earth's memo that it was time to go to seed and die, apparently determined to be youthful spring, seasons be damned. Tony looked at the concrete and the flowers, wishing he knew what came next.

"Wait, I just thought of something," Luis said.

"Was it painful?" Tony said.

"You're a jerk," Luis said.

"Only to you," Tony said.

"Child support," Luis said, apparently deciding it wasn't worth his time to prolong the snipe-fest. "How many kids did Roj say he has? Twenty?"

"He told you he had fourteen. That he knows of."

"Fourteen kids. What are the odds he paid child support on all of them?"

"Brilliant," Tony said, scratching his chin thoughtfully. "But that gets you Roj. What about Joey?"

"Investigating Roj for child support gives me an excuse to question his cousin," Luis said. "They're obviously close, close enough that Roj told Joey to go be his proxy at the diner to listen to local gossip." He stuck his lips out, a visible indicator of thinking, for him. "And maybe there's a financial connection. I'd have to do a little digging first, figure out if Roj and his cousin are engaged in any kind of official business together. Something that would give Roj a place to quietly park his money so the mothers of his kids couldn't find it."

"Then what are you waiting for?" Tony said.

"Another insult from you," Luis said.

Tony grinned, only semi-sheepishly. "I'm all out," he said.

*    *    *

Of course, the problem with an official interview conducted by a licensed detective was that no one from the café could listen in. The rest of the crew watched in frustration as Luis informed Joey that he'd like to talk to him privately, saw Joey try to get out of having to talk to Luis, and heard Luis state flatly that he'd be happy to take Joey to the station in the squad car waiting outside the restaurant. (The officer in the squad car was actually there to protect Tony, though Luis didn't tell Joey that.) Or, Luis said, he could get a warrant, if that's how Joey wanted to play it. Joey didn't want to play it that way, apparently, so he finished his meal, paid with cash, left a pile of nickels and dimes as a tip ("Cheap bastard," Walt said), and followed Luis out the door.

The rest of Tony's shift was uneventful, and although uneventful should have been welcome, under the circumstances, he chafed at the not-knowing, and paced and sighed like a child restlessly awaiting the moment his parents picked him up from daycare.

The others clearly felt the same. "God, I hope he finds something to hang on that dickwad," Nancy declared angrily, flinging herself through the swinging door to the kitchen.

"For a second there I thought you said God I hope he hangs that dickwad," Tony said, looking up from the greasy dish water.

"Maybe I did," Nancy said.

Later, while cleaning up after closing, Tony told Nareen that Luis had asked how she was feeling. She was sitting on one of the swiveling stools at the counter, looking pensive. A few weeks ago—pre-Leesa-blowout—Nancy had told Nareen she could skip cleaning duties, now that she was getting closer to her due-date, and Leesa had commented that giving pregnant women a break was actually a kind of sexism, as if they were too delicate to do anything while their bodies made a baby.

"I'll go for sexism, just this once," Nareen had said, grimacing as she leaned over to retie her shoe. "Good lord how did my feet get so far away? I can hardly reach them!"

"You should have someone rub your feet to keep the circulation going," Leesa had said, oblivious to the fact that it's obnoxious for a non-pregnant person to say to a pregnant person *Here's what you should do, you know*. Especially if the lecture involves foot-rubbing and the pregnant person has no one to rub her feet. "Here," Leesa'd said, apparently feeling the dual glares Nancy and Walt directed at the back of her head. "Let me." And then tenderly, and more gently than anyone would have suspected she could, Leesa knelt on the hard floor, removed Nareen's shoes, and rubbed her feet.

Now, as he wiped down tables and dumped old coffee down the drain, moving with Nancy in a complicated dance around the empty restaurant, Tony remembered the scene, Leesa's dimpled and freckled fingers moving in circles around Nareen's stockinged feet, the look of pain and then bliss that covered Nareen's face like an opaque mask, and he felt like weeping at what he'd lost. Once again he was reminded that he'd ruined everything. There was that moment, when the Vice President of Product Safety said sign here, Giles, there is some risk but it's an acceptable risk, when he could have said No! Dammit, there's no such thing as an acceptable risk. Over and over that moment and his failure to do the right thing had obliterated all the warm and the kindly and the light-hearted from his life. Leesa's friendship was just another casualty at the end of the line.

# Chapter 16

Caroline didn't answer the phone that night, or the next. Tony realized he had not called her during the days he'd lain in a drug-induced stupor, and wondered if she had tried to call him without leaving a message, or if she was punishing him for the lack of contact.

Or if she just didn't care any more.

Could a person give up a marriage-worth of memories—red velvet cake and surreptitious love-making in the game room and performance art in SoHo—all at once? Without prior notice, no *Your account is now thirty days past due and at risk of closure?*

Tony went to work the next day, and the day after that, and the day after that. He alternated between fretting over not hearing from his wife and fretting about not hearing from the detective whose competence he seriously doubted. He spilled coffee on someone's lap, failed to bring out silverware and napkins for several customers, and neglected to wipe down tables properly, until Nareen made a crack about the LaBrea tar pits having nothing on the tables at Sunnyside Up. Tony smiled weakly, and wiped one of the tables down again, leaving it only marginally better than before the exchange.

For three days, they saw neither hide nor hair of Roj, his cousin Joey, or Luis. On Friday afternoon, Tony took his clothes to the laundromat. (He mostly had it down, now—no more tie dye.)

The officer on duty drove his unmarked car slowly behind Tony, and parked outside the squat building housing ten washing machines (one of which was always broken) and eight dryers. (Tony didn't understand the inequity between washers and dryers—another of life's little mysteries.) The police presence made Tony feel ever so slightly ridiculous, but also protected, and grateful. He thought about asking if the officer would give Tony, and his laundry, a ride to the laundromat, but then Tony pictured himself sitting in the back of the police car, as if he was in the process of being arrested, and decided hauling his own laundry was the better option.

He sat in one of the hard, plastic, violently purple chairs lining the wall of the laundromat. There was a crack in the chair that tugged at his pant leg every time he shifted position. He alternated between watching someone else's clothes tumble in the dryer in front of him, the regular flash of a green-striped t-shirt interspersed with the yellowed white of men's briefs and the faded blue of several pairs of jeans, and attempting to read a Louise Penny novel. Normally, he enjoyed the philosophical musings of Inspector Gamache, and could lose himself in the trials and tribulations of a Canadian murder mystery. Today, his mind was too full to concentrate on the book in his hands. His brain felt like a Google search, one image or thought or memory leading to another, and another, and another, out of chronological order and jumbled together, until his neural synapses were stretched to the breaking point and beyond: the girl in the Urgent Care waiting room, teardrops on an ill-fitting sequined dress, dark eyes that no longer dared to express fear, and the empty faces of the hospital staff, as if the girl wasn't really there; the dusty warm smell of the pavement as he lay face down on the sidewalk, hearing the gruff voice warning him to *Back off* but not yet feeling the pain in his face because a body can only take in so many sensations at one time; Leesa's shrill voice piercing him like a dagger, or like a shard from a pint glass knocked to the floor, a glass one had hoped was sturdy and would hold, *What the hell is wrong with you, you mother-fucking child-killing-bastard* reverberating in his head and in his heart; Walt's caustic disdain as Tony tried, ineffectually, to assist with digging Sam's grave, the still predawn silence punctuated by the dull thud of clods of red clay hitting a body that has already passed from stiff rigor mortis back to flexibility, because it had been more than twenty-four hours since the life the body housed had fled the scene.

Thud. Thud. Thud.

"Dude, your laundry's unbalanced."

Tony looked up to find the officer who had been assigned to him pointing at one of the washing machines across the room. For a nanosecond he wondered if the statement was some kind of code, telling him his mind was unhinged, or perhaps intimating that he was in danger, but then he realized the thumping he had been hearing wasn't a memory of grave-digging but a real sound emanating from the machine, because his laundry was, in fact, unbalanced.

"What do I do?" Tony said, looking up at the young man helplessly.

"Fuck," the officer said, and Tony was reasonably certain that was not a set of instructions on how to address unbalanced laundry, though as a general proposition it would not have been an entirely unwelcome suggestion.

"I haven't had sex in forever," he said, trying to smile. It was true. His months of exile were just the latest in sexless nights for Tony. After the trial started, Caroline had continued to be a model wife in public, but in private any displays of affection were perfunctory at best, and she had made it clear, with the greatest gentility, that intimacy was out of the question.

The officer ignored the comment and walked over to the machine. Tony followed and watched as the officer yanked open the lid and pointed to the innards, where the clothes were still spinning around the agitator. "As soon as they stop going around," he said, "you take some of the clothes out and kind of rearrange them so they're not all on one side like they are now. If it happens again, you just do the same thing."

It had been over four months since Tony'd had Addy or anyone else to balance his laundry for him, and much, much longer since he'd had sex. Tony wasn't entirely sure which he missed more, sex or having a personal assistant to make sure his life was not perpetually out of whack.

\* \* \*

That night he called Caroline, and this time, she answered.

"I think I need to go clothes shopping," he said without preamble, as if his last call to her had not been about an attempt on his life, as if they hadn't shared a moment of tenderness and fear, as if they hadn't been out of contact for nearly a week.

On the other end of the line there was something that sounded like an exasperated sigh ending in a slight chuckle. Tony curled the phone wire around his finger, thinking this run-down motel in the middle of nowhere must be the last place on earth to have a phone with a curly cord. He felt (and looked) like a teenager waiting for a response to the question *So, you wanna hang out, or something?*

"Giles," Caroline said.

"I'm sticking with Tony while I'm here," he interrupted. "Everyone here knows me as Tony."

"Whoever you are," Caroline said, "you don't need me to buy new clothes."

"I kind of do," he said. "I'm not allowed to go online, and the only clothing store in town is a western store called Rancho. They have metal horse heads in a bucket and a painted cow's skull on the wall. There's nothing else within my five-mile radius."

Caroline really did laugh then, but Tony waited to see if she was laughing at or with him. "Well, honey," she said, "maybe you should pick up a few metal horse heads to decorate the flat. We could start a new trend. I'll bet no one else in Manhattan has metal horse heads in their foyer."

And then he allowed himself to feel glad because, at least for now, there was going to be an "our flat," because the teenager on the other end of the line had said *Yeah, sure, we can hang out.*

Caroline agreed to have her new assistant Daryna order a few pairs of jeans and casual button-down shirts, since that seemed to be the proper attire, as far as Tony could tell from his time in Motte and Bailey. She also agreed to send a few sweaters, in anticipation of winter.

"And I'd like exercise clothes and sneakers," Tony said. "I'm getting a bit thick around the middle."

Caroline said "fine," but the tone of her voice made Tony wonder whether that truly was the last straw. Criminal conviction and a destroyed reputation and exile to the-middle-of-nowhere Oregon were bad enough, but an overweight husband might just be too disgraceful to bear.

"Are you still under police guard?" Caroline said, speaking softly.

"Twenty-four hours a day. But nobody's seen the men who broke into my room and then followed us to the health clinic." He told her about Joey, and Luis's decision to question him in the course of investigating potential child support fraud. "We haven't heard anything from Luis since Tuesday, and I'm thinking that if Joey or Roj hired the thugs, maybe Luis's questioning has convinced them to back off. Either way, I'm feeling pretty safe." He paused, and Caroline murmured, but he didn't know whether it was an I'm-relieved-you're-safe murmur or merely an inarticulate sound of civility, because that's what you do when your spouse says something and then pauses.

"What would you think of getting a dog, when I come home?" he asked.

"Well!" Caroline said, giving another little laugh. "What is the saying? 'You could knock me over with a feather'?" And then it was her turn to pause, and there was a scritching sound, and Tony pictured her running her elegant fingers through her impossibly soft hair. "I thought you were afraid of dogs," she said.

"I am," he said. "But I went to Crackers' and Jems's ranch, and met their dogs. They have eight dogs. Or maybe nine. I lost count. One of them is this German Shepard. Her name is Lipton, like the tea. She is gentle, not at all your average ferocious German Shepard type. Anyway, I've been thinking it over, and I think a dog would be a good addition to . . . ." He stopped just short of *a good addition to our family*. Is that what they had? A family? A family where one partner had been sentenced in a court of law to live thousands of miles away in a rundown motel with telephones from the sixties and the television bolted to the wall while the other partner played bridge and went to board meetings with the excruciatingly handsome Jack Tollefson?

"You know that dogs drool and shed and bark and pass gas, don't you?" Caroline said.

"I'm sure that would be an impediment to someone who has to clean his own home," Tony answered stiffly, before realizing she was joking. Then there was that laugh again, and hearing it freed something that had been imprisoned in his chest.

"Where is this coming from, Giles?"

He didn't correct her, this time. "I just . . . ." More finger-in-the-phone-cord twiddling. "I just feel as though, when this is over, we need a way to . . . start something. Something new. Together."

"We always had a dog, growing up," Caroline said. "Sometimes two."

Tony had seen many photos of Caroline as a child, most showing her perfectly coiffed and staring into the camera with a succinct, practiced smile. None of the photos included dogs, as far as he could recall. But his favorite was a picture of Caroline at maybe eight years old? Or nine? Old enough to know she's breaking family protocol by being filthy and unkempt, young enough to do it anyway. Wild hair escaping from two braids, clothes hanging askew on her body as if she longed to run naked and free, her arms flung around the neck of a pony so muddy and disheveled it must have made the entire family *and* household staff shudder to know there was a photograph memorializing the moment.

He imagined Caroline now, fussing over a big-pawed puppy, maternal, broody, ignoring the messes and the smell, and the image was gladness itself.

"I wouldn't mind having a dog," she said.

And then she added, "Since we can't have children."

\* \* \*

It wasn't as though he'd forgotten. One doesn't forget when one's wife is told her womb is barren.

But he hadn't thought about it in years.

Caroline had immediately sought a second opinion, and after that yielded the same result, she'd told her parents, and Tony, in that order, and asked them to please consider the subject closed. She did not want their suggestions about new treatments, adoption, or fostering, she'd said.

That night, after getting up to go to the bathroom and making his way, in the darkness, back to bed, he thought he heard her crying, but when he rolled over to put his arms around her, she turned away.

"I'm fine," she said.

\* \* \*

Saturday morning was cloudy. It was one of the few days since Tony had arrived in Motte and Bailey that the sun had not stared down at the earth like a foreign agent of a governmental body so powerful it doesn't need to hide its spying.

"It's kind of a relief," Tony ventured to Walt (since no one else was in the kitchen at the time). "To see clouds, that is. I was surprised when I got here. I'd always heard Oregon was very rainy."

"That's the other Oregon," Walt said.

"There's more than one Oregon?" Tony said, fumbling to pick up the oversized carton of salt with one hand.

"Northwestern Oregon is rainy," Walt said. "Portland, Salem, Eugene. I heard they had a whole campaign about it for a while in the seventies to try to keep everyone else out. 'Welcome to Oregon, Please don't stay,' and 'In Oregon, we don't tan, we rust.'"

Tony pictured the map of Oregon he had pored over since coming to the state. "That's not a very big part of the state," he said.

"No duh," Walt said, which Tony thought, understandably, was an amazingly inarticulate comment from a poet and English-teacher-wannabe.

"There are so many beautiful places in Oregon," Nareen said, joining them in the kitchen. "My favorite is Ashland. I'd move there if I could." She grabbed an apron from the hooks by the door, pulled it over her head, and tied it around her ample waste. Then she picked up a pen and a partially-used order pad, and shoved them into the pocket of the apron.

"What's stopping you?" Nancy said, coming in to see why her entire staff was gathered in the kitchen less than a half an hour before opening.

"Mostly just that I'm not white," Nareen said. "Did you know they didn't even let black people into Oregon until 1920-something? And Ashland, Southern Oregon, that was really bad. Worse than the rest of the state."

Walt looked up from counting slabs of bacon, pink-on-white-on-gray like a display at a kids' science fair demonstrating the layers of the earth, a towering mound that was visually interesting but didn't look particularly appetizing. "I knew that," he said. "Everybody's been trying to cover up that history ever since. Trying to say they aren't racist. Trying not to *be* racist."

"Isn't trying better than not trying?" Tony said.

"Yeah," Nancy said. "It seems like every time somebody white tries to do something good somebody else says they're not doing it the right way." She shook her head. "I'm not even white, or at least I'm a tiny little bit Cayuse, but still, I can see it."

Tony, Walt, and Nancy looked at Nareen, as if she held all the answers, as if it was her burden to unlock and resolve for them the whole vast universe of systemic racism and implicit bias. Nareen looked at them looking at her, frustration and exasperation competing in her eyes. "I don't have time to educate you on the ins and outs of being woke," she said.

"I don't even know what that means," Nancy said flatly, looking resentful and hopeful all at once.

"And that's part of the problem," Nareen said. She walked—or rather, waddled—to where Nancy stood and put her arms around Nancy, in a rare display of physical affection. "I love you, Nancy," she said. "Woke or asleep. Just remember that. But woke is better."

"Unless you have insomnia," Walt said.

Nareen looked torn between laughing and making a scathing remark, but the conversation was interrupted by the sound of the front door being jiggled.

"Goddammit!" Nancy said, more loudly than was strictly necessary. "Can't they read the sign? We're not open yet!"

They peered through the order window and saw Luis standing uncertainly by the door. Tony noticed with some surprise that he was wearing a relatively stylish burnt-orange button-front shirt, and a pair of jeans that looked new and, even more surprisingly, seemed to fit him well. Luis was a shabby, baggy-pantsed detective no more.

Was it possible the Sunnyside Up crew was having a positive effect on Luis?

"I can come back later," Luis said through the door.

"You're here now," Nancy grumbled. "Might as well sit down." She bustled out of the kitchen, still muttering, unlocked the door, and let him in. "It's not like you ever order anything difficult. Decaf and dry toast. Gives me the shudders just to hear you order it. Why not have an egg or two once in a while? Good God Almighty you're kind of a waste of space in a diner."

"Are you finished yelling at me about my breakfast choices?" Luis said, sliding into "his" booth.

"That," Nancy said, "was not yelling. When I yell at you, you'll know it."

Luis scowled. "Then are you finished scolding me?"

"Yes," Nancy said. "I'm done. All right, what'll you have?"

"Decaf and dry toast," Luis said, and there was the tiniest of smirks around the corners of his mouth. "But that's not why I'm here. I came in early to tell you all something."

As if they were players in a *Star Trek* episode, as if no actual movement on their part was necessary when important information was in the offing, the three in the kitchen materialized next to Nancy.

"I got nowhere on the child support angle," he said, and four faces fell. "It appears most of the women must not have even filed for child support, and for those few who did, Roj made timely payments."

"I wish Leesa was here," Walt said.

"Why?" Tony said.

"Somebody needs to say godfuckingdammit."

"I wish you people wouldn't take the Lord's name in vain," Luis said. "It really bothers me."

"Hi, my name's Nareen," Nareen said angrily, extending her arm as if she were going to shake Luis's hand. "This is Tony, or at least that's his alias. That's Walt, and this nice woman here is Nancy. We are not now, and never will be, 'you people.'"

"Bravo," Walt said. "That's even better than godfuckingdammit."

"You should know that," Nareen continued. "You're Latino. You and every Mexican, Costa Rican, Cuban, Spaniard, and even some poor schmucks from the Philippines and India have been lumped together by the ignoramuses of America, time out of mind, all 'you people'd' practically into oblivion. So let's drop the 'you people,' okay?"

Luis sighed and rubbed his forehead with his fingertips. "I see your point," he said heavily. "I just wish we could keep God out of it."

"Fair enough," Nareen said. "She's off the hook."

Luis really did smile then, a full, warm grin that transformed his face from annoying to almost friendly.

"Anyway," he said, "Remember I told you I thought maybe Joey and Roj had some business dealings together?" He looked at Tony, who nodded. "I was right. Joey and Roj are partners in a lavender farm in Washington."

The others looked at each other triumphantly.

"So," Luis said, "if Roj *had* been squirrelling away income to avoid paying child support, the farm would have been a valid target for my inquiry. But even though the child support thing was a dead end, still, at least now we know the both of them must have regular dealings with lavender, which connects them to your attack, Tony. And I'm convinced Joey is hiding something. When I pressed him on the farm operation, he suddenly got very vague. I've alerted the IRS that they might want to audit, and if they do, Joey'll know where that came from. Maybe if he's worried, he'll do something stupid, and then we'll catch him."

"But we can't just wait around!" Nancy said. "You're trying this and that and Tony's getting beat up and I'm getting put in jail and all the while Sam's body is rotting in the ground outside of town!"

"What?" Luis and Nareen said, simultaneously.

Nancy gave a tiny groan and covered her mouth as if she could manually prevent any more revelations from tumbling out.

A palpable silence enveloped the small group clustered around Luis's booth, cotton batting insulating them from the rest of the world, stopping clocks and breath and thought and sound, leaving only this: the resounding echoing *What?* from Luis and Nareen, overlaid with the collective unspoken *No!* from Tony and Walt.

"Nobody here killed him," Tony said, deciding that silence was not what was needed in this moment. "We found him dead."

"Oh. My. God." Luis said.

"I thought you asked us to leave God out of it," Nareen said, and she sounded small, and uncharacteristically timid.

"You realize I have to arrest you. All of you," Luis said.

"Nareen didn't know anything about it," Tony objected.

"Obviously," Walt added, and Tony could tell from the barely suppressed tremor in his voice that Walt was terrified. He knew that, in addition to worrying about Nareen, Walt was afraid for himself. Was it really possible, Tony wondered for what felt like the hundredth time, that Walt could go to jail for deserting from the army so long ago? What was the penalty for going AWOL? Was it worse if you were also found guilty of secretly burying the body of a man no one wanted, in the desert, in the middle of the night?

"We were trying to protect you," Nancy said to Nareen.

Tony expected Nareen to argue, to say she wasn't fragile and didn't need protecting, but she seemed to be momentarily stilled, the fiery substance that coursed through her veins temporarily turned to ordinary blood. She nodded a mute thanks.

"If you arrest us you'll never get to the bottom of this," Tony said.

"I don't know why you'd say that," Luis said, grabbing onto the table as if he needed support. "But it doesn't matter. Even if you were right, I'd still have to do it."

"But it was Roj who did it!" Nancy shouted.

Luis took a long, deep breath, and exhaled slowly. "You keep saying Roj is responsible. For this and every other problem in town. I get that he's no candidate for sainthood, but I'm still in the dark. Help me understand. Why do you think Roj killed his son?"

"Because he was still alive when I dropped him off at Roj's house the night before!" Nancy shouted, slapping the table.

The reaction was instantaneous. Walt and Tony shouted inarticu-
lately, surprise and fear and anger echoing in the diner, as if Nancy's
words had excavated a cavernous space, a canyon of the improba-
ble, and Luis jumped to his feet, accidentally flinging a (luckily still
empty) coffee cup across the room, which made far more noise than
a single item of crockery should have.

In the midst of the shouting and shattering the front door jangled,
barely piercing the cacophony, and Jems peered around the door at
them. "I know it ain't quite eight o'clock yet," he said, "but I saw you
all setting there and figured maybe it'd be okay if we come in."

The others looked from Luis to Jems and back again. A deep scowl
took over Luis's face but finally he gestured to Jems to come in, and
then he said to the crew, "Nobody leaves the restaurant after closing.
We're not done here."

The rest of the day was a blur. Luis parked himself at the tiny
table in the kitchen (presumably to ensure no one slipped out the back
door), so there was no opportunity to grill Nancy about her shocking
revelation. That didn't stop Walt from expostulating nonstop over
the grill, stabbing ham steaks viciously and later stormily flattening
hamburger patties as if exorcising demons from the lumps of meat.
Occasionally Tony could make out phrases like ". . . *thought* we
were friends," and ". . . who knows what *else* she's hiding," liberally
interspersed with his signature expletives. Once, when Walt dropped
a fried egg onto the floor, spattering warm egg yolk in a starburst
pattern, Tony distinctly heard, "*Et tu*, Brute?"

Tony was grateful for the distraction from his own frantic ponder-
ings. What would happen when the judge found out Tony had per-
formed no community service during his time in Motte and Bailey?
Had instead busied himself with still more criminal activity, obstruct-
ing justice and burying bodies and god-knows-what-else? Would he
go to prison?

"What kind of food do they serve in prison?" he asked himself,
quietly, aiming the question at the sink full of dirty dishwater.

Somehow, Walt overheard. "Shit on a shingle," he said. "Real
shit. Real shingle."

At forty-eight minutes after one o'clock the last guest left, having
lingered interminably over his pastrami on rye. Nancy locked the
door and turned the sign to CLOSED.

"Now then," Luis said.

"We . . . have to clean up."

"No," Luis said. "I'm done waiting."

"Okay," Nancy said, fear spilling over the edges of the word. "Let's go to my place. This will take a while, and we might as well be comfortable."

It seemed like an odd suggestion to Tony—why give up your most closely guarded secret to The Enemy and then invite him into your home?—and judging by the surprised expressions on the others' faces they apparently felt the same. But the entire day had seemed more and more surreal, so what was one more anomaly?

Luis shrugged, and agreed.

"We can finish cleaning up later," Nancy said, running her hands nervously up and down her thighs, and Tony understood that was a message of optimism, translating as *I hope we'll be back to clean up later, not sitting in jail.*

Nancy's house was just outside the town boundaries, she told Luis as she led them out of the restaurant and down the street to where her car was parked. Since the town was less than two miles across at its widest point, she usually walked to work. "It helps me keep my girlish figure," she said, just like she'd told Tony, and he understood this was her go-to joke, her talisman against reality. Luis did not smile. "But I've been driving lately," she added, "so I can bring Nareen with me and she won't have to walk, you know, in her condition."

"I'll follow you in my car," Luis said. "Please don't do anything stupid." He stopped, and put his hands on his hips, and shook his head. "I still can't believe I didn't arrest you all this morning."

Everyone except Luis piled into Nancy's car, and waited until Luis had started his car and signaled to them to lead the way. Tony wondered if the officer who was assigned to him was going to follow them, or if Luis was calling for backup from his car. Wasn't he afraid they'd gang up on him at Nancy's house, overpower him, leave his body to rot in a dumpster like poor Sam?

They drove slowly through town, and turned into a driveway in a small suburban development. Luis pulled his car up beside Nancy's, and joined them at the gate to the yard.

Unlike Walt's house, Nancy's house was exactly as Tony would have pictured it, had he given it any thought: a baby blue two-story fifties-era house, with a yard decorated in lava rocks and a few potted drought-resistant succulents.

"I don't have the time or energy to mow a lawn," Nancy explained as she led them up the front walk, as if they had asked, as if anyone was thinking about her landscaping.

She pointed to a set of stairs leading to what appeared to be an apartment over the garage. "That's where Nareen is living," she said.

Nareen looked away, mutely distancing herself from the house, from Nancy, from the whole situation.

The entry hall was dim, and clean, and quiet. Faux-wood laminate covered the floors, and scuffed baseboard lined scuffed walls, suggesting that at some point the hall had been the scene of Things Happening. But now no dog bounded to greet them, no cat stalked their arrival, no children's toys peeked shyly from doorjambs. No spouse puttered in the kitchen, no television sounded from a den or family room beyond the hall. In the midst of his worry for himself and for Nancy and Walt, and overlaid against his curiosity about Nancy's revelation at the diner, Tony found himself thinking *I guess this is what it's like to be middle-aged, unmarried, without money, hoping for a visit from your grown daughter who is named after a woman named after Gertrude Stein.* And then he was ashamed of himself, because he recognized he was feeling pity, and maybe a little contempt, and Nancy deserved better than that.

And besides, before this latest incident he would have said Nancy seemed happy, in spite of her scuff-walled two-story house in the suburbs, which is more than he, Giles Anthony Maurice Gibson, could say.

"This is my parents' house," Nancy said. "They spend a bunch of time in Florida or Arizona or someplace like that. They flitted off to California last week, so I have the house to myself I. I offered to let Nareen sleep in one of the rooms in here but she said she'd rather be alone in the apartment over the garage. Gives her space to think, she said." She looked at Nareen for confirmation that she was telling the truth, but Nareen again refused to meet Nancy's eyes.

They followed Nancy to a formal dining room and sat down around a mahogany table with a braided-rope design carved into the edge. Nancy touched the design with her index finger, rubbing it as though for luck. "This was my grandparents' dining set," she said, and opened her mouth to say more, but Luis cut her off, clearly uninterested in information about the house or the table. "Okay," he said, taking the chair nearest the doorway, blocking the exit. "Now," he said. "Tell me about Roj's son."

# Chapter 17

Luis looked at Nancy, but Tony looked away, hoping to minimize for her the sensation of being the center of attention. Tony was comfortable in the spotlight, having been born to it, but he knew others might feel differently. Here they were, assembled around Nancy, as if on a set for a play, waiting for curtain call: Nareen, the set of her mouth reflecting simultaneously distress for and about her friends and resentment, an I-didn't-hide-out-in-Motte fucking Bailey-to-have-to-deal-with-all-your-shit; Walt, his deeply lined forehead furrowed with worry, one hand rubbing the battered t-shirt bearing traces of the day's cooking (a little egg-yolk, a splash of Tabasco sauce, a couple of grease stains that might or might not be new); and Luis, whose dark eyes were trained on Nancy, as if he thought he could extract the truth from her by staring.

Nancy opened her mouth, closed it, opened it again but only to let out a whoosh of nervousness, and ran her fingers through her short-cropped gray hair. Tony saw a hint of her Native American heritage, a suggestion of a broad face and full lips and proud nose that were hidden most of the time. Perhaps fear raised them to the fore, he thought, and then rejected that thought; of all possible emotions, fear did not define this woman.

Finally, she spoke.

"I've always felt kinda motherly toward Sam. His own mom was such a mess, but she was a victim of That Bastard same as me, and she didn't have her own parents to fall back on like I did. I never did drugs, so I had that on her, too."

She took another breath and held it, and it was as if their hearts and lungs were synchronized. No one else breathed until she did, and then there was a collective exhale.

"I'd stop in every so often. That little house what Roj gave Sam and his mom was right on my way home from Sunnyside Up. Sometimes he was there, and I'd fix him some dinner to heat up later, and just talk to him quiet-like. He wasn't the brightest, but then I'm no Einstein myself. We'd talk about the weather, other folks in town. Just that kind of thing."

Walt nodded. "I heard from Maggie who lives next door. She noticed you coming by every so often."

And here was another mystery, though some might have said it couldn't hold a candle to the Nancy-and-Sam story. Who was Maggie? Tony wondered. Did Walt have a "thing" with someone named Maggie? Had Walt ever had a romantic partner? Was he lonely?

"Sam tried to get clean lots of times," Nancy continued. "But he failed lots of times. Sometimes it was booze, other times it was harder stuff. Mostly it was both. If I came over and found him out of it, I'd stay with him 'til he sobered up. A couple times I took him to the clinic if he was so bad I thought someone else should keep an eye on him, but they got no overnight stay there, so when he was really rough I'd drive him over to the hospital in Walla Walla."

Tony pictured Nancy hoisting/heaving/shoving a dead-weight Sam into her car, and then out of her car and into the clinic or the emergency room at the hospital. The strength in that diminutive body amazed him.

It appeared Walt felt the same. "Nancy, you're like the Volkswagen Bug of human beings," he said. "How many clowns can fit in that heart of yours, I wonder?"

"Get to the point," Luis said.

"That day, the day before Walt found him in the dumpster—it was the Fourth of July. You were still out sick, Tony, you remember?"

He did remember. It seemed an eon ago. At least that got him off the list of suspects, he thought, but then he saw the expression on Luis's face and realized Luis was already calculating the odds that Tony had been faking illness, or maybe had dragged his body, between bouts of vomiting, to the house of a stranger, to do him in.

"You're open on the Fourth of July?" Luis clarified.

"Always," Nancy said. "Anyways, I dropped Nareen off at my house after work and then came back into town to run some errands. I went grocery shopping, and thought I'd pick up some food for Sam while I was there. I went to the post office, and then to my sister's house, and she said whyn't you just stay for dinner and then we can all watch the fireworks together. Nareen, I invited you but you said no thanks."

Another shrewd look from Luis.

"So I put my groceries in their extra fridge so they wouldn't go bad, and then we had hot dogs and hamburgers and the grandkids ran around like little monsters, and then we oohed and aahed over the fireworks. Her grandkids're just as cute as can be, the little stinkers." Luis drummed his fingers impatiently on the beautiful table, and Tony felt a momentary sympathy. He, too, wanted to hear the story's denouement. Nancy's sister's grandchildren were not the stars of this show.

"It was pretty late by the time I got to Sam's house," Nancy said. "I don't remember exactly when, but it was after eleven o'clock. It was dark, anyway."

More impatient finger-drumming.

"So yeah," she said. "And you can just stop with the tap-tap-tapping. You police-types always want details. I'm trying to remember."

Nareen shifted a little in her seat, her body visibly vacillating between uncomfortable and downright miserable at this stage of the pregnancy.

"On my way home, I stopped at Sam's to give him the groceries I'd picked up for him," Nancy continued. "When I got there, every light in the house was on, and Sam was lying on the kitchen floor, out cold. Not dead," she said quickly. "Just out. The place was even more of a mess than usual. There were chairs upended, drawers open, even a little table on its side. I guess I should have thought something was up, but I just figured he'd been on an extra bad bender. Which made me really sad, because he'd seemed to be going in the right direction, lately. Roj wasn't lying when he said that."

Tony tried to absorb that thought: Roj wasn't lying. It felt as if someone had declared the Easter Bunny was a duck, this year, or someone had installed basketball hoops on the baseball field, for a change of pace.

"But I didn't really take that in," Nancy said. "I was just mad. Madder than I can remember being in a long time. All I could think was where the hell is Roj? Here's his son lying in his own drool, and his dad's probably off banging some poor girl. So I decided it was time for him to have to deal with it, just for once."

Everyone in the room sat up and leaned in, so as not to miss a word.

"I poured water on Sam's head, and bullied him into getting up. He opened his eyes, but he didn't really seem like he knew who I was. He kept saying, 'I don't do that no more.' Over and over. I told him, 'Sure you don't. That's why you're high as a kite right now.' I don't think he heard me." She rubbed her eyes. "Now I think of it, I should have known he needed to go to the hospital again. I guess I thought Roj would take him. I don't know why." She sounded small then, a child who has just discovered that the fairies she'd seen in the fields were really bugs with lightbulbs on their butts.

"Somehow or other I got him into the car, drove to Roj's house, got him out, and dumped him on the porch swing in front. Roj's house was dark, like the old fucker'd already gone to bed, but I pounded on the door, and hollered for him. I didn't wait to see if anyone came out, just ran back to the car and drove away."

"Why didn't you say anything when I found his body?" Walt said, speaking more gently than Tony had heard him speak in the over four months he'd known him.

"Okay, wait," Luis interjected. "Walt, you found the body? Where did you find it, and when?"

"I found it in the dumpster behind the restaurant," Walt said. "I'm the first one in every morning. I'm usually there by six to do the prep work. I found Sam's body, sitting on top of the garbage like he was somebody's unwanted omelet."

Exactly like that, Tony thought.

"I tried to tell Nancy quietly that I found a body, but Leesa over-heard and started carrying on so I told everyone to calm down, it was just a dead cat. Then when everybody left, we went out back to talk about it."

"And why the *hell* didn't you report it to the authorities?" Luis said grimly.

"Because we thought right from the get-go that Roj did it," Nancy said. "Who else could have? Last I saw, Sam was alive, on Roj's front porch, and I'd, uh, alerted Roj to come get his son."

"There didn't seem much point in reporting the fox to his fellow foxes, if you get my meaning," Walt said to Luis.

"*The point* would have been that you wouldn't now be the prime suspects in a young man's death," Luis said. "And you don't *know* there wouldn't have been an investigation. Whatever you may think, Roj doesn't own the sheriff's office."

"Maybe not," Nancy said, "but when push comes to shove he still calls the shots."

"Why are you so sure about that?" Luis asked.

"If you were from around here you'd know," Nancy said sullenly.

"How else do you explain the fact that Nancy's bail was set at fifty thousand dollars?" Tony pointed out. "If Roj no longer has significant influence, how is it that he can turn his wounded pride into a ridiculously high bail at a moment's notice?"

Luis nodded, acknowledging the truth of his words. They waited, and Tony wondered if this was the moment when they would all be arrested.

"And yet Roj also paid the *'ridiculously high bail.'* So, there's more going on here than all your assumptions and supposings." Luis shook his head again, apparently the only gesture left to him in this strange world. "Okay, Nancy, what do you think happened after you left Sam on Roj's porch?"

"I don't know," Nancy said, and every part of her body sagged, as if she had been holding herself upright by sheer force of will until she got the story out. "I guess I just figured Roj decided to put an end to the one black spot on his record—the one kid who turned out rotten."

"How?" Luis said.

"What do you mean, 'How?'" Walt asked, visibly trying to redirect the attention away from Nancy.

"I mean, how do you think Roj killed his son? With a gun? A knife? Strangled him? Poisoned him?"

"I don't know!" Nancy said.

"That's my point," Luis said. "If you'd reported this, a coroner could have examined the body, and we'd at least know how he died." He shook his head. "Did it even occur to you that Sam might have just OD'd after you left? Maybe Roj just left the body behind your restaurant in revenge, to get you back for dumping Sam on his porch. I mean, you said you shouted at him through the door, so he must have known you were the one who brought Sam."

Tony pictured the scene: Nancy kicking at the door, screaming *Roj come and get your son you no good rotten shithead*, Sam lying on the porch, moaning softly, a light in a back room, then footsteps.

"I don't know," Nancy said again. "I didn't wait around to see if Roj came to the door. Maybe he wasn't even home." And then, sullenly, "I don't know why you expect me to know anything. That's your job, isn't it?"

"A job that has been made exponentially more difficult by your collective obstruction of justice," Luis said, with remarkable calm. He placed his palms on the table, almost precisely parallel to his shoulders, as if preparing to issue judgment. Once again, there was a collective holding of breath.

"I'm probably going to lose my job for this," he said. "I may even go to jail myself. But God help me I believe you, and I can't see what good it will do to arrest you."

Four pairs of lungs exhaled.

"But we are going to have to exhume the body," he continued. "And before we end this little party, I want the whole truth from each of you about why you're here, and what you're hiding."

Tony folded his arms across his chest.

"The Cliff Notes version," Luis added.

Tony started to speak, determined to take charge, but before he could say a word Walt leaned in and snarled, "I'm AWOL from the army. About forty-seven years ago. That's all there is to tell."

There is much, much more to Walt than desertion of military service, Tony thought. There are shallots and coffee cake and omelets. And poetry. And Percocet.

Luis looked up at the ceiling as if seeking divine patience. "And the reason you wear fatigues and army boots after leaving the army would be?"

"Fatigues is about all they've got at the thrift store," Walt said. "And I need the boots for support." He glared at Luis. "I've got weak ankles."

Even in the midst of this fraught, airless moment, it took every ounce of self-control Tony had to keep from laughing.

"And you?" Luis said to Nareen.

"I just finished my junior year at PSU," Nareen said. "Portland State University. I was studying accounting. I hope to finish someday. I got pregnant. Well, really, my boyfriend and I got pregnant. Everyone was telling me what to do so I decided to visit my cousin in Spokane, just to get away from them and think for myself. Decide if I wanted to get an abortion or go through with the pregnancy. The bus broke down outside Motte and Bailey, and Nancy found me and took me in. Like a stray kitten."

"More like a stray mountain lion, I'd say," Walt said.

Nareen smiled.

Nancy jumped in, having rallied more quickly than Tony would have imagined possible. "I was born and raised here. Roj and me were together when I was fifteen. I thought it was grown up, maybe even romantic. He told me he loved me. I got pregnant, had my daughter, Gertie. I never told my parents who Gertie's dad was. They thought it was one of the boys at school. It's true what Roj said, that time I dumped coffee on him, about him asking me to marry him, but it was just because he was running for re-election and he wanted a ready-made family to make him look respectful and shit."

Nareen stared at Nancy, and Tony was pretty sure Nareen was thinking of a hundred and one ways to hurt Roj, to vindicate the slightly dumpy, warm-hearted, foul-mouthed protectress who had rescued her.

"Your turn," Luis said to Tony.

Tony sighed. "I would have thought you had 'detectived' my background already," he said.

"Not knowing your real name made that difficult," Luis said testily. "But I did eventually figure out who you are. Interestingly, the sheriff's office knows your identity, of course, since they're charged with monitoring you. But Roj didn't know, at least not at first, which is one of the reasons I think you all overestimate his power. I think he's more out of the loop than you imagine." He looked at each of them in turn, and Tony read in his gaze an accusation: they should have known half-assed decisions based on assumptions would only end in disaster.

"But I still want to hear your version," he said to Tony, "and I want to know how you fit into the whole Sam-thing."

*The whole Sam-thing.* That was the crux of it, wasn't it? For Nancy and Walt and himself—and now, Nareen—in this moment "the Sam-thing" was the sum of the parts of their lives.

Luis continued to stare at him, waiting.

Everyone at the table already knew the basic outline of his reason for being in Motte and Bailey, after Leesa's outburst, and Tony wasn't sure what else Luis wanted from him. Whatever he said, the most likely result would be a further erosion, or maybe even utter destruction, of the fragile, nascent bonds of friendship. *It doesn't matter what someone in a tiny town in Oregon thinks of you,* Caroline had said. But it did matter. He felt his heart contracting, readying itself, if necessary, to return to the pale place where nothing signified except the winds of fate on which he floated.

"My name is Giles Anthony Maurice Gibson," he said finally. "Of the Long Island Gibsons."

"'*Giles*'?" Walt said, his voice pock-marked with incredulity.

There was a snort from Nancy. "Now you see why I told him he'd have to go by Tony," she said.

Walt shook his head, signaling that he'd forgiven Tony much but he might not be able to get over the name Giles.

"I was—I *am*—the president of ABC Toys," Tony went on, wanting only to get through his explanation, not wanting to stop and defend his name. "I have final authority over every financial development plan, every marketing strategy, and every new toy. Whenever there's a question about whether to move forward or scrap an idea, I have the ultimate yea or nay vote. I have a whole army of people below me, designing new toys, setting up focus groups and recording the results, trading advertising jingles. But as the old saying goes, the buck stops with me. We developed a plush toy called Poppy Panda. It was the height of the panda-craze. It was a charming toy, actually. Very soft and appealing. But the specifications for the eye-connections were inadequate—a cost-saving measure, I guess—and the little button eyes sometimes popped off under stress. After everyone had run all the safety tests, the VP of Safety told me there was some risk, but he said it was minimal, 'an acceptable risk,' he called it. I told myself later I hadn't really thought about what that meant, but that's not completely true. The truth is, I knew what it meant. It meant that if something went wrong, the cost of a settlement would be less, much less, *acceptably* less, than the hit to our profit margin." He wanted to keep going, to get from point A to point B so he could stop, but he was afraid, so afraid of what came after, the point C in his life, what the others would do when they heard him say the words aloud, heard him confirm that he was in fact every sordid, profane thing Leesa had called him.

"One of the children who choked on a Poppy Panda was a little girl from Motte and Bailey," he said, for Luis's benefit. "Her name was Libby."

And then he stopped again, realizing in astonishment that he was weeping. He could not recall crying over anything since the day his father came into his room and told him his mother was gone, and he wanted to ask *Where did she go?* but he was old enough to know gone was just a euphemism for dead.

Nancy handed him a paper napkin from a basket in the center of the table, and he blew his nose.

"There was a class action civil suit from Libby's parents and others, and criminal charges," Tony continued, after looking in vain for a place to set his mucus-laden napkin and finally stuffing it into his pocket. "On the civil side, there was a significant damage award," he said, and then, seeing the look of confusion on Nancy's face, "I had to pay a lot of money," he added.

Walt's face was hard, and Tony understood that Walt at least was not mollified; having to pay a lot of money is no atonement when the payment is blood-money for a child's life.

"On the criminal side, there was also a fine," he continued. "And in lieu of jail time, the judge sentenced me to perform community service here, in Libby's home town. He also said I'd have to pay my own living expenses by working, and he said it would have to be a minimum wage job. I'd have to go where I was nobody important, he said."

The phrase hung in the air, and Tony realized too late that he was once again condemning everyone else who worked at the diner as "nobody important," just as Scooter had said.

Luis raised an eyebrow. "I've seen my fair share of criminal sentences," he said. "And that was a new one on me. I was surprised when I saw that in your file."

"The judge's clerk convinced Nancy to hire me," Tony said. "I don't think the clerk told Nancy what I'd done, only that I had to work at the lowest level possible." He looked at Nancy for confirmation, but she was looking down at her hands, rubbing the space between her thumb and forefinger as if to purge some smudge or smear from the web of her skin. "I know it must have been a shock to find out what I'd done, Nancy," he looked at the top of her head, willing her to look up, "and I was so grateful that you didn't send me away. So grateful I didn't have to go work at McDonald's." He laughed, but it was a strangled sound, less like the sarcastic chuckle he'd intended and more like barely-contained hysteria.

"Nobody has ever assigned me any community service," he said. "I guess I should be worried about that, but I figure it'll catch up to me, or not. Whatever." He smiled ever so briefly at the Leesa-ism. "My sentence is for one year," he said. "It's been nearly five months. Sometimes it feels like I've always lived here."

Arrogant omnipotent company bigwig. Grieving penitent. Hysterical. Pleading. He'd run the gamut of identities and emotions, but he wasn't finished. Not yet.

"I'm married, but my wife, Caroline, refused to come with me to Motte and Bailey. I don't know what will happen when my sentence is up. The Gibsons don't really do divorce, but it's easy enough to simply live parallel lives. Then again, Caroline is only a Gibson by marriage." The word marriage hung in the air, a question mark rather than a statement. He was tempted to say *mawiage*, like the priest in *The Princess Bride*, to force them all to laugh, to ease the tension. Why had he mentioned Caroline and his secret, private fears? Surely that wasn't part of the Cliff Notes version of his life.

"When Walt told me we needed to bury Sam, when he said it was the only decent thing to do, I said yes. That felt more like community service than anything else I could have done."

There was no The End or Happily Ever After, but at least he was done with his part of the story. He waited then, longing for someone to say something. Questions. Recriminations. A pardon.

But there was only silence.

"Do Leesa and Scooter know all this?" Luis asked finally.

"They know about Libby, and why Tony's here," Walt said, "at least, now they do, after Libby's aunt and uncle made the connection and told Leesa. But they don't know anything about finding Sam's body."

"Or about Nancy dropping Sam off at Roj's house," Tony offered. "We didn't know anything about that until now, either."

Luis rolled his head, stretching his neck and possibly his brain to make room for all the information. "So far, Tony, you haven't told me anything I hadn't already discovered about you—anything relevant, that is. But what I want to know is this: why do you think someone in Motte and Bailey is coming after *you*?"

Tony was infinitely, irrationally glad they were sticking with *Tony*, rather than insisting on *Giles* now that they knew his given name. "I truly have no idea," he said.

"Is it possible there's a price on your head because of Libby? A local gang affiliated with that family?"

"No," Nancy and Walt said, speaking in tandem, and Walt added, "You'd just have to be part of this town, and you'd know. There's nothing like that."

Luis made a sound of disgust. "I don't think you know as much as you think you do. But I can say this part of our little conversation has been pretty much a waste of time, about as useful as—"

"—as a one-legged man at an ass-kicking competition," Walt interjected. "I could have told you that, before we started."

"But we do appreciate your decision not to arrest us," Nancy hastened to add, clearly worried that Walt's mean-spirited comment might cause Luis to change his mind.

"That's a temporary decision," Luis cautioned them. "I can't promise you anything about the future."

And that's really what it came down to, Tony thought. Nobody could promise them anything about the future.

Ever.

# Grade A Egg

After the impromptu interrogation, Tony walks the streets of Motte-fucking-Bailey, followed by his police shadow, ambling purposelessly through the purple sunset hours, the words in his head drowning out the sights and sounds of the town around him. He wonders what the Sam-thing will look and smell and feel like when it's been dug up, and whether there really is an afterlife and if so, does one's spirit look down on the rest of humanity and sigh, seeing the whole panoply of existence and understanding the grand scheme of things, or does it fret over whether one's spouse remembered to prune the roses by Presidents Day, as myopic in death as in life?

His existential musings are interrupted, literally, when he nearly trips over Lipton.

Crackers greets him cheerily, an almost physical interruption to Tony's thoughts, and tells him Lipton went to the vet on Friday and got a clean bill of health, and the vet said to bring her into town for short walks, to exercise the ligaments. Tony notices the pressed trousers, immaculate black button-down shirt, and perfectly styled hair (in spite of the late October breeze—Tony suspects hair gel is involved).

Lipton sits down, one half of a hairy black and brown buttock resting on Tony's shoe, and looks up expectantly. Tony's hand hangs just about level with her head, and it seems the most natural thing in the world to stroke her ears. Lipton's eyes half close, and there's a sound of bliss, almost like purring.

Crackers says Tony's obviously a dog-person, and claims dogs always know who likes them.

It is almost impossible to stay stuck inside one's own head with a hairy dog-butt resting on one's shoe. "I am a dog person," Tony says, thinking maybe it's not a lie, right this minute, thinking maybe it's an announcement of future predilection rather than an assertion of fact.

And then Crackers tells him Jems is a cat person, and says something about to each his own I suppose, and nods a goodbye.

As if she carries color and sound with her, the town opens up in Lipton's wake. It is no longer the silent backdrop to Tony's life. Seeing the mural of activity springing up around him like paint filling in a paint-by-numbers scheme, he realizes again that (a) the town is a vibrant, living community, not a ghost town, and (b) he is irrelevant to this town, not the other way around.

"That's it!" he feels like shouting, Lucy shouting to Schroeder when Schroeder finally recognizes all she wants is plain old ordinary Jingle Bells, no grand orchestra, just the notes, one after another after another.

# Chapter 18

As if they hadn't spilled their guts to a detective, as if they weren't waiting for the results of an exhumation and autopsy of Roj's son, and a final determination on whether they were all going to jail, the same crew that had gone to Nancy's house the day before arrived at Sunnyside Up the next day.

Sundays were blessedly busy, so—other than a quick confab in the pantry, where Walt told Tony he'd taken Luis to the burial spot, and Luis had just about lost his shit, Walt said—there was no chance to talk about what had happened in Nancy's dining room.

The Maxes hadn't come in since they'd tried, ineffectually and bumblingly, to warn Tony off, but all the other regulars were there: a few older folks who liked to come in before the rest of the town was awake, to have a quiet cup of coffee and one of Walt's cinnamon rolls (made with a hint of cardamom and almond extract, and generously drenched with brown-butter frosting); a steady stream of atheists, agnostics, Jews, and other non-Sunday-church-goers; and then, starting at around noon, the chattering, squabbling, humming, purse-lipped, pondering and pontificating church-goers.

At one o'clock Roj showed up. Restaurant crew and customers alike did a double take, to see if it was really Roj, not his Okie from Spokie cousin, and then a third take, because no one could quite believe he'd have the gall to come in after being doused with hot coffee and getting Nancy tossed in jail for it. Roj's booth was taken, so he headed over to one of the tables near the window. Walt whistled loudly at Tony who, lost in daydreams, worries about the investigation, and dirty dishwater, had not seen Roj come in. When Tony looked up, Walt jerked his head toward the place where Roj was sitting. Tony dried his hands and hurried out of the kitchen, hoping to

200

head off Nareen and, more importantly, Nancy.

"I thought I asked you to stay away," he said sternly.

Roj shrugged. "You did," he said. "And so did that detective. But I figure it's been long enough, since I ain't done nothing wrong."

"You've done plenty, mister," Nancy said, beetling over to where the two men were eyeballing each other like fighters in the ring.

"I'll have the usual," Roj said, smiling at Nancy with an obvious attempt at charm, or affection, or whatever approximated the veneer of friendship in Roj's fetid brain.

Tony caught Nancy's arm as she took a step forward, and pulled her away. He wasn't sure what she was planning to do, and she probably didn't know, either, but one thing he was sure of—whatever it was, nothing good would come of it. Not for Nancy, anyway.

Walt made Roj's "the usual," and Tony wondered how Walt could restrain himself from spitting into the Western omelet and hash browns, and then wondered whether Walt *did* restrain himself.

Tony picked up dirty dishes and refilled water glasses and coffee cups until Roj's meal was ready, chatting lightly with all the regulars and taking pleasure in the fact that they knew him by name.

There was Nancy's sister sitting by the door (sitting in Roj's booth, which earned her the female equivalent of *attaboy* from Tony), wearing the same worn pink slippers, her hair pulled back into a graying ponytail that stretched her face tight and brought into sharp relief the similarities between the two sisters' features. Tony asked her how her grandkids were doing, and she said, "Rascally and full of theirselves, just the way I like them," and then she laughed her throaty, smoker's laugh, and Tony laughed with her.

Here was the elderly couple whose names Tony had never asked but who always murmured *thank you young man*, with benign grace, when Tony checked in on them.

And in the corner booth was the family with the little girls who tried hard to behave "like ladies," at their mother's exhortation, but who usually gave it up within a few minutes.

When the food was ready Tony brought it to Roj's table, set the plate down with a slight but noticeable clatter, and walked away without speaking to Roj.

A few minutes later he heard a sound. He was wiping a table with a circular motion, soothing and rhythmic (though not necessarily calculated to eliminate remnants of food, much less bacteria, in any efficient manner), humming a little as he worked. This new sound intruded upon his cleaning and humming and the background noises of the diner, insistently, and he stopped for a moment, as if an invisible maestro had lowered his baton to signal a *caesura*. He heard the sound again, clearly, because the restaurant had grown silent, the rest of the orchestra responding to the conductor's command. Tony turned, slowly, in an arc, toward the sound. And when he had completed the arc, he saw Roj, hunched over his plate, one gnarled hand clawing feebly at his throat, and the other clutching the edge of the table.

Tony thought, words streaming through his consciousness with lightning speed and honeyed sloth, I-don't-know-Roj-and-I-don't-like-him-why-should-I-help-him-someone-else-will-help-no-not-this-time-this-time-it's-me-I-can't-turn-away. He walked through the swirling storm of words to where Roj sat, confirmed that Roj was indeed choking and no air was going in or out, squatted slightly so that he could reach around the back of the chair, encircled Roj's not-inconsiderable girth with his arms, placed his fist at a spot that he hoped was midway between Roj's navel and the bottom of his breast bone, cradled his fist with his other hand, and gave five quick, sharp, upward thrusts. Each thrust jerked the man's body, making his head bob up and down as if on a spring. On the fifth thrust, a chunk of what might have been toast flew out of Roj's mouth and landed on the table in front of him.

Tony stepped back, expecting Roj to cough, or sputter, or vomit, or perhaps all three, as he had been taught in the First Aid and CPR class he took when he first arrived at Sunnyside Up. But Roj did none of those things. Instead, he collapsed out of his chair onto the floor and lay in a semi-fetal position, curled over but with one leg splayed out to the side. Tony leaned over, watching Roj's chest for signs of breathing, and rested his finger lightly on Roj's neck.

No breathing.

No pulse.

There was no time for more existential philosophizing, though he did fleetingly wish it could have been Leesa or Nareen who needed resuscitating. Hell, even Scooter would have been better than putting his mouth on this foul old man who surely deserved to die. Taking a deep breath, Tony rolled Roj onto his back, pinched Roj's beer-reddened nose, adjusted Roj's jaw to ensure an accessible airway, sealed his lips around Roj's, and blew twice into Roj's lungs. Then he pushed on Roj's heart with the heel of his hands, thirty times in rapid succession (having since learned that his mantra from the class, the *one-two-three-four breathe*, was wildly out of date).

After a few repetitions there was a gasping cough, and then the conductor lifted his baton again, and the symphony resumed, someone shouting at Tony across the diner *Congratulations maybe you oughtta volunteer for the fire department*, someone else wanting to know, sarcastically, why he bothered, one of the not-ladylike girls asking *mommy does that man have an owie?*, the girl's father talking to the 911 operator on his cell phone, the soft clicks from other patrons who had also taken out their otherwise-forbidden cell phones not to get help but to take photos of the death throes of a man few, if any, would miss.

And as Tony helped Roj sit up, another instrument joined the orchestra, and this one was oh so familiar to Tony.

"You have got to be the weirdest man alive," Leesa said loudly, shrilly. "I don't know whether to hug you or punch you."

Tony stood up and faced her, shaking uncontrollably. "I'd prefer a hug, if it's all the same to you," he said, weakly.

"If you were going to go and be a hero, why'd it have to be for that slug, that slimy pig, that . . . ," she seemed to run out of words, and after looking up at the ceiling as if casting about for the most appropriate terminology, settled on a soul-deep scowl.

"What are you doing here?" Nancy said to Leesa.

"I came to talk to Tony, or whatever his name is," Leesa said.

"Are you sure that's a good idea?"

"No," Leesa said, "but I'm doing it anyway."

Nareen, who had been leaning against the counter throughout the drama, sighed and shook her head and said, "Isn't that just the way for all of us?"

"The restaurant is closing early!" Nancy bellowed, as if in response. "If you're not done eating, too bad. Anyone out of here in the next five minutes pays half price."

That got everyone moving, and it was amazing, Nareen commented later, how many of the customers demanded half off even though they had clearly finished eating long before and were simply being asked to leave a few minutes earlier than they'd planned.

For reasons known best to herself, while Nareen closed out the customer tickets and worked the cash register, Nancy sat with Roj and waited for the ambulance. Tony's ubiquitous shadow from the sheriff's office was sitting in a car outside, and the unpleasant task could easily have been handed off to him or to anyone else in the restaurant, yet there Nancy sat, glaring at Roj but refusing to leave his side.

The EMTs arrived, loaded Roj onto a gurney, and rolled him outside to the waiting ambulance. Tony watched while the gurney was put into the ambulance, then he moved into the kitchen, followed by Leesa. They sat down on either end of the tiny table near the back door. Walt gave up any pretense of working at the giant prep island in the middle of the kitchen that was, as usual, covered with various remnants of food and implements of culinary destruction, and stood watching them.

"I had to save him," Tony said.

"No," Leesa said, holding up her hand. "I get to talk first. And I know you had to save him. It would have been wrong to just let him die without trying. I just wish he'd choked to death, alone in his home, so nobody had to make that choice to save him or let him die. That's what he deserved."

Tony nodded in agreement but said nothing, having been ordered to listen. While Leesa gathered her thoughts, he marveled at the strange and fickle fate that brought him to this moment in which he, the wealthy and influential president of an international company, a member of the infamous One Percent, sat meekly obedient to a freckle-faced, f-bomb-dropping, part-time server at a run-down diner in a tiny town in rural Oregon.

"I haven't forgiven you," Leesa said after taking a breath. "I know the whole story now, and I know you didn't *actually* kill Libby. I understand the crime is more in what you didn't do. But it's still a crime, and . . ." she seemed to struggle, again, for the right words.

" . . . morally repugnant?" Walt suggested.

"Yeah, that," Leesa said. She twisted a few strands of strawberry blond hair around her index finger. "But Scooter and me—I mean Scooter and I—we talked about it for a long time." Tony pictured the two of them, closeted together, Scooter gently talking Leesa down from her righteous wrath. He hoped the conversation had ended with a kiss, or some passionate necking, or maybe even the whole shebang. Leesa's face went a little pink, as if in answer to Tony's unasked question about that long talk. "He said you and I were friends before I knew all this, and I thought you were a good guy then, so maybe that shouldn't change."

Tony silently reminded himself to thank Scooter. And to find out if Scooter'd kissed Leesa.

"He said it's like the whole cancel culture thing," she said. "Erasing what's good when someone's made a mistake. And I said yeah, but this was a big fucking mistake, not a little oops. And even though you're sorry and all, that doesn't fix it. But I thought about it some more after that, and I decided you can't just hide away here in Motte and Bailey and call it good. Washing dishes at a diner doesn't make up for what you did."

Tony waited, wondering what additional punishment Leesa was going to pronounce. Walt leaned in, apparently curious, too.

"Here's what I decided," Leesa said. "You've got to face them."

"Face who?" Tony said.

"Libby's aunt and uncle," Leesa said, and Tony flinched, as if she'd slapped him.

"Her mom and dad moved away," Leesa went on, ruthlessly. "They couldn't take it, staying here, where everything reminded them of her. But her aunt and uncle are still here. Remember I told you they recognized you, and told me who you were. I want you to talk to them, to let them tell you what she was like, what they lost when you signed off on that stupid toy."

He wanted to protest. I've changed! Look what I did today—I saved a man's life with my bare hands (and lips). I helped Walt investigate the Lavender Bandit. I paid for the girl's hospital bill. I tried to get Nancy out of jail. Isn't that enough? How long do I have to keep paying for that one decision? But he knew the answer: as long as it takes. Maybe as long as he lived. He sighed, and nodded his agreement, unsure whether he was allowed to talk yet.

Leesa looked at Nancy, and then at Walt, and Tony hoped for a split-second that Walt would rescue him, would tell Leesa this was a terrible plan, but Walt pushed his lips together in what may have been intended as a smile. "You're a smart kid, Leesa."

"Thanks," Leesa said, obviously pleased. Then she turned back to Tony. "Their names are Gloria and Rick," she said. "They were born and raised here, same as just about everybody else in town. They're Hispanic. Is that what we say now? Or is it Latino? Whatevs. I don't think Gloria and Rick care what we call 'em, so long as it isn't, like, really bad."

And Walt said it was true, if you're born here you're one of us, and then he added, "It's only strangers we get all racist on," And then he went back to his somewhat erratic clean-up efforts, having apparently heard as much as he needed to hear.

"You told me you're married," Leesa said, tugging on that same bit of hair. "That time you walked me home. You've got a wife back in New York City, right?"

Tony was surprised, both that this should follow a discussion of Libby, and that Leesa should care.

"You've got some nerve messing around with a small-town girl like me when you're married," she said, though the look in her eyes suggested she was teasing him, not piling on new accusations. Tony considered pointing out that she was the one who kissed him on that dark night outside Joe's Bar & Grill, and that he had pulled away, and squashed all further attempts at flirting, but he decided a smile was the better response. "Don't you miss her?" Leesa asked.

"I do," Tony said. "Deeply. But she wouldn't come with me. I'm sure she doesn't want to fly across the country and live in a tiny town in Oregon," he was always careful to pronounce it correctly, now, "with a man who wears an ankle monitor and works in a diner."

"Have you asked her?" Leesa said.

Walt stopped scraping the grill and stood still.

Tony could hear the last customer talking to Nareen, a querulous elderly woman insisting that she shouldn't be charged full price, even though the five-minute deadline Nancy'd imposed was long past. Nareen muttered something like *Just because you're old and slow doesn't mean you shouldn't have to pay,* but the ding of the cash register drawer told Tony she had conceded the fight.

Had he asked Caroline to come with him? He could hear his father's voice in his head, reminding him that one doesn't ask such things. A Gibson doesn't say, "I'm frightened, will you take this journey with me, so I won't be alone and afraid?"

"Well, she told me before I came that she wouldn't be joining me in Oregon. But if you're wondering whether I've asked since then, the answer is no," he said.

"Maybe you should," Leesa said. "Maybe she just needs to know you want her."

\* \* \*

There seemed to be a shared feeling that it would be nice if everything calmed down for a while, but the universe was not finished springing surprises on the crew at Sunnyside Up.

Nancy assured Tony and Walt that she would find a time to fill in Scooter and Leesa on the new information (dead body Walt found in the dumpster last summer wasn't a cat, it was Sam; Nancy'd found Sam high and put him on Roj's front porch but he died later; he'd OD'd on meth but it wasn't his fault—and she said it just like that, like it was a series of headlines about nothing more significant than the weather: rain on Monday, sunny Tuesday, local kid murdered and left in a dumpster behind Sunnyside Up).

Leesa was on the schedule on Tuesday, for the first time since Nancy had sent her away. She and Tony worked together without incident, though she pointedly ignored his anxious hovering until she couldn't stand it any longer (approximately fifteen minutes into her shift), and told him to take a chill pill, she hadn't talked to Gloria and Rick yet but she'd let him know when they were ready to meet him.

The next day, Scooter was serving, and he was positively ebullient. No shy skulking, no timid shuffling.

"Thank you for talking to Leesa," Tony said, when there was a brief lull in busyness.

Scooter shrugged, and then grinned.

Tony shoved aside the thought *What business is it of mine?* and said, "So . . . you and Leesa?"

Scooter's grin broadened and deepened, until it was not just his mouth but his eyes and his whole face lit with happiness.

"Yeah," he said, "me and Leesa."

Luis came in right in the middle of the lunch rush and told Nancy there'd be a meeting after the restaurant closed for the day.

"Maybe I should just hand you a coffee pot and put you on the payroll," Nancy said, "as long as you're gonna keep hanging around every day."

Luis didn't smile, and Nancy looked worried.

"Don't mind him. He's got no sense of humor," Tony assured her.

After closing, the crew took care of the basic cleanup but decided the rest could wait until Luis had said what he came to say. This time, everyone else squeezed into the booth, and Luis sat in the position of power in a chair at the end of the table.

"First things first," he said. "Nancy, your hearing's been put off. You'll get a notice in the mail, but it looks like it'll be January at least before you'll be back on the docket."

"Good god almighty," Nancy said. "Here it is, what, October 23? And they wait until *now* to tell me the Halloween hearing has been put off?"

"I thought you'd be relieved," Luis said.

"I just want it over," Nancy said, worry draped on her shoulders like a heavy shawl.

Luis shrugged and then shared the news he'd brought. "The body was exhumed," he said. "I said I got an anonymous tip."

"You lied to the authorities?" Scooter said.

Luis rolled his eyes. "Maybe 'anonymous' means more than one person told me," he said archly. "Anyway, I got the results of the autopsy last night. They confirmed it was Sam Meluka." Tony looked at him quizzically, and Luis explained that Sam had his mother's last name, not Roj's. "They also confirmed that he died of an overdose of methamphetamines."

Nancy yelped as if she'd been hit. "I knew I should have taken him to the hospital," she wailed, and tears burst from her eyes. Like everything else about this woman, crying was no mild-mannered business, Tony thought. Scooter put his arm around her and squeezed her shoulders.

"It's unlikely that would have saved him," Luis said loudly but not unkindly, so as to be heard over Nancy's wailing.

"How do you figure that?" Walt said.

"He had so much meth in his system, the coroner was pretty sure death would have been inevitable."

"He was trying so hard to be good," Nancy said, still crying.

"Well," Luis said, "that's consistent with something else the coroner discovered."

"What else?" Scooter said.

"Apparently, the concentration of meth in the blood increases rather than decreases after death," Luis explained. "Then it remains at a fixed level. Although it was difficult to extrapolate with precision, since the body's been buried for so long," he paused, and glared at Walt and Tony, "the concentration was still so great, the coroner is

reasonably certain it must have been administered by someone else."
He paused again, letting that sink in, while Nancy tried get control of
her breathing.

"Even taking into account the increase after death, the amount
they believe was in his system at the time of death was extremely
high.   Anyone taking meth would have achieved their high and
stopped long before reaching that point," he finished.

"But why?"   Tony said into the stunned silence that followed.
"Why force some guy nobody cares about, who's apparently shaken
his addiction, to take drugs?"

"Presumably, the person or persons who administered the meth
knew Sam was a former addict, and the intent was to cause death
and make it look like an accidental OD," Luis said.

"Poor bastard," Walt said. "The world had it in for him from the
get-go. He never really had a chance."

There was a moment of silence then. No one had suggested it, but
the thought was there, shared without articulating it, a moment for
all that Sam had suffered, in living and in dying.

"So," Nancy said, between sniffles, "Roj . . . didn't kill Sam?"

"Unless you think he administered the fatal dose," Luis said, but
Nancy and Walt shook their heads simultaneously.

"He's a conniving, soulless bastard," Walt said, "but I can't see
him plunging the needle in. Though maybe he ordered it done?"

Nancy shook her head again.

"He did seem to be genuinely worried about Sam," Tony said.

"Who knows?" Luis said. "But I still need to talk to him again,
hopefully before he's released from rehab. He had emergency bypass
surgery," he explained, "and since he's got no one at home to take
care of him they're sending him to a rehab place to recover."

Nancy dipped her finger into the glass of water she'd brought with
her to the table, and traced the edge of the glass, but there was no
sound, as if even the drinking utensils had been struck dumb by this
strange turn of events A miraculous redemption from death, only to
be consigned to the dingy halls of a rehab center because no one cares
enough to make sure you get fed and do your daily walk to the end
of the hall and back.

"We believe you may be right that he's involved in running the
drugs," Luis continued. "And I want to know how his son went from

nearly comatose on his father's porch to dead in the dumpster behind the diner."

"Go get 'em Magnum," Walt said.

"'Magnum?'" Scooter said.

"*Magnum P.I.*," Walt explained.

"What?" Scooter said.

"Eighties television. Hawaiian detective. Heart throb Tom Selleck, flashy guy. Oh good lord," he said in disgust. "You're all too young. But you must have seen it. Lying on the couch when you're home sick, eating boxed mac and cheese and popping cough drops?" He looked at Scooter expectantly, but there was no flash of recognition. "No? Never?" He smacked the table and slid out of the booth. "Getting old sucks!" he declared. "Don't do it." He took a step toward the kitchen but Luis held up a hand. "I'm not done with you," he said.

Walt sat down again, looking wary.

"You are all still subject to arrest, and you most of all, Walt," Luis said. "But I'm way more interested in stopping this particular thread of the drug trade and—now—solving Sam's murder, than getting you court martialed for something you did nearly a half a century ago when you were young and desperate and stupid."

Walt looked relieved but said only, "I guess being old has its perks."

"I did some research," Luis said, "And it may be possible to get your desertion pardoned, or at least get a sentence that doesn't involve jail time. It turns out Ford—President Ford—issued pardons to deserters and draft-dodgers in 1974." He pulled out his phone, ignoring Nancy's head-shaking in his direction, and read from the screen:

> *Desertion in time of war is a heinous offense; failure to respond to the country's call for duty is likewise unacceptable. The objective of reconciliation of differences among our people does not require that we condone these acts. Rather, the forgiveness contemplated by this Proclamation is an act of mercy, intended to bind the nation's wounds and heal the scars of divisiveness.*

Tony looked at Walt, to see the effect of Luis's words. There was disbelief, lodged in the worry-lines running from the sides of his eyes, but there was also something else, hidden in the set of his mouth: a vision of a different life than the one he'd led for so long.

"I'm assuming you didn't know about that?" Luis said, setting his phone down.

Walt shook his head. "I heard about an offer, but didn't trust it. And then it disappeared."

"The problem," Luis said, "is that the offer was limited. You had to turn yourself in by the end of the year, before January of 1975, pledge allegiance to the country, and perform two years of community service."

"We could have done our service together," Tony joked, trying to lift the despair that had settled once again on Walt's face. "If only I'd been born then."

"Not helping," Walt said tersely.

"I bring this up both because it is astounding to me, as I sit here now, to read about a US president talking about mercy." He stopped, looking the part of an astounded man. "But also because I'm wondering if you could turn yourself in and say you never heard about the amnesty option."

"I can confirm the man doesn't even have a computer in his house," Tony offered. "It actually makes sense that he has no clue what's going on in the world."

"Still not helping," Walt said.

"The thing is," Luis continued, "even if I ignore your obstruction of justice with Sam, and even if by some miracle we can get you off the hook for desertion, the IRS might have you on their radar for tax evasion."

Nancy groaned. "That's what Nareen said."

"Nareen knew about Walt's desertion before our little chat last weekend?" Luis said testily.

Nancy nodded.

Luis rolled his eyes and clenched his fists. "Moving on," he said. "Walt, you've been hiding out here for years, using the name Walt Whitman. Am I right that you have paid no taxes, haven't applied for Social Security or Medicare?"

Walt didn't answer, but Luis, apparently assuming he was on the right path, continued. "Which must mean you've been paying him under the table, Nancy."

Nancy looked like a small animal tossed from its safe hidey-hole into the cold and unfeeling world. "It's not like I ever paid him much," she said. "Even with no damn taxes taken out, I'm guessing he can barely keep up with the rent on that little house."

"Taxes are a bitch for everyone," Luis said dismissively.

Tony wondered if that was really true. He and Caroline had accountants and lawyers to keep his taxes at bay, and ABC Toys had a small army of them. But he'd never really *thought* about taxes. Never had to wonder if, after paying taxes, he'd have enough to pay for housing. Discussions of the Occupy Wall Street movement had been purely academic, for him.

"By helping Walt avoid paying taxes," Luis continued, still speaking to Nancy, "and not paying into Social Security and such on his wages, that makes you complicit." He sighed. "And the IRS, uh, doesn't forget, and doesn't forgive. Not unless you come forward on your own, and get some kind of settlement. Your only hope is that between their 'antiquated software and chronic staffing shortages,'" he held up his fingers to show he was quoting some article or headline, "they haven't figured out that you—the real you—are alive and well and have been hanging out in Motte and Bailey, earning money all this time."

"F-fuck the IRS!" Scooter shouted, and it was so utterly odd and unexpected they all laughed, at which Scooter's face and neck and even the scalp beneath his prematurely-thinning hair turned a deep crimson.

When the laughing was done Luis said, in his tired and tiresome voice, "You do realize that without the IRS no one would pay taxes, and without taxes there'd be no schools, or roads, or firefighters, or . . . ."

"Armies," Walt said.

"I think we're getting a little far afield," Tony said, trying not to sound like he was criticizing.

"You think?" Luis said. "Look, the point is, your whole life here is a house of cards, built on the lie that you're, what, dead? Is that what you've been hanging your hat on all this time, Walt?"

Walt didn't answer, but Nancy smacked her hands on the stained and scarred table. "My uncle!" she said. "I just thought of him. He used to be the coroner all the way over to Pendleton. He maybe could make a . . . a fake death certificate, or something."

The "or something" hung in the air between them like a shimmering thread.

"Yeah, we could swear we heard he died," Scooter said.

"My sister does the taxes for the restaurant," Nancy said. "I could ask her—

"—Stop!" Luis said, his voice an unimposing screech. He stood up, banging his hip on the corner of the table so that when he grimaced it was difficult to know if it was pain or disgust that twisted his features. "I'm not listening to any more of this," he said. "Your uncle! Your sister! Does your whole family tree have some kind of genetic predisposition to lying? You're talking about perjury, falsifying records. Just stop already!"

Nancy set down her cell phone, which she had presumably taken out, hypocrisy be damned, to call or text the possibly-open-to-perjury uncle, or maybe the sister who had already been looking the other way for decades.

"This is what it comes down to, people," Luis said. "I need to focus on the drugs, and your other *crimes*," he emphasized the word as if he thought they might have forgotten that's what was at issue, "aren't relevant, which is the only reason you're all still free and not in jail. But if someone shows up to take you away, Walt, it doesn't matter if it's the military police or the IRS, there's not a damn thing I can do for you. Hell, I'm probably already in trouble, as a law enforcement official, for not reporting you myself. When this is over, we may all be sharing a cell in the hoosegow." He gave them a ghost of a smile, but no one smiled back.

He sat down again, closed his eyes, rested his elbows on the table, and held his face in the V of his hands. "I'm trying to tell you something," he said. "If you would just stop interrupting and coming up with new ways to break the law for one blessed minute. I'm trying to tell you that I did find some avenues to maybe, after all this is over, unwind everything. Officially."

"You did that for Walt?" Scooter said, sounding amazed.

"Yes," Luis said shortly. "Don't worry, Walt, I don't like you any more now than I did when we first met. But I also don't think there's any justice in you going to prison now."

"Thanks," Walt said.

"Oh go on," Nancy said, switching instantly from cowed to commanding. "He saved your bacon, Walt. At least for now. Give him a hug and make him a burger."

"I'll make him a burger if that's what he wants," Walt said, standing up again. "But it'll be an ice cold day in the lowest level of hell before I give that man a hug."

# Chapter 19

It was both easier and harder than he ever could have imagined.

Halloween came and went, with miniature lions and princesses and Darth Vaders scampering down Main Street collecting candy from all the businesses, and then spreading out to the residential areas to demand more sweets. And then, a little over a week after Roj died and Tony brought him back to life again—November first, All Saints Day, which might or might not be a good omen—Tony found himself in front of a small and tidy-looking house. The house where Libby's aunt and uncle lived. As he got out of Scooter's car (it was working again, at least temporarily) and followed Leesa and Scooter up the walkway, he noticed that, like Nancy, the owners had conceded the battle of lawn versus high desert, and had filled their yard with lava rocks. Tony stood on the front porch looking down at his feet while Leesa knocked, waiting with growing unease and wishing he could spirit himself forward to the time when he could say he'd done this thing he'd agreed to do.

The woman who opened the door was petite and trim, with short molasses-colored hair curling neatly around her face. The beginnings of wrinkles framed her eyes, even though she looked to be in her early thirties, and it seemed to Tony as if her face was used to smiling, accustomed to being warm and welcoming, though the expression in those eyes now was guarded, and weary.

"Come on in," she said.

No "Hello," no "I'm Gloria, Libby's aunt." Just "Come on in."

She led them to a small living room where her husband was already seated on a loveseat of nineties' vintage, faded navy blue with large coral-colored flowers. Rick was tall, dark-haired with light brown skin, his long legs folded awkwardly in front of him. He stood up when Tony came in, and started to extend his hand, but then dropped it to his side before Tony was within reach.

Tony, Leesa, and Scooter sat on a matching couch that formed an L with the loveseat, which meant Tony had to turn to face Gloria and Rick. On the side table between the couch and loveseat, and on the coffee table in front of the couch, there were about a dozen framed pictures of Libby. Everywhere he looked, Tony saw the dark hair and laughing eyes. Libby as an infant, ensconced in a pink blanket and balanced on a young woman's lap, staring solemnly up at the young woman's face. Libby as a toddler, wearing a garish red holiday dress and patent-leather shoes, beaming in front of a small Christmas tree that was covered with cheap-looking decorations and practically buried under a mound of gifts. Libby wearing nothing but a pair of grubby underpants, standing in someone's yard, holding a hose while the water ran over her feet, her bare belly liberally spattered with mud.

There was no introduction from Rick, either. For the entirety of Tony's life the social niceties had been observed in almost every situation, no matter how tense or unusual. It was deeply uncomfortable to be on the receiving end of an intentional decision by these two obviously decent human beings to ignore propriety and civility.

Tony had been instructed by Leesa to say one thing only, and then shut up, and he was getting pretty adept at following Leesa's instructions. "Tell me about Libby," he said.

Rick moved his long legs to one side, and then the other. "She was always worried about how other people were feeling," he said. "She once told me, 'Don't worry about me, Tío.'" He mimicked the lisping voice of a little girl. "'I won't die until I'm ready,' she told me."

Tony waited, thinking that was an odd choice for an opening anecdote.

"I was in the community center pool with her," Rick continued, "and she slipped out of my hands and someone else accidentally pushed her away from me so it took me a few seconds to reach her and grab her out of the water. She coughed and choked but she was okay, and I made her come sit with me by the side of the pool for a little while. I told her I was scared for her, and I didn't want to get back in the water right away. She sat next to me on one of those lounge chairs they have, her pigtails sticking up every which way, and she patted me on the knee, like I was the kid and she was the grown up, and she told me not to worry about her."

"That was when her mama (my sister) decided to sign her up for swimming lessons," Gloria said.

"She loved animals, every kind of animal," Rick said, continuing as if it was a list, as if the person who was Libby needed to be catalogued, like a library book, before it could be put back on the shelf.

"She cried when she found me throwing away a dead mouse we'd caught in a trap," Gloria said. "'He was hungry,' she told me. 'Why'd you have to kill him just because he was hungry?'" Gloria shook her head and gave a little laugh. "I've felt guilty about putting out traps ever since," she said.

"She liked all the things little girls like," Rick said. "Disney princesses and ice cream—though she couldn't eat very much. A lot of Latinos are lactose-intolerant, you know."

Tony didn't know, but he nodded as if he did.

"She was a good big sister to her baby brother," Gloria said. "She was just a little bit of a thing, but she lugged him around like a doll as soon as he was old enough they didn't have to worry about holding up his head or anything." Rick nodded in agreement. "But she could be a stinker to the others," she said with a smile. "I don't know if you were aware she had an older brother and sister."

Tony shook his head.

"She'd wait until they were watching TV or something, when they weren't paying attention, and she'd yank on their hair or whack 'em on the back of the head with a plastic baseball bat."

"Baseball is big around here," Rick explained, as if that was part of the story. "Pretty much every kid gets a ball and a bat for Christmas or their birthday as soon as they're big enough to stand."

"And soccer," Gloria said. "We go to church to worship God, and then we come home and worship *Iglesia Maradoniana* on TV."

"The church of Diego Maradona," Rick explained, looking a little sheepish and a little defiant all at once. "El Diego is from Argentina. He played for Argentina, and Spain, and Italy."

"Lots of people from Argentina are mad about the whole *Church of Maradona* and *El Diego* thing," Gloria pointed out. "Because of the drugs and drinking and all."

"This man didn't come here to listen to us talk about Diego," Rick said sternly, and Tony had the distinct impression Rick was shutting down heresy as much as redirecting the conversation.

"Did Libby play soccer?" Tony asked, thinking this might be an acceptable deviation from Leesa's directives.

"Of course!" Rick said.

"Even though she was only five years old," Gloria said, rolling her eyes a little.

Rick shook his head. "Old enough to know better than to chew on her toys," he said, and then suddenly it seemed they were spent, their most precious memories laid at Tony's feet.

That seemed like the right time, so Tony gave the speech he had practiced, alone, in his motel room. "There is no apology or explanation I could give that would make up for what your family went through," he said, trying but failing to look them in the eyes, "but I do want you to know how very, very sorry I am. And I want to promise you that never again on my watch will anyone at my company sign off on a toy until we know with as much certainty as anyone can have that the toy is completely safe."

He waited, and ventured again to make eye contact, and saw that there were tears in both Rick's and Gloria's eyes, though the tears stayed put, hovering on the edges of their lower lids, stubbornly refusing to spill out, lest they be the first leak in a burst dam.

"Don't expect us to forgive you," Rick said finally, his voice breaking.

Tony tried to look as if he had not come here for forgiveness. That was a lie, of course, but he was beginning to know there were some things he could not buy or order, and he was beginning to remember the lesson learned when his mother died: peace cannot be had simply by wanting it badly enough.

"But we do appreciate your coming to see us," Gloria said. "And we want you to have something." She got up and went to a massive faux-oak TV cabinet on the other side of the room. She opened the door of one of the cupboards, and pulled out a two-by-three inch unframed photo. Without a word, she returned to the loveseat, and handed it to Tony.

It was another picture of Libby. In this photo, she was wearing a beruffled pink dress and smiling that smile that took up her whole lovely face. And she was hugging a stuffed panda.

"Please promise us you will keep this picture with you, so you won't ever forget."

Tony took out his wallet, swallowing over and over again as if he could swallow his shame. He carefully slid the photo into a pocket of the wallet and said in a low voice, "I will carry it with me always."

\* \* \*

When he called her that night, Tony didn't tell Caroline about meeting Gloria and Rick. He had at least earned the right not to relive the experience, he thought.

He filled her in on the budding romance between Scooter and Leesa, and assured her that no one had threatened or mugged him lately. She told him about meeting an old friend from college. "We met for coffee," she said. "And she asked about you." Caroline breathed, audibly. "I didn't know what to say."

Didn't know what to say because she didn't want to disclose where he was, he wondered, or because she didn't want to tell an old friend that they were splitting up, the marriage the friend had witnessed floundering under the weight of the tragedy he himself had caused.

"I wonder," Tony said, and then he paused, afraid of the enormity of what might happen after he'd said the words. "I wonder if you would," he paused again.

"If I would what?" Caroline said, her words carrying curiosity across the miles.

"I would like it, very much, if you came to visit me," Tony said.

"I would like that, too," Caroline said.

\* \* \*

It felt like he was making things happen, for once, instead of letting things happen.

Within a couple of weeks after meeting with Libby's aunt and uncle, he had nudged Scooter to move the relationship with Leesa forward, asked Caroline to work with their accountant to set up a college fund for Libby's siblings (the accountant told Caroline to tell Tony that the families had already been compensated through the settlement, but Tony told Caroline to tell the accountant this was different, and she didn't ask different how, and once again Tony didn't know how to interpret her silence), and talked with Luis about how he wanted to get Roj to drop the charges against Nancy. Hadn't he, Tony, saved the man's life, he said, and shouldn't that be worth something?

He shared his plans with Nancy, and said aloud what he'd been thinking: "I'm making things happen, for once."

"What do you mean?" Nancy said, sounding skeptical, "Don't you *usually* just sit around ordering everyone around, telling them what to do? In a fancy big office in New York City?"

"Yes," he said, "but that's my job. I mostly sign papers and go to meetings. I have 'people' to make the difficult decisions for me."

And then he had an epiphany, albeit a miniscule one, something that probably should have been obvious to him long ago. "Maybe that's why Jack is finding it so easy to take control," he said, stopping in front of a half-clean table, his rag suspended in mid-air. "I'm not really necessary. The company could probably run itself in my absence. But as long as I was there, I had at least nominal authority. I was just a paper-signer and a figurehead, but no one could usurp my role. Now that I'm gone, he's free to step in and provide actual leadership in the void."

Nancy appeared to be only half-listening to his musings, but then she turned to him and asked, "Who's Jack?"

"My vice president," he said.

Maybe Nancy was prescient, or maybe it was something in his voice that tipped her off. "Is Jack trying to take over more than just your office?" she said.

"Maybe," Tony said.

"Well, it's a good thing your wife is coming out here," she said, thumping Tony on the back. "A couple of nooners'll set things straight."

Tony laughed loudly to cover the waves of desire that rolled over him at the thought of a nooner, or an any-other-timer, for that matter.

He felt even more vindicated in his optimism when Scooter took his advice, and asked Leesa to marry him, right there in Sunnyside Up.

The Closed sign was in place, and everyone except Scooter was working that day. It was a scene that had somehow become even more familiar to Tony than the ABC Toys boardroom, his living room in Manhattan, or the gracious estate where he grew up: Nancy bustling among the coffee pots, Walt scraping the grill and blasting Grateful Dead or Credence Clearwater Revival, Leesa sweeping or mopping and chattering ceaselessly about nothing in particular, Nareen sitting in a chair watching like a tired, bulbous queen overseeing her subjects, hanging around even when she was not on the schedule, because she really had no better place to be.

Scooter showed up wearing a new-ish brown sweater and truly new khaki pants, his sandy hair slicked into place, and stood just inside the door. "Leesa," he said loudly, so that everyone stopped bustling/cleaning/talking/singing along to the music, and looked at him.

Leesa frowned slightly. "What?" she said.

Scooter took a couple of steps forward, and grabbed her hands (one of which was unfortunately still holding the broom handle). "Will you marry me?" he said, and then he dropped her hands and fumbled in his pants pocket, where a slight bulge suggested he had a jewelry box with a ring (unless he was just anticipating marital bliss, Tony thought), but it turned out he had a balled-up piece of paper. Having extracted and flattened the paper, Scooter held it up to his face, and began to read.

"I love the way you smile, and laugh, and tell me what to do. I want one thing in my life and that is you. Please make me happy and say you'll say 'I do.'"

He read smoothly, and it was clear he had memorized the little poem, but it was also clear Walt had worked a minor miracle in something like two months.

"Walt helped me write the poem," Scooter said, his face colored with pleasure and embarrassment and pride.

"For God's sake, Scooter," Walt yelled from the kitchen, "don't make it sound like I wrote that tripe. You came up with the Hallmark verse, I just showed you how to spell the words."

Scooter ignored Walt (really, the only option with Walt, sometimes), and looked steadily at Leesa. Emotions played over her face, like one of those videos where the clouds rush across the sky and create a constantly changing tableau. The rest of the crew waited.

"No," she said, speaking so quietly Tony wondered whether Walt, watching from the kitchen, could have heard her answer.

"No?" Scooter said, and his entire body wavered, and Tony thought he could hear Scooter's heart breaking, an audible crack in the fabric of Scooter's being. "I thought—I thought you loved me," he said.

If Tony had tried to describe the scene to someone, he would have said it looked as though there was a volcano erupting in Leesa. There was silence for just a few seconds while the lava bubbled to the top, and then the shouting started, erupting from her mouth in a stream of words.

"I don't want to marry you!" she shouted. "Don't get me wrong," (still shouting), "I love you! I think I've loved you since we were little kids, and I just didn't know it until you kissed me!" Scooter looked joyful and appalled all at once. "But I don't want to be Lisa spelled the boring way married to Scooter who works part-time at a goddamn diner and part-time at the goddamn gas station in goddamn Motte and Bailey. I want to *do* something. Or *be* somebody."

As if frozen in place, the others could only watch.

"On *American Idol* you're always seeing someone who was nobody and then they were somebody," Leesa said. "I want to sing like an angel," (I've heard you sing, Tony thought sadly, and that's not very likely), "or write a book that wins a prize," (Do you even like to write? he wondered), "or save someone from drowning." (Where would they be drowning? Tony wondered, but then he remembered the reservoir.) "I want to get away, I want to escape. I want to be *you*," she turned to Nareen and flung the words at her, tears and desperation running together down her face.

"Leesa, you cry way too much," Nareen said, breaking the spell that seemed to be holding them all at bay. She spoke roughly, but she stood up, groaning slightly at the effort, walked to where Leesa stood, and put her hands on Leesa's shoulders, giving them a little shake. "Look at me," she said. "I'm Black, and I live in a state where nice people pretend they don't notice, as if that's the opposite of racism. I'm twenty-one years old, and pretty soon I'll have a baby but no husband, and I didn't finish college. Yet," she added, the lift of her chin daring anyone to suggest that was the end of her story. "If I was a little younger and lived in the projects with my Momma and a handful of crack-dealing brothers I'd be every neo-cons' favorite stereotype. Never mind that in Portland you're more likely to find white trash out on the farms, all that ickiness tidily tucked away out of sight of the nice neighborhoods where they may or may not have a token person of color to show how not-racist they are."

"Speaking of stereotypes," Tony said.

"I'm just saying truth," Nareen said, not letting go of Leesa's shoulders or looking at Tony. "Here's my point." She shook her head, a little of the heat going out of her voice. "You *don't* want to be me,

Leesa. *I* have enough trouble being me. I'm not going to tell you to marry Scooter and settle down in a three-bedroom house with a picket fence. I left home to get away from people telling me what to do with my life, so I'm not going to start in on you. Marry him. Don't marry him. Stay here in Motte-fucking-Bailey," (Tony noticed they all seemed to have adopted Leesa's nomenclature, as if that was the town's real name), "or move somewhere else. But don't try to be me. I'm not some patron saint of Really Living. My life is mostly the shits."

Leesa listened, looking dubious and then just defeated. Turning back to Scooter, she said, "We're happy. Why do we have to get married and change everything? Why can't we just let things be the way they are now?"

There was a long pause, and Tony could almost see Scooter searching his brain for the best response. "Because the way things are now we're running in place, or maybe even just standing still," he said at last. "And I'm tired of standing still."

Walt came out of the kitchen, wiping his hands on the greasy apron tied around his waist.

"Leesa, I'm not as nice as Nareen—" someone, Tony wasn't sure who, snorted "—so I'll tell you right now you're being an idiot. If you love the man, marry him. Marry him and go have all those adventures you want to have, but have them together. It's not an either/or proposition, you know."

Leesa glared at Walt, and then, inexplicably, at Tony. Finally, she looked at Scooter. "Fine," she said, "I'll think about it." And then she threw down the broom she'd been holding the whole time, and stormed out, dashing through the kitchen and then the back door.

"Dammit!" Nancy yelled, and Tony assumed she was referring to Leesa's ungracious response to Scooter's proposal, but then realized she was staring at the broom. "She wasn't done cleaning," she said. "I swear if that girl has one more tantrum at work, she's history."

"I'll do it," Nareen said unexpectedly. "But someone else is gonna have to get the broom up off the floor. Bending over's a bitch, these days."

# Chapter 20

Caroline arrived on the Saturday before Thanksgiving, and Tony's gladness knew no bounds.

Crackers and Jems, sitting in their usual spot at their usual time, alerted everyone else in the diner when the gleaming Lexus pulled up and parked just behind the ubiquitous sheriff's car. Tony dropped the glass he'd been about to place in the dishwasher (it didn't break, luckily), and rushed outside just as a straight-backed stony-faced man emerged. It was Pete, Caroline's driver, and Tony was fleetingly embarrassed, knowing he'd have to explain to the Sunnyside Up crew that Caroline never travelled anywhere without her driver. Pete opened the rear passenger door, and held out his hand for Caroline, before Tony could intercept the gesture.

In spite of having travelled most of the night, Caroline looked impeccable, not a hair out of place. She also looked small, misplaced, uneasy. Tony kissed her over and over, drinking in her hair, her eyes, her scent, determined to erase or maybe overwhelm the uneasiness.

"Pete got lost several times," Caroline told him, extricating herself from his embraces. "GPS doesn't seem to work out here."

"I've heard," he said, and even his commiseration sounded joyous in his own ears. "It's strange, as if we're not really part of the modern world out here."

"Except for the drug rings and murderous thugs and sex trafficking," Caroline said with a faint smile.

It didn't matter—nothing could dampen his enthusiasm.

He led her into the diner like a child leading a prize goat or lamb he'd won at the fair, and made introductions. Caroline shook hands with Nancy and Leesa, though the interchange was the very soul of awkward. Caroline was wearing black silk- and wool-blend slacks and a burgundy blouse, discreet pearls in her ears and an abalone clip holding back her hair. Her makeup was so perfectly applied it looked as though she wasn't wearing any, as if she arose each morning with unblemished skin and rosy lips. Nancy and Leesa looked positively dowdy by comparison, and everyone in the hand-shaking moment seemed to feel the comparison keenly.

Luis introduced himself, his expression intimating he understood how Caroline felt, and Tony was annoyed at the unspoken understanding that passed between the two of them. What right did Luis have to be exchanging knowing glances with his wife? Luis was a shifty-eyed baggy-pantsed detective, and he should stick to solving crimes.

After the introductions, Nancy told Tony, "Leave, go, git, vamoose, I don't want to see you here!"

"Let's go for a walk," Tony said. "It's only a few blocks, and I want to show you around. Pete can drive the car over to the motel and get settled in his own room."

Caroline agreed, and they walked the length of Main Street side by side, almost but not quite touching. Tony pointed out Tio Mio's, and Peet's Coffee (with an almost-obligatory joke about the likelihood that Caroline's driver would want to get his coffee there), the veterinary clinic where yoda-cats went to be healed, the law office with the lizard-faced man who may or may not have been an attorney, the playground at the park ringing with shouts: *You're the unicorn and I'm the fairy princess! I don't want to be a unicorn and you can't make me—I'm a frog! Ribbet Ribbet Ribbet!*

She was only staying for seven days, she told Tony later, leaving the day after Thanksgiving. The subtext was this: at the end of a week, I'll know where we are, and what I'm going to do. The unspoken moment-of-truth hung between them, and their first night together since mid-June began and ended with a chaste kiss, to Tony's intense frustration.

"Heigh ho, heigh ho, it's off to work we go," he said the next morning.

Quietly. More of a whisper than a raucous dwarfish chant.

Nancy had offered to let Tony take the week off, but Tony declined, thinking he couldn't take Caroline anywhere out of town, because of his ankle monitor, and a week of sitting in a room in a Sleepy Time Motel would probably push Caroline over the edge.

Caroline came in later, looking just as lovely, and just as uncertain, as she had the day before. At Tony's invitation, she found a place to sit and watch the morning chaos. She perched in one of the booths (Roj's booth, but of course she didn't know that, and no one thought to tell her), a bird poised to fly away should the need arise. She tried to find something to do with her hands, her eyes—Tony could see her testing, and then discarding, each action: for a little while, she read a novel she'd brought in with her; she wrote a letter in graceful cursive on monogrammed stationery; she looked at god-knows-what on her ipad (she hadn't noticed the no-cell-phones sign, and Nancy, mercifully, seemed to have decided Caroline was exempt from the rules).

She didn't speak to anyone unless spoken to.

She ordered only coffee and toast, though unlike the oh-so-annoying Luis, at least she ordered real coffee, and she had her toast with what passed for butter at Sunnyside Up, and smeared the toast with jam from the little plastic tubs that came with the toast.

It seemed to Tony, as the morning wore on, that her easy elegance ceded to the tawdriness of her surroundings, as if there had been a battle and the cheap Formica tables and worn linoleum had won.

The others moved around Caroline, watching her out of the corners of their eyes (or, in Leesa's case, staring directly at the back of her head). They were unfailingly polite but seemingly mystified about whether or how to talk to her. Tony overheard Nareen say something to Nancy about "seems nice," speaking in a low voice, as Tony was coming into the kitchen, and they both looked up when he entered, their faces drenched in guilt. Guilt about what? Tony wondered.

In between the Sunday breakfast rush and the Sunday brunch rush, Walt made Caroline an omelet with artichoke hearts and feta, and like the Grinch (*he, he himself, the Grinch, carved the Roast Beast*), personally placed the plate, somewhat roughly, on the table in front of her. She looked up, surprise and mistrust in her attractive hazel eyes, but years of good breeding stood her in good stead, and she said simply, "Thank you." After she ate, she came into the kitchen, instantly in the way of the bustling bodies around her. Walt was flipping hash browns, adjusting sausages for equal browning, and pouring pancakes onto the griddle, seemingly simultaneously, as if he had three scarred and age-pocked hands instead of two.

"Thank you," Caroline said. "That was delicious."

Walt turned his head but not his body. "Of course it was delicious," he said. "I'm a damn good cook." And then as Caroline was retreating, he added, "Manhattan doesn't have a fucking monopoly on good cooks, you know."

Tony came into the kitchen as *fucking monopoly* echoed off the greasy walls and stove hood, and he flinched. Caroline eased past him without looking at him, returned to her booth, and sat down again, curling one leg under her bottom. It looked to Tony, watching through the pass-through window, as though she had pulled an invisibility cloak around her, as if she was not just shutting down but somehow making herself *not there.*

He turned toward the stove and addressed himself to Walt's broad, bent-shouldered back, anger and fear competing in his head like squabbling siblings vying for the best seat in the car. "Don't swear at my wife!" he said, speaking loudly but not shouting, because a Gibson doesn't raise his voice in public, not even in the kitchen of a diner, not even when one is terrified that the curmudgeonly chef is going to drive away one's wife, and she will be lost to him forever.

"I swear at everybody," Walt yelled, directing his words to the impossibly fluffy and golden pancakes.

Tony made a sound of frustration, the sound of an animal that had been kicked and was not seriously injured but was quite peeved at the affront.

He went to where Caroline was sitting. "Honey," he said, "this is Roj's booth. It's—it has bad karma. You should pick another table."

Wearily, Caroline moved to the next booth. Luis's booth, Tony realized, but that was somehow not as dire. He smiled at her, and then, looking at the coffee pot in his hand, feeling the touch of divine inspiration or perhaps a more contrived *deus ex machina*, he said "Here," and he placed the coffee pot in front of her. "I could use a hand refilling coffee." He returned to the kitchen and watched, covertly, as she made the rounds at the tables, checking and filling coffee cups and promising to return with water for those who needed it. He wouldn't have said she looked comfortable in her role, but she made others comfortable with her genuine, gentle smile framed by the odd wisp of honey-brown hair escaping from the hair clip (an antique bronze clip, today).

That night, Tony slid into the miserable Sleepy Time Motel bed wearing nothing but his ankle monitor. Caroline was sitting in bed wearing a pale blue satin sheath that sat on her shoulders like royalty. She was reading, and she didn't look up when Tony joined her, or when he put his arms around her waist, shoving one arm behind the small of her back, and rested his head on her thigh. He breathed deeply, taking in the scent of the soap used to wash Caroline's clothes, the lingering odors of the diner, and the smell that was uniquely Caroline. He sniffed again, and buried his head in her lap, nuzzling through the silky material into her groin as if he was a child rejecting birth, desiring only to crawl back into the womb and leave living to braver souls.

Caroline pushed his head away.

"This isn't a situation comedy on the television," she said.

The precise articulation stopped him, *situation comedy on the television* unfurling from Caroline's mouth with an almost imperceptible trace of her mother's British accent. This was not the Gibson way, and he was surprised by her willingness to tackle their discomfort and name it rather than pretending it wasn't there.

"I'm not some confused rich socialite who will suddenly realize she loves slinging hash," she said. "We're not all going to burst into song at the end of this scene, bosom friends forever."

He lay still, willing her to finish with words of comfort, to say *but I love you and I'm glad I'm here*, or something along those lines.

"I don't like it here," she said, and Tony sat up as if he'd been shoved into place by her words. "I don't like how the restaurant smells, there are too many odors at once, and they're competing, sweet syrup and bitter coffee and savory whatever it is that Walt is making. The only tea you have is Lipton. You don't have Sugar in the Raw or organic honey. I don't like how Nancy looks at me, and I wish Scooter would stop just staring at Leesa like a lovelorn kid. And Walt is rude. Being a good cook and having had a difficult life—that doesn't excuse him from simple courtesy."

"Walt is rude," Tony agreed, cautiously. He rubbed his hands across the cheap sheets, noticing that his nascent erection had disappeared under Caroline's diatribe. "He's gruff, and sarcastic, and sometimes I think he says what he says just for the purpose of hurting people." He paused, trying desperately to think of the perfect words, the letters and phrases that, when pushed together, would make her understand, and see Motte and Bailey as he did. Would make her take back the words *I don't like it here*. "But I prefer Walt's open rudeness," he said, "over the veneer of civility of someone like Jack or the rest of the sycophantic management team. At least you know what you're getting with Walt. Jack will extend every 'simple courtesy' while stabbing you in the back."

Caroline looked at him, and it was deeply unnerving to see the sense of betrayal in her eyes. "This is not my world," she said. "I know how to deal with charming back-stabbers. I don't know what to say to a man who responds to 'Thank you' by swearing at me."

"Walt swears at everyone," Tony said, trying to block the word *charming* from his mind. "He even swears at the food as he's cooking it."

"So I've heard."

"Please," Tony said, desperation eliminating any ability he'd ever had to be articulate.

"Please what, Giles?" Caroline said, once again ignoring his request to call him Tony. "I'm here. I served coffee today. But at the end of the week I'm going home to Manhattan. I'll play bridge and attend dull board meetings and make plans to meet my parents in St. Moritz over Christmas. The only question is what will you do, when your year is up? Will you come back and pick up the reins of the company and renew your attempts to improve your golf game because it's what people like us do, or . . ." she trailed off, apparently unsure what the alternative was.

"Of course I'll come back," Tony said sullenly, thinking but not saying *if you'll let me*. "I hope I haven't left you with the impression that I'm enjoying the gracious accommodations offered by the Sleepy Time Motel, or that I've found a cultural Nirvana in Motte and Bailey. I do care about Nancy and Leesa and Scooter and Nareen, and I was hoping you'd see them for who they are." He paused, wishing he could describe *who they are*, but all the words that came to mind were insufficient. "But they're not my family," he said. "You are."

"Then why are you trying to get me to fit in? Why are you acting like *you* fit in?" Caroline said.

"I don't know," Tony said. "Maybe there's some pleasure in doing real work, washing dishes and stocking the sugar dispensers. At the end of a day at ABC Toys I'm not sure I could point to anything I've accomplished. When I'm done at Sunnyside Up, there is a stack of clean plates, and every table has sugar. Maybe I feel like I'm a more meaningful human being as Tony in Motte and Bailey, than I ever was, than I ever would be, as Giles in Manhattan."

"Giles," Caroline said, "you were sent here as a punishment, because you were so careless about your job as company president that a child died." She stopped, and Tony saw that there were tears in her eyes. "Whatever revelations you've had," she said, "whatever pleasure you've found here . . . you're forgetting the little girl. Working a menial job and trading insults with the cook doesn't bring her back, and it doesn't make up for the fact that you ruined our lives. We were happy before. *I* was happy before."

There was no answer to that, to the Truth with a capital T. Tony wasn't here to become a more meaningful anything, he was here to make atonement for his sins. Somehow he'd lost sight of that, or maybe he'd just hoped when he was through his debts would be paid in full, not only to the State of New York but to Caroline, to Libby's family, to the universe.

"That's the thing" he said finally. "That's why I want to be Tony instead of Giles. *Tony* never killed anyone. *Tony* never destroyed his marriage."

Caroline pressed her fingertips against her tear ducts, as if she could forcibly hold back the flood. "You can't be both," she said, barely audible. "You have to choose."

*I don't want to be a unicorn and you can't make me,* Tony thought. *I'm a frog!*

*Ribbet Ribbet Ribbet!*

* * *

The next day was Monday, without even the distraction of work to keep the questions at bay. Caroline joined Tony with visible reluctance on his Monday morning jaunt to Peet's Coffee for a latte and a stale butterhorn most likely purchased from Safeway by the young woman staffing Peet's. Caroline accompanied Tony to the bunker-style public library, and found (O miracle of miracles) a recently published book on Gertrude Stein, to give to Nancy so she'd know something about the woman who inspired her best friend's name, and by extension, her daughter's name. Tony leafed through Peter Nicholls' *Modernisms: A Literary Guide*, reading excerpts to Caroline in a hushed voice. "'For Stein,'" he read, "'language is to be grasped

not as a means of reference to a world of objects which can be domi-
nated, but as a medium of consciousness.'"

Caroline looked at him with mock surprise. "I never would have
taken you for a closet feminist," she said.

"I'm a man of mystery," he said, grinning.

He felt for a moment as though they were college students again,
studying together.

And after all these years, he still longed to find an excuse to put
his hand on her thigh.

They left the library without the book, having agreed that it would
do nothing to enlighten Nancy about her friend's (or her daughter's)
nomenclature. They returned to the motel with a couple of cheap pa-
perbacks, and spent the afternoon in companionable silence, reading,
together but separate.

Tony had already introduced Caroline to Tio Mio's, so they tried
the Italian restaurant, which Scooter had recommended, calling it
*the eye-talian place over on Fourth Street.* As they ate their mediocre
spaghetti, sitting in a lacquered booth and drinking cheap red wine,
he felt her cool toward him and he knew: he would not be touching
her thigh tonight, either.

* * *

Caroline had said he should go to work without her the next day.
She wanted to sleep in, she'd said, the time change was wreaking
havoc with her body clock. She thought maybe she'd take a drive
around the countryside, she'd said.

With fear nibbling at the corners of his mind, his wife breathing
softly in the lumpy, undersized bed, and nothing else to do, Tony
decided to go to work even earlier than usual. He knew he'd probably
beat Walt in, but waiting outside the diner alone was better than
waiting in his hotel room watching his wife sleep and wondering if
this was the last time, if after this week he'd never find himself in bed
beside her again.

It was late November, and the street was cold, and dark, and quiet.
The officer guarding the front of the motel was asleep in his car (fat
lot of good he was doing, Tony thought, and made a mental note to
talk to Luis). As he approached the diner, he saw a familiar figure
walking toward him. It was Nancy, but there was something wrong.

"Hey you," Tony said, echoing the greeting Leesa often used. "What are you doing here so early?"

Nancy looked to one side. "I just felt like coming in," she said, shrugging, but it was a furtive shrug, and she wouldn't meet his eyes.

He stood behind her as she unlocked the door, and realized what the something wrong was. She was disheveled. Nancy was not what anyone would call a sharp-dressed woman. She typically wore faded jeans, a worn blouse or even a sweatshirt, and black "sensible" shoes. But her clothes were always clean, and she always looked tidy. This morning, Tony could just make out in the flickering light of the spotlight over the diner's door that her blouse and jeans were rumpled, and her short hair was flattened on one side of her head. One shoe was only half tied.

And there was this: Tony had watched her walk or drive home at the end of her workday, and he knew which direction she went; this morning, she had been coming from the wrong direction.

She pushed the café door open and started to enter, but stopped when he put his hand on her shoulder.

"Nancy," he said. "Where were you coming from?"

She pushed through the doorway and turned to face him. "Roj's place," she said, looking as though there was simply no more fight left in her fiery soul.

"Roj's place," Tony said, too stunned to do anything other than repeat the words.

"Yes, Tony, Roj's place," Nancy said.

"What, are you *sleeping* with him?" he said.

Her eyes never wavered from his. "Roj holds the mortgage on this building," she said.

* * *

The rest of the day a red haze of disbelief and then, inexplicably, rage, fogged his mind. He could not have said with whom he was angry—Nancy, or Roj. Surely there had been other options besides prostituting herself to that despicable worm of a man, Tony thought. And why was Roj demanding this price from Nancy, who'd had a lifetime of trouble already, and often enough shouldered others' problems on top of her own? Had he given up preying on teenage girls?

Caroline showed up just after lunch, expounding on the beauty of the Blue Mountains, but Tony hardly acknowledged her, and she subsided after a few minutes, looking puzzled and hurt.

He dropped two glasses, one after another. He accidentally tripped Leesa, setting off a small but potent blast of profanity. Jems said *Howdy Pardner* but Tony scarcely cracked a smile, causing Crackers to say *Methinks the man has something else on his mind, could it be the fair sex?* (The two men had come in on a not-normal day, very obviously hoping to see more of Caroline.)

Tony desperately wanted to ask Walt if he was aware of the situation with Nancy and Roj, but he didn't want Nancy or Leesa to overhear.

"I have to do something after work," he told Caroline. "I'm really sorry. I'll be back at the motel as quickly as I can."

She looked at him quizzically. "Did you find out something about Sam?" she asked quietly.

"No," he said. "At least, I don't think this is related. I don't know, really. This town is ridiculously convoluted."

"Worse than New York?" Caroline said, skeptically.

"In some ways," he said. "When millions of people are engaging in outrageous conduct every day, the insanity is spread out over the whole population, a little bit everywhere. Here, the insanity is concentrated. Incestuous."

"Well, hurry back," she said, and then Tony really did take notice, allowing a tiny flower of hope to germinate. "I want to show you the photos I took," she said, and the flower blossomed and danced in a summer breeze.

* * *

When the restaurant had emptied and the cleaning and prep work were done, Tony approached Walt.

"May I come over to your place for a few minutes?" he asked.

Walt rolled his eyes. "We're not BFFs because I rescued you after you got mugged," he said.

Tony laughed, Walt's ludicrous words overcoming, momentarily, the dire emotions roiling in his gut. "I never thought I'd see the day when a short-order cook who escaped from the army used the term 'BFF.'"

"I was being ironical," Walt snapped.

"Understood," Tony said, but he was still smiling. "So, may I come see you?"

"I'll give you fifteen minutes," Walt said, glaring. "Any longer, and you're liable to be forcibly removed from the premises."

"Fine," Tony said.

\* \* \*

The little cottage was just as trim outside as Tony remembered it (Walt had even cleaned up the dead flower stalks and refreshed the pea gravel in the walkway), and just as filthy and unkempt inside. A giant soup pot with the moldering remains of what might have been chili took up most of the tiny kitchen counter. A pile of laundry of questionable vintage and cleanliness tottered on the couch. Tony looked around and wrinkled his nose, an expression that was not lost on Walt.

"I didn't know you were coming or I'd have had the housecleaner over," he sneered.

"Did you know Nancy was sleeping with Roj?" Tony asked, without preamble.

Walt stopped looking mean and angry, and just looked tired.

"I knew she used to," he said. "I didn't know she started again."

Tony was at a loss for words, and could only splutter for a second or two. Finally he said, "How? Why? Is it just because he holds the mortgage? Is he forcing her to have sex with him?"

"I don't think he's forcing her," Walt said. He looked at Tony, and shook his head, and Tony once again felt, as he so often did in Walt's presence, that he had been tried and found wanting.

"Didn't you ever wonder why she never got married?" Walt said. "She's still a fine looking woman, and she was damn attractive when she was younger. She never went to college but she's got her own kind of smarts, and she owns her own business. She's got the heart of an angel and the chutzpah of a biker chick. She could have had any number of guys in the county."

"Are you saying she's in *love* with Roj?" Tony demanded.

Walt sighed heavily. "I don't know about love. But when the first and only man you sleep with gets you pregnant, and you're only fifteen, and he says he loves you, there's some kind of bond there that . . . I don't know. It's hard to break."

Tony remembered, suddenly, how Nancy sat with Roj while they were waiting for the ambulance, even though the deputy outside could have been called in to stay with him. And he remembered when they found Sam's body in the dumpster, and Walt decided they'd bury the body rather than reporting it. Standing next to the dumpster, Nancy'd said, "I won't be any part of this," and Walt had said, "Some day you might want to take a stand." Was this why? Because she still had *feelings* for Roj?

"I think he tried to get her back into his bed when he was married—both times—and she refused him," Walt said, though he didn't explain how he knew these things. "But after his second wife died, I think she ended up with him. Once in a while. I doubt she went there after the whole thing with Sam, but maybe now, now that Luis says it wasn't Roj who killed Sam, well . . . old habits die hard."

He cuffed Tony on the shoulder, a little harder than was perhaps strictly necessary, and then he said, "Besides, you know, even us old farts have 'needs.'" He grinned, and it was disarming to see the angry lines of his grim face stretched by a smile.

"I don't begrudge Nancy intimacy," Tony said, rubbing his shoulder where Walt had hit him, "But can I just say: Ew."

"Now who's talking like a Valley Girl?" Walt taunted. "But yes, I agree, at least when it comes to sex with Roj: Ew."

# Chapter 21

Nancy had invited them all over to her house for Thanksgiving dinner. Gertie was driving down from Seattle. Walt was invited, and Scooter, Leesa, and Nareen (of course—she only had to walk down the stairs from her room over Nancy's garage). Tony and Caroline were the putative guests of honor. Even Luis had been invited. When questioned about that last one, Nancy had shrugged and said, "The man's gotta eat. Besides, maybe he'll give us an update. He's been sniffing around for months. Seems like he must have found something more by now."

"You think he's holding out on us?" Scooter said.

"Maybe," Nancy said. "But that's not why invited him. Like I said, he's gotta eat. I just figured he might as well eat turkey with us than have a candy bar alone in his hotel room."

Ah, Tony thought. Luis was just the latest stray, in need of rescuing.

The guests arrived in ones and twos, and squeezed into the kitchen, ignoring the spacious and scrupulously clean living room in favor of the chaos and camaraderie where the meal was being prepared, in the time-honored tradition of holiday guests everywhere.

Everyone except those living in temporary housing (*i.e.* a hotel) was required to contribute to the meal. Nancy provided roast turkey and mashed potatoes and made gravy from a powdered mix that came in little red and brown packets. Nareen was technically or figuratively a member of Nancy's household, so she could have gotten away with claiming credit for the turkey and mashed potatoes, but she found out Nancy liked all the middle-America traditions, so she made green bean casserole and sweet potatoes with miniature marshmallows on top. Walt hauled an enormous pot of stuffing into the kitchen, the aroma of parsley and thyme and sage and onions from his garden setting off an explosion of food lust in Tony. Leesa brought a Jell-O salad, pistachio pudding with Cool Whip and maraschino cherries and pineapple chunks. Tony was fascinated.

"What, they don't eat Ambrosia in New York?" Leesa said.

"Not that I'm aware of," he said.

An internal battle waged in Leesa's eyes: snub hometown food and sound urbane, or defend her rural roots? Jell-O won. "They're missing out," Leesa said.

Scooter brought eight packages of Hawaiian rolls.

"In case of the zombie apocalypse?" Nancy said.

"You never know," Scooter said.

Gertie arrived last, bringing with her a blast of cold air from the outside that seemed to cling to her like an aroma, or an aura. Tony studied her surreptitiously, looking for traces of Roj. Mid-thirties, short brown hair, full lips, and warm brown eyes that looked as if she was warding off worry, minute by minute. No trace of the unctuous, the disingenuous, the conniving, Tony decided. Just a younger Nancy with an added splash of angst.

In spite of assurances that he didn't need to bring anything, Luis had picked up a couple of pies. Walt growled audibly at the Safeway boxes on the counter, but since no one else had thought to address dessert, there wasn't much he could do about it.

Tony and Caroline brought a floral arrangement. It hadn't occurred to Tony to ignore the instruction not to bring anything. "You always know the right thing to do," he said to her when she suggested flowers. "I'd be lost without you." He hoped she understood that wasn't hyperbole.

Just as the noise and heat and smells in the kitchen reached critical mass, Leesa turned to Caroline and said, "Where's your driver guy?"

Caroline looked at Leesa, surprise stamped on her face. Tony stared at his feet. He'd suggested bringing Pete, but when Caroline balked, he'd let it go. He knew now what he'd felt without articulating it at the time—a truly improved Giles/Tony would have insisted, not left his wife's driver to have tamales at Tio Mios or go hungry on Thanksgiving.

"Time to eat!" Nancy bellowed, her voice blasting into their discomfort. As Tony turned to move into the dining room, she grabbed his elbow and whispered roughly, "Is her guy outside?" Tony shook his head, having seen Pete drive away after dropping them off. "Well crap," Nancy said. "He's staying at the Sleepy Time, too, right?" Tony nodded. "All right. I'll pack up some leftovers for you to bring back with you."

Once again, Nancy had saved Tony from himself.

The dining table was exactly the right size for nine people and a feast. There were jokes about needing to add a few guests so they could be the twelve disciples (Did that make Nancy their savior?), and jokes about not having enough food and maybe we should run to McDonald's for some burgers, and Nareen said she was going to have a baby in a couple of weeks so she was already eating for two and they could just leave the food at her end of the table, no need to serve her up she'd eat right from the serving platters.

Leesa and Scooter sat next to each other, and every couple of minutes, at the slightest provocation or for no reason at all, one of them touched the other, on the forearm, on the shoulder, on the hand. At one point, Tony was pretty sure (judging from the angle of his arm) Scooter was resting his hand on Leesa's thigh. Walt apparently noticed, too, and loudly asked the question on everyone's mind, with the possible exception of Luis, "So, Leesa, have you decided?"

"Not that it's any of your fucking business," she said, blushing so that her cheeks glowed pink and her freckles deepened. "But yes, we're getting hitched."

There were whoops and cheers and one *Thank god you came to your senses.* Tony looked at Leesa; unlike Mrs. Darling in *Peter Pan*, Leesa kept no box hidden in her heart, but left it all on display, all the time. Everyone in the room knew or sensed her longing for something other than *small town girl marries small town boy and has babies*, and her fear of abdicating all other future options, all other iterations of *Leesa.* He wondered whether the decision would stick, but decided it didn't matter right now, all that mattered was this instant of gladness.

"Scooter's promised he'll take me out of this middle-of-nowhere place," Leesa said, once everyone had had his or her say. The room grew quiet, as everyone realized what that would mean for Nancy. Leesa, oblivious as always, forged on. "Maybe we'll start over, kinda reinvent ourselves. Maybe we'll even use our given names," she said. "Lisa with an 'i,' and Glen."

"Glen?" Nareen said, looking at Scooter. "Your real name is Glen, but you went with Scooter?"

Scooter grimaced. "It's what I grew up with. I never really thought about using any other name."

Tony looked at Nancy, and saw that she was fighting tears, but she said only, "I'm real happy for you."

To distract them all so Nancy could cry in peace, Tony turned to Luis and said, "Any news, Mr. Detective?"

Luis shoved back his chair and folded his hands over his stomach. "That was an excellent meal," he said. "Thank you for inviting me."

"Hear hear," Tony said. "But seriously. Any news?"

"I was getting to it," Luis said, looking annoyed. "I just wanted to thank the hostess first." He unfolded his hands and placed them on the table, on either side of the plate that looked as though he'd done everything short of licking it to get the last drop of gravy. "As a matter of fact, we are very close to the end."

That could mean so many things, Tony thought. Solving the case, giving up, the end of the world as we know it.

"We've identified at least one of the contacts in town, and we think we've traced it back to one of the sources in Los Angeles," Luis said. "I'm afraid that's all I've got for now."

Nareen groaned, and they all looked at her. "Heartburn," she explained. "It's killer at this stage. Nancy warned me it'd be bad with stuffing, but I don't care. It was worth it."

"I've heard that about pregnancy," Gertie said. Her voice was rough, and throaty, like her mother's. "One of the many reasons I decided not to have kids."

"Well, that and the lack of a husband," Nancy quipped, starting to gather the dishes.

"That didn't stop you," Gertie shot back.

Nancy pressed her lips together but seemed to decide it wasn't worth continuing the fight. She carried a load into the kitchen, and then returned for more, as the rest of the guests (all except Nareen), slid their chairs away from the table and stood up to help, many of them groaning with the effort.

"We don't even have pregnancy to blame," Caroline said, after Tony'd added his own over-stuffed groan to the chorus. "We're just gluttons, we've got no excuse." It made Tony smile, to see her joining in the banter.

The others noticed, too. Leesa looked at the emerald earrings glinting demurely from Caroline's earlobes and asked where she got them. It was a noble effort, though patently ridiculous, as if Leesa was thinking she might be able to run out and buy a pair for herself, if she only knew where Caroline got them. Walt rolled his eyes at the question, but seemed to approve when Caroline said only, "Thank you. My mother gave them to me." He nodded at Caroline as he reached past her to pick up the platter with the turkey carcass. "Nice flowers," he said, and Caroline looked at him with a mixture of apprehension and gratitude but said nothing, having apparently learned already, in her short time here, that effusive expressions of emotion did not go over well with Walt. Scooter seemed to want to say something to Caroline, to confirm the impression that the Motte and Bailey residents were glad to welcome her into their fold, but gave up after staring at her shyly for a minute or so, and contented himself with reaching for her plate (accidentally hitting her in the nose with his elbow in the process, for which he apologized profusely, and she said it was fine, she wasn't hurt). Tony saw her rubbing her nose discreetly a few seconds later.

Many hands in the kitchen did not actually make light work, but after an hour or so Nancy's grandmother's china was clean and dry, and the leftovers were crammed somewhere in the refrigerator or tucked onto the back porch where the cold night air would substitute for refrigeration. Then they gathered in the living room for tea and coffee and whisky. ("Finally!" Nancy said. "You all are like a pack of vultures hanging around the kitchen when a body's trying to get stuff done!" "We should get you a red velvet rope like they have at the movie theater," Walt suggested, "to keep the riffraff out of the kitchen.")

When they were settled with their various after-dinner libations on the eclectic collection of worn couches and chairs, someone suggested they watch the game. Tony didn't know who was playing, but he knew that on Thanksgiving even in the gracious homes in Oyster Bay on Long Island families gathered around the television to watch The Game. He understood the players were essentially unimportant, it was the act of shared viewing that made it a time-honored tradition, as important as gathering around the fire to the Neanderthals, a communion of shared experience and expectations. But Nancy put the kibosh on the idea, saying there was no television. Her parents had one, she explained, but she'd put it in storage the last time they went gallivanting off to Florida.

"As far as I can see, there's nothing but a bunch of bull-crap to watch," she said. "Sorry, Tony."

Caroline looked at him quizzically. "I seem to have become the profanity police," he told her. "I'm not quite sure why."

"You must have some pretty virgin ears," Gertie said, "if 'bull-crap' gets you all in a tizzy."

"It doesn't," Tony said, a little stiffly. "I didn't ask Nancy to apologize."

Walt tried to press Luis for more details on what he'd found so far, but Luis excused himself and said he thought he'd serve the pie. Walt snorted at the word 'pie,' as if something from the grocery store could ever qualify, but he made the mistake of snorting and taking a sip of whisky at the same time and spent the next few minutes coughing and spluttering, while Nancy thumped him ineffectually but sympathetically on the back, and Leesa asked, grinning, if he needed Tony to give him the Kiss of Life like he gave Roj.

Once again, Caroline looked at him with questions in her eyes.

"Didn't he tell you?" Leesa said. "Our Tony's a regular hero around here. Roj nearly choked to death, and your hubby gave him mouth-to-mouth. Brought him right back from the dead."

"Did you?' Caroline said, and it was unclear, perhaps even to her, whether it was respect or revulsion that tinged her voice.

"Of course if it'd been up to me," Leesa said, "I'd have let him die a slow, painful death, rolling around on the floor, foaming at the mouth and begging for mercy." And then she added, in case there was any doubt, "Pigs would fly out of my ass before my lips would touch his."

"Don't you think that's a little harsh?" Nancy said. Walt had stopped coughing but she continued to rub his back in a circular motion, as if comforting herself and Walt at the same time.

They all looked at her then, the woman who had been induced, at the age of fifteen, to have sex with a man more than twice her age, who had been the victim of his manipulations and sleazy machinations ever since, and whose child, having been conceived from that unholy union, had grown up without any of the benefits Roj could easily have bestowed. Tony remembered vividly the moment Nancy poured hot coffee on Roj, and had to be restrained from smashing the empty pot on his head when the coffee was gone. And here she stood, invoking decency and calling for pity for that same man, a man with whom she had apparently resumed what used to be quaintly called "relations."

"Oh my god," Gertie said, glaring at her mother.

"What?" Nancy said, glaring back.

"You're sleeping with him again, aren't you?"

Nancy said nothing, just stood beside Walt, her hand resting on his shoulder now.

"You're insane," Gertie said. "And I'm done." She stood up, looked around the room, and said, "Tony and Caroline, nice to meet you. You too, Nareen. Good luck with the baby. Scooter and Leesa, I'm real happy for you. Walt, try'n slap some sense into my mom, won't you?" She skirted the coffee table and walked through the arched opening to the front door, lifted her jacket from the coat tree staggering under the weight of multiple parkas and other winter wear, and then turned to face them again. "Mom," she said, "don't call me. You make me sick."

Just then Luis appeared in the doorway from the kitchen, holding a tray. "Pie, anyone?" he said.

\* \* \*

After they returned to the motel, and dropped off the leftovers with Pete ("surprised" and "grateful" were inadequate to describe the look in Pete's eyes), Tony and Caroline sat in bed and watched television. Tony felt vaguely guilty, not only for enjoying the "bull-crap" Nancy had so correctly called out, but also because by unspoken agreement they refrained from talking about anything substantive. Anything that mattered. *But it's so pleasant to pass the time this way*, Tony thought, recognizing the slight petulance in his inner voice.

They scrolled through the news, and watched the last half hour of *It's a Wonderful Life* (a Thanksgiving requirement, for Caroline, and Tony wondered whether missing the full movie this year would be added to the list of his offenses, in her mind). After the last swelling chord of "Auld Lang Syne," they channel-hopped again, and the television froze on one of the Spanish stations. Caroline translated a few sentences, calling on her high school Spanish classes, though she quickly lost the thread, the words slipping through the crevices of her memory.

"I think he might have just said something about hamsters and pizza," she said, laughing.

"Not on my watch," Tony said. "Any hamster that comes sniffing around my pizza will have me to answer to. A fight to the death."

"A duel for pride and pepperoni?" she asked.

"Not a pacifist where peppers are concerned," he said.

"An activist for anchovies. I can get behind that," she said, and they laughed again, together.

Laughing. Talking about tailless rodents. Ignoring ugliness and uncomfortable truths and unnamed fears, as if by pretending they didn't exist one could unmake them. This was the Gibson way. Or maybe it was simply exhaustion, the weariness that comes from prolonged grappling with intractable problems, and the aching unknowability of the future. Nancy's inexplicable feelings for Roj and Gertie's rage at her mother, Walt's terror of being court-martialed, Leesa's fear of being trapped, Nareen's anxiety about adulthood and parenthood, Sam's death. And, of course, their own relationship.

It was all too much, really.

So he was surprised, and deeply, deeply glad, when Caroline rolled over, later, in the close darkness, and wrapped her slender, smooth arm around Tony, and slid her soft hand down his belly, moving with easy grace over the familiar territory, the dips and concaves of his body, known to her from years of exploration and re-exploration, and touched that seat of longing that had been deemed untouchable for what seemed like an eternity. Possibly two eternities.

They made love, and then, after a while they made love again, and Tony wondered, listening to Caroline's breathing grow softer and steadier as she slid into sleep, whether it was a welcome back lovemaking, or a goodbye lovemaking.

# Poached

The predawn darkness feels abandoned, as Tony walks through the town, having slipped out while Caroline was still sleeping. This is not the quiet of a big city before the earliest of the morning commuters fill the streets with the sounds of motors and heels clacking on the sidewalk and automobiles honking and shopkeepers opening their stores and garbage trucks with their infernal beeping, nor is it the quiet of the farm, before the cows begin to low and the sheep begin to—whatever it is sheep do. Baa? Is that what it's called, Tony wonders. How has he reached the age of thirty-five without knowing how to describe the sound sheep make? Clearly, his parents read him the wrong sorts of books and sang him the wrong sorts of songs when he was a child.

It seems a grievous error, suddenly, like the failure to teach him how to say *I love you* and *Don't go*.

He has loosed the bonds of all ties, for a time. The deputy stationed outside the main entrance to the Sleepy Time Motel is once again asleep in the unmarked patrol car, his face mashed against the driver's side window, a faint snoring audible even from the street. It is eerie, passing the vacant shops and shuttered houses, seeing no one, hearing nothing. Perhaps he has imagined everything—the people in the town, and their lives of mystery and drama. Or perhaps he has been living for the last nearly six months in a television show—*The Twilight Zone*, or maybe *The Truman Show*. He pulls out his wallet, and finds the photo of Libby, and looks at her face again as he has done every day since Rick and Gloria gave it to him. She steadies him, as surely as an anchor holds a ship while its crew rests, before they must again put hand to line and tiller and guide the vessel to its destination.

She is real. The people in the town are real. This is not a made-up journey in a carefully-scripted life. And he realizes once again, as if it's a fresh and new idea rather than something he has to keep learning, that he's just not that important. What happens to him is, quite simply, not significant enough that others would be orchestrating it. He's stuck in this life muddling along like everyone else, one splash of paint on a massive canvas, one word in a script of monumental proportions.

He feels a little sorrow but mostly relief. There is an enormous, heady freedom in being a small, anonymous part of something bigger.

But also, weirdly, a sense of responsibility. If he's only one drop (one drip?) in the painting, he'd better make sure his drop is right. It's not just Libby's death, or Sam's death, it's Nancy trapped in Roj's manipulations, and Walt barricaded against intimacy, and Leesa flailing around searching for meaning and purpose but never actually confronting the search—somehow their lives and his own have melded to form a highway sign or maybe just a fortune-cookie revelation: there is darkness in inertia, and evil in standing still when action is called for.

He turns back, then, suddenly anxious to wake Caroline in spite of the hour and tell her what he's discovered, to see if she will go with him into the unknown, take that leap into being Nobody In Particular but accountable for being the best damn Nobody you can be. Will she believe him? (Or will she just say *Can't it wait until it's properly morning?*)

And if she doesn't, what then?

Is it his job to convince her?

Is it ever anyone's job to convince anyone else?

As he rounds the corner, stepping up the pace a little, eager to get on with it, to prove to the universe that he's learned his lesson and he's brave enough to take whatever comes next, with or without Caroline (but oh how he hopes it's with Caroline), he looks up, and sees two men sitting on a low wall in front of someone's yard. They are sitting next to a Pontiac Firebird, of all things, a bright metallic blue car with a ridiculous bird image painted on its hood. Its passenger-side door is open, and Tony is momentarily distracted by the automobile, until his brain registers the sight of the two men.

One of them is the bull-headed man he saw in the Urgent Care Clinic.

Bull-Man looks up just as recognition dawns. What an apt phrase, Tony thinks. Walking the streets of Motte and Bailey as dawn breaks over the town, and *recognition dawns*. Bull-Man appears to recognize Tony at the same time, and he elbows the man sitting next to him, and grunts, also an oh-so-appropriate sound, Tony thinks, and the two men stand up in one surprisingly graceful motion, and Tony knows he should run, but the impulse seems to be stuck in his brain, traveling with agonizing sloth through his neural pathways, down his spinal cord, and into his legs, so that by the time he moves his feet to escape, the smaller man is hitting him over the head with something—a baseball bat? How common! How gauche!—and there is pain, but only for a second, until there is darkness, and the last of his thoughts flutters gently into the void.

# Chapter 22

It's amazing what you can know without seeing. It's not just the sense of smell, or hearing; it's as if your whole body becomes a vibrating tool, complete with echo-location like a bat, canine olfactory glands, and an almost absurdly heightened tactile awareness.

Tony smelled dust, the kind that comes from the rich red clay soil in the fertile valley at the foot of the Blue Mountains, an odor he'd grown accustomed to without realizing it. There was another smell, mixed in, and his brain locked onto "agricultural chemical," though where he would have come into contact with such a thing so as to recognize it by smell alone, he could not have said.

He heard whispers floating upward, getting entangled overhead, lost among what he assumed were the rafters of the building he was in. The sound carried in a way that wouldn't be possible in a home or an office building, a sound unique to the warehouses he visited several times a year in his role as company president, to let "his" people know that he, the president of ABC Toys, cared.

After being hit with a bat (a fact which still rankled), he'd regained consciousness to find himself tied to a chair and blindfolded. His initial panic gave way to an odd kind of peace because, he reasoned, that was the only option open to him, and that's when his other senses took over.

Across the hours that seemed like miniature eons, he heard three distinct voices, all male, each speaking in a slightly different key as if singing harmony to a central tune.

As he sat in what his spine and fingers told him was a metal folding chair, he could feel cold cement beneath his feet, through his socks and his shoes. Every so often, a massive-sounding furnace would roar into life, and there would be a rush of air, mixing the smells and the sounds and temporarily confusing his nose, his ears, his skin.

His captors had not, thus far, been cruel to him, for which Tony was overwhelmingly, embarrassingly grateful. He and Caroline were fond of James Bond movies, and every time they watched Double O Seven, he thought to himself that it was a good thing he wasn't a spy, because he'd crumble under the slightest pressure. Hell, he'd once said to Caroline, I'd never survive a minute of torture, a hangnail keeps me awake at night; and Caroline had laughed, and he had been glad she wasn't ashamed to be married to someone as not-spy-worthy as he.

Five times since coming to and finding himself tied to a chair, a paper plate had been set on his lap, with food. The first couple of times it was a plain piece of bread, an apple, and some rubbery cheese-ish slices that Tony took to be American cheese, and his hands were released (but not his feet), so he could feed himself. Yesterday, there was a piece of cold, greasy pizza that recalled as if from the distant past the hamsters-and-pizza conversation, and Tony choked, and then vomited, and one of the nameless captors swore at him. After each meal, someone handed Tony a plastic water bottle with the stale, slightly metallic-tasting water he had come to know as the product of Motte and Bailey taps.

And every few hours, one of the three Voices spoke to him, told him they were going to untie him, not to try anything funny (a good Groucho Marx joke would not go amiss, Tony thought), so he could go to the bathroom. Then someone would lead him to a restroom, and he would walk almost sure-footedly, because he could tell they were in an empty warehouse, and he now knew it took twenty-one of his steps to walk from the chair where he was imprisoned to the place, somewhere along one of the outer walls of the warehouse, where there was a restroom with multiple stalls (he could tell by the tinny-clang of the door behind him, and the proximity of the metal walls on either side of the toilet). He hadn't had a bowel movement yet, but he knew that was coming, and the thought was the source of some anxiety, crowding out other thoughts, thoughts of whether he was going to die here in this warehouse, and whether it would hurt.

And twice since having his head clonked and passing out and coming to and finding himself blindfolded and bound, someone released him from the chair and led him to a hard mat with a rough wool blanket and a musty pillow that appeared to be down, from the feel of it, though a down pillow that had seen better days, perhaps even better decades, and then someone tied one of his ankles to some kind of metal pipe running vertically up from the floor, a pipe he could feel with his foot when he moved it.

So he could sleep.

In short, the various messages tapping at his brain like Morse code told him he had been kidnapped about forty-eight hours ago, and transported (probably in the preposterous Pontiac), to an empty warehouse that housed or used to house agricultural supplies, located in Motte and Bailey or very close to it.

Wouldn't an abandoned warehouse be the first place the police would look? he thought. That's where the SWAT team always started in the movies. He was surprised, quite frankly, at his captors' lack of creativity, holding him in the same place all the other thugs and criminals hid their captives.

And then he wondered if anyone would even be looking for him. Caroline had given him an ultimatum: be Giles when your sentence is up, or be Tony and we are no longer *we*. Silly bantering and (beautiful, beautiful) lovemaking aside, there had been no obvious change of heart. She'd thrown down the gauntlet, and he had missed his chance to give her an answer. He'd been kidnapped Friday morning, she had a ticket to fly back to New York Friday night, and by now she was home, living her life, the life he used to share with her.

Of course, it was Luis's job to solve crimes, including investigating the kidnapping of a company-president-turned-convict, but certainly there was no love lost between him and Luis.

Walt seemed to think he was an annoyance at best. Nancy would worry, he was pretty sure of that, but he had been nothing but trouble for her, and perhaps she'd decide, guiltily, that it was good riddance.

Would Nareen care? Or Scooter? Or Leesa?

It is harder, maybe, when you are a company president used to living in Manhattan and all the *yes sirs* a man could want, to see that you are not the star of your own show, to realize you are not even the protagonist of the particular play you're in at the moment. Then again, realizing your own insignificance could be very liberating, as he'd noticed just before being kidnapped.

At least until you understand it means no one will come after you when you go missing.

He had a brief, wild burst of hope when he remembered his ankle monitor. Aha! he thought. Oho! Surely Luis would undertake the minimal effort of tracking him down with the monitor. And then he realized he could no longer feel the monitor rubbing against his bony leg. Someone had managed to remove it, or cut it off, while he was unconscious. His tether to Motte and Bailey, severed.

Two days should have been an eternity. Tony would have expected to feel restless, would have expected that boredom and fear and physical discomfort would paralyze all rational thought. Instead, deprived of sight, and relieved of all burdens and obligations other than the requirement to sit in a chair and think of anything except death, Tony found himself almost (but not quite) content.

At one point he heard one of his captors whisper something about ransom, and another voice respond that it wasn't worth the risk, and a bullet to the head was the ticket.

The ticket to what? Tony thought. A ticket to the movies would be nice. Or how about an airplane ticket home? That would be perfectly lovely, thank you very much.

There were other conversations, too. It sounded as though his captors had given up hunting him down long before Thanksgiving, but when he showed up out of nowhere at dawn on Friday morning, they made an extemporaneous decision. It also sounded as though at least one of the Voices was angry about the kidnapping. There was a terse *What the hell were you playing at?* and a *What are we supposed to do with him now?*, and something that sounded like an attempt at an explanation. Tony gleaned that there had been a vague plan, some time ago, to use him as a distraction, to throw the police off what one man called "the scent," and also to make some extra cash, because they had found out he was "filthy rich." They spoke as if referring to a seasonal lemonade stand, or a side job delivering pizza. The kind of thing one does (if one is not "filthy rich") to make ends meet: kidnap a wealthy man, and demand ransom.

Tony knew he should listen to their conversations carefully, to determine whether there were any clues to his whereabouts, and a possible way out, but he also knew he wasn't terribly clever in this regard. He was the ultimate Winne the Pooh when it came to nefarious schemes. Give him an international negotiation over the price of cotton batting and he could hold his own, but now he could only sit and think, a bear of very little brain. Nothing in his life so far had equipped him to hatch an escape plan after being kidnapped and tied up in a warehouse in rural Oregon. So he didn't try to analyze their conversations, just waited and was humbly grateful when they brought him food, and metallic-tasting water, and led him to the bathroom to relieve himself, or to the mat, to sleep.

On what he determined might be Sunday (it was difficult to be sure), Tony woke up with the kind of revelation that, perhaps, comes only to a blindfolded kidnapping victim: he had to try to escape. Maybe it was true that nobody cared, maybe it was true that he'd wasted every opportunity in his life thus far to be someone worth rescuing, but if so that was all the more reason for him to fight for the chance, now, to change.

And so as he was led away from the mat for his morning pee he tried to orient himself, to see if he could sense where the warehouse door might be. He allowed himself to stumble a little against the captor who was leading him to the bathroom, to ascertain how large or small, muscular or weak, this particular person was, and whether he would succeed in a fistfight. Afterward, as his legs were once again being tied to the chair, he made them twitch slightly, hoping to create space for sliding his bony feet out of the ropes. His inadequacy at each of these tasks, his shortcomings vis-à-vis heroism, nearly overwhelmed him. Nearly, but not entirely. He had no reserve of Zen, no ability to say ah well if it's my time it's my time, but what he did have was a determination not to take the easy way, not if trying meant somebody somewhere would be glad he was born, would find his or her or their load lighter, by whatever miniscule margin.

Sitting in the hard, hard chair, surreptitiously moving his legs up and down and trying to come up with a plan, he heard a sound, faintly, wafting from somewhere outside the warehouse. His head still hurt where they had hit him, and he couldn't be certain he wasn't imagining the sounds. He wondered if he had a concussion, or if his brain was swelling inside his skull. Maybe he'd die from brain-swelling, and they wouldn't have to use that ticket they'd referenced.

All things being equal, he thought, I'd prefer to die from a swollen brain than from a bullet. People die of brain swelling all the time. A gunshot seemed so messy, so ignominious. A statement, once again, that he was expendable.

Then he heard the faint sounds again, only they were louder, and as his extraordinarily-sensitive but likely fatally-swelling brain sorted through the sounds, he recognized a dog barking. Almost before he could process that sound, the Voices inside the warehouse yelled *Get the car* and *There's no time* and *We have to shoot him now,* and then there was the sound that could only be a massive bay door being slid on its tracks to one side, and more voices shouting, and footsteps on the concrete floor, the footsteps and shouts and grunts tangling in mid-air until they were silenced by the one sound Tony had been dreading most of all, a gunshot.

Tony waited for pain, or death, but instead he felt someone cutting through the ropes binding his hands, and then his feet, and roughly removing the blindfold. The sudden light and relief from the pressure on his eyes made him almost blind, temporarily, but he recognized the voice saying, "Get up, Tony."

It was Luis.

As his vision cleared, Tony looked around. He was in a warehouse, just as he had surmised. Bull-Man lay on the floor, not too far from where Tony stood, blinking. There was a puddle of blood around Bull-Man's head, and Tony was momentarily mesmerized by the bright, almost cheerful color forming a halo around the large head. There were officers in bullet-proof vests sweeping through the warehouse, presumably to see if anyone was hiding, and other officers applying handcuffs to the two men who had not been shot. Tony thought at first that one of his captors was Roj, but almost immediately realized he'd fallen prey to the same mistake as before; it was Roj's cousin Joey who was being cuffed, not Roj. Tony could hear the officers giving the Miranda warning to Joey and the other not-dead man, even as another officer picked up a gun that Bull-Man had apparently been holding when he was shot, crouched beside the body, and confirmed that Bull-Man was dead. And then there was an alarmingly hairy face, and two heavy paws on his shoulders, and a somewhat putrid-smelling tongue was applied to his cheeks, his nose, and his right ear.

"The dog helped us find you," Luis told Tony. "I think its name is Iced Tea or something."

"Lipton!" Tony said, genuinely pleased to see her, if not necessarily pleased with her ministrations to his face. She wagged her tail and returned all four paws to the ground, apparently satisfied that he was unharmed.

Another officer appeared at the open door on the far side of the warehouse, through which the mid-morning sunlight was pouring as if anxious to fill the dark building with light. Following closely behind, looking more miserable (and therefore more human) than Tony had ever seen him, was Roj.

Roj was also handcuffed, and Tony gathered from the muted conversation between Luis and another officer that they had brought Roj along in case their search was successful, because they believed he might be useful in the aftermath. "Let's see if he can get '*Cuz*' Joey to talk," one of the officers said now.

Luis said, "Tony, I'll take you back to the motel in a few minutes, but we need to question Joey right away, so you'll have to wait a little while longer. I'm sorry."

Tony was touched by the apology. As if his feelings, his desire to return to whatever passed for normalcy at this point in his life, mattered. "I'm fine," he told Luis. "But if you don't mind, I'd rather go back to Sunnyside Up." There would be nothing for him, he knew, at the Sleepy Time Motel. Caroline was gone, and the thought of sleeping in the empty bed, stripped clean of her scent with the changing of the sheets, in a room barren of all sounds except perhaps the television and the occasional car passing in the street below, was unbearable.

Luis nodded, and then turned to the task at hand.

The warehouse, though clearly unused at this time, was not completely empty. There were folding chairs set up in a small circle a short distance from the chair and the mattress where Tony had spent the last two days. One officer directed the handcuffed Joey and Roj to sit facing each other, while another led the nameless not-dead captor outside. Miranda warnings were repeated, and Joey did not seem inclined to provide any information. Tony heard Joey say "Yeah, I choose to remain silent," and demand to call his lawyer, but then Roj spoke.

"You had my son killed?" he said to Joey. Five words, five tiny words, none of them even of the twenty-five cent variety, three to six letters each, nothing you'd find on a high school vocabulary test. Five words that broke through the other sounds echoing through the warehouse, and stilled, momentarily, all other movement.

"He was a liability," Joey said, and his voice was gruff, and simultaneously pleading. "He knew everything, and he stopped using. We couldn't control him if he wasn't using. You know that."

"You killed my son," Roj said, and the subtle shift was not lost on

Tony, the change from having someone killed to killing him.

* * *

If there's anything nicer than receiving a hero's welcome after being kidnapped and thinking no one would even care enough to look
for you, Tony couldn't imagine what it might be. Leesa hugged him,
Nareen hugged him, turning sideways because she could no longer
reach her arms past the protuberance of her belly and around Tony's
body, Nancy hugged him fiercely, Scooter shook his hand so vigorously it hurt a little, and even Walt clapped him on the shoulder awkwardly and thanked him for not dying.

But it was Caroline's tears of joy and kisses of relief that made
him so deeply glad he'd missed that bullet-to-the-head ticket. She
jumped up from the corner table, where she had been sitting before
he arrived, and threw her arms around his neck and whispered that
she'd cancelled her flight when he disappeared, and she said I love
you, I thought I'd lost you. He said I love you back, over and over, as
if it was a mantra to ward off any more hurt. And he told her there
was something else he needed to say, but it would have to wait until
later, and she said that was okay, she had something she wanted to
tell him, too, but she just wanted to hug and kiss him for now.

Everyone started talking at once, after that. Leesa said they'd
all been trying to help Luis find him since the day he disappeared,
and she told Luis she didn't understand why they were so stupid and
couldn't just track Tony using his ankle monitor thingy and that's
when Luis said the monitor didn't really work, the sheriff's office told
him, privately, they hadn't figured out a way to make the monitor
track anything short of house-arrest, so they just *told* Tony he couldn't
go more than five miles from the Sleepy Time Motel. Tony was astounded: all the care he'd taken never to exceed his restrictions, and
the whole time it had been a ruse, a lie to keep him in Motte and Bailey and prevent him from running away to . . . Pendleton? Spokane?
Where would he have gone, if he had known the ankle monitor didn't
work?

Nancy had closed the restaurant when Tony disappeared, she told
him. Walt jumped in and pointed out, lest Tony miss the significance,
that it was the first time he'd seen it closed on a not-Monday in over
twenty years. Jems said they saw the Closed For Emergency note on

the door and they went right to Nancy's house and told her she had to open the restaurant just for people who wanted to help find Tony, so she did, though not 'til Sunday, which made no sense to him, he said, but Crackers took over the story and said Well, you know, she was distraught. He explained that he and Jems had told Nancy she should get that shifty-eyed Mex—that detective guy to use Lipton to find Tony, because Lipton and Tony, they had a special bond. (And Tony was amazed, that a dog had formed a special bond with him and he hadn't had to do anything to earn it.) Of course, Crackers said, Lipton had no formal training as a tracking dog, but she figured it out anyway.

"We took her to the closest warehouse outside of town," Luis said, sounding somewhat exasperated. "The plan was to check each of the warehouses, moving in a circle from Motte and Bailey. We'd made the plan already, and we were just waiting for the SWAT team, when these two offered their dog. I'm not a fan of untrained animals," he added. "And she almost ruined everything. She started barking as soon as we got out of the car."

Tony wanted to protest that he was glad to think she'd found him, but decided that might sound dismissive of Luis's efforts, the careful planning on his behalf. "Thank you for rescuing me," he said to Luis, who nodded, curtly.

Turning to Crackers and Jems, he said, "Please give Lipton an extra pat on the head from me. I am so grateful."

Crackers smiled and Jems slapped his hand on his knee and said, "I never woulda thought you'd be a dog-person, but the world's just full of surprises, ain't it?"

"The world's just full of surprises," Tony agreed.

As if to prove his point, Tony looked up and noticed Caroline's driver, Pete, sitting in a corner booth. Here indeed was another surprise, a living, breathing demonstration that, perhaps, Motte and Bailey was working its magic on Caroline, too.

Everyone clamored for more information, and Luis explained what had happened at the warehouse. After enduring a barrage of questions, he said the investigation was far from over, but with the kidnapping and what amounted to a confession from Joey, they were a hell of a lot closer. He told them the task force had identified what they were pretty sure were the key players in the drug ring, at least on this end of the line, and he was reasonably confident they had enough evidence for a conviction of Roj, Joey, and the other two men (whose names were Marco and Carl, though no one at Sunnyside Up seemed terribly interested in them).

"So how did Sam's body end up in my dumpster?" Nancy asked, curiosity and fear vibrating on conflicting frequencies in her words.

"Roj claims he never knew you'd left Sam on his porch," Luis said. "He said he went downstairs when you were hollering and making a fuss (his words, not mine), then he looked through the front window and saw you get in your car and drive away, and he figured your hissy fit was over, so he went back to bed." He looked searchingly at Nancy. "It looks like he was telling the truth, for once, when he was asking around, trying to figure out where Sam was."

"Meaning you were right when you said Roj didn't kill him, or even just . . . leave him on the porch to die," Nancy said.

And Walt said quietly what no one else would have dared to say: "You're setting the bar pretty low if you give the man a pass just because he didn't murder his own son."

Nancy looked at her feet and nodded, almost imperceptibly. "I've never stopped hating him, you know," she said. "I just couldn't stay away, somehow."

After a moment of silence to honor the age-old admission of loathing that masked itself in yearning, Leesa said, "But you still haven't told us how Sam's body ended up in the dumpster."

"We haven't completely pinned that down," Luis said, "since everyone clammed up after Joey and Roj's conversation at the warehouse. But here's what we think happened: when you showed up at Sam's house, Nancy, and tried to rescue him, Joey's men were probably watching the house. They would have been worried you'd spoil the plan, so they would have followed you, and as soon as you left Roj's house, we think they grabbed Sam and took him to the diner, and left him in the dumpster."

"Do you think he was still alive when they threw him away?" Leesa said.

As one, they looked at Luis, willing him to say no, to say Sam hadn't suffered the ultimate humiliation, hadn't languished in pain, alone, amongst the refuse. He shook his head. "I don't know," he said.

Weariness descended on Tony suddenly, inexorably, falling like a heavy curtain descends upon a stage, signaling the end of a dark play or a lugubrious symphony piece played by oboe and bass and mournful French horn.

"I'd like to go back to the motel now," he said.

"That's fine," Luis said, "but you all need to know we're not done here. There's still the issue of your obstruction of the investigation."

Leesa opened her mouth to protest, and Nancy made a noise that was a cross between a squeak and a sigh. Walt managed to look simultaneously thunderous and terrified. Nareen lifted her finger in obvious preparation for unleashing on Luis, and then she stopped, and put a hand on her ample belly, and said, "Ow."

"Not again!" Luis said. "Don't you think it's a little lame to keep using your pregnancy to get your friends out of trouble?"

Nareen didn't look at him, didn't even appear to have heard him. She groaned, a low, guttural, animal sound.

"Oh for the love of . . . " Luis said. He went to the door and shouted for the nearest officer, and when he appeared—the same irritable-looking young man who had helped Tony with his laundry—Luis told him to take Nareen to the hospital.

"We're coming too," Nancy said.

"All of us," Scooter said.

"Including us," Caroline said, and the others turned to her with astonishment written on their faces. "Unless you're too tired, Giles," she said, and then she smiled, shyly, and added, "I mean, Tony."

"Plenty of time to sleep when I'm dead," Tony said, misquoting Benjamin Franklin (and hoping the venerable Franklin wouldn't have minded too much, under the circumstances).

"Tony can come with me, and I can fit one more in my car, as long as one of you doesn't mind sitting up front with the driver," Caroline said. "With Pete, I mean."

Pete nodded.

"I've got my car here, too," Nancy said.

"Could you all play musical cars later?" Nareen said through gritted teeth, hunched over and clutching her stomach with both hands now. "I need to go. Now."

The caravan of cars traveled through Motte and Bailey, led by the police car with lights flashing and sirens blaring. They passed the boarded-up theater, the drug store, Tio Mio's, the law offices, the sundries shop ("Trish's Place"), Peet's Coffee, McDonald's. They drove through the small suburb where Nancy and Gloria and Rick lived, and

Tony watched as the modest houses ceded to farms, yellowed early winter yards giving way to brown early winter fields. He absorbed the sensations so long missing from his daily life, the smooth leather upholstery, the sound of Miles Davis gently playing in the background, the soft air, heated to exactly seventy-two degrees, and he thought to himself that an ancient Ford truck was an interesting adventure but, given the choice, it seemed likely he'd take the Lexus.

He imagined he wasn't alone in that. Walt would probably choose luxury and comfort, too, if he had the option. Certainly Leesa and Scooter would enjoy a little opulence, he thought. Maybe even Nancy would go for it, if no one else would be the poorer for it, if she could have her cake and eat it too, and no one would go without, because of her.

Or maybe she'd still choose the cherry red Chevy truck with the shiny chrome hub caps.

# Chapter 23

At the hospital, Tony felt again how superfluous he was. Nareen was admitted right away, identified by the intake nurse as clearly being in labor even though her due date was still nearly two weeks away. Nancy was allowed to remain with Nareen in the hospital room, but all others were ordered out. "I'm not spreading my legs and airing my hooha to the world with you all in the room," Nareen said angrily, between contractions. "Get out!"

Luis left, but not before warning Tony that everyone needed to be at work on Tuesday so they could discuss "what comes next."

Caroline offered to call Nareen's mother, but Nareen said she'd already texted, on the way to the hospital. Tony was surprised at the offer, but Caroline said, "It doesn't matter how independent you're trying to be, you want your mom when you're having a baby." Tony was mystified that she would know this, but chalked it up to innate feminine knowledge.

Walt paced the floor and muttered bits of poetry, speckled with profanity. Over the din that is seemingly requisite in every hospital waiting room Tony could just make out, "'Keep your face always toward the sunshine, and shadows will fall away'—fuck, that's not right—'shadows will move behind'—fuckity fuck fuck."

Scooter and Leesa sat on a sort of divan, holding hands and touching knees and talking in low voices, their faces bright with the thought that someday it could be Leesa in that room, having their baby.

Tony lay down on a row of hard plastic chairs next to the two of them, and slept.

When he woke up, there was a puddle of drool beneath his left cheek and his breath smelled like some vile combination of dead fish and used diaper. *Eau de Poissons Morts.* He wiped away the drool with his hand and asked Leesa how long he'd been asleep, and where Caroline was.

"Dude," she said, "your breath smells like dead fish."

"You've been out for like three hours," Scooter offered. "I think your wife went to get coffee."

"Nareen's mom is here," Leesa said, "and so is her grandpa and her boyfriend. They just got here. I guess Nareen's family has a friend with a private plane, and he flew them here."

In spite of the lingering exhaustion that colored his world in a gray haze, Tony was curious to meet the others in Nareen's life, the people who knew her "BMB," as Leesa put it (Before Motte and Bailey).

Another few more hours of waiting, kept upright by hospital coffee and sandwiches, until finally everyone was called into the room.

Nareen was sitting in the hospital bed looking weary and puffy-eyed and holding a tiny bundle that Leesa immediately christened Baby Burrito.

Nareen's mother introduced herself as Gizelda. She was tall and slender, wearing a flowing bright blue wrap with white batik symbols and a green scarf around her head. She had intelligent eyes that looked shrewdly at the motley crew crowded around her daughter's bed, apparently weighing each in turn. Tony was keenly aware of the smell of his breath, the dried saliva on his cheek, his rumpled clothes, his wild, greasy hair, and the vivid blue-green mark on his temple where he had been whacked by his kidnappers. If she was Quality Control in this setting, he felt sure he'd be stamped Insufficient and Rejected.

Nareen's grandfather was similarly tall but more conventionally dressed. He had eyes only for Nareen.

Nareen's boyfriend was surprisingly nondescript. Tony learned that his name was Derek, but he could not have said, later, what he looked like, other than that his hair wasn't quite blonde and wasn't quite sandy brown, and he was average height and build. He just wasn't very memorable. Derek was holding Nareen's hand, and look-ing at their baby, shyly, with a hint of terror. Tony looked at the frightened young man and realized with a whoosh of recognition that Derek was a younger and poorer Giles, a life-happens-to-me-and-I-just-let-it kind of guy. Tony hoped Derek would buck up and become someone else, at least to Nareen and their baby.

"It's a boy," Nareen said, when they were all gathered.

"Wait, I thought you told us it was going to be a girl," Leesa said.

"I did," Nareen said, smiling. "His penis must have been hiding when they did the ultrasound."

Leesa grinned, and Derek looked embarrassed.

"What are you going to name him?" Nancy asked.

"Not Ophelia, I hope?" Tony said, smirking, thinking the joke was on Walt for offering such a ridiculous suggestion.

"We're naming him Theodore, for my granddad," Nareen said, giving her grandfather a warm, tremulous smile, "and his middle name will be Walter."

They all looked at Walt, and Tony was sure that, like him, they expected some quip, or a gruff suggestion that Nareen pick another name, but Walt pursed his lips and blinked furiously and finally said in a voice hoarse with suppressed tears, "Thanks."

They talked a little, sharing those snippets of life stories that complete strangers share when they're thrown together by a common love, and everyone who was family held the Baby Burrito and kissed him and called him Little Man before handing him back to Nareen, and everyone who wasn't family took turns touching the tiny bit of his face that was peeking out from his blanket, as if newborn baby cheek was a talisman against all that was wrong with the world.

"What are you going to do now?" Leesa said, with her unerring sense of the one question no one else dared to ask, the one question Nareen likely didn't want to consider.

But it seemed the issue had been settled before the Sunnyside Up crew entered the room, and Nareen didn't even look irritated at the question, though possibly she was just too tired to be irritated.

"We talked about it, and we both agree getting married right now isn't a good idea," she said, giving Derek's hand a reassuring squeeze. "Though we're not ruling it out someday. I want to finish school," she said, "and get my degree. So I'm going to move in with Mom, and we'll figure out childcare between the four of us—me, Mom, Granddad, and Derek."

Nancy reached for a rough hospital tissue and blew her nose noisily.

"I'll miss you too," Nareen said, smiling.

Nancy and Caroline began nudging the not-family toward the door, working together as if it was the most natural thing in the world, and then Caroline and Tony said goodbye to everyone, and

Caroline's driver took them back to the Sleepy Time Motel, cradled once again in luxury, for just a little while.

\* \* \*

There was an interlude of showering and teeth-brushing and the lovemaking that only happens when you are relieved beyond measure to be alive, and then sleeping, and Tony's last thought as he drifted off was Oh God sleeping is a marvel and a revelation, an event unto itself.

The next day was Monday, so Tony and Caroline were free to spend their time together, sharing what it was like to be on either side of a kidnapping. And then Caroline told him what she'd wanted to say, when he was first rescued.

"I called Martin, and told him you had authorized an appeal," she said, almost giddy in her eagerness to tell him what she'd done. "He was a bit frustrated with me, calling over the holiday weekend, but I reminded him how much we've paid his firm over the years, and he finally agreed to fax me the forms. I had to pick them up at a place called Rite-Aid. Isn't that an odd name?" Tony nodded, mesmerized by the sound of her voice more than the words. "I got the forms, and I forged your signature, and sent them back." She didn't look ashamed, though Tony imagined there had been at least some internal dialogue about the ethics of the forgery.

"We were all dying to be useful, while the search was going on, so I got everyone at Sunnyside Up to write letters to the judge," she continued, "saying you have been rehabilitated. Martin thinks there's a pretty decent chance your sentence will be shortened, and you can come home, probably not by Christmas, but maybe by Valentine's Day, or Easter."

It was Tony's turn to weep, though he tried to hide it. "What if it's not a holiday?" he said, trying to control the quaver in his voice. "Can I still come home?" Caroline answered him with a kiss.

"I have something to tell you, too," he said, running his hands up and down her arms and reveling in the feel of her skin and her Caroline-smell. "You asked me to choose, and I did." For once, the words flowed out of him. Maybe that's what happens when you have to sit in a hard chair and listen to faceless men discuss a bullet to the head. Maybe the words had been there all along, barricaded inside by generations of so-called good breeding. "I chose a long time ago," he said. "Not just since I was banished to Motte and Bailey, not just since you flew here and told me I had to choose. I chose ten years ago, when we stood in front of all those people and ate that hideous red velvet cake. I choose you, my lovely, gracious, intelligent, sexy, funny Caroline."

And then his sudden fluency was spent, and his body went taut with desperation that she would understand what he was going to say next. "But I'm going to stay here until the end of my sentence, and I'm going to do whatever community service they finally assign to me, and I'm going to stay Tony," he said. And then he added the words he hoped would not break her, would not break them: "I'm not sure what happens after that."

Confusion descended in her eyes like the curtain coming down at the end of a play, but Tony thought, or maybe he just hoped, there was also a sliver of comprehension at the last minute, a line of light where the curtain didn't quite meet the stage floor.

"Haven't you been punished enough already?" she said.

"'Punished'?" he said. The past six months tumbled into his memory. The smell of biscuit mix, confabulations in the pantry, Walt muttering obscenities over his omelets as if swear words were an incantation to the cooking gods, Lipton's head resting on his bony knee, Nancy patting his behind. Was it really punishment to share these lives? And if the goal was penance, had he really done enough, could there ever be an *enough*, to make up for the death of a child, for extinguishing the light in those luminous, mischievous eyes? It wasn't a new thought, just the pounding of the same drum, a rhythm rat-a-tat-tatting on his brain or his soul again and again and again, until that moment when the tempo became as much a part of him as his heartbeat.

He tried to explain what had seemed so clear on the morning he'd been kidnapped, about being an insignificant nobody and the obligation to be good at it, but the words he had learned in the gracious empty halls of his childhood home and the stilted air of the boardroom were insufficient, and he had to leave it that he didn't want to forget the people he'd met here, or the lingo he'd learned, that sometimes life is *Shit on a shingle*, and the answer to *Why bother?* is *Because that's what we're meant to do.*

"I don't know if I can go back and just . . . take up where I left

264                                    *Lane: Two Over Easy*

off," he said.

He rebelled against the idea that those were the only options, staying here and being Tony or going back and being Giles. He needed more time to figure that out, and he needed to be sure, if he did return, the next time the Vice President of Safety said there's an acceptable risk he would reject the toy, maybe even shout everyone else down the way Jimmy Stewart did in *Mr. Smith Goes to Washington*.

There were, it turned out, many things he didn't know, and many more he couldn't articulate. His repeated "I love you" would have to carry everything, uncertainty and defiance against either-or, and hope that Caroline would join him in figuring out how to stop taking the easy way.

*All day long.*

And then Caroline said, though her lip trembled in the saying of it, "I know."

* * *

Tuesday dawned clear and cold and dry, but for some reason the sunshine and the blue sky felt ominous to Tony. Everything had worked out just fine, better than fine, even, and he couldn't identify a reason, only knew he felt inexplicably anxious.

The entire crew was at Sunnyside Up, in complete disregard of the schedule. Even Nareen was there (although of course she wasn't working)—Nancy had convinced Nareen's family to stay at her house for a few days, to give Nareen and the baby time to get used to each other, she said. By which they all understood Nancy meant *Give me time to say goodbye.*

It was a good thing everyone was at the restaurant, because it seemed the whole town was there, too. Sunnyside Up had been closed since Thanksgiving, first because of the holiday and then because Tony had gone missing, and the Motte and Baileyites missed Walt's cooking and their communal gathering place. People came in waves—everyone wanted to see the man who was lost and then found, and congratulate Crackers and Jems for Lipton's role in the finding, and cheer about the downfall of Roj, and touch the Baby Burrito. Nancy, Walt, Scooter, Tony, and Leesa had all they could do to keep everyone fed and stay on top of the dishes.

Even Max and Sandy and their three boys came in, and Max reached for Tony's arm, and Tony flinched, and Max flinched too. "I came to say I'm sorry," he said. "We did what Roj told us, because I'd of lost my job if we hadn't."

The explanation was so simple Tony knew it must be true.

"Thank you for telling me," he said, and though he wasn't sure he *felt* forgiveness, he hoped it *sounded* like he did.

Luis was there, of course, taking up a whole booth and nursing his infamous decaf coffee and dry toast for several hours.

As the breakfast rush was finally petering out, Baby Theodore (who was now going by "Teddy") began to wail, and Nareen rose to leave, jiggling the crying baby in that instinctual bounce a mother's body seems to know without being told—but she found the doorway blocked. A small group of men, some with cameras and one with a ridiculous grin on his face, was crowded around the door, holding it open and letting the frigid December air blow in.

"Close the damn door!" Nancy yelled, and then something about the look on the grinning man's face stopped her.

"We're here to see Jerome Robleski," the man in the front said.

"You've got the wrong place," Nancy said.

"I don't think so," the man said.

"Look, bub, I've lived in this shithole my whole goddamned life. If there was a Jerome Rumplestiltskin I'd know it."

"Robleski," the man corrected.

"Him neither," Nancy said.

"Jerome Robleski?" the man said loudly, looking past Nancy.

From the kitchen there was a crash and a "fuck," but the word sounded oddly soft and quiet, like a plea.

It didn't seem possible that a man could smile so broadly. "I'm sure Mr. Robleski will want to see me," he said. "I'm from the *Oregonian*, and I'm here to do a story about his prize."

"His prize?" Nancy said.

"He's been awarded the Walt Whitman prize for poetry," the man said, looking at her as if she ought to have guessed.

"Well I'll be damned," Nareen said, still jiggling Teddy, who was crying a little less vigorously, as if even he was curious about this strange turn of events.

Tony took charge. "Oh *that* Jerome Robleski," he said. "Sorry, gentlemen. I think the folks around here knew him as . . . Jerry."

He put his hand on Nancy's shoulder. "Nancy, you know Jerome. Good old Jerry." Nancy looked utterly baffled.

"Jerry, who likes to grow shallots? Who left the, ah, service some time ago?"

Recognition woke in her eyes, and she started to giggle. "Jerry? Jerry writes *poems*?"

The remaining customers were silent, watching the exchange with interest.

"The Walt Whitman award is nothing to sneer at, ma'am," the reporter said. The men behind him nodded. "It's a national award of some prestige."

The customers gawked. Nothing "of some prestige" happened in Motte and Bailey.

"So where is he?" the man pressed. "This is the address on the contest entry, though this certainly doesn't look like a residence. I'm starting to wonder if we got it wrong."

"GPS doesn't work out here, you know," Caroline piped in. "Your system probably made a mistake."

"Probably," the man said. "So where is one-two-seven Main Street?"

"That's us," Nancy agreed, nodding her head as if it had come unhinged. "But Jerome isn't here."

"Jerome is dead," Walt said, coming out of the kitchen. Someone in the restaurant gasped, and Tony almost laughed. Who was feigning shock over the death of a person they never knew existed?

"He died a few years ago," Walt said. His face was drawn and pale, and Tony could see the emotions written in his eyes like a recipe: one cup pride to two cups fear, mixed well and baked in an old soul for decades.

"I submitted his poems, in his memory."

Tony could see understanding dawning in Nareen's eyes, and then Scooter's, and finally Leesa's, but thankfully they all kept their poker-faces on (even Leesa).

The journalists were not thrilled to hear they'd driven to the middle of nowhere to record the awarding of a prize to a dead man. After some grumbling and a request to see Mr. Robleski's grave (which was firmly rebuffed, with yet another lie about Jerry having moved away before he passed on), they asked for Walt's name, and requested a picture of Walt with the plaque. Walt refused.

Tony couldn't have said what made him do it, whether it was a stroke of brilliance or a morsel of revenge for all the slights and hurts

Walt had flung, carelessly, at his wounded psyche, but whatever the motive he seized the moment. "Wait," he said, as the men turned to leave. "Why not take a picture with Nancy here? She," he nodded at Nancy, "is Walt's common law wife."

In all the time Tony had spent working side-by-side with Nancy, six days a week from six a.m. to three p.m., Tony had never seen Nancy speechless, but for a second or two she could only stare, the left corner of her mouth twitching dangerously.

Walt looked at Tony, and looked at the men, and then he put his arm around Nancy's shoulders and squeezed. "That's right," he growled. "She's my wife. If you want a photo to go with your story, take a picture of her."

So they handed the plaque to Nancy and took her picture with it, memorializing forever the bemused smile floating above the award.

And then they left, followed by Caroline and Nareen, still jiggling Teddy, whose sporadic fussing had turned into a determined roar that followed the men out the door and continued to reverberate from outside as Nareen strapped him into the car seat temporarily housed in the Lexus. (Caroline had put Pete-the-driver at Nareen's disposal for a few days, while Nareen recovered from giving birth and the rest of the family camped out at Nancy's house).

None of the restaurant patrons had any idea what had happened, though they understood there was some subterfuge at play. Under Roj's dominion, subterfuge had become a way of life, so that alone was neither surprising nor terribly interesting. That the gruff and crusty Walt should have cared about someone so much he'd submitted a poem to a contest on his behalf was another matter altogether.

"This's better'n a Hollywood spy show," one of the regulars declared.

"Who's this Jerome fellow? Did he really write the poem?" The question came from Crackers, who looked genuinely interested to find out there had been a man of letters in their midst, a possible kindred spirit in a way his Jems could never quite match. The question was seconded by an elderly woman wearing a polka-dot dress, and a young mother wiping egg off her toddler's face nodded, too.

"Hell if I know!" Walt said angrily, even though that made no sense, since he'd said he was the one who submitted the entry.

Luis was the only one present who already knew Walt's real name, but he hadn't known Walt was a poet, and he could not resist a jibe at the man who had missed no opportunity to insult him: *"O captain my captain,* may I have another cup of coffee?" he said.

At which Crackers called out, *"I have known the evenings, mornings, afternoons. I have measured out my life with coffee spoons."*

And then Scooter, turning his native shade of red, stammered:

> *L-love at the lips was touch*
> *As sweet as I could bear*
> *And once that seemed too much*
> *I lived on air.*

"Walt made me memorize some real poetry when I was trying to write something to ask Leesa to marry me," he explained.

Leesa looked at him with a mixture of adoration and exasperation. "You doofus," she said.

Tony looked at her looking at Scooter, and time was suspended for less than a second, as he pondered the fact that her love for Scooter and her "you doofus" were waging a war and the winner had not yet been declared. He wondered if even Leesa knew who would be victorious, and thought again that the time he'd spent rubbernecking into their lives had not been quite the onerous sanction the judge intended.

The questions and the joking and the impromptu poetry slam subsided, and the diner slowly emptied out, and then filled again with the lunch crowd, plus a few others who'd heard about the award and wanted to rib Walt about his soft heart—though of course no one dared to tease him directly; they just stood in the general vicinity of the pass-through window and tsked and said things like, "Who'd a thunk it of the grouchy old cuss?" and grinned slyly.

They worked through the lunch rush, answering a steady stream of questions about Tony, Roj, baby Teddy, and now Walt. Luis left briefly and returned cradling his phone in one hand, and something in his face signaled Houston-we-have-a-problem. Tony remembered the vague feeling of doom playing on the cold air this morning, and shook his head, as if he could shake off whatever it was by the movement of his body.

When the last customer left, and the crew moved into clean-up mode, Luis took his phone into the kitchen and held up a screenshot in front of Walt. Tony followed him, and leaned over Walt so he could see the phone. It was the story of "Jerry's" award, which had been posted on the web version of the *Oregonian*, shortly after the reporters left.

"Why on earth did you use your real name?" Luis demanded.

The others crowded into the kitchen, and Tony thought briefly, wildly, of suggesting that they move into the pantry; that's where important meetings take place at Sunnyside Up, he thought.

"Dunno," Walt said, sounding momentarily like a sullen teenager.

"You understand the risk, don't you?" Luis said. "You understand that you've put the name and address of a fugitive into the public domain."

"I hadn't thought about that," Walt said. "Not until those damned reporters showed up. How was I supposed to know I'd win? Or that winning would be national news?"

"Can we discuss this after we finish closing?" Nancy said, and Tony translated: I have no more capacity for worry, I just want to clean the coffee carafes.

"Fine," Luis said.

Reluctantly, the others returned to their tasks, and Tony knew they were sharing the same thought, once again a single organism bound by their communal fate, each wondering how long they had before the next moment of catastrophe.

Not long, it turned out.

Tony was washing a massive stainless steel bowl, scrubbing the remains of dozens—possibly hundreds—of eggs that had been used that day, when he heard Leesa squeak. He looked up and over the top of the swinging doors, and saw two more men standing outside the diner. They were wearing somber suits and somber expressions, and neither was carrying a camera or an oversized microphone. He turned to say something to Walt, but Walt had slipped into the pantry and was pressed against the back wall as if by sheer force of will he could meld with the Crisco and the biscuit mix.

In any other place, at any other time, Tony would have been sure Walt was overreacting. Two men in suits . . . they could have been anyone. Hungry businessmen looking for a late lunch. Mormons offering salvation. Men in Black tracking little green aliens.

But here, and now, it seemed obvious that they were agents of some kind, come to make Walt answer for his sins.

Nancy seemed frozen in place. Leesa dropped the broom (again), and reached for Scooter, who was at her side in less time than it would have taken her to say I need you. Luis sighed, audibly, got up from his booth, and let the men in.

They introduced themselves as Mark Gillespie, no relation to the famous jazz musician, and David Strong. They showed identification to Luis, who gave a curt nod, leaving the others to wonder whether they were agents from the IRS, the army, or some horrendous hybrid prosecutorial arm of the federal government.

"We're looking for Jerome Robleski," the not-jazz-musician said.

Nancy said, "Don't you people read the news? He's dead, like I told those reporters earlier."

"Died a f-few years ago," Scooter agreed, shaking almost imperceptibly.

"I don't know what you have to come sniffing around here for," Leesa said. "We're about full up on law enforcement these days."

Under the circumstances, Tony thought, Leesa was showing amazing restraint.

"I'm Giles Gibson," he said, extending his hand with the confidence of years of being company president, an oily sheen that never quite leaves a person, even if that person has been working in a diner and living in a Sleepy Time Motel for a while.

"We know who you are," the one called David Strong said, taking Tony's hand with obvious distaste, as if he would have preferred not to but was compelled by the force of convention. "We're not here to talk to you."

"Mr. Delgado," Mr. Strong said, turning to Luis, "I understand you're in the process of concluding a bust."

Luis nodded.

"Congratulations," he said.

"Thanks," Luis said. "Your folks were a big part of that operation, of course."

"You say Mr. Robleski died?" The question was directed at Nancy, who nodded mutely.

"A few years ago," Scooter said.

"We only heard about it from a friend of a friend," Leesa added.

"Heart attack, isn't that what you said?" Tony looked at Nancy, and felt the arc of hope pass from him to her and back to him.

Again, she nodded.

At that moment Nareen returned, carrying Teddy, who was now sleeping. Caroline followed her into the restaurant, their eyes speaking questions.

They introduced themselves, but the government agents were focused on the hunt, and they knew neither Nareen nor Caroline had anything to do with their quarry.

"Ever see any documentation of this 'death'?" Mr. Strong pressed Nancy.

"Yeah, I mean no," Nancy said, finding her voice. "But why would we? We weren't family or nothing."

"These gentlemen are asking about Jerome Robleski," Tony told Nareen and Caroline, and they moved from the door to stand beside the others, a human wall facing the agents.

"Hardly knew the man," Leesa said.

"That's why we didn't know who they were talking about, when those reporters showed up with the award," Scooter said, with a flash of inspired genius.

"And what about your cook?" Mr. Gillespie gestured toward the kitchen. "According to the article, he submitted Robleski's poems. They must have been friends."

Everyone spoke at once. "Oh I don't think so," Leesa said, and Tony said, "Never heard him speak of it before now," and Nancy said, "That old fart isn't anybody's friend," so loudly they all laughed, nervously, uproariously, as if that was the funniest thing anyone had ever said.

"That's right," Walt said, coming out of the kitchen, "I'm nobody's friend." There was resolution and terror clothing him like a second skin.

"I'm Walt Whitman," he said, extending his hand, just as Tony had done. "Pardon the name," he said, and there was the slightest tremor in his voice. "My parents really liked *Leaves of Grass*."

"*I am large; I contain multitudes*," quoted Mr. Gillespie, squinting at Walt with obvious suspicion.

Walt nodded, having apparently spent his courage for the moment.

"Mr. Delgado, did you have any occasion to look into Jerome Robleski while you were here?"

One body, one wildly beating heart.

Luis nodded. "I did, though it was peripheral to my investigation into the drug ring," he said.

"And can you confirm what these people are saying, that Mr. Robleski passed away several years ago?"

One body, one pair of lungs squeezing oxygen from the miserly air.

Luis looked down, as though searching his memory, or his conscience. Then he stepped away from his booth, and stood beside the others, and nodded. "I didn't see any documentation," he said. "But I have reason to believe they're right, Mr. Robleski is dead."

Tony could not have said what happened next, except that the men asked Luis a few more questions and the others went back to trying to appear to be cleaning, all the while exchanging surreptitious glances of joy and relief. Finally, the two agents left.

And then the joy erupted in earnest, and there was laughter and a few tears and Walt thanking Luis and Nancy hugging Luis, and Leesa talking shrilly about how we sure pulled the wool over their eyes and what a bunch of stick-up-their-butts they were, and Scooter hyperventilating and having to breathe into a bag while Nancy expressed herself in a few choice words Tony had never heard before, and Nareen striking up a chorus of *You gotta march down, march down, march down to Jordan, Hallelujah!* until Walt could no longer take the chaos and frivolity and camaraderie, and he retreated to the kitchen and shouted over the din, "Will you all just knock that shit off!"

Tony looked and listened, drinking in the scene the way a man gulps water before crossing the desert: ridiculous cantankerous Walt clattering the pots and pans in the kitchen; Nancy bustling around getting things done and simultaneously radiating warmth like a short, compact fireplace, a miracle in motion; Nareen singing and swinging her baby in a circle, smiling at last the smile her face was made to hold; Scooter sitting at the counter holding the bag he'd been breathing into, and looking at Leesa with palpable love and maybe a little lust; Leesa wielding a broom with absolutely no effect on the food scraps on the floor. It was a mental photograph Tony would carry with him to New York or wherever he landed, whenever the time came, as surely as he carried the physical photograph of Libby, a reminder that he had shed his Pinocchio-puppet self. He was real, and grounded, one foot in the teeming metropolis and one foot in the middle of the middle of nowhere, a string or a rope or a line that would pull him back to the center, *this* center, if ever he was tempted to forget that he was always and forevermore nothing more or less than a dishwasher at a diner in Motte-fucking-Bailey.

# Acknowledgements

I owe a never-ending debt of gratitude to my children, Marty and Amanda, who have been the best cheerleaders; to my dad, David, who always believed in me; and to my sister Jessica (ditto). Thanks, too, to my husband, Justin, for his patience as I tap-tap-tapped my way to finishing this book. To Kathy H, whose friendship over the years has meant more than I could ever express: Love you to the moon and back! A huge thank you to the women in my first-ever writing group, Kara and Celia and Arlene, and our beloved June, who left us in 2019 for the greatest adventure of all. And another huge thank you to the women in my writer's group, Valerie and Kathy and Kathleen and Gini and Marna and Criss: it's your turn to share your amazing talent with the world. To our fabulous writing coaches and writing retreat leaders, Charlotte and Debbie, without whom this book would never have been possible—"Thank you" is wholly insufficient.

Last but definitely not least, tremendous (colossal, monumental, stupendous) thanks to Betsy and Neal Delmonico—my heart is full because of your passion for good books, and your enthusiasm for *Two Over Easy All Day Long*. I feel so lucky the universe brought me to you and to Golden Antelope Press!

# About the Author

    Shari Lane was reading voraciously by the time she entered kinder-garten, and she has been writing for almost as long. (Her first full-length novel, hand-written at the age of ten and stapled together for her family, followed the adventures of magical guinea pigs.) Her adult bio is as multi-dimensional as the characters in her book. With an MA in Classics she taught Latin to middle school students and operated a Montessori preschool. Eventually she headed back to uni-versity for a Juris Doctor. In addition to her work as a lawyer advising employers about civil rights and related laws, she became a certified mediator, served on the board of a Head Start organization serving primarily the children of migrant farmworkers, and volunteered with organizations serving houseless and food-insecure people. Seeing two sides, building bridges. Along the way she wrote *The UnFairy Tale* series for middle grade readers and began an adult novel titled *What the Dogs Know.* (A chapter is available at **alaughingdog.com** .)

Whenever and however possible, Shari surrounds herself with books, writers, and readers. In addition to being Managing Editor of *SHARK REEF Literary Magazine,* she is on the Lopez Island Library's Board of Trustees, and hosts WORD!, an open mic for local writers. It is her ardent belief that good writing can provide a much-needed escape, a chance for a cathartic cry, or a healing belly laugh. Just as importantly, in these divided and divisive times, she believes stories can build bridges, as we see through another's eyes, and feel through the beating of another's heart.

Her short stories have been published in *Evening Street Review, Adelaide Literary Magazine, Cape Magazine, Antithesis*, and other literary magazines. *Two Over Easy All Day Long* is her first traditionally-published novel for adults.

Find Shari online at **sharilane.com,** with links to follow her on Facebook and on Instagram (ReadWriteBreathe38).

Pioneers
David mCCulbugh

Printed in the USA
CPSIA information can be obtained
at www.ICGtesting.com
CBHW081557040424
6385CB00006B/115

9 781952 232862